I0760995

A MAGIC+CITY WONDERS NOVEL

TAYLOR THOMAS SMYTHE

LAMPLIGHT
UNIVERSE

WEST PALM BEACH, FLORIDA

Cover design and interior layout by Taylor Thomas Smythe

Published by Lamplight Universe
ISBN: 978-1-959345-12-1

Lamplight Universe
West Palm Beach, FL

www.lamplightuniverse.com

For all of us
who dream crazy, big,
unfathomable dreams—
and then take the leap
to turn them into reality.

MAGIC✦CITY WONDERS

TIMELINE

1980

1981

GOLDIE

NIGHTMARE
ARRAY

COMING 2024

ALSO BY TAYLOR THOMAS SMYTHE

KINGDOM OF FLORIDA SERIES:

I. The Golden Alligator

II. The Lamplight Society

III. The Place Beyond the Sea

IV. The Fountain of Youth

V. The Curse of Coronado

VI. Coral and the Treasure Hunters

VII. Guardians of the Willow

MAGIC CITY WONDERS SERIES:

Goldie

The Dream Team

Nightmare Array (Coming 2024)

More stories coming soon!

Visit lamplightuniverse.com *for more.*

Table of Contents

(continued)

(continued)

The DREAM TEAM

A

MAGIC✦CITY WONDERS

NOVEL

CHAPTER 1

South Beach. Miami, Florida. Summer 1981.

Hotel Florian boasted a sleek facade; after all, it was one of the crown jewels of South Beach's famed Art Deco-speckled main strip, with signature glowing block letters illuminating its name at night to the sidewalk passersby. Rounded peachy overhangs flanked the corner windows of the narrow building (which abutted a conjoined twin structure of about the same size), with two massive coral-colored circles like eyes along the top wall looking past the road to the roiling dark ocean. Mint green columns rose the height of the first floor, while a pair of vertical stripes in matching paint ascended the proceeding two levels up to the roof.

The open-air patio above the final floor—the rooftop—had grown quiet some hours ago, save for the breezy rustling of the palm trees that sprouted and waved their fronds from the ground level. In one corner, a sweaty couple lay sprawled across a dewy couch, fast asleep with a number of half-empty glasses peppered around them. There was a slight movement discernible in the shadows at the other end of the roof: two figures in black—one about an average build, the other at least a head taller and considerably bulkier, wearing what looked like an oversized backpack.

The larger man nodded toward a glowing, bubbling vat of steamy water. "Sure there's no time for a dip?"

"Maybe later," the smaller of the two grinned, tucking a swath of chestnut hair under his beanie as he glanced at the hot tub. "If we can pull this off without a hitch."

When they reached the corner of the building, the smaller man moved his finger to an earpiece. "Me and Buster are in position."

"Roger that," came a woman's voice between static blips. "I've got eyes on you and Smith. He's watching TV. Can you see me?"

The man bent his neck to look over the edge, down toward the alley between it and the next building. He squinted in the dark to get a better look at one of the corner windows in the adjacent building, which appeared to be blacked out with a thick, drawn curtain. "Negative, Mira," he replied, baffled. "You're completely invisible."

"Perfect," answered Mira with a satisfied smile in her tone.

The other, larger man—Buster—shook his shaven head and muttered to himself, "Gets me every time. Wild."

The first man removed his beanie, breathed in the fresh, salty air, and closed his eyes, running a hand through his brown hair. A moment later he opened his eyes and returned the hat to his head. From a pocket on his belt, the man removed a small pneumatic syringe gun and rolled up one of his sleeves.

"Uh, Declan," whispered Buster. "You okay? You aren't feeling another, uh, *episode* coming on, I hope?"

"No," the man said. He pulled the trigger, releasing a sudden burst of air. Declan winced. "All good. Don't worry about me." He stuffed the injection device back into his belt.

"Good," replied Buster, tightening the straps to the large mass on his back. "Kiki should be in place by now."

Declan spoke into his earpiece again. "Kiki: ready when you are."

A moment later, the radio chirped back with a young woman's voice: "These wigs are itchy and I'm swimming in a housekeeper's dress at the moment."

"Swimming?" Buster contorted his eyebrows and whispered to Declan.

"Think she means it's a little big on her," he muttered, then spoke into the transmitter again. "Is it gonna work or not?"

"We'll make do," Kiki answered with a puff.

Declan nodded to reassure Buster. "What's your crowd like tonight? Just two?"

Kiki's voice shot back: "Two's company, Dec; three's a crowd."

Buster muttered, "I thought *three* was company?"

"No," Declan shook his head quickly. "That's the show with Suzanne Somers."

"Who, by the way," shot Kiki's half-garbled voice, "is *not* returning next season and, if you ask me, that's an absolute tragedy."

Mira's rich voice resurfaced in a stern tone. "Time's ticking, team. Are all three Kiki's ready to roll?"

"Roger that, Mira," Kiki answered. "It's showtime!"

Three identical young women huddled in the janitor's closet, pressed under the hot, dim light of a dying fluorescent bulb. One of the women, garbed in a knee-length yellow housekeeper's dress, fastened a pair of bobby pins into a bun on her blonde wig. The second woman had just zipped up a set of janitor's coveralls and adjusted some of the dark brown hair that spilled out from under a faded ballcap.

The one in the housekeeper's dress turned to the third woman: "Can you tighten the ties on the back? This dress isn't flattering in the slightest."

The third woman tucked her chin-length, hot-pink hair behind her ear and twisted the dress straps into a practical bow: "You always look fantastic, Kiki, if I may say so myself."

"You absolutely *may* say so, *Kiki*," the housekeeper smiled. "But I'm a little jealous you don't have to wear one of these wigs like us—they're wildly uncomfortable."

"Hey, you came up with this plan," said the pink-haired Kiki defensively.

"Mine's not too bad," quipped the janitor. "I kinda like being a brunette for the night."

"Eh, hot pink's more fun," said the blonde Kiki in the

housekeeper's dress. "Soon as we're done, I'm burning this blonde mess." She arranged a few items on a small service cart that pressed against her side then turned back to the others. "Alright, so Mr. Smith is in the room at the far end of the hall. One member of his private security team is guarding the doorway at all times, and another's camped out undercover in the room right next to his. For me to get into Smith's room, we need this to run like clockwork." After a moment to breathe, Kiki added, "Why am I telling you all this? You already know everything I'm thinking."

"What can I say? We like to talk," quipped the pink-haired woman. "Well, I'm up first—barf bag's loaded." She motioned toward a small purse with thick straps slung over her shoulder and hanging at her side, then cracked a smile as she moved to the closet door. "It's been nice knowing ya, gals."

Without another word, the pink-haired Kiki pushed through the door, leaving the other two carbon-copies of her likeness in the dank closet. As she moved to round the corner toward Mr. Smith's hotel room, she adjusted her black dress and tousled her hair. Then, with a quick half-glance to make sure she could see the security detail posted in front of Smith's door, Kiki began to alter her steps into a conspicuous, drunken stumble.

The guard turned his attention to the staggering woman immediately. Kiki was a convincing enough actress, but tried not to show the deep, anxious elevation in her pulse as she moved closer under the light of a row of gaudy wall sconces.

"'Scuse me, officer," she slurred. "W-which way to—d'you

know where my room is?"

The security guard took a deep breath and exhaled slowly, wanting so badly to ignore this domestic crisis unrelated to the more important work of standing watch over his employer's hotel room. But Kiki's feigned jitters must have got to him, for he finally spoke: "Sorry, lady. Sounds like you maybe had a little too much to drink. And I, uh, think you're on the wrong floor. Elevator's back that way." He gestured in the direction she'd come.

"Too m-much? 'Scuse me?" Kiki enjoyed going over the top when pretending to be an intoxicated club-goer. "Who d'you think you are? The *drink*-police? Hmm?"

As the guard took another large breath, his eyes grew wide. Kiki covered her mouth and began to bob her neck, a minor convulsion like one that would precede an expulsion of vomit. "Onesecond," she slurred again, wagging a limp and lazy finger toward him with her free hand.

"Please, miss, I think you're going to want to—"

"*Blahhh!*" Kiki retched, ducking her head toward the man's shoes, and squeezed her purse against her side using her elbow. A convincing potpourri of processed vegetables and baby food streamed out of a hidden tube in the high neck of her dress and splattered across the bottom half of the stoic guard. He instinctively raised his arms up to avoid further contamination as Kiki forced a second, larger burst of homemade faux-puke.

The pink-haired Kiki ran her forearm across her face to wipe her mouth, and looked up toward the guard with puppy-dog eyes. "S-sorry, ossifer."

The guard shook his head silently, muttered, "I just had this dry-cleaned," then motioned back toward the elevator. "If you'll leave, I need to get this cleaned up."

Kiki nodded slowly and obligingly moved down the hall. While she pressed the elevator button, she watched as the officer disappeared down another hall where she heard a room door open then click closed. Kiki tapped the glowing button for the first floor and smiled as the doors closed on her.

"Alright, you're up," the blonde-wigged maid snapped to her mirror image in the janitor suit. She added, almost under her breath: "Gonna miss that one—she had spunk."

The brunette Kiki in the janitor's coveralls bobbed her head as she pushed open the closet door and stepped into the hall. "Yeah, yeah, I get it. You like the pink hair better."

The door closed and the brown-haired Kiki moved swiftly around the bend. She gave a firm rap on the door of the room adjacent to Mr. Smith's and waited as she heard the faint sound of footsteps on the other side.

A cold, gnarled face appeared in the space of the half-opened door. "Can I help you?" The man's voice was deep and grim, marred by cigarettes and a few too many jabs to the jugular.

Kiki nodded and adjusted her cap. "Yes, sir, uh, got a report of a possible electrical issue in this room and need to take a look—if that's alright."

"It's not alright," the man said and began to close the door.

Thinking fast, Kiki thrust a boot-clad foot to stop the door from closing all of the way. "Unfortunately, sir, it's actually a very dangerous issue—fire hazard, you get what I'm saying?"

The man loosened his grip on the door and allowed it to open slightly.

"Shouldn't take more than a few minutes for me to locate the issue," Kiki said, smiling awkwardly.

Without another word, except for the clear irritation indicated by the ascent of his bushy eyebrows up his smooth forehead, the man opened the door and allowed the counterfeit janitor to enter.

As soon as the hotel room door closed, the remaining Kiki—the real, *original* Kiki in the blonde wig and maid's uniform—wheeled her housekeeper's cart out of the linen closet and toward Mr. Smith's room. She touched her earpiece and spoke a quick confirmation: "Alright, crowd control's done. I'm going in—wish me luck!"

Declan's grainy reply shot back. "Ready to drop in when we're all clear. Just say the word."

"Stand by," Kiki nodded and switched the walkie off as she reached the door to Mr. Smith's room. The young woman took a deep breath then gave an elaborate knock. "Room service," she emphasized in a higher-than-usual, sing-songy tone.

Just as her counterpart had sensed moments earlier, Kiki now heard footsteps approaching the thin door. Her pulse raced as she heard the slide of the chain at the top of the door followed by the turning of the deadbolt. Finally, the door opened, revealing a well-groomed man in a silk bathrobe.

The amount of hair on the man's exposed chest immediately distracted Kiki's focus, but she quickly moved her gaze to his face and smiled, recognizing Mr. Smith's face from a photograph. "Room service?" She gestured to the cart beside her, upon which sat pitchers of water and orange juice, several empty glasses, a bucket of ice, and a variety of covered silver platters. "Midnight breakfast—it's complimentary."

After a deep sigh that felt like a small eternity to the nervous housekeeper, the man nodded his head and motioned for her to enter. Kiki relaxed slightly, but kept up her guard as she wheeled the cart into the main room near the bed. Mr. Smith seemed distracted while he slowly closed the door behind her.

Kiki glanced out the window to the adjacent building. As her partners on the roof had witnessed earlier, all the young woman could see was a thick shade covering a darkened room. Satisfied, she grabbed the pitcher and quickly sloshed orange juice into one of the glasses.

"Orange juice?" Kiki smiled and she extended the cup toward Smith.

The man raised a skeptical eyebrow.

"Freshly-squeezed; Florida-grown," the nervous housekeeper doubled-down.

With a roll of his eyes, Mr. Smith snatched the juice from Kiki's hand and took a swig. Then, when he'd swallowed, the man nodded toward the cart. "And what's for breakfast?"

Kiki made a nervous glance at the cup of juice—he'd taken a large enough gulp, but there was still a good bit of pulpy juice left in the glass. The young woman swung around and lifted the metallic coverings over a pair of dishes. "Sausages; diced potatoes; some scrambled eggs if you like?"

Smith seemed to be staring off out the window toward the beach.

Why isn't he drinking the rest of the juice?

"Anything strike your fancy?" Kiki said, hoping to interrupt the train of thought. "Sir," she added for good measure.

"You know," he answered, a slight contortion in his face, "I'm actually not hungry anymo—"

The half-empty glass of orange juice shattered to the floor. Kiki lunged forward to catch Mr. Smith as his eyes drooped and his body tumbled into a heap. The young woman managed to keep his head from hitting the tile entry. A limp arm gave Kiki the final confirmation she needed. "Sweet dreams, Mr. Smith," she whispered in his ear.

Kiki spoke into her earpiece: "It's go time."

The ocean roiled in the distance and a couple cars whizzed by the hotel. Buster and Declan slid down through the shadows on the side of the building, fastened to thin wires from the roof, and made their way around the stucco overhang so that they could see through the large window beneath it. Inside, Kiki dragged the limp body of Mr. Smith toward the bed.

Declan slid the window up and open, then entered first, easily fitting through the gap.

"A little help?" Kiki grunted. Smith wasn't a large man, but he felt heavier and less cooperative while unconscious.

When he'd unclipped himself from the cable, Declan hurried over and grabbed Smith by the legs. Together the two managed to slide him onto his back and lean the man's neck against a couple of pillows and the headboard.

Buster first unstrapped the large apparatus attached to his back and tossed it through the window and onto the floor. Then the hulking man squeezed his way through the window, careful not to push too hard and risk damaging glass or frame.

"Hurry," said Kiki with a nod toward the wall. "Thing Two is running out of places to check for electrical problems next door."

Buster opened his large pack and removed a sleek device. It consisted of two main parts: a round-edged casing that housed a tangle of computer machinery with a small viewscreen, and another segment resembling a futuristic bicycle helmet. The two were connected with electrical cords and cables.

"I'll get the helmet on," Declan spouted, extending his hands. "Fire her up."

The large, bald man gripped a top handle and moved the machine closer to the bed then handed the headpiece to his counterpart. Buster let his finger hover near a switch on the side of the machine, next to a series of metallic letters: *Dreamcatcher 3000.*

Buster breathed in. *Click!*

The machine rumbled briefly, then began to whir—the sound of dozens of tiny cogs and rotors and circuits coming to life.

When the helmet was securely strapped to Smith's head, Declan stepped back. "Alright. Let's see what Mr. Smith's got on his mind."

With a deep breath, Declan entered a sequence of keystrokes then pressed a large red button. An audible electric pulse emanated from the device and illuminated a panel of tiny lights in seemingly random patterns along the outside of the metallic helmet on Smith's head. Finally, the viewscreen switched on.

"Mira, you seeing this?" Kiki clicked into the walkie.

"Transmitting and recording," Mira's voice assured her.

A grainy, moving image began to form on the screen. Abstract shapes and blobs at first, but then people, places, scenes. Declan and Buster watched intently, while Mira did the same from her place in the next building.

"Guys!" Kiki exclaimed quietly and pointed toward Smith. "Did he just move?"

Buster's eyes grew wide. "I thought you gave him the dose!"

Kiki shook her head. "He only drank half!" The shattered glass in the corner dripped with orange liquid. Kiki reached for her earpiece: "Mira, he's waking up!"

Mira's voice shot back: "Shoot! You know what that

means: you've got 90 seconds before that dream evaporates—maybe less."

"That's not enough time," Declan shook his head.

"It's what we've got." Kiki took a quick breath. "Or the dream fades and he doesn't remember where he left off." She turned to the window to look toward the darkened, shaded room in the opposite building. "Mira: can you hide us while we finish up?"

For a brief moment, the illusion faded; the image of a shuttered, unlit room morphed into one that was brightly lit, with curtains wide open. A woman stood with her hands against the glass, a mass of wavy dark hair falling in loose bunches over her wide shoulders. "I can try." This time, Kiki watched Mira's mouth form the words she heard in her earpiece. "But if you make a sound *or* touch him, he'll see right through it," Mira added.

Kiki nodded to her, then the bright room faded back to darkness. She turned back toward the bed and waited for a change. Smith's eyes flickered and he took a deep, drowsy breath.

"You three and the *Dreamcatcher* are now invisible to him," Mira's voice whispered. "He can't see any of you."

"What about the headset?" Kiki wondered quietly.

"He'll feel it, but he can't see it. This is *not* exactly an ideal scenario."

So we just wait? Kiki bit her lip.

The viewscreen continued to flash scenes from Smith's dream, but it played like a poorly edited film—cutting from moment to moment, skipping around in a nonlinear fashion. Still, the team might be able to glean something valuable from the scattered imagery.

"60 seconds." Mira sounded calm enough. "We need more of the dream."

Mr. Smith's eyes fluttered open slowly and his brow furrowed; he could sense that something wasn't right. Kiki, Buster, and Declan held their breaths. Smith tossed and turned onto his side, his head propped at an awkward angle because of the unseen helmet strapped to his head, and the trio exhaled as quietly as possible. He was still sleeping—barely.

Kiki knew she wasn't supposed to make a sound, but quickly whispered to Declan: "Bad news: our Kiki next door just got found out by the bodyguard!"

"Tell her to distract him!" Declan shot.

"Too late. They're already on their way here."

Again, Smith began to writhe. He opened his eyes and looked up as if he'd heard the voices. "Is someone there?"

"30 seconds! The dream's slipping," Mira noted. "Get out of there!"

Carefully, Declan reached his hand near Smith's chin. To remove the helmet, he'd have to press the clip's release clasp, which was sure to be felt by their groggy new friend. Without making a sound, Declan inhaled slowly then grabbed the clasp and pushed it. The faint clicking sound and the sharp pinch caused Mr. Smith's eyes to jolt open, and he swung a hand to feel the spot on his face. Declan pulled away with no time to spare, lifting the whole apparatus from the confused man's head in one swift motion.

Heavy footsteps resounded through the gap beneath the hotel room door, coming to rest just in front of it. *Tap-tap-tap!* A knuckle with a metal ring rapped on the hollow door. "Mr. Smith—everything okay in there?" The bodyguard's voice held a hint of concern. "Stop squirming," he added in a volume obviously not intended for Smith.

Smith looked around the room, trying to surmise from where the strange pain and whispers were coming. He felt a sudden breeze through the window, which he hadn't remembered opening. "I'm not sure," he answered back to the guard, barely loud enough to be heard through the door. The bathrobed man hurried off the bed and stuck his head through the window. The crisp ocean breeze and distant, echoing disco-beats put him at ease; these sensations were familiar and expected. *Must've had too much to drink.*

Tap-tap-tap! "Mr. Smith?"

"I'm coming," he muttered with irritation and stumbled to answer the door.

When the door swung open, the guard was distracted, looking frantically around the entryway like a child searching for its lost favorite toy.

"What's going on?" Mr. Smith sighed.

"She was right here!" The man's thick hands gestured toward the space beside him. "Some kid posing as a repairperson—gone! I was worried it was a ruse to get to you."

Mr. Smith exhaled slowly and shook his head. "I'm fine,"

he waved his hands. "Just a little woozy, actually. Maybe went a little too hard at the bar tonight." After a glance down either direction of the hall, Smith leaned close to the hulking bodyguard. "Not a word to Ducane, you hear?" He quickly added, his lip quivering.

"Secret's safe with me, boss."

Apparently satisfied with this response, Smith took a deep breath, motioned for the guard to leave, then closed the door. As he turned back, he nearly stepped on the shards of broken glass along the wall. Mr. Smith cocked his head, trying to remember what had happened.

There was a maid—her cart's still here.

But what about the voices? Whispers. A strange machine?

Must have been a dream, Mr. Smith surmised. He slumped back into the silky sheets and drifted off to sleep once more—the salty Miami breeze gliding through the open window.

CHAPTER 2

Donna Locke navigated the maze of hospital hallways as she had so many times before, her high-heels clacking with each hurried step. The woman's mass of blonde hair was extra voluminous and smelled as if she'd applied gallons of hairspray. She entered the hospital wearing a pair of Ray-Bans, but now removed them with gloved hands and smoothed out her blush-pink skirt as she knocked softly on the door to a patient's room.

A young nurse greeted Donna with a nod of acknowledgment and opened the door wide enough for her to enter.

"Dare I even ask?" Donna raised a cautious eyebrow.

The nurse shook her head and took a deep breath. "No visible progress since the last time we spoke," she said meekly.

Donna exhaled slowly and stepped further into the room. "Thanks, Darly. Can you give me and my sister a moment?"

"Of course, Miss Locke," replied the nurse. "I'll just be

down the hall if you need anything." Darly quietly closed the door halfway and disappeared.

Donna approached the bed where her older sister lay—a pallid, silent ghost of the woman she once was.

"Hey, Sondra. Miss me?"

As she took a seat beside the cot, Donna swept a lock of Sondra's wispy brown hair out of her face. Donna, the younger sister, could barely recall the color of the other's eyes; they rested shut, and occasionally one could see them flutter—usually when her daughter Starla was in the room.

"Don't you worry. I'm taking good care of her for you," Donna said. "Starla's almost done with school for the year, if you can believe it. She loves her art class and she's so, so talented—especially for an eight-year-old." The blonde woman spoke as if her sister could hear. She smiled softly and clutched Sondra's limp hand. "Starla's special—I know you knew that. And now she's got everything she needs and more."

For a moment, Donna's gaze drifted toward the window and out across the crystal-clear bay waters. She took a deep breath. "I haven't given up looking for Marcus," she muttered, wiping a shimmering tear with a glove-covered finger. "I know he's out there somewhere. It's just a matter of time before I locate him—wherever Angela's got him. Somebody has to know *something*. I'll find him."

After a moment of silence, save for the slow, steady blip of the life support machines and air conditioning, Donna turned her attention back to her sister. "Why I really dropped by today was to share the big news," Donna smiled. "You're finally coming home!"

Donna thought she spied an almost discernible jitter of Sondra's eyelids as she continued:

"Now that Starla and I have the new place, we've got a *little* bit of room for you to stay with us. I figure it's been over a year that you've been like this and you deserve better. You'll be safer and well attended to, and she'll get to see you more. They're going to make the move this afternoon. It's a modest place, really, but I think you're gonna love it." Donna envisioned the scene as she rose from her seat.

"Well, see you later, sis." Donna bent to plant a soft kiss on Sondra's forehead. Then she gave one more light squeeze of her sister's hand, placed her sunglasses back on her face, and turned to leave the room.

Just as swiftly as she'd entered, Donna now clacked back down the hall, took the elevator, and sauntered through the main lobby. The automatic double doors slid open, ushering in a gust of humid, thick air that threatened to undo Donna's immaculate coiffure.

As she peered out across the hospital parking lot, Donna thought she felt someone looking at her out of the corner of her periphery. When she turned to get a better view, the woman sighed; there was no one there. Just a sapling rustling in the wind.

"Is this your car, miss?" An almost accusatory voice interrupted her thoughts.

Donna turned. A small, rusting maroon sedan with no hubcaps idled at the curb without a driver in sight. The hospital staffer motioned to the scene with an agitated look in his eyes then put his hands on his hips.

Donna lowered her glasses halfway down her nose and raised an eyebrow. "*That* old thing? Not a chance." She turned when she heard the rev of a more refined engine. "*That* is my car."

The valet driver wheeled a sleek, shiny convertible under the covered entryway, stopping precisely in front of Donna. The driver's side door flew open with care as the man hurried around the vibrant yellow Corvette to greet its owner.

"All ready for you, Miss Locke," the young man smiled as he motioned for the door. "I always look forward to your visits. She's a real beauty."

"Thanks, Skip." Donna ran a hand across the glittering surface as she rounded the hood. "I've had a few little modifications made since she's been mine." She glanced up at the bright blue sky then gracefully slid into the leathery driver's seat, where she pressed a button on the dash. Immediately, there was a faint droning sound from within the back trunk. The canvas top of the car began to retract, folding slowly down into the back of the car.

"Rad," Skip nodded.

"Isn't it, though? Well, I'll try not to be a stranger." Donna adjusted her glasses and smiled at the boy. "But for now? Clear skies, top down, gotta roll."

Donna revved the engine, clicked on the radio, shifted into drive, then peeled away out of the hospital parking lot and down the street. Soon, she ascended the ramp to the causeway that led over Biscayne Bay toward Miami Beach and the greater Atlantic Ocean beyond it. The rush of wind swept back her glorious mane and she took deep breaths of the salty air as she swerved in and out of the morning's light traffic.

About halfway up the causeway, Donna slowed and veered down an adjoining bridge that split off from the main one. The brief road flanked by quaint lanterns was the gateway to Star Island, a small and exclusive private key where only the wealthiest of businesspeople and movie stars owned homes and land. The island, shaped like a stretched-out oval, had a palm-lined interior road by which one could access each of the water-facing properties.

The yellow Corvette zipped around the oblong ring until it reached the north end of the island. A guard manned a gate at plat No. 46, opening it as soon as he sighted the shimmering sportscar rounding the bend. Donna waved as she passed and drifted up the long Chicago-brick driveway to a huge house. The woman brought the car to a stop right in front of the immense mansion—a wonder of craftsmanship assembled meticulously in the Mediterranean style, the majority of the house rose to two stories high, with a third story parapet that doubled as a stairwell with roof access.

Donna disembarked and left the car running. A pair of youthful doormen appeared. One hurried to the Corvette and quickly drove it off to a multi-car garage at the side of the house; the second attendant waited at the front steps and swung open the large door as Donna reached it.

"Thanks, hun," she nodded to the young man as she stepped into the arctic gusts generated by the home's air-conditioning.

When the door closed behind her, Donna stopped and stared up toward the ceiling of the expansive atrium in which she now stood. She took a deep breath and allowed the morning's tension to be released from her shoulders. She closed her eyes and muttered with a smile: "Home, sweet home."

Not more than a few seconds later, the blonde woman heard the high-pitched squeals of a young child hurrying barefoot across the carpet upstairs: "Aunt Donna! Aunt Donna!"

Donna looked up to the landing at the top of the curving staircase. A freckled girl with tangly reddish hair flashed a toothy grin to the just-arrived aunt.

"Is it true?" The girl wondered aloud as she began to hop down from step to step. "Is mom really coming home today?"

"Now why would I lie about something like that?" Donna grinned as the girl reached the bottom steps. "Come here, Starla."

The girl hurried toward Donna's outstretched arms, but slowed as she came nearer.

Her brow furrowed—a look of worry: "Is it *safe?*"

A little over a year prior, Donna's participation in a scientific research study had yielded the curious side effect of turning everything she touched into gold. In an unfortunate accident, Starla herself had been one of the casualties of an untimely gilding. With the help of friends, Donna managed to succeed in breaking into the lab to secure an antidote which was able to restore the girl to her lively self, though her memories of the incident were nearly nonexistent. Donna had made the difficult choice shortly thereafter to tell the girl the truth about what happened—after all, it was the best way to prevent another such incident. Ever since that conversation, though, the child had kept her distance, afraid to get close to her aunt—afraid to touch.

Donna crouched a little and wiggled her gloved fingers. "It's safe," she assured the girl. "I've got the special gloves, remember?" Still not sure the girl was convinced, Donna exhaled and added, "Dr. Lansing did extensive tests, and it's been almost three months without any incident."

Starla took a couple steps closer, but stopped just shy of her aunt's touch.

"You need more time, don't you?" The woman asked softly, lowering her arms.

The girl nodded slowly.

"That's alright," Donna forced a smile. "Take all the time you need, little Starling." The woman rose to her full height. "Why don't you make a card—something nice—for your mom? I've got to check in with the doctor—I'll be right back and we can have lunch."

The little girl flashed another endearing smile before scurrying back up the stairs. Donna sighed and moved down a hall to her left. She took a turn at the end of the long, narrow corridor and began to ascend a curving staircase. At the top of the steps, Donna was confronted with a simple, thick wooden door. She gave it a light rap.

A few moments later, she heard fingers fumbling with locks on the other side of the door. It swung open, revealing a young bespectacled man whose hair shot up in all directions. He grinned when he recognized Donna.

"Oh, Miss Locke! What are you doing awake at an hour like this?" The doctor grimaced. "Are you having trouble sleeping, too?"

"It's almost noon, Roger," Donna smirked.

"Oh," he replied, dumbfounded. "Hadn't realized. Come in." Dr. Lansing opened the door wider and allowed his visitor to enter the room. It was a large studio apartment above the garage that doubled as the doctor's laboratory and living quarters.

"Maybe," Donna said, moving toward a window with a thick curtain, "you should let a little light in every once in a while." She quickly drew back the cloth, revealing a burst of blinding Florida sunlight.

The newfound beams illuminated a long worktable upon which sat an assortment of vials, measuring cups, and sheets of looseleaf notepaper. A bunsen burner gurgled in the corner.

Roger made a sudden exclamation and quickly crawled on all fours under a desk. "My favorite pen! *That's* where it went." On his way out from under the table, the doctor's head bumped the bottom surface with an audible *thud!*

"Yikes," Donna winced. "You alright?"

The doctor stood up, rubbing the bump. "Just a flesh

wound." He placed the favored writing implement on the tabletop. "Have you made any progress in locating Officer Myles?"

Donna shook her head. "None." She seemed to sink into a memory. "I just can't understand how Angela could get him and keep him off the grid like that for so long."

"She's a powerful woman," Roger noted. "Believe me—I would know."

Donna chuckled. "Powerful and deranged," she muttered. "A wonderful combination. Well, she can't hide forever. I'm going to find her *and* Marcus—whatever it takes."

"Well, when you do," the doctor started as he moved toward his assortment of vials, "I will *hopefully* have a cure devised for his, um, condition—and yours."

"How close are we?"

"I can't know for certain," he began. "But cracking the science behind the lining of those gloves I made for you certainly helped me get a better grasp of what we're dealing with. Months and months went into testing and crafting the original compound that gave you your, er, *abilities*," he continued. "You'll recall we used the last of the antidote to bring little Starla back to life. I haven't yet been able to recreate it or reverse-engineer its effects, but I promise you, Donna: we'll find a way to turn your dear Marcus back from a golden statue to his rightful, dashing, human form."

As the man finished, Donna sighed and stared out the upstairs window at the cerulean waves outside. "Thank you, Roger," she said finally. "I know you're trying your hardest.

I'm just grateful for everything you've done so far."

"It's the least I can do, Donna," he muttered. "After all, it's my fault the treacherous compound that brought all this about even existed in the first place."

Donna turned and looked firmly into the man's eyes. "This is *not* your fault, Roger. You may have crafted the compound, but you aren't responsible for how others misused it. If there's anyone to blame, it's Angela Hyde—and the rest of those awful people at Pelican."

"I appreciate that, Miss Locke."

"Alright then," Donna said, moving toward the door. "I'll leave you to it. I've got a big day ahead—the medical staff is moving my sister into the house in a few hours and they'll need some space, and I have the big fundraising gala tonight." She paused as she opened the door. "Actually, could you keep an eye on Starla for me tonight? Normally, I'd ask the girls, but they're going to join me as my guests."

"S-sure," Roger stuttered. "I haven't had many adventures in babysitting, but I suppose I can give it a try."

Donna smiled. "She's old enough to entertain herself. Just keep her safe and alive, okay?"

The man nodded affirmatively and forced a hesitant, awkward smile.

"Catch ya later, Doc." Donna closed the door behind her and returned to the house.

The handsome, disheveled man closed his eyes. The

sun had nearly set, and the sky and his skin were bathed in salmon hues. Enrico Castillo inhaled a gust of salty air. He sighed deeply then returned his gaze to the perspiring glass on the table in front of him, filled to the brim with a bubbling, colorful liquid. A pair of matching glasses rested haphazardly beyond the other—balancing between the slats of the table—their contents already consumed.

A speaker pumped a twangy, meandering tune about a pineapple-centric beverage—a track that had been on loop throughout The Uplander since the song became a radio hit almost two years prior. Rico didn't care if he'd heard it a million times, though; if there was anything that made him feel at ease now, it was the familiarity of a song about piña coladas.

As he took the first sip of his sweating beverage, Castillo glanced across the street. A clean, white conversion van sat parked in one of the beachfront parallel spaces. It had sat there unmoved for most of the afternoon. The vehicle was void of passengers, its doors were locked, and the parking meter was now ticking precariously close to its expiration. *The driver will be here within the hour,* Rico noted. *These types of lowlifes aren't ones to waste a dime or risk the attention of a parking ticket.*

So Castillo waited and watched. It was a simple enough assignment—wait for the driver, then follow them to a deal—which was why the officer felt no shame in taking in a few afternoon drinks while he passed the time. Sure, his supervisor would have something to say about it. *But what Chief doesn't know can't hurt him.*

The sun sank quickly, as it does in the last moments of afternoon, and dusk soon grew near. On cue, the neon lights along South Beach flickered to life, revealing the names of hotels, clubs, and eateries as well as formerly-hidden beams that accentuated the distinctive lines and curves of the decadent low-rise architecture.

As he took another swig, something else caught Castillo's eye; a man with a smooth, dark complexion and a distinctive jawline crossed the intersection beside The Uplander. The officer nearly choked, then swallowed with a wince before taking a second look at the pedestrian.

Marcus? Can it really be—?

Castillo quickly rose from his seat and tried to get another look at the man, but the figure walked briskly with his back to the officer. Rico prepared to shout his partner's name, then paused with his mouth agape. The man turned. The officer's shoulders and pulse slumped. It wasn't Marcus. *Just another anonymous, transient face on South Beach.*

A loud noise shifted Castillo's attention abruptly. An engine sputtered. A van. *The* van. The officer whipped around and instinctively felt for his holster under the side of his linen blazer while he kept his eyes on the white van. Its windows boasted a heavy tint which made it impossible for the officer to discern the identity of the driver in the dim twilight.

Drat!

Before he knew what was happening, Castillo witnessed the van lurch out of the parking space and start down the street. Traffic was picking up as people flowed to the main drag for dinner and a taste of the seaside nightlife, so the vehicle lumbered slowly at first. Gradually, though, the van was picking up speed—and getting away.

Realizing his squad car was too far in the opposite direction, Rico moved his hand away from his holster, threw a few bills on the table, and sprinted across the outdoor bar area toward the sidewalk. He reached the steps, stumbled, and nearly lost his balance, narrowly avoiding a faceplant on the concrete. Castillo quickly regained his composure and looked up. The van continued to rumble down the street. Rico once again reached under his jacket and, this time, removed a loaded sidearm.

By this time, the van was nearly a block ahead of him. With a woozy glance up the crowded sidewalk, Castillo began to run. The image of an armed man running beside a busy street caused several passersby alarm; many ducked into the alcoves of shops and restaurants to hide.

"Metro-Dade!" Castillo identified himself as he shuffled past. "Metro-Dade PD—keep out of the way!"

The van picked up speed now. Castillo realized that if he didn't act fast, the vehicle would get away and there would be no hope of catching up on foot. So, as he ran, the young officer aimed his handgun toward the van, dashing in and out of clear shots between lampposts and cabs. He half-squinted to get a better shot and pulled the trigger with confidence.

Crrrack-pling!

He was aiming to shatter the driver-side window, but

Castillo's bullet ricocheted off the side of the van—several feet from its intended target. The young officer leaped over a sidewalk grate and raised the gun again.

Last chance.

Castillo squeezed.

Crack!

Glass flew everywhere. The window burst over the asphalt and Castillo lowered his gun and bit his lip. The bullet had shattered the glass of a window on a building across the street; the van's glass was still intact, and the vehicle careened around a corner and out of Castillo's sight as the man slowed to a light jog, then a full stop. Out of breath, the man hunched over and groggily tucked his weapon back into its place.

"Are you insane?" A pair of women with short, sequined dresses and massive hair shot disgusted, fearful glances at Castillo as they clacked past atop high heels and disappeared into the throng.

The officer looked up and around. Crowds had gathered on every corner and watched with nervous anticipation for what he might do next. A couple of cameras flashed.

"Nothing to see here," Castillo shouted to no one in particular. "You can move along."

Gradually, the onlookers returned to their nighttime revelry and Castillo slumped back down the sidewalk to find his car. He decided the whole incident would be better left unmentioned to his superiors.

What Chief doesn't know can't hurt him.

CHAPTER 3

"What the hell were you thinking?" The chief was nearly a foot shorter than Rico but now towered over him as the officer sat unflinching in a chair across from the desk. "Firing off a sidearm into a crowd of civilians? Tell me this isn't true, Castillo." There was no immediate response. "You're kidding—it *is* true?"

Castillo slumped in the stiff chair and clenched then opened his fists. "I didn't fire *into* a crowd exactly," he began cautiously. "But yes, there were civilians nearby. The driver was getting away—"

"That's the least of our concerns; there'll be another runner that crops up tomorrow." He shook his head. "You've gotta be kidding me," the chief muttered and spun toward the glass-block window behind him, backlit by streetlamps outside the station. He massaged his glistening forehead for a few seconds before facing Officer Castillo once more.

"You've been with Metro-Dade for how long now, Rico?"

"Four or five years," Castillo mumbled.

"Right. So you are well aware that this kind of behavior is *not* acceptable for a member of our force." The chief began to pace behind his desk.

The officer nodded slowly. "So, what, then? Is this it for me?"

A rotating box fan in the corner sputtered, filling the otherwise silent and stale room with an ambient buzz and a burst of lukewarm air. The chief sat down on the corner of the desk and inhaled deeply. "I'm a firm believer in giving people a chance to prove themselves, but you're about *this* close to the edge, Castillo." The diminutive man held out his thumb and forefinger a few millimeters from each other. "Unfortunately," he continued, "it's been a trying year for the city, so we're short-staffed as it is. Which is why I'm going to give you the opportunity to make up for this." He held up a trio of fingers on his pudgy hand. "Three strikes, you're out. Tonight? That was strike one." He lowered one of his fingers.

"So you're giving me two more strikes?" Castillo shifted in his seat, relaxing slightly.

"Well, I hope you won't *intend* to strike out," the chief said as he rose to his feet and started to pace again, this time a few feet from the seated officer. "Listen, I know this past year has been tough on you—what with losing Officer Myles and all—but the past few months you've really started to slip. I'm, well, *concerned* to say the least. Which is why I'm going to need you to turn in your weapon."

Castillo's eyes shot wide and he gripped the arms of the chair to keep from springing out of it. "You're taking away my gun?"

"That's what I said."

"With all due respect, Chief," Castillo started, shaking his head, "how do you expect me to do my job without my sidearm?"

The chief stopped pacing and grinned at Castillo. "Don't worry. Your partner's going to be armed."

"My *partner?*" Castillo started to sink back into his seat as the chief punched a few numbers on his desk phone. "Marcus Myles is my partner, sir. He's still out there somewhere and I'm going to find him. He's coming back—"

The chief held up a finger for Rico to quiet down. The phone began to ring softly through the receiver.

"Yes, thanks, Marge," the chief muttered into the phone. "Send in Officer Jones. Thank you, Marge." When he was done, the chief hung up the receiver with a clunk and turned back to Castillo. "For the time being, I'm not comfortable sending you out into the field on your own."

Castillo jumped to his feet. "But Marcus is—"

"We don't know *where* Marcus is right now, but it definitely isn't here." The chief's words were stern and decisive. "The point is that you need a new partner for now."

"Whoever this Officer Jones guy is, he better not get in my way—"

Castillo was cut short as the office door swung open with a light creak and the two men turned. A sturdy, uniformed silhouette appeared, backlit by the fluorescents in the hall, and sauntered confidently into the room. Castillo raised an eyebrow as he realized that the approaching officer was a dark-haired young woman, around his own age.

The chief gestured toward her. "Officer Rico Castillo, meet Officer Tracy Jones: your new partner."

Officer Jones extended a firm hand toward Castillo, which he shook hesitantly.

"Officer Jones joins us from the mean streets of New York City," the chief explained.

Jones smiled, revealing a pronounced dimple on one cheek. Her voice was smooth and refined, with a hint of grit. "Just got off the plane a few hours ago, actually."

"Then I guess I should say, 'Welcome to Miami,'" Castillo quipped and released his grip with haste. "Listen, no offense, but I don't need a babysitter."

The woman chuckled, and the chief sighed: "Officer Jones is your partner—your equal. She isn't here to hold your hand."

"Good."

"However," the chief added, "if you step out of line, Tracy here will be obligated to share that with her supervisor—that's me."

Castillo breathed in and exhaled slowly. "Noted."

After another moment of stuffy silence, the phone on the chief's desk rang. As the chief went to pick it up, Castillo asked, "So, are we done here?"

The chief held up a finger as he placed the receiver to his

ear: "Just a sec. It's dispatch."

The two officers attempted to avoid all eye-contact or interest as their supervisor nodded along to the voice on the other end of the phone line. Castillo took another glance at Officer Jones out of the corner of his eye. In the freshly-ironed Metro-Dade trappings, she looked serious and stern, but Castillo thought there was something intriguing in the way the light caught her deep brown eyes. He hurriedly shifted his glance back to the chief as the shorter man slammed the phone back into its resting place.

"Looks like you two are gonna get a chance to know each other a little better." The chief forced a half-smile before proceeding in a somber tone. "We just got a report of a possible homicide over on the strip—Hotel Florian. A guest found in an alleyway with what were described as wounds from a knife or blade. Dispatch will give you a file with the rest on the way out."

"Thanks, Chief. We're on it." Tracy nodded respectfully and started toward the door.

Castillo followed, but stopped when the chief called out.

"Not so fast, Castillo," he said. "Aren't you forgetting something?"

For a moment, he actually had forgotten. Then Castillo's mind turned to the weight under his coat. Castillo's eyes pleaded, but he knew it was useless to argue. Slowly, reluctantly he slumped toward the chief and removed the handgun from its holster. With a *thud* he placed it in the center of the desk, accompanied by the second, softer *thud* of an extra magazine.

"It's for your own good," the chief said with a hint of sympathy. Castillo rolled his eyes and moved back toward the door. "Be careful out there."

"Yes, sir," Tracy answered. She followed Rico out of the office and shut the door behind her.

When they'd grabbed the file from dispatch, the duo moved swiftly to the garage at the back of the building. Castillo pulled a set of keys and started toward the driver's side of a squad car.

"I think you should let me drive." Officer Jones waited for Castillo to turn toward her.

Castillo nearly laughed as he turned to her. "Let *you* drive? Not a chance, Miss Officer. I know these streets way better than you."

Jones gritted her teeth and exhaled through her nostrils. "So you're saying I should tell the chief I smelled alcohol on your breath and let you drive a motor vehicle anyway?"

All at once, Castillo's demeanor sank, but he remained calm. "Tell him what you want." He started to insert the key into the driver's side door.

"I'll tell him you were drinking on the job." Tracy crossed her arms.

This time, Castillo didn't look at her. "And I'll tell him it was part of my cover." He fumbled with the keys and finally unlocked the door.

Tracy raised an eyebrow. "How much?"

"How much *what*?" Castillo rolled his head lazily to face

her once more.

"How much did you have to drink?"

"That's not relevant." The young man quickly opened the door.

"Seems pretty relevant to me," said Officer Jones, moving closer. She held out her hand. "So I'll say it again: I think you should let me drive." The woman moved her outstretched palm closer.

Finally, Castillo exhaled then handed over the jangling keys to the car. He puffed, shook his head, then rounded the vehicle to enter via the passenger side. Tracy quickly slid into the driver's seat and shut the door. Castillo pulled and slammed his as hard as he could, then stared straight ahead. The engine roared to life and the car sped out of the garage and onto the dark street.

The shimmering yellow Corvette glided along Ocean Drive under a starlit sky with the car's top down and the music blaring. Donna steered the car to pass in the opposite lane, her head bobbing along with the radio, while her two passengers flailed their arms haphazardly in the cool, salty night air. Flashes of neon reflections zipped across the glossy hood as they neared the south end of the bustling island.

"This is *totally* what I needed after a long week," shouted a red-haired woman from the back seat.

"I second Lisa's sentiment," added the woman with poofy dark hair and large hoop earrings in the front passenger seat.

"A night on the town!"

"Totally," Donna nodded. "Thanks for being my wing-women, girls!" She turned her attention to a glowing sign that came up on their left: *Aquatica Tower Condominiums*. "Welp, we're here."

The car careened through a small roundabout and approached a second larger one with a gurgling fountain in its center. After passing a guard who waved them through without a word, Donna wheeled down the curved driveway and braked with a screech right in front of the building's entrance. A well-groomed valet hurried to open the driver's side door to let Donna out.

The blonde woman smiled and stepped gracefully onto the pink-paved drive, allowing the valet to take her by one gloved hand to maintain her balance. Sue and Lisa slid out the other side and swooned as the young man drove away with the Corvette.

"Quit staring," Donna muttered, elbowing Sue in the side.

"What! He's just my type," Sue retorted.

Lisa shook her head. "Susana! The valet's *way* too young for you."

The trio could hear the trickle of the ornate fountain and the faintest sound of waves crashing just beyond a row of low-rise structures to their side.

"C'mon, Sue," Donna nudged her to follow as she started toward the entrance to the towering building.

The lobby doors slid open on their own, prompting a gust of ice-cold air to wash over the women as they entered. Inside, they slowed their steps as their heels clicked over massive, polished white marble tiles. The entry was bright and vast, and stretched up nearly two stories high, with an entire wall covered in living green plants and a triad of small waterfalls.

"Well this is lavish," Sue muttered into Donna's ear.

Donna smirked. "Tell me about it."

A young twenty-something with long legs and a short cocktail dress approached bearing a red-lipstick smile and a clipboard. "Welcome to Aquatica Tower. Are you here for the gala?"

"Thank you; we are." Donna nodded. "Donna Locke plus two guests. They should both be on there—Susana Castillo and Lisa Jorgenson."

The attendant scanned her list then forced a smile. "Welcome, Miss Locke." She nodded to the others. "Ladies. Right this way." She began to walk toward a set of large elevators beyond them.

Lisa whispered, pushing up her red coif to keep its hair-spray-saturated shape: "How do you ever get used to all this opulence?"

Donna turned to her and raised her eyebrows. "You don't."

The lady with the red lipstick pressed the elevator call button and turned back to the three friends. "You'll just press the letter 'P' and that'll take you to the penthouse suite."

"Thank you," Donna smiled and the other woman sauntered away to attend to another newly-arrived guest.

A moment later, the elevator chimed softly to signal its arrival to the ground floor. Its frosted-glass doors opened.

When the prior passengers had departed, Donna, Sue, and Lisa filed in and pressed the button. Immediately, the doors closed and the elevator car began to rise, swift but smooth, while a saxophone track lulled the riders in the background.

"Geez," Lisa shook her head. "I don't think I've been this high up since I visited the Sears Tower with my folks a few summers back." The redhead turned to Donna. "Are they making you give a speech at this thing?"

Donna bit her lip. "They'll probably ask me to say a few words."

"A few words?" Sue's eyes grew wide. "This whole thing is because of *you*, Don."

"I know," she nodded. "If they ask me to speak, I'll make something up. Don't worry about me. You two, on the other hand—go easy on the finger food."

The elevator chimed and came to a stop. Before the doors even opened, the women could hear the thump of a bassy dance track. When the glass slid away, Donna led the way into a loud, large space with warm, moody lighting. As the blonde woman stepped into the room, she realized that it was unusually dark for a reason—with the lights dimmed, one could better see out the wide glass windows that stretched around the entire circumference of the penthouse level, framing an incredible, picturesque panorama of the glowing Miami Beach nightlife and the surrounding area of the bay. Donna started toward the window to view it for herself, with her friends in tow, but she was startled by a voice resounding over the music.

"Miss Locke?"

Donna, Sue, and Lisa turned toward the sound behind them, finding a handsome man in an expensive suit and tie. The man's hair was a dusty brown and his jawline was sharp and freshly-shaved.

"Miss *Donna* Locke?" He repeated her full name just to be sure it was her.

"Yes," Donna raised an eyebrow and extended one of her covered hands. "I'm Donna. And you are?"

"I'm... intrigued by your fashion sense," the man smiled with a sparkle in his eye as he shook Donna's hand and examined its enshroudment. "Gloves in the summer? That's a bold choice—even in Miami."

"She's a bold lady," Sue tilted her head with a hint of attitude. "And I think she asked you a question."

"Sue!" Lisa whispered and gave her counterpart a light smack on the shoulder.

Again, the man chuckled and smiled winsomely. "Of course. I'm Declan," he said. "Declan Draven. It's a pleasure to meet you."

Donna's eyes narrowed in a look of recognition. "Wait, *you're* Declan Draven?"

"In the flesh," Declan replied.

Sue leaned to Lisa and muttered in her ear: "Who's that?"

"We are *very* grateful for your generous gift, Miss Locke," he continued. "I was delighted to hear that you'd be joining us this evening." The music began to fade. "Oh, I think we're about to begin. Follow me." He motioned with his hand as he began to move toward a sort of stage near the middle of the room. Hesitantly, the three women followed closely behind.

"How do you know this guy?" Lisa asked Donna as they walked.

"This is my first time meeting him," Donna responded, seeming distracted. "He's the director of the research foundation that I made a very large gift to this year."

"I don't buy it," Sue added in a quick whisper. "He's too attractive to be a researcher."

Donna rolled her eyes and shook her head as they reached the edge of the stage. Declan motioned for Donna to wait while he stepped up to a spotlit microphone. The dozens of patrons who were present immediately began to quiet down and turn their focus to the man.

"Well, good evening, friends," Declan's voice resounded over invisible speakers. "It's a pleasure to have you all here for the annual gala in support of The Draven Foundation." The patrons, mostly elderly couples with fake tans, erupted in a measured applause. "I want to thank each one of you for your generosity this year, which has enabled us to raise an impressive, record-breaking amount of fifteen-million dollars."

Again the attendees clapped and smiled.

"But there is one, exceptional woman to whom the Foundation owes an incredible debt of gratitude," he continued, turning to look at Donna with his signature smirk. "Please show your appreciation for the incomparably generous Miss Donna Locke."

With a deep breath, Donna held her chin high and stepped onto the stage. She smiled out at the crowd and approached Declan and the microphone, where she waited several moments for the applause to die down.

"Thank you," Donna said at last. "When I saw the work that The Draven Foundation was doing to help make this world a better place, I knew that I wanted to ensure that they could carry out their mission. I believe that money is merely a thing to make the world better, and there's more than enough money in this room—" This elicited a chuckle from the audience. "And more than enough work to be done. So won't you join me in raising a glass to thank the true hero of the evening?" Here two attendants handed the speakers bubbling champagne flutes, and Donna turned to Declan as she spoke: "To Mr. Declan Draven—a man who's done far more good than he takes credit for." Donna leaned her glass toward him, raised an eyebrow, then took a sip.

Declan hesitated a moment before tipping his head back to take a large swig. When the audience had taken their own sips, they began to applaud once more. Donna smiled, waved, then returned to her friends at the edge of the stage.

CHAPTER 4

As she looked out across what looked like a miniature model of Miami from so many floors up, Donna pressed a gloved hand against the glass. Sue and Lisa had disappeared to the bar and allowed Donna a chance to take a breather after her stint in the spotlight; she hadn't realized how much she needed the moment of solitude.

The music drifting about the penthouse ballroom was far more mellow now, and the patrons indulged themselves in jollification with the occasional—almost startling—outburst of drunken laughter. Donna squinted with one eye and ran her gloved finger along the window, tracing the sparkling South Beach coastline in the dark.

"Spectacular, isn't it?"

The voice was clear and smooth, prompting Donna to whip around. It was Declan.

"Oh, yes," Donna smiled and nodded her chin toward

the glass. "I've spent so much time down there, I never even dreamed of what the city or the island could look like from so far up."

"She's really showing off for you tonight," Declan grinned as he stepped beside her.

He exhaled slowly and fogged the glass. Donna barely noticed her own breaths quicken.

"You were looking for something," Declan said after a brief lull, gesturing down toward the city lights below.

Donna hesitated, then shook her head, "It's nothing."

Declan's eyes narrowed and he turned his whole body so that he was now leaning against the thick glass. "No, really—it's alright," he urged softly. "What was it? Your home?"

The blonde woman closed her eyes and inhaled deeply, then looked out once more. "It's silly, really," Donna muttered. "There's this little hole-in-the-wall pizza place just off the strip—Jaci's—and I wondered if I'd be able to see it from all the way up here."

"Well?" Declan turned again to face the view.

Donna breathed in deeply then sighed. "We're too high up." She shook her head, then slumped her shoulders slightly.

By that time, a pulsing song concluded and gave way to another. Someone spilled a drink and a patron shouted, but Declan's attention was laser-focused on Donna.

"I'm guessing there's more to Jaci's than just a good slice of pizza?" His pronounced jawline loosened as he smiled.

This broke the tension and Donna responded with an involuntary chuckle. "Yeah," she replied. "Jaci's is where I met someone very, um, dear to me."

The handsome host shifted his feet a bit, as if deciding whether he should say what he was thinking. Finally, he moved closer to Donna and spoke softly: "It's where you met *Marcus?*"

Donna's brow furrowed and her eyes grew wide. "Y-yes, how did you know—?" She took a half-step back.

"I know a lot of things," he said, glancing around the room before returning his determined gaze to Donna. "I know why you wear those gloves. I know about Angela Hyde. And I know about what she did to Marcus Myles."

"Where is he?" Donna blurted, then lowered her voice when she remembered the crowd nearby. "Do you know where Marcus is?"

Declan lowered his head and exhaled slowly. "No. I don't know where Angela's taken him." Just as Donna's shoulders began to sink, he continued, "*But*... we know who does."

Donna's jaw hung open for a moment before she clenched her teeth and leaned toward Declan. "*Who? Who* knows where he is?"

At this point, Donna glanced toward the bar to witness Sue and Lisa stumbling out of their seats. The two women scanned the room until they located Donna, then waved and began to move across the room.

Declan ran the tip of his tongue along his lips and noticed the women coming toward them. "Not here." The man shook his head and reached into a pocket of his coat. He placed a small slip of paper into Donna's gloved hand. "Meet us tomorrow. The details are all there. There's far more to this story than you know, Miss Locke."

She barely had a moment to glance at the slip before Sue and Lisa shouted, "Don! You ready to go?"

"Almost!" Donna hollered back with a forced smile, then quickly returned her attention to Declan. "Wait—what's this all about? Meet '*us*'? Who's *us*?"

Declan straightened his coat and smiled. "The *team*."

Before Donna could ask any more questions, her friends arrived at her side to greet her. When she turned back to Declan, Donna found that the man had already vanished to another part of the room. Sue and Lisa's voices faded into the background as Donna's mind raced to understand what had just occurred. In the flurry of questions, a single truth rose to the top of Donna's mind:

Declan knows how to find Marcus.

An ambulance arrived outside Hotel Florian moments before the squad car, bouncing crimson shadows across the building's facade in rapid succession. Officer Jones slowed the vehicle as they approached, noting a small crowd of pedestrians gathering across the street. When the car came to a stop, Castillo heard a click as he started for the door handle. He squeezed the handle to unlatch it and disembark, but he was met with resistance. The door was locked. Irritated, the man sighed and turned to Tracy.

"You gonna let me out or what?"

Tracy raised an eyebrow. "Depends. You gonna do anything stupid?"

Castillo exhaled sharply. "I'm fine," he muttered, gritting his teeth. "Now are you going to continue to criticize every single thing I do, or are we going to do our jobs?" The man glared at the other officer.

Officer Jones cracked a half-smile and unlocked the doors while she maintained her eye-contact with Castillo. "Chief told me about the strikes: two more and you're out. Don't make this difficult, okay?"

Instead of replying, Castillo rolled his eyes and opened the door. Jones followed suit and the two moved swiftly toward the hotel and the flashing siren lights.

The pair was greeted at the front steps by a distraught, older woman with graying hair tied back in a hurried bun. She introduced herself as Mrs. Menken, the hotel manager. "Oh, thank God you're here," she said with the voice of a lifelong smoker. "The paramedics are here to check out the body now, but they're waiting for you before they touch anything. Didn't want to disturb the crime scene, tamper with evidence, yada yada."

Mrs. Menken led the cops around the corner and into the alley, where a few medical personnel hovered over a lifeless lump in the shadows. The old manager stood at a distance while Jones and Castillo moved toward the scene, producing small flashlights that they clicked on.

"Metro-Dade," said Tracy to the paramedics as she flashed her newly-minted badge. Castillo lazily waved his own to the medical examiner, who took a step away from the body. "Any signs of life?" The limp and wounded man wore a silken bathrobe, tattered and ripped.

One of the medics shook her head. "He's gone," she said quietly, but confidently. "Most likely bled out from the incisions." The woman gestured to a series of fresh, bleeding parallel wounds across the neck and body of the pale corpse.

"We get a name?" Castillo asked, cocking his head to examine the face. The skin was pale and pasty.

The woman gestured toward the hotel manager a short distance away. "She said he was signed in under the name of a Mr. Wesley Smith."

Tracy turned toward Mrs. Menken as the older woman pointed up and shouted: "That's his room up there—third floor, corner!"

"Thanks," Officer Jones hollered back. She craned her neck to look up to the room on the corner of the building, where a window hung wide open with a glowing warm light seeping through it. Tracy turned back to the body.

"There's no wounds to indicate he died from falling," said the chief paramedic, anticipating Tracy's next thought.

Officer Jones sighed, then looked closer at the series of gaping slashes across the body. "You think those are from some kinda knife?" The officer instinctively pointed toward the red lines across Smith's neck.

"No way," chimed Castillo. "They're perfectly parallel and too evenly-spaced to be a knife. It looks like there's *four* slashes here—and another set there." The incisions ran across Smith's torso and neck.

Tracy knelt to get a closer look, confirming Castillo's observation. "I've never seen anything like that," she muttered after inspecting the cuts for a few more seconds. "We'll need some photos of this before you take him away." The paramedics nodded as Tracy hurried back to the car and returned with a Polaroid camera. She captured photos of the body from a few different angles. The square images gradually faded from gray to color, highlighting the details of the strange wounds.

When she was satisfied, Officer Jones stepped back to allow the paramedics to carry the body away and handed the camera to Castillo, who reluctantly accepted it. She glanced back up at the open window on the third floor. "So he didn't fall," Tracy began to Castillo, "but I'll bet there's something up there that can help us understand what happened down here."

In quiet agreement, Castillo followed Tracy and Mrs. Menken into the hotel. They passed through the lavish lobby and up the tight elevator to Smith's room on the third level. When they came near the door, the hotel manager's voice lowered to a whisper and she motioned for the officers to move in closer.

"Mr. Smith had a number of *men* that came with him," she said, looking over her shoulder.

"Men?" Castillo raised an eyebrow. "You mean like—"

"Bodyguards," Menken clarified. "Booked rooms nearby so they could keep an eye on him. They vanished as soon as all this happened."

Tracy cocked her head. "Do you have any more information on these *men?*"

Mrs. Menken shook her head, then waved for them to follow her to Smith's door. She gave a light rap on the door, then smiled to herself as she remembered it was unoccupied. "Old habit," she muttered then produced a ring of master keys from a deep pocket.

The two officers kept an eye on the quiet hallway while Mrs. Menken fumbled with the lock. A moment later, they heard the click of the latch and watched the woman turn the handle to open the door. As she pushed inward to open it, the door lurched and caught a snag, preventing it from opening more than a few inches.

"Been chained from the inside," Mrs. Menken remarked with a hint of surprise.

Officer Jones reached for the handgun holstered at her side as a precaution while the hotel manager wriggled her fingers between the gap of the door to try and undo the chain. After some time and significant struggle, Menken finally released the chain from its fastening and the door swung open. Instinctively, Tracy whipped her gun out and stepped in front of Mrs. Menken. Castillo followed closely behind as they entered the room and left the manager to wait in the hall.

The room was quiet, save for the sound of a whistling breeze and street noises flowing through the open window. Officer Jones crept as softly as possible, inspecting the bathroom then the hall as the duo moved into the main space of the room.

The covers were strewn across the bed. A housekeeper's bar cart rested in a corner, while a shattered glass cup lay in fragments near the entryway, covered in a sticky, yellow-orange liquid. Oddly, there were no personal belongings—no suitcases, toiletries, wallets. Castillo approached the big window and stuck his head through. Below, he watched the paramedic team finish zipping up a body bag, which they promptly carried out of the alleyway.

"Room's clear," declared Tracy when she'd completed a sweep of the closets, the bathroom, and the space under the bed. "So Smith didn't fall from the window, but he also couldn't have left out the front door."

Castillo inspected a bit of fiber stuck to the edge the window. "Either way, something definitely happened here—a struggle by the looks of it." He snapped a photograph.

"But with who?" Officer Jones lowered herself closer to the broken glass on the floor.

Neither had an answer to Tracy's question, but Castillo looked closer at the threads caught in the window. They were accompanied by what appeared to be a few strands of thick, brownish fur. "Uh, Jones? Take a look a this." He pointed to the two bits of evidence as Tracy leaned over his shoulder.

"Silk. Looks like thread from Smith's bathrobe," Jones noted, holding up one of the Polaroid photos to compare. Both were a distinctive crimson color. "Could've climbed down."

"But what about *that*?" The other officer gestured toward the tuft of brown fur then clicked the camera.

"Hair—from Smith or his attacker?"

"Or maybe neither?" Castillo looked closer. "That's like *animal* hair—fur. Like a dog or a wolf or something."

Tracy let a laugh slip. "Animal hair?" She turned and shouted to Mrs. Menken, who waited patiently in the hallway: "Did Mr. Smith have any pets? A fur coat, perhaps?"

Mrs. Menken's face contorted. "He sure as heck better *not* have had any pets! Hotel Florian has a *strict* no pet policy." When she'd calmed down a bit, she added, "But no, I hadn't seen him bring any pets in or out. And it's summertime, lady—no one's come in here with a fur coat in months."

"Bag it and we'll take a closer look back at the lab," Tracy instructed.

Castillo slowly turned toward her and rolled his eyes. "I know how to deal with evidence from a crime scene." He reached into a pocket and removed a pair of rubber gloves and two small plastic bags, into which he carefully placed the two sets of curious fibers. Castillo then tucked them away in a pocket.

While he did this, Officer Jones took another look around the room. She carefully moved around the edges of the room to inspect behind the furniture. Her search seemed fruitless until at one point she crouched low, with her head and hands near the floor to look underneath a dresser; a glint of a small, shiny object caught her eye. Tracy slipped a glove onto her hand and reached for the item.

"Ouch!" She winced. The side of it was sharp, so she adjusted the placement of her fingers and was able to lift the object out from under the dark bureau. It was a small shard of glass, not more than a few inches long. There appeared to be two different syrupy substances clinging to its ragged edges.

Castillo craned to look over Tracy's shoulder and took another photo. "Is that *blood?*"

Without answering, the woman moved quickly across the room toward the entryway. Mrs. Menken hovered at the door, watching to see what the officers had discovered. Tracy ignored the woman and crouched near the pieces of the broken glass cup. As she held the fragment from the bureau beside it, she knew she had a match: a thin, patterned decal ran around the rim on both the shard and the shattered cup, fitting together like puzzle pieces.

"It's blood," Tracy affirmed finally. "Blood—and orange juice." Carefully, Officer Jones sealed the blood-smattered piece into another evidence bag.

"So Smith put up a fight," Castillo posited, beginning to pace. "Dropped his OJ. Things got a little... *hairy*. Then both Smith and his attacker left through the window—but without falling?" Once more the young officer angled his head to look out the window toward the three-story drop below. After a moment of inhaling the salty air, Castillo quickly walked back to the entryway. "Mrs. Menken, does room service usually leave their carts in the rooms unattended?"

Mrs. Menken shook her head slowly. "Not often."

"We're going to need the list of all of the staff who had shifts this evening," Tracy instructed. "And headshots, too, if you have them. If you can gather that, we'll just be wrapping up here."

The hotel manager nodded and hobbled off down the hallway to the elevators.

When she'd left, the two officers took another look at the scene.

"Something's off," Tracy muttered, mostly to herself.

Castillo smirked. "Welcome to Florida. Things can get a little weird here."

Officer Jones rolled her eyes. "Finish gathering photo evidence and let's get out of here, alright?"

The man inhaled slowly then raised the Polaroid camera to his eye. "Say cheese." His face was muffled behind the camera.

"Huh?" Tracy turned toward him.

Click! The camera flashed and Officer Jones squinted. Castillo smiled in satisfaction as the camera spit out the instant photograph. After a few seconds he held it up for the woman to see.

"Yep, that one's a keeper," Castillo grinned from ear to ear.

Officer Jones, on the other hand, had never looked more serious. "Careful, *Rico*," she nearly spat the name. "You're walking dangerously close to another strike."

The man sighed, shook his head, and resumed taking photos of the remainder of the crime scene. When this was complete, the pair returned to the hotel lobby, where

Mrs. Menken handed them a folder full of their requested information. The two officers thanked her and returned to the squad car. Tracy revved off into the midnight city, the car bathed in neon.

CHAPTER 5

The late morning rays pierced through the thin, gauzy curtains of Donna's second-story bedroom. A glittering, golden stripe of sunlight fluttered across her sleeping eyes, compelling the drowsy woman to stir and wake slowly. Donna could hear the soothing murmur of the bay waters lapping outside the thin glass, a peaceful reminder of how much her life had changed in just a few short months. She glanced through squinted eyes at the items on her bedside table: a watch, an alarm clock, and the slip of paper from the mysterious Declan Draven upon which were scribbled the details for a covert meeting later that day.

Suddenly, a small voice began shouting, accompanied by heavy pattering footsteps down the hall. "Aunt Donna! Aunt Donna, wake up!"

The woman ran a gloved hand through her voluminous blonde hair, which fell in a mangled heap as she slid herself to sit at the edge of the bed. The door burst open and Starla stood over the threshold with a huge smile.

"Is she home now? Can I see her?" The girl's eyes were bright and sparkling, and her reddish hair hung just above her shoulders.

Donna stretched and yawned, then stood up and shuffled toward the girl. "They moved her in last night," she smiled.

"Has she said anything?" Starla wondered. "Has she asked about me?"

Her aunt exhaled softly then crouched to the girl's level. "How about we go and find out?"

An even wider grin spread across Starla's freckled face and she nodded eagerly.

Donna smiled. "Alright, let me freshen up and we'll go together."

After a few moments, Donna met Starla in the hallway. The woman had managed her hair and changed into a comfortable sundress with short sleeves and mustard-yellow floral designs. The pair made their way through the narrow maze of doors along the second floor until they came to one at the other end of the house.

"Go ahead," Donna urged Starla. "The nurses should've already attended to her this morning, so it's just us now."

At Donna's urging, Starla slowly opened the bedroom door and entered the carpeted room. The morning light filled the space with a calming glow, and as Starla's eyes alighted on her sleeping mother, she thought the woman appeared like some kind of angel tucked underneath the covers.

"Hey, Sondra," Donna spoke softly, though she knew her sister couldn't hear. "Someone to see you." Donna settled into an upholstered armchair beside the bed while Starla threw herself across her mother's sleeping figure. "Be gentle—she may not be in the hospital anymore, but she's still got a few of those tubes keeping her alive."

Starla stood back to her feet and took her mother's cold hand in her own. "Mom, it's me, Starla. Can you hear me?"

Donna watched as the girl waited for a response, tense and expectant. Then, something changed in Starla's expression—slight but barely discernible. A contented smile just to be in her mother's presence, it seemed.

One step closer to a normal life for us, thought Donna. She reached into a pocket of the sundress and took out a slip of paper. The scrawled ink letters were difficult to read, but she managed to make out a downtown street address followed by brief instructions: *Meet at noon. Wear something comfortable.*

Donna took another look at Starla and Sondra, sharing a brief moment of peace. *Almost peace. I'll really be at peace when we find Marcus.* She only hoped her forthcoming mysterious meeting would move her closer to finding the man she loved.

Donna's glimmering yellow Corvette screeched over the causeway, weaving between the mid-day traffic. A pair of slick Ray-Bans blocked the glare of the road while the radio blared over the rushing diesel-exhaust breeze from a nearby semi-truck. At last, the woman crossed onto the mainland

and wheeled toward the designated rendezvous point, backing the car into an alley so as not to attract too much attention.

When she'd disembarked, Donna walked quickly down the sidewalk. She had changed into a pair of high-waisted jeans and an oversized light jacket patterned with blocks of color. *Declan said to wear something comfortable,* she smiled to herself as she fished in a small handbag for the slip of paper.

A city bus barreled by, nearly blowing the paper from Donna's grasp. She gripped it tightly and scanned the address. A quick glance at the road signs indicated she was at the proper intersection. Donna looked around. Three of the four streetcorners were occupied by large dilapidated warehouses, while the fourth contained a parking lot, but there was no hint of anyone waiting for her. Donna checked her watch. It was noon. *On the dot.*

The woman took a deep breath and orbited to glance around her shoulder, wanting to be sure she didn't miss something. After a few long seconds had passed with no signs of the other half of the rendezvous, Donna's shoulders slumped a little. *I'm too late.*

Before she could start back for her car, Donna caught the blur of a blue van out of the corner of her eye. She turned to see the unmarked vehicle approaching quickly from the narrowest of the intersecting streets. Her pulse quickened and she clutched her purse. *Declan?* The windows of the conversion van were heavily tinted, so Donna couldn't tell who was driving. *I can't turn back. They know about Marcus.*

She took a deep breath as the van squealed to a stop.

The driver's window rolled down slowly—a manual crank—revealing a large man with dark eyes and a shaven scalp. He seemed to barely fit in the tight space of the van's front seat. "Donna Locke?" His voice was deep and firm, but his eyes were almost soft.

Donna anxiously adjusted the strap of the small purse over her shoulder. "Y-yes," she nodded. "Are you with Declan's team?"

The big man cracked a smile and puffed, "*Declan's* team? Is that what he's calling us now?"

"Uh, no, I just meant—"

"Get in, Miss Locke," the man nodded toward the passenger side door.

With a deep breath, Donna obeyed, her heels clacking across the pavement. She yanked open the door and climbed up into the high seat. She slammed the door shut. Donna turned to the large man and stretched out her gloved right hand: "And *you* are?"

The man smiled again as he finished rolling up his window with one hand. "If I *shake* hands, I *break* hands," he said without reciprocating Donna's greeting. Her brow furrowed and she recoiled as the man added, "But you can call me Buster."

"Nice to meet you, Buster." Donna didn't know what to do with her hands, so she folded them awkwardly across her lap.

"Nice to meet you, too, Miss Locke," Buster replied, reaching into a compartment between their seats. The man handed Donna a thin strip of torn cloth. "I'm sorry, but I'm going to need you to put this on."

Donna hesitantly received the long piece of stain-splotched fabric and held it with as few fingers as possible. "What do I—?"

"It's for your face," he interrupted. "Blindfold."

The woman took a deep breath and wrapped the cloth so that it covered her eyes. Donna ruffled her nose as she brought the strip close to her face. "Smells weird," she muttered as she tied the blindfold in a knot at the back of her hair.

When the task was complete, Buster shifted the van into another gear. "Alright. Hold on tight, Miss Locke."

Before she could respond, Buster pressed *play* on the tape deck. Instantly, a grainy classical track began to play. For a moment, the string music calmed Donna. Then she lurched back suddenly as the van barreled forward and made a sharp turn. Donna grasped blindly for the armrest as she felt the vehicle rumble and sputter in a dizzying route toward some unseen location. She tried to map the route in her head, but she became confused after the first few turns.

Only a few minutes passed before the motion of the van stopped. Buster clicked another button to stop the tape. "We're here," he said.

Donna slowly removed the blindfold, her eyes squinting as she expected them to be met with the bright, sunny light of the afternoon. Instead, the woman was surprised to find that the van was parked inside of a large, pitch-black room—a warehouse.

Buster disembarked, so Donna quickly followed suit, leaping the final few inches to the concrete floor before looking around at the space. "Where's '*here*' exactly?" Donna's voice echoed into the cavernous space. A few flickering lights hung from the rusting rafters above.

"This," started a familiar voice from the shadows, "is the team's headquarters."

Donna turned toward the sound of approaching footsteps as a man emerged from the dark. "Declan?" She wasn't sure why she felt surprised—after all, he was the one who invited her. "Was all of this cloak and dagger business really necessary?"

"Just a precaution," Declan smiled and extended a hand, which Donna shook quickly.

"I thought you knew everything about me," Donna smirked. "Don't you trust me?"

"It's not you I'm worried about, Miss Locke. We had to be sure you weren't being watched—you can never be too careful these days." Declan turned and started walking back in the direction he'd come.

Donna took this as her cue to follow. Hesitantly, the blonde woman gripped her purse and tried to keep up with Declan's strides. Before she had taken more than a few steps, Donna heard a loud metallic clunk. A series of fluorescent lights flickered on above, revealing more of the vast warehouse, including a seating area, a number of nondescript vehicles, and a table draped in a lumpy, textured dropcloth. A number of cords and wires ran from underneath the cloth toward another larger mass draped in sheets—this stretched at least a foot higher than Donna.

"What's all this about?" Donna pointed toward the coverings.

"We'll get to that," said Declan over his shoulder as he led her toward another corner of the warehouse where the lights had yet to come on. "First, there's some people that I'd like you to meet." Buster followed them, casting a wide shadow over Donna.

Donna heard the sound of a distant door creak open then slam shut. Audible footsteps moving to meet them. Finally, the last of the fluorescent lights sputtered on, revealing two figures—women—walking toward Declan. They stopped a few feet away, giving Donna a moment to catch up to her host. She hovered a few feet behind him.

"*That's* her?" The shorter of the two women dropped her jaw dramatically and sized up Donna. The diminutive woman looked young—Donna thought she might still be in high school. Her hair was a vibrant pink, chopped just below her chin, and she was dressed in a ripped denim jacket sewn with a variety of bespoke patches.

Declan shook his head. "You'll have to excuse Kiki," he said quietly to Donna, though he fully intended for the pink-haired young woman to overhear. "She sometimes forgets her manners." Declan raised his eyebrows in Kiki's direction.

Kiki rolled her eyes. "Manners are just dishonesty in fancy wrapping paper," she muttered.

Here Declan motioned toward the second woman, whose

long dark hair draped down her back in waves. "And this is Mira." In contrast to Kiki, Mira looked mature and poised, dressed in comfortable clothing that accentuated her effortless beauty. *She looks like she could be a supermodel*, Donna noted.

Mira extended a hand to Donna: "Pleased to meet you, Miss—?"

"L-Locke," Donna stuttered as she reciprocated the handshake. "Donna Locke. It's a pleasure to meet both of you." She flashed a genuine smile to Mira, then Kiki, who rolled her eyes again.

"And of course you've already met our friend Jacob Alabaster," Declan said with a sweeping gesture toward the imposing figure that towered over Donna. "We call him Buster for short."

Donna nodded timidly. The man's largesse made her nervous.

"Together, we comprise the Dream Team," Declan explained as he turned back to Donna.

"The Dream Team? Real original." Donna crossed her arms and smirked.

"But *entirely* accurate," Kiki chimed in.

Donna raised an eyebrow. "How do you mean?"

No one responded immediately.

Mira turned to Declan. "You think she's ready?"

"I can hear you," Donna said, flabbergasted at being talked about in the third person.

Declan nodded toward the lumpy dropcloths beyond the

group. Mira, Buster, and Kiki started toward them. "Mira's right, Donna—er, Miss Locke," he said. "This is going to be a lot to handle and I need to know you're ready."

"Ready?" Donna puffed. "I'm ready. Listen, I don't mean to be rude," the blonde woman said as she shifted her eyes across the curious assemblage. "But what's all this about? I thought you were going to tell me how to find Marcus. Do you know where he is or not?"

Declan bit his lip lightly. "We're getting to that," he said calmly. "But first I think you need to understand what we *do*." He paused for a moment then smiled. "Follow me. Please," he added as he began moving in the direction the others had walked.

As she didn't see many other viable options, Donna reluctantly trailed behind Declan until they came to a series of large objects covered in sheets and cloths.

"The reason we're called the Dream Team is because of *this*." Declan, the apparent leader of the group, motioned toward one of the covered masses. On cue, Buster tugged effortlessly on a heavy dropcloth, generating a cloud of dirt and dust. Beneath the cloth lay a strange, shiny apparatus atop a well-worn folding table. Donna instinctively took a step toward it to get a better look, noticing a number of wires and conduits spewing from one of its ends, but she could not immediately discern the object's purpose or function.

Donna shot Declan a quizzical look. "What's that supposed to be? A vacuum cleaner?"

The suave host moved closer to run a hand along the sleek,

chrome casing of the machine. "Technically, it's called the REM-Sleep Visualization Synthesizer," Declan stated. "But we prefer our own little pet name for it: the Dreamcatcher 3000." He pointed to a custom-made label along one side, fashioned in mid-century script lettering that resembled the type one might find on an old household appliance. "As for what it *does*," Declan smiled back at Donna, then nodded toward Mira and Kiki, "it's easier if we show you."

As he said this, the two women removed the sheets that covered the other larger mass, revealing a monolith of boxy television sets stacked several rows high. There were at least a dozen by Donna's quick count, and each showed an identical moving image of black and white static on its screen. A tangle of cords connected the monitors to a dusty VCR.

Here Declan muttered to Mira: "Can you cue up the tape from last night?"

Mira nodded and rifled through a small bookshelf full of VHS video cassette tapes until she found the one she was looking for. She quickly inserted the tape into the VCR and hit *stop* then *rewind*.

"We're what you might call *investigators*," Declan said as he began to pace in front of the wall of TVs. "We use our technology—and um, *talents*—to extract vital and confidential information."

"What kind of information?" Donna sized up the strange team once more, trying to put the pieces together.

Declan inhaled deeply. "Miss Locke," he said finally. "The information our team gathers isn't hidden in a file folder or some penthouse office suite—it's hidden in *dreams*."

"Dreams? You're kidding right?" She glanced at Kiki and Buster, hoping either would reveal that the last several minutes had just been a convoluted practical joke. But both shook their heads.

"Declan doesn't kid," Buster's deep voice echoed off the warehouse walls.

"I say you just show her the tape," Kiki said, shaking her head.

Mira nodded. "Kiki's right."

After a moment, Declan nodded. "Of course. Go ahead and play the tape."

Mira pressed *play* on the VCR. After the brief sound of small machinery spinning and clicking inside the player, the TV screens turned to black. A small white arrow appeared in the corner of the frame.

"Am I supposed to be seeing something other than a black screen?" Donna whispered facetiously to Declan.

"You'll see," he said quietly. "Just watch."

With an impatient sigh, Donna turned her focus back to the screens and mindlessly tapped her foot. Then shapes began to appear—blobs that morphed and contorted from blurry abstracts into clear, distinctive outlines of people.

Two people stand tall, hovering and towering over the smaller man. One of the two is a woman, the other a man. The woman places a piece of paper in front of the small man and he looks down. He's now sitting at an old school desk and the paper is a test in mathematics. To the right of the test sits a clunky calculator.

You may begin, the woman seems to say to the small man. The tall man stands with his arms crossed, a disapproving scowl painted on his wrinkled face. He moves so that he stands over the shoulder of the test-taker. The small man in the desk looks over the opposite shoulder and sees a tiny dark blur in the distance.

He turns back.

Beads of sweat begin to form on the forehead of the man in the desk. He's a grown-up. His teeth begin to fall on the desk, one-by-one. He covers his mouth to try and stop their escape, but somehow they slip through his fingers nonetheless. The man tries to ignore it.

If you ignore things, then they'll go away.

The small man looks over his shoulder again. The dark blur is closer than before.

He turns back.

Now he's a boy—grade-school-age—tapping a strange rhythm on the desk with his fingers while he reads the test questions:

What is the square root of pi?

He scrawls the number 1,204. It doesn't look right, but he writes it anyway.

What is the sum of seven and seven?

Again, he writes 1,204. *Wrong.*

The woman looms and raises a massive, skeptical eyebrow.

The dark, fuzzy blur is closer than ever. *He's coming to get me.*

The boy puts his head down, back to the task at hand, and solves the next question:

What is the product of pink and seven?

The answer is, of course, 1,204, though the boy doesn't know why.

Before he can read the next question, the boy feels something wet at his feet. He looks under the desk to find that a cool ocean wave has lapped up over his bare feet. The tide is coming in. The desk—and the boy's feet—begin to sink into the moist sand. Slowly, slowly he sinks, downward. He is halfway submerged when—

Click. Mira paused the tape.

"And *that* is what a dream looks like on VHS," Declan smiled.

Donna's jaw hung loose. "B-but how—?"

"That's what the Dreamcatcher is for," Declan moved back toward the large machine. "When the brain frequency cap is appropriately affixed to the subject's head, the Dreamcatcher interprets and transmits brain waves into images—like what you see here." He waved at the television stacks and the jittery, final image of the paused tape. "It's truly a revolutionary technological advancement."

Donna was growing impatient. "What does it *mean*?"

"Nothing, really, without other context. The only way we're going to make sense of this is if we have more content to compare to, correlate, find the overlaps…" Declan let the thought trail off as he waited for Donna to respond.

Donna was silent for a moment, apparently baffled by what she had just seen. Then she shook her head and let out a burst of laughter, which rolled out somewhat uncontrollably.

Now it was the others who looked confused. Kiki raised her eyebrows dramatically at Declan, who angled toward Donna: "What's so funny?"

"I'm sorry," she managed to say with a wave of her hand. Finally, Donna composed herself. "I get it now," she said. "The name? The *Dream* Team? It's a little on the nose, don't you think? Listen, if you really wanted me to believe all this stuff was real, the least you could have done was ratchet up the production quality of your video."

No one spoke.

Donna's smile quickly faded as she looked from face to face. "Wait a minute—you're serious?"

"Dead serious," Kiki replied.

The others nodded slowly and Donna took a deep breath. After a brief moment, her mind returned to its most pressing question: "So what does all this have to do with Marcus? Can you help me find him or not?"

Declan tapped his chin. "Have you heard of a man named Rolf Ducane?"

"I don't think so," Donna's eyebrows furrowed. "Should I have?"

"Mr. Ducane is the very wealthy man who runs Ducane Enterprises," Declan continued. "Ducane Enterprises is the parent company of a little research organization called Pelican Innovations—now *that's* something you've heard of, no?"

"Of course I have," Donna puffed. "Angela Hyde worked for Pelican—they're the reason for... everything that happened to me and Marcus."

Here Declan began to pace toward a corkboard near the wall. "We have reason to believe Ducane's planning something big—something that involves Miss Hyde *and* Marcus. What's more, we have a short list of every person who knows where the next phase of that plan is taking place." Declan pointed at a grouping of black and white headshots pinned to the board. "They're called the Inner Circle."

"So if we can find the members of this Inner Circle, they'll tell us where Marcus is?" Donna took a few steps toward the board to get a better look.

Kiki chimed in: "They won't just *tell* you what you want to know. This is top secret stuff."

"What are you suggesting then?" Donna glared at the young woman.

"She's suggesting we do what we do best," Mira added. "Gather intelligence." Her eyes drifted toward the static television sets.

Donna's mouth hung agape. "What, you mean look into their dreams?"

"Exactly," Declan nodded.

"Without them knowing? Is that even possible?" Donna ran both gloved hands through her mass of blonde hair, trying to make sense of the information she had just been given. "This is crazy," she muttered under her breath, loud enough for the others to hear.

"I think you know the answer." Declan started back toward her. "And I know why you wear those gloves, Miss Locke. They're all the evidence I need to know you've seen stranger things than these dreams."

Donna locked eyes with him. "How do you know all this?"

The man smiled, a glint in his eye. "We're just like you, Donna."

CHAPTER 6

The darkened warehouse was strangely quiet, save for the faint voltaic murmur from the muted TVs and a distant hum of traffic beyond the four walls of the large building. Donna scanned the eclectic lineup before her: diminutive but fiery Kiki with her short pink hair; Mira—measured, mature, and perfectly poised; Buster, the hulking but soft-spoken giant of a man; and Declan—handsome, well-groomed, and dripping with charm. His words echoed in Donna's ears: *We're just like you.*

"What do you mean you're just like me?" Donna's words hung in the air, waiting for any of her new acquaintances to answer.

"He means that we've all been burned by Ducane," Mira said finally. "Because of him, each of us has suffered terrible consequences—he's ruined our lives. Isn't that what happened to you, too, Miss Locke?"

"If he's the one behind Pelican, then yes," she replied somberly. "More terrible than even I like to remember." Donna looked down at her gloved hands. "He's the reason for my *curse*."

Buster loosened his cross-armed stance. "What curse?"

"It's just what I call it," Donna said dismissively. "They'd probably call it a *side effect* of the experiments I took part in."

Mira stepped forward and asked softly, "Will you show us?"

Donna took a deep breath then nodded. She looked around the room. "Do you have anything—any small object—that you don't mind parting with?"

The members of the team looked at one another and began turning out their pockets. Kiki removed her hand from her pocket and held out a stick of chewing gum wrapped in a white wax paper package. "How about this?"

"That'll do," Donna nodded. "Give me just a moment." Carefully, she began to remove one of her gloves, revealing her pale hand. She moved toward Kiki. "Now, drop it into my palm. And be sure not to touch my hand," Donna warned.

Kiki hesitantly stepped closer and held the gum over Donna's outstretched bare hand. "What's gonna happen?"

"You'll see."

Curious, Kiki released her two-fingered grip on the wrapped piece of chewing gum. It dropped quickly into Donna's hand. As soon as the first corner of the wrapper touched Donna's skin, the gum's color and form began to change. In an instant, the item was no longer a normal, average stick of gum; instead, it had turned into a chunk of solid gold, while maintaining every fold, contour, and detail of the original.

Donna took the golden gum between the fingers of her still-gloved other hand and held it out for Kiki and the rest of the team to inspect. They craned their necks and stepped closer, their mouths agape at what they had just witnessed.

"Wait—is that *real* gold?"

"See for yourself." Donna dropped it into Kiki's hand.

"Woah!" Kiki remarked. "It's heavy."

Mira looked over Kiki's shoulder. "That's incredible. Does this happen to everything you touch?"

"It *did*," Donna nodded as she slipped her other glove back onto her exposed hand. "Until my friend—Dr. Roger Lansing—invented these." She wiggled her fingers in the well-fitting gloves.

"Must be nice to never have to worry about having enough cash," Kiki joked.

"I thought it would be, too," Donna lowered her head, lost in a sudden memory. "Then everything started to go wrong. I could no longer be close to the ones I loved—in fact, I hurt them. First my niece, Starla. Then Marcus."

The others were reverent as Donna continued:

"There was only enough of the experimental antidote to cure Starla. I kept myself from getting too close to Marcus, but Angela—" Here Donna choked up. She wiped a few stray tears with the back of her glove. "Angela shoved him and I reached out and—I realized too late. As quick as that stick of gum, Marcus turned to cold, solid gold. Then she took him.

They vanished. I've been looking for him for a year now—but no luck."

"I'm so sorry, Donna," said Declan.

The others nodded and mumbled their agreement with the man's sentiment.

"Still," began Kiki, "that's way cooler than any of *our* powers—"

Mira nudged Kiki with her elbow and gave her a stern look.

Donna caught a whiff of the apparent tension and cocked her head. "What do you mean *your* powers?"

Buster was the first to nod. "You're not the only one to experience—what did you call them?—*side effects* of Ducane's experiments."

"Do you mean you—?"

"Yep," Kiki interrupted. "We've each got our own little *curses*, thanks to that old creep."

"And yes," added Mira. "They've also ruined *our* lives, too. Caused irreparable fractures in our relationships with those we love—and loved." She lowered her head.

Donna shook her head to herself, then muttered: "I thought I was the only one."

"Far from it," Buster smiled softly.

Realizing the conversation had gone on for some time and her feet were starting to feel sore from standing on heels, Donna leaned against a table to rest her legs. "So, what are all of your, um, *powers?*"

"I'll go first," Mira said as she moved toward Donna. She looked intently in the blonde woman's eyes, maintaining eye-contact just long enough for Donna to start to grow slightly uncomfortable, and then extended both of her hands in front of her, palms facing upward.

"Um, what are you doing—?"

"Turn around," Mira instructed, maintaining her outstretched palms.

"Why—?" Donna started, then rolled her eyes. "Fine."

As Donna turned around, she let out a scream and took a step backward. The table upon which the Dreamcatcher sat was engulfed in huge flames. "Get away from there! Quick!" Donna shouted to Declan, who stood near the flaming table. She staggered backwards, but her heart rate slowed when she saw the man smirk.

"Don't worry," Declan said. "It isn't real." He nodded at Mira.

Donna turned around slowly. For a brief moment, she thought Mira's appearance was different than before—broader shoulders, curlier hair, her skin a bit less unblemished—but it must have been her mind playing tricks. Mira stood there with her eyes closed, just as before, and made a motion with her outstretched hands. She pointed back toward the table.

Donna looked over her shoulder. The flames were gone. There were no burn marks on the table, and Donna could not smell any smoke.

"Wait—that was all *you?*"

Mira nodded meekly.

"Mira can make things appear quite different than they

truly are," Declan added.

"I'm still learning how to master it," the woman explained. "Right now, I can easily maintain the illusion until someone interacts with it or touches it—but soon I'll be able to confuse *all* of the senses—even touch. Just need a little more practice."

"I'm impressed," said Donna. "Can the rest of you do things like Mira?"

"My abilities are different—and a little more obvious," said Buster. He reached his thick fingers around the edges of the table and effortlessly lifted it a few feet off the ground.

"Buster's the brawn," said Declan.

"And Dec's the brains," Kiki nodded.

"Thanks," he smiled. "Ready to show Donna what *you* can do?"

"Gladly." Kiki closed her eyes and seemed to tense her whole body. Suddenly, a mass of particles began to form at her side, which materialized into a mirror image of Kiki—an identical woman who stood right next to her.

Donna gasped and covered her mouth. "Is this another illusion?"

Kiki's double smiled and walked toward Donna. "I'm as real as you are." She swung a light punch at Donna's shoulder.

"Ouch! Hey!" Donna nursed the spot with a gloved hand.

"See?"

When the brief sting faded, Donna inspected the twin, pink-haired women. "You're a carbon copy of Kiki?"

"Just one," Kiki explained. "I can make more of me, but it's pretty draining to make even just one exist. It's like part of me is split off—we share thoughts, ideas, that sort of thing."

"That's amazing," Donna said. The original Kiki closed her eyes again and—with a puff—her double vanished in a cloud of particulate matter.

Donna turned to the last member of the group. "What about you, Declan? Any special powers?"

"Nothing worth mentioning," he smiled. "As Buster said, I'm the leader of this ragtag group." Then, shifting the attention back to Donna, Declan added, "So—are you *in*?"

"Wait, you mean you want *me* to help you pry into people's dreams?"

"I want you to help us bring down Ducane," Declan clarified. "And, if we're lucky, we'll find your Marcus—and a way to fix things."

"Fix *us*," Buster added.

Donna raised an eyebrow.

Declan continued: "We believe Ducane's secret meeting of the Inner Circle is taking place somewhere off the grid—in a secure facility with a vault where he also happens to keep backups of all his company's research and work. It's the kind of place where he'd keep Marcus *and* the antidotes to cure the damage he caused our friends here—" He nodded toward Buster, Kiki, and Mira. "And possibly even to counteract the experiments done to you. Your *curse*—is that what you called it?"

"You know a lot about this Ducane character," Donna noted. She wanted to ask more questions. Her mind was spinning, racing.

Declan smiled. "I've done my research, Miss Locke." He crossed his arms. "So? Are you with us?"

The others patiently awaited Donna's response.

"I don't see what I have to offer this team," she said finally. "Turning things to gold isn't exactly as practical of an ability as the things these three can do." Donna motioned toward Buster, Mira, and Kiki.

"Miss Locke," Declan took a deep breath. "There are few things as powerful as an unshakeable desire to see justice done. And I've seen how you are at parties, Donna—I know you can be winsome and persuasive when you want to be."

Donna tensed, narrowed her eyes.

"You'd make contact with the members—undercover, of course," Declan continued.

"What, like a spy?" Donna put her hands on her hips. "If you think I'm going to be some sort of Bond Girl and seduce some creep—"

"It isn't seduction," Declan interrupted. "Think of it more as acting—pretend you're onstage. We'll be right there with you through it all. We won't let things get too far." Here he paused, then added. "We could *really* use one more on our team—someone like us. You want to find Marcus, don't you?"

She exhaled. "Of course."

"Good. *They* are out there—Marcus and Angela—and we can find them. We *will* find them." Declan moved back to the monochromatic photos on the corkboard. "We'll do whatever it takes to retrieve the dreams from each member of the

Inner Circle—that should tell us how to find Ducane's secret vault and find your dear Marcus." He spoke to the whole group now. "Using the intelligence we've retrieved so far, we were able to gather the whereabouts of the next member of the Inner Circle. We move on him tonight." Declan smacked one of the photos with a pen.

The group shifted their attention back to Donna, who stood near the stack of television sets. "What about Starla? Am I supposed to just leave her by herself while we do this?"

"Who's caring for her now?" Declan inquired.

"Dr. Lansing, but—"

"It sounds like she's in capable hands. And we won't be far away." The man urged. Donna didn't offer another excuse. "So, Donna, have you made your choice?"

After a moment, Donna crossed her arms and nodded with a hint of a grin. "Yeah. I'm in."

The others cheered as Declan sauntered back across the space toward her. He extended his hand to her. "Welcome to the Dream Team, Miss Locke. We'll see you tonight."

It was late afternoon when the air-conditioning at the Metro-Dade Police station decided to stop working. One of the administrative clerks, Miss Marge, displayed her usual reliable wizardry by producing a number of dusty box fans from a storage closet. She hastily set them up throughout the crowded space to offer a slight reprieve from the oppressive summertime heat; with the fans, the difference in temperature was negligible. Everyone seemed to slug around the office as they carried out their duties—even the wall clocks seemed to struggle to keep up.

With the back of his hand, Officer Castillo wiped a few droplets of sweat from his sun-kissed forehead and flipped through a file folder. His oily fingers left moist ripples at the edges of each once-brittle sheet, which were accompanied by headshots of the employees of Hotel Florian. For the moment, Castillo wished he hadn't let his hair grow out so long.

"Almost done with those rosters?" Officer Jones nearly shouted above the rotating fan that Miss Marge had placed in the corner of the conference room.

"Yeah," Castillo nodded wearily and flipped the page. "Last one. No sign of an abnormally-hairy housemaid yet, but I'll keep my eyes peeled."

Tracy continued her inspection of the hotel blueprints, which had been photocopied and pieced together on the corkboard. The woman leaned on a table and tapped her finger against its surface. "There was no other way in or out of the room," she mumbled to herself.

At last, Castillo turned the final page, flipped the whole stack over, and dropped it with a thud back on the table. "That's it!"

"And?" Tracy rose and took a few steps toward him.

Castillo grinned. "Nothing," he said smugly.

Officer Jones cocked her head. "What do you mean '*nothing*,' Rico? Who was working Mr. Smith's room last night?"

"No one," he shook his head. "That's just it—no one was working that wing of the building last night."

"That doesn't seem right," Tracy said, moving closer.

"It doesn't," Castillo repeated and flipped through the stack of employee files, "but it *is*. There was a woman assigned, but she called in sick. Never clocked in." He held out the file of a diminutive old lady with gray hair, which Tracy snatched from his sweaty hand. "She doesn't exactly fit the description when it comes to her, um, body hair."

After a moment of skimming the document herself, Officer Jones nodded and handed it back to her partner. "Might be something there," she said. "Or it might be a coincidence."

"Either way, we have no way of establishing a motive if we don't know anything about this mysterious *Mr. Smith*." Castillo tucked the absent maid's file back into the stack and closed the folder.

"Maybe the hair or blood samples from his room will tell us something," Tracy mused. "Could be Smith's blood, or could be from his hairy attacker. It'll be a bit before they can cross-reference with other samples in the database."

"I won't hold my breath, then," smiled Castillo.

Just then, Miss Marge entered, handed a folder to Tracy, then disappeared. Inside, the officer found a black and white photograph paperclipped to a stack of xerox-copied documents. She held it out for Officer Castillo to see: "Ask and you shall receive. It's everything we've got on Smith." The portrait matched the face of the body they had found in the alleyway. Tracy walked over to the bulletin board and pinned it beside the Polaroid from the crime scene.

"So what else did Marge find for us?"

"Bank statements, records of his investments and philanthropy—the usual." Tracy set the folder on the table so both of the officers could read.

"Guy was loaded," Castillo noted as he ran his finger down a ledger of six- and seven-figure donations to various organizations and foundations. "How did he end up with all this cash? I've never even heard of the guy."

Tracy flipped the page and read a few lines, then pointed. "There you go," she said. "He was a long-time investor in a company called Ducane Enterprises, which appears to be where most of his funds came from."

"Ducane Enterprises?" Castillo repeated in a whisper under his breath. "There's something familiar about that name..."

Again, Officer Jones flipped a page, revealing something akin to an organizational chart, etched in inky, typewritten characters. "Evidently they're the parent company to dozens of other smaller organizations." Here she began to skim the list, reading a few out loud: "*South Coastal Electronics, Texas Implements, Operation Nueva, Pelican Innovations, Coronado Geological Resources*—"

"Stop," Castillo said suddenly.

"What is it?" Tracy furrowed her brow.

"That last one—"

"The Geological Resources one?"

"No, before that."

"*Pelican Innovations*," Jones repeated. "That mean something to you?"

Officer Castillo took a deep breath. "Yeah," he nodded. "Pelican—they're responsible for what happened to Marcus." He shook his head slowly. "That can't be a coincidence."

Something in Tracy's expression seemed to show a hint of compassion, but her eyes quickly turned serious once more. "Rico, c'mon. Really?"

"What? You don't think they could be connected?"

"Don't you think you're being a little too hasty?" She offered. "That's an incredibly loose connection—if any—to our Mr. Smith."

Castillo nodded reluctantly and picked up a loose manila folder with which to fan himself. "You're right," he said. "It is hasty. But something in my gut tells me this is significant."

Tracy raised an eyebrow. "I swear, if that 'something in your gut' is another piña colada, I'm going straight to the chief—"

"Hey, cool it, Tracy," Castillo lifted his hands defensively. "Haven't had a drop all day." Here he lowered his voice. "But that sure sounds nice right about now." The officer stuck a finger between his neck and collar to let in some cool air from the fan.

After a moment of flipping through a few more pages, Officer Jones said, "Are you saying you think someone from this company killed Mr. Smith? Because it seems like Smith had an amicable relationship with Ducane Enterprises, judging by the size of his paycheck. I'm sorry, Rico, but I just can't see how someone would slice and *literally* sever one of their top employees then leave him to die in a dark alley."

"Listen," Castillo started defensively. "I can't explain the scars—or how it all connects—but we don't have a lot to go on right now. I think there's something here."

"So, you suggest we waltz into an office building and tell them—*what?*—that someone was killed who has a connection to them that's tertiary at best?"

The man thought for a moment then smiled. "I know someone on the inside," Castillo nodded. "Look, let me see if I can set up an appointment for me to chat with her tomorrow."

"Again, we have very little to go on here, Rico—"

"Just humor me, okay? It's the least you could do."

Finally, Officer Jones exhaled. "Fine. Set up the appointment."

"Thank you, Officer Jones—"

"But," she held up a stern finger, "I'm coming with you." Before Castillo could protest, Tracy shook her head. "Chief said we're partners, so we're doing this together."

Castillo puffed hot air through his nose. "We are *not* partners," he muttered, gritting his teeth. Then he added: "But... I'll let you know when the meeting's set."

Satisfied, Officer Jones moved back to the bulletin board and surveyed the information they had collected. Castillo flipped through the pages of Smith's file while the clock inched slowly on.

CHAPTER 7

Starla's fork scraped against the ceramic dinner plate, scooping up the last bit of butter-drenched mashed potatoes. Donna winced but held her tongue. With the girl already keeping her aunt at a literal arm's length, the last thing Donna wanted to be was critical.

"All done?" Donna rose from the table and reached out for her niece's plate.

Starla nodded affirmatively as Donna swooped the dish onto her own and moved toward the kitchen. There was hired help for such things, but Donna had made it a point to try and keep dinners just between the two of them. As she placed the dirty dishes in the sink and began to rinse off potato residue, Donna hollered to Starla: "It's nice to have your mom around again, huh?"

The girl slid her chair back and moved over to a closet, where she removed a plastic box full of crayons. "Uh huh!"

Starla answered back, her mind half-attentive. She grabbed a couple pieces of colored construction paper and returned to her seat at the table. "It was a little bit hard to talk with her while she was in the hospital," continued Starla as she selected her favorite shades of crayon. "Now we can talk whenever I want—just the two of us."

Donna gave an inquisitive glance at the girl. "What sorts of things do you two talk about?" In many ways, Donna still felt ill-prepared for the task of motherhood, though she always thought her sister seemed to be a natural.

"The usual stuff," said Starla, leaning her head as she scribbled. "My friends at school. Toys. Movies. Questions about my dad."

When she'd finished rinsing the plates, Donna returned to the dining table and sat down across from Starla. "I never met your dad," the woman leaned forward. "Were you close with him?"

Starla shook her head, keeping her eyes on her drawing. "Not really. I don't remember much about him." She switched crayons. "He's the reason for *this*, though," Starla smiled and pointed to her ruddy hair.

"Well I assumed it wasn't from Sondra." Donna chuckled. "A lot of things run in our family, but red hair is *not* one of them, little Starling."

For a few moments, the two were quiet as the girl scribbled and scratched words with the dulling crayons. From the angle at which she sat across the table, Donna couldn't discern what the drawing was supposed to depict.

"Your mom's a good listener," said Donna finally. "I'll bet she loves having you sit by her side and tell her about everything in your world."

"Yeah," Starla replied. "She listens. And sometimes she tells me things."

Donna's brow furrowed. "Tells you things? How do you mean?"

"I dunno. She doesn't talk, but it's like I know what she *wants* to tell me—if she could speak, I mean." The girl leaned back in her chair to get a better look at her creation.

"You've got an active imagination." Donna angled her neck and inspected the drawing: a tropical sun beat down on a bird colored in purples and blues, with stick figure women on either side—labeled as *Aunt Donna* and *Mom*. Underneath the bird, the girl had scrawled *Starling.*

"I learned about starlings in school," Starla explained. "Now that's what I think of when you call me that—a colorful bird like this one."

Donna smiled as she watched the girl explain with childlike exuberance—a simple joy, unfettered to the circumstances around her. "It's beautiful. Want to add it to the fridge?"

"I wanna show mom first," the girl grinned. "Then I'll put it on the fridge."

"Okay, kiddo." Donna started to rise. "Listen, I've gotta go, um, take care of something tonight, and I'll be away for a couple days." She searched for the words. "While I'm gone, I'm putting Doctor Lansing in charge—and the girls will stop by from time to time to check on you, okay?"

Starla shoveled her crayons back into their box. "Where are you going?"

"I, uh, made some new friends who are going to help me find Marcus," she said with a bit of hesitation. "I've gotta help them with a few things first." The girl didn't seem to hear her response, so Donna moved back to the kitchen while Starla finished cleaning up.

"You go get ready for bed after you take that to your mother," Donna called out as she placed an empty plate on the counter. "I'm gonna bring some of these leftovers to Roger." She scooped a dollop of potatoes, meatloaf, and steamed vegetables onto the dish. "Who knows if he's eaten today," Donna added under her breath. She grabbed a set of silverware and issued down the hall.

The sun had set by the time Donna and Starla finished eating. As she rounded a corner, Donna caught a glimpse of shimmering light through a small alcove window as she passed it on the way to the garage apartment. She stopped and backpedaled, brushing a gauzy curtain with her free, gloved hand. The bay waters were black and brackish, splashing up along the seawall at the edge of her island property. *I could've sworn there was a light out there.* Donna lingered for a moment. Finally, she conceded that it must have been a reflection on the glass.

Donna cautiously ascended the steps to the doctor's apartment, a sense of unease welling inside of her. *Is it really a good idea—leaving Starla for so long?* Whatever her paranoid fears were telling her, she also couldn't shake the feeling of promise and hope offered by her newly-found comrades.

Marcus—this may be the only way to find him!

Donna checked the clock as the car idled in the dark: 11:15. She turned off the ignition, grabbed a duffel bag from the passenger seat, and slung it over her shoulder as she exited the vehicle. Dressed in black from neck to toe, the blonde woman's mass of hair stuck out like a shimmering, wispy beacon as she locked the car and started down the shadowy road. As she reached the agreed-upon intersection, she looked down at her golden wristwatch.

A rumbling engine startled her, and she looked up to find the familiar van pulling up to the curb with Buster's hulking figure visible in the driver's seat once more. This time, the passenger side window rolled down, revealing Declan and his signature grin.

"Ready to go, Miss Locke?" He nodded toward the back of the van, and the door slid open from inside.

Kiki jumped out onto the sidewalk, also garbed in black, and gestured toward the seats where Mira sat safely buckled. "Well, what are you waiting for?"

Donna took another glance over her shoulder. She had the same feeling she'd had before—that someone might be watching—but this time it was most definitely in her imagination, she determined. She nodded, took a deep breath, then leaped up into the van's cabin. Kiki followed suit and slammed the door shut behind them.

Buster floored the gas pedal and the van sailed around a bend. While Donna gripped an armrest with her gloved hands, Declan bent around from the front seat of the vehicle so that he could address the whole team.

"Alright," he started. "We've tracked a member of Ducane's Inner Circle to a nightclub on South Beach called Casarosa. The subject is the Reverend Juan Delacorte." The man held up a photo of their target.

Kiki chuckled as she snatched the photo, then handed it to Donna. "Ooh, a reverend at a nightclub? Those should be some juicy dreams."

Declan rolled his eyes. "Since this is Donna's first dream heist, I figure we should go over a few ground rules." His expression became very serious. "Don't use your real names. Don't let anyone see you fraternizing with another member of the team in public. And under *no* circumstances are any of you to give the subject even a *hint* of what we're up to."

"What happens if we do?" Donna asked, studying the photograph.

"If this guy catches wind of what we're doing, he'll raise a warning flag to the rest of the Inner Circle that will make it impossible for us to get to the dreams of the other members—*and* it would mean they'd likely change their plans—or worse: move or destroy the vault."

Mira leaned to Donna and summarized: "It means our chances of finding your Marcus would be kaput."

Donna let the words linger for a moment before nodding that she understood.

"Oh, and let's keep the cops out of this, too," Declan added with a nod to Donna. "That means any friends who may have worked on the force with Marcus." He made sure to add, "Don't worry, Donna. I've done my research."

All of a sudden, Donna was starting to feel more nervous. Officer Castillo had been her key support system in the search for her missing lover. But she couldn't compromise the mission at hand—not when it seemed to hold so much promise. She pushed the thought aside to make space for a more pressing question: "Don't we need your Dreamcatcher device?"

"Everything's in the back," Buster added from the driver's seat, taking another sharp turn that caused the van to lurch. "I'll handle its transport."

"There's a green room at the back of the club," Declan continued. "It *should* be unoccupied—that's where Buster and I will set up our equipment. Mira, you'll do what you do best and make the door invisible. Kiki, keep watch and create diversions as necessary, and one of your, um, *selves* can man the recording equipment in the van. Donna, you get the most important job for your first gig." He smiled.

Donna felt more uneasy than she already had up to that point, but waited for the team's leader to continue.

"You're going to get the Reverend to warm up to you, then follow you back to the green room."

"Warm up to me?" Donna's eyes grew wide. "You mean like—?"

"Just lead him on a little," Kiki said with a pair of playful fist-pounds to Donna's shoulder. "You can do that, right?"

"S-sure." Donna returned her focus to Declan. "But doesn't the Reverend need to be *sleeping* in order for you to see his dreams?"

"Yes. That's what these are for." He handed Donna a few small packets—but not before shaking them to indicate the grainy, powdery substance inside. "Thanks to our friends at Pelican Innovations, we can make sure our subjects jump straight to REM sleep in no time."

"No time?" Donna turned the packets over in her hand.

"Well, you'll have just a few minutes before it knocks him out." Declan could sense the woman's uncertainty. "Trust me, we've done this many times—it'll work."

The van made a sudden stop, then swerved around a corner. "Sorry," Buster muttered as the vehicle kept moving. "Arriving in two minutes."

Declan nodded, then looked back to Donna, Mira, and Kiki. "Excellent. Any questions?" Before waiting for a response, the man directed another question at Donna: "You bring what I asked?"

"Yeah," Donna said, reaching for her duffel bag.

"Good. You can change back there." He angled his chin toward the back of the van.

Donna raised her eyebrows as she examined the wide open space of the van's main cabin. "How about a little privacy?"

"I'll close my eyes," Declan shrugged. "You have two minutes."

The man turned back in his seat so that he faced forward

once more. With a deep breath, Donna rolled her eyes and unzipped the duffel bag.

The van pulled into the alleyway behind Casarosa, splashing through a shallow puddle with its front tires. Declan was the first to exit the vehicle, moving swiftly toward a door beneath a flickering neon pink sign that read: *Stage Access.* He opened it, turned his head in both directions to ensure no one was around, then waved for the others to follow. Buster killed the engine and rounded the back of the van while the women hurried toward the door.

"Ladies first," Declan smiled and made a dramatic flourish with his free hand.

Mira and Kiki hurried through the door into the shadows, but Donna lingered a moment longer, straightening out the front of a gold sequined dress with her gloved hands. "How do I look?"

Declan flashed a grin. "Like a million bucks." Then, as Donna started past, he clutched her forearm. "Donna—"

She cocked her head back toward him, glancing first at his gentle but sure grip.

"You can do this. Remember, this is how we're going to save your precious Marcus. This is how we make things *right*."

His gaze was oddly intent, Donna noticed, but she raised her chin and freed herself of his grip. "Right," she nodded and feigned a smile. "See you in a few, Declan."

The space behind the stage was pitch black, so Donna

threw her arms in front of her and cautiously followed the growing thrum of bass and synthesizers that issued from some unseen hallway. The dim, red glow from an exit sign guided her like a hellish north star in the distance, and Donna finally managed to escape from total darkness. With her gloved fingers brushing along one wall to keep her balance, Donna was startled when her hand bumped a cold, metallic object. She strained to see better, but the wall appeared to have no visible extrusions. As she moved to examine the strange phenomenon closer, the woman heard a voice whisper in the shadows.

"*That's* the door where you'll bring the Reverend." It was Mira's voice.

Donna whipped around. She hadn't noticed the woman's figure lurking in the shadows of a thick curtain, but the red exit light now cast its harsh glow along her face. Something about Mira's appearance looked different to Donna, but the dim light made it difficult to get a clear look.

Mira whispered. "Pretty convincing, huh?"

"You mean—?" Donna pointed toward the place where she had felt—but not *seen*—the metal door handle. In fact, Donna didn't even see a *doorway*—just a smooth wall with cracked and chipped paint.

"The illusion usually falls apart when people start touching things," Mira explained softly. "Kiki will do her best to keep anyone out of this corridor, but in case anyone finds their way back here, I'll keep things under wraps." Here she closed her eyes. For a moment, the door became visible, with the words *Green Room* depicted in faded vinyl lettering on its surface. Then, Mira waved her hands and it was gone again. "Go get 'em, Donna."

Donna took a quick breath then continued down the dim hall. When she pushed through the door at the end of it, a flood of sound and humid air washed over her. The pulsing dancebeats throbbed in her ears, and the chatter of young twenty- and thirty-somethings made the entire room feel alive. For a moment, it was disorienting. Donna reached into her mind to conjure up the image she had seen on the photograph just a few minutes prior—the Reverend.

CHAPTER 8

Where are you? She scanned the crowd, searching for any signs of the mysterious holy man. Donna's eyes flitted from one couple in matching tracksuits to another sipping drinks at a high-top table. The scene quickly brought back memories of nights dancing with Lisa and Sue and—

Marcus?

Donna tensed. Her breaths grew short. A man sat with his back to Donna, his thick black hair trimmed with an immaculate fade. His posture and physique were eerily familiar. *It can't be.* Donna started toward him. She had to know if it was him—

The man turned, revealing a face that was equally as charming as Marcus', but far less familiar. Donna's heart sank, then she recalled her goal:

Find the Reverend.

The blonde woman slinked along the edge of the room so

that she could get a better view of the full space. Across the dancefloor, Donna spied a man sitting by himself, sipping from a glass that was filled mostly with ice. Donna's eyes wandered to his face. *Gotcha.*

Donna inhaled, drawing in a whiff of sweat and cheap cologne, then made a beeline for the Reverend. She slowed as she drew nearer, taking care to pass in front of him to divert his attention from the slinky college girl flailing on the dancefloor who clearly had a few too many moscow mules. Her instincts were correct; the man couldn't help but notice Donna in her gold sequined dress—shimmering like a living disco ball.

"This seat taken?" was all Donna could muster as she motioned toward an empty seat near the man. Her heartbeat throbbed, raced.

The Reverend grinned. "Actually I was saving it," he said.

Shoot. Donna started to rethink her plan.

"—saving it for you," he stammered quickly, then forced another overstated smile.

"Oh," Donna feigned a chuckle of amusement to keep from cringing. "That's kind of you." She slid into the seat, glancing up at a rosy neon swoosh mounted to the wall above them. *Alright, Donna: think!* She eyed the man's drink. The leftover ice was melting into water. "Another round?" Donna pointed at glass.

"If it means I get to spend a little more time with an angel like you, then of course."

Donna tried not to barf. "Uh—what's your libation

of choice?"

"Libation? Now there's a woman who knows her stuff." He chuckled to himself. "Vodka. On the rocks." The Reverend held up the glass and jingled the remaining ice cubes.

"Sounds like a classic." Donna glanced around. A waiter finished helping the table next to them and headed their way. Finally, the young man moved over and Donna flagged him down. "Hi, can we get a vodka on the rocks and uh—actually, make that *two*."

The waiter nodded and disappeared briskly toward the bar.

"Wow, quite forward of you," the Reverend said with an impressed look. "Quite progressive."

"It's 1981—can't a woman order drinks for herself?" Donna said dismissively.

"I, uh, didn't get your name," the man said.

"I'm D—" Donna stuttered. She hadn't planned that far ahead! "—D-Demetria." *Donna, what on earth?* "And *you* are?"

"Juan." The man raised his eyebrows. "So, Demetria the Independent Woman, what do you do for work?"

Donna gulped. "I'm in, uh, acquisitions... boring stuff, really." It wasn't *technically* a lie. She pivoted quickly before he could ask her any more questions: "And how about you?"

The man smiled to himself and nodded, then spoke quietly. "You probably wouldn't believe it, but I'm actually a priest." There was a glint of both pride and shame in this revelation, as if his expression expected his hearer to say: *a religious zealot patronizing a salacious, hip bar? How rebellious!*

"Oh!" Donna pretended to be surprised. "You, uh,

could've fooled me." *Donna: keep this up and you'll blow the whole thing!* She bit the end of her tongue to keep from making a visible reaction. "Doesn't seem like the kind of establishment that religious folks usually hang out at."

"There's something about a place like this," the Reverend mused, looking out at the lively dancefloor. "Everyone's free to be whoever they please. No pretending. No masks. I guess it just feels a little more honest."

"And you haven't found that in your, er, profession?" She leaned in.

The man sighed and shook his head, then looked into Donna's eyes. "If you want others to be honest, you've got to be willing to put *your* guard down first." His gaze was piercing. For a split-second, Donna was sure he could see through her cover.

Donna was scared but something intrigued her about the man. "That's a challenge for you—being honest, I mean?"

"If the people knew all of the things I've done," the Reverend looked away again, "I don't think they'd keep showing up to my little parish."

"Or," Donna speculated with a wave of her hand, "maybe they'd show up in droves—just like they do every night out here." She observed giddy laughter and bouncing perms, lost in a brief daydream. Donna wasn't sure if the man heard her over the music, for his eyes drifted off beyond her.

"I think those are ours," the Reverend nodded toward the approaching waiter. "Let's forget about what I've done for now, Demetria. How about we look *forward* instead?"

The waiter set two identical glasses on the table, the ice cubes clinking. Before either of the seated pair could reach for them, the cups had already created sweaty rings on the table.

Donna was starting to feel sorry for the man when her thoughts shifted: she wondered how she was going to get the sleeping powder into the drink without the Reverend noticing. He took a sip from his glass and smiled at Donna, keeping his eyes locked on hers.

Suddenly, a woman from the dancefloor moved quickly backward, bumping straight into the Reverend. Miraculously, he balanced his glass to prevent it from spilling, but whipped around with a stern look at the surprise interloper.

"I am *so* sorry!" The woman made dramatic gestures with her hands as she faced the pair. It was at this moment that Donna recognized her: she wore a huge, poofy black hairdo and chunky eyeglasses, but underneath the disguise it was clear that this was Kiki. *Or at least one of her.*

"You almost made me spill my drink!" The Reverend snapped, turning his attention to Kiki. In an instant, the two began to bicker about whose fault it was that she had fallen into him. The man was starting to turn away to try and ignore the conversation when a second, nearly-identical woman walked up—this one sporting platinum blonde.

"You do *not* talk to my sister like that," the blonde, carbon-copy of Kiki spouted, getting in the Reverend's face.

"Well, if your *sister* hadn't run into me, I wouldn't *have* to talk to her like that—!"

Quickly, Donna reached her gloved fingers near the shoulder strap of her dress and withdrew the small package of powder—it was labeled to look like a sugar packet. With a careful rip, she lifted the pouch over the Reverend's glass. As he had already consumed a few drinks prior to her arrival, the man's hand bobbed aimlessly while he spoke to the first Kiki and her double, making the cup a tricky target for Donna. Finally, the glass hovered in place long enough for the woman to dump the powder into the drink. Almost instantly, the dust dissolved in the liquid, turning as clear as the glass itself.

The first Kiki, noticing the deed was done, gave a wink to Donna then wrapped up the conversation with the Reverend with a smug, "Enjoy your drink, *sir!*" She and her twin hurried away into the crowd.

"I apologize, Demetria," the Reverend said, lifting the glass to his lips. He took a long, drawn-out gulp, then coughed and scowled momentarily. When he'd wiped the spittle from his mouth, the man set the glass down. "Now, where were we?"

Donna eyed the level of the liquid in the glass. Declan hadn't specified how much the man needed to drink for the drug to kick in, but the Reverend had consumed nearly a third of it in one swig. She waited as he took another drink of nearly the same volume.

"Hey, uh, it's pretty loud in here, huh, Juan?" Donna motioned toward the door from which she'd emerged earlier. "You wanna go in the back and, uh, find someplace a little more..." She searched for the right word to seal the deal. "...*intimate?*"

The Reverend gave a smirk and threw back his head to consume the rest of his drink. When he finished, he slammed the glass down, stood up, and made a not-so-graceful flourish of his hands. "Lead the way."

Donna took this as her cue to grab him by the hand, pulling the Reverend along as she pushed through the door into the dark, hazy hallway. She pretended not to know her way around, feeling along the walls, until she saw the door to the green room—to keep others from walking in, Mira would make it invisible once they entered.

"Let's try in here," Donna muttered.

The Reverend's eyelids were drooping as he mumbled, "Maybe a little nap first?"

The sleeping compound was taking effect. Donna quickly opened the door. The man slumped and she caught his body to keep him from falling to the ground. Mira must've been working her magic, for immediately a sort of mist seemed to fall from the room, making Declan and Buster visible. The latter of the two held the brain frequency cap, ready to place it on the drowsy Reverend.

"Good job, Donna," Declan whispered. "Let's get him in the chair."

Donna struggled to keep the man from slipping through her arms as he nodded off. "A little help!" He wasn't a particularly large man, but his now-limp body felt extra heavy.

Declan hurried to Donna's side and the two managed to get the sleeping Reverend into a floral-patterned armchair.

Donna heaved a sigh of relief as she let his weight slip from her grip. As soon as the man was in place, Buster strapped the helmet on his head—its wires jutting out in every direction before they joined in a braid of cords that connected to the Dreamcatcher.

"Alright," Declan ordered to Buster. "Fire her up!"

Buster flipped a switch and pressed a large button. The device began to hum. Buster put a finger to his ear. "Kiki, you getting anything?"

"We're live," she crackled back through his ear speaker. "Entering REM cycle...n—" She drew out the sound as if she was waiting, then finished quickly: "*Now!*"

A deep breath.

This is the street I grew up on.

The thought runs through his mind, following a glance of recognition. The man looks left, then right, before choosing to cross the street. It's a sunny day—typical for a summer morning—and a breeze rustles through the tall hedges that line the sidewalk. He runs his fingers through the small green leaves. Strangely, they don't really *feel* like anything, but he doesn't seem to notice.

The man keeps his eyes on his feet—bare—and does his best to avoid stepping on cracks in the sulfur-stained sidewalk. *Best not to break my mother's back,* he muses, thinking back to a grade-school rhyme oft repeated by his classmates.

It's at this point that he has two observations. The first is that he is clothed only in a pair of faded boxer shorts. The second:

I'm late!

He picks up the pace, moving swiftly down the street. Now it's not a street but a garden, and the hedges grow taller here. The man weaves through a garden maze, its living walls constricting, pressing in, shifting with each step forward.

Over the top of the hedge, he can see a roof—a tower—jutting toward the sky. And the sky isn't blue; it's dark and gray, then a roiling green that's almost brown.

Across his shoulder, the man glances at a rustling motion. There is a white bird with dusty feathers and a large, orange, spoon-like beak. The man continues to jog and the bird begins to chase him. First it waddles, then it runs. At some point, it begins to fly and squawk, nipping at the heels of the man who is late.

He runs. He peers around each corner of the hedge maze while trying to avoid the snapping of the hungry seabird. Finally, he reaches what he presumes to be the garden's center. At the middle of the space—which seems impossibly vast—the man sees a glint from the sun's meager rays. An object, shining and glittering and gold, sits on a pedestal. The golden item is a cube with each of its six sides at least as wide and long as the man's handbreadth.

The man reaches out for the cube and extends his hand to touch it—

Tap-tap-tap!

At the sound of the knocking, Donna whipped around toward the green room door.

"I thought they couldn't see the door?" Her eyes betrayed her fright to Declan and Buster, who maintained focus on the sleeping Reverend.

"They *can't* see it," Declan assured her.

"It should be right here—!" came a muffled voice from the hall.

"But it's only a matter of time before they *feel* the handle and barge in here," the leader finished. "Kiki, do we have the dream?"

Kiki's voice sputtered back through Declan's earpiece: "Yeah, he's stuck in some sort of loop but I think we got what we need—"

The handle to the door jiggled. "It's locked—what the—!"

As the unseen intruder fiddled with a mass of keys on the other side of the door, the trio inside the room scrambled to unhook the Reverend from the Dreamcatcher and its accoutrements.

Again, Donna uttered a shrill whisper. "How do we get out of here without them seeing us? There's no other doors!" She waved her hand toward the other three walls of the sparse room as the two men flipped switches and unclipped the brain frequency helmet.

"Mira," Declan's voice wavered. "A little help?" There was no reply, but that was to be expected, for the woman lurked in the shadows just outside the room. If she spoke, she would give away her position and the whole operation. "Alright, get to that wall and *whatever* you do, don't make a sound!" Declan pointed toward the spaces on either side of the room's door. Buster lugged the heavy device and Donna scrambled to follow. Under his breath, Declan exhaled and muttered, "Mira? Come on..."

Click! The intruder found the proper key and the door swung open. Two burly men—both bald and covered in tattoos—entered and laid their wide, piercing eyes on the sleeping Reverend, who was drooped over the floral armchair on the far side of the room. A quick survey of the room yielded no other signs of life, so the two crept slowly toward the slumbering man. For a moment, the man was so still that the others feared he might be dead. One of the pair waved a meaty finger under the Reverend's nostrils and felt a wisp of breath, verifying that he was indeed only sleeping, then turned to his companion.

"Something isn't right," he muttered and then started to inspect the rest of the room again.

Even with the muffled, bassy pulse flowing from the hall, the room felt quieter than it should—the sound dampened ever so slightly. The man thought he saw movement—light playing strange games in the shadows of the doorway—and he moved toward the threshold.

The second man, who remained close to the first, ruffled his nose. "Ladies' perfume," he noted, furrowing his brow.

Suddenly, they heard a metallic *clunch!* from the hall—the sound of the building's back door being thrust open from the inside. The two men hurried into the hallway and rounded the corner quickly, watching the door swing back into place. The first man hustled and heaved toward the opening. A loud rumble of an engine sputtered through the shrinking gap. Finally, the men reached the door and nearly tumbled into the poorly-lit alleyway. A large van screeched away and disappeared around a shadowy corner and out of sight.

The first man muttered a curse and shook his head, then the two sulked back into the nightclub. The rusty edges of the door creaked as they slammed it shut behind them, trapping the pulsing bass rhythm inside.

CHAPTER 9

The sun had not yet crept up to its highest, hottest point in the sky the next morning when the squad car screeched into the driveway loop of a magnificent tower. A marvel of modern architectural prowess, the headquarters of Pelican Innovations climbed toward the cloudless, cerulean sky—a wordless glass and ivory beacon of the organization's outward and upward intentions.

The officers parked the car and started toward the building's lushly-landscaped entryway.

"Never seen it this close," remarked Officer Jones. "Impressive."

"Yeah," nodded Castillo. "I'm just surprised they're still in business after, uh, what happened last year."

By now, Tracy knew better than to bring up the man's missing partner, but her curiosity prompted further questioning: "Why *didn't* they shut down?"

"They've got one heck of a public relations department," the man smirked. "Always pushing out stories about all the 'good' they're doing. You know: community service, life-saving research breakthroughs—that sorta thing."

"Usually a business doesn't survive a huge incident like that." Officer Jones stated. "Are you sure they're responsible for what happened to—?"

Castillo shot a quick glance in her direction and cut her off. "I was there, *Tracy*. I saw what happened with my own eyes. I know that Angela Hyde took Marcus."

Jones gave a respectful nod of acknowledgment as they continued walking across large, pressure-washed pavers. "And this... *contact* of yours?"

The door swooshed open, letting a silent gust of cool air sweep over them. The lobby was voluminous and bright, which caused the two officers to take their next few steps in silence, captivated by the room's strange, tacit magic.

"She's one of the good ones," Castillo answered finally. "At least I think she is. She agreed to meet with us, so let's hope she's in a helpful mood."

The two checked in at the front desk, then filed up one of the elevators toward the uppermost levels of the towering structure. When the doors opened on the twenty-fourth floor, just one floor below the penthouse, both Jones and Castillo felt their jaws loosen; the view from the top of Pelican headquarters was stunning, with large floor-to-ceiling glass windows that bounced a sky blue reflection over the otherwise muted space. As they stepped forward, the duo could see the ocean's horizon line stretching far in the distance, with the Miami mainland skyline visible as well.

"Mr. and Mrs. Castillo?" A young woman's voice interrupted the momentary serenity.

"Yes, uh—I mean *no*!" Castillo scrambled, a faint rosiness growing in his cheeks. "We're not, uh—I mean, I'm Officer Castillo and this is Officer Tracy *Jones*." He made sure to emphasize the last name to ensure the young secretary was abundantly clear on their relationship status.

Officer Jones grinned as the man stumbled over the words.

"Oh!" The secretary's eyes grew wide and she started spewing in a panicked tone: "I am *so* sorry—I didn't know—I only had Mr. Castillo on my list and I just assumed—"

Tracy shook her head and chuckled. "It's fine, hun," she said at last. "No harm done."

The young woman nodded furiously and forced an awkward smile. "Wait here, please. I'll just let Miss Underhill know you're here." With that, the secretary disappeared through one of a large set of wooden double doors, stained a rich mahogany.

"Nice save," Tracy snickered.

Castillo rolled his eyes then asked her, "Do we *look* like a couple or something?"

"Not a chance." The expression on Officer Jones' face became quickly more serious—evasive, even.

Before either of the two could say anything more, the secretary returned and held open one of the large wooden doors. "Miss Underhill will see you now."

"Let me do the talking, okay?" Castillo leaned to whisper to Tracy.

Officer Jones took a deep breath and exhaled slowly, then gave a reluctant nod.

The officers moved toward the door. Officer Jones started for the opening first, but Castillo edged himself between her and the door, causing a momentary awkward shuffle in the tight space. Finally, the man stepped back and gave an exaggerated flourish of his hands: "Ladies first."

Tracy raised an irritated eyebrow and walked into the office. Castillo followed closely behind. The first chance he got, he shifted so that the two again stood side-by-side.

The office was enormous and spacious. A woman sat at a large desk, behind which wrapped the continuation of the bright glass window-walls, silhouetting her short brown hair. She looked up as the two entered. She offered a pleasant smile.

"Officer Castillo," she remarked as she rose from her seat. She wore a knee-length skirt and matching blazer that boasted formidable shoulder pads. The executive moved around the sharp corners of the desk and extended a hand to greet the man. "Been awhile!"

"It certainly has been," Castillo flashed a smile and shook the woman's hand.

"And who is this?" The woman turned to Officer Jones, sizing up the stranger.

Castillo spoke up before Tracy could introduce herself: "This is Officer Tracy Jones. She's, uh, filling in as my partner temporarily." The man gestured toward the executive. "Officer Jones, meet Debra—I mean, uh, Miss *Underhill*, is it?"

Debra swatted the air then shook Tracy's hand. "Please. Debra's fine." She smiled again and returned to her desk. "Won't you have a seat?"

The pair obliged and settled into the leather seats of two chairs that looked more like modern art sculptures than typical office seating. Castillo took another look around the room: on one of the two sides that contained an actual solid wall, he noted a bookshelf, an assortment of oddly-shaped glassware, and a huge painting of a majestic stag with a massive tangle of antlers.

"That was found in one of our vaults," Debra explained of the artwork. "They were going to throw it out, but I thought that would've been a shame. I can't quite tell how I feel about it, actually."

"It's, uh, *nice*," Castillo mumbled. He quickly swept the rest of the room with his eyes. "This whole thing's your office? It's nearly the size of a two-bedroom house!"

"It is a bit much, isn't it?" Debra's tone suggested that she actually didn't have a problem with the room's size. "But sometimes you just have to take what life gives you, right?" She forced a smile.

Neither of the officers was sure if the question was rhetorical or not, but Debra quickly continued speaking.

"Now, what brings you two up to the exciting world of Pelican today?" The executive rested her arms on the desk and interlocked her fingers. Her slight tilt of the head seemed calculated, a power move to appear more inviting. *Probably a technique she learned at one of those weird business conferences,* Rico mused.

Officer Castillo inhaled and began: "Well, first off—thank you for seeing us. Officer Jones and I are working on a case and thought that you might be able to help us out."

Debra shifted in her seat. Castillo thought he noticed her fingers tense, but he couldn't be sure.

"Of course," Debra feigned an eager, compliant attitude. "Anything to help out the 'boys in blue'—oh, and *girls!*" She added quickly with a nod to Tracy. "I'm an open book."

Castillo glanced at Jones, which she took as a signal to open a folder she had carried in. Tracy removed a photograph and stood to pass it across the desk.

"Do you recognize this man?"

Debra took the photo in her hand and quickly covered her mouth with the other. "Oh, my—! What happened? What are those strange markings?"

"We aren't quite sure yet," explained Tracy. She pressed back into the unanswered question: "Do you know who this is?"

Debra became uneasy and handed the photo back to Tracy. "To be honest, it's a little hard to make out the face with all the, um... *lacerations*. But no—I don't know this man." The executive shifted her eyes away from the officers as she said this, causing both of them to become suspicious.

"You're absolutely *sure* you don't know who this man is?"

Castillo's eyebrows furrowed as he pressed in.

Debra gulped, then eked out another mechanical grin. "That's correct."

Officer Castillo breathed quickly through his nose. He could feel his pulse quickening. *She absolutely knows who this is. Why is she hiding?*

"So, I guess you all came up here for nothing?" Debra cocked her head slightly and stood up from her desk chair. "If you like, I can have one of my staff members give you a tour of the facility? The radio tower on the roof is a popular—"

"I don't know that we have time for a tour." Tracy matched the executive's movement and stood as well. "Maybe another day—"

"Um, Officer Jones," Castillo said suddenly, gripping the arms of his strange chair, "would you step outside for a moment? I need to talk to Deb—, er, Miss Underhill alone." He held out his hand toward the photograph in Tracy's hand.

If they weren't in front of a suspect, Jones would've shown her displeasure with the man's request more flagrantly. Instead, she inhaled deeply, shoved the photo into Castillo's grip, clenched the other hand behind her back, then gave a slight nod. "Sure," said Tracy with a smile that Castillo knew was laced with a secret fury.

Debra said nothing as she watched the female officer leave the room.

"And close the door on the way out," shouted Castillo. "Please."

Click. The latching sound indicated that the two were

now the only souls in the room.

"Alright, good," said Castillo, finally rising from his chair. "How about you get comfortable, *Debra*." He nodded toward her chair.

"An officer of the law ordering me around in my own office is *hardly* enough to make me comfortable, Mr. Castillo!" By now, she had dropped the smiling charade, but settled back into the chair with a huff.

"You know the man in the photo." Castillo pushed the tiny image in her face.

"I already told you, I don't—"

"Cut the act, *Debra*! My partner—my *friend*—is out there somewhere because of *your* company. So either you tell me what you know about this man *right* now, or I bring this whole company down—including you!" His eyes were wide and starting to show their bloodshot edges. "Your choice," he added.

The executive was quiet, her gaze transfixed on the photo that Castillo had thrown down on the desk in front of her.

"I know you know who he is," Castillo pressed. "And I know he's connected to Pelican—that's why we're here."

"Look around," the worried woman gestured toward the light-soaked office. "This all didn't just *happen*—I was in the right place at the right time, I worked hard, and stuck with it long enough to see myself move up the ladder. I'm not about to lose it all!"

Castillo was frustrated, but managed to speak calmly. "I understand, Miss Underhill. But if you know anything about this man that can help us find his killer—or if you know anything about where Marcus is—then you need to tell me now. Every second that ticks away is another moment where a murderer roams free. Do you really want to live with that on your conscience?"

The room was silent, and Rico could hear the faint tick of a fancy clock near the doors.

Finally, Debra nodded. "Alright," the woman said quietly. "I'll tell you what I know. But I had *nothing* to do with his death and I have *no* idea who would do such an awful thing—!"

"Fine. Start with what you know then."

"Of course," Debra calmed herself. She breathed in deep then said, "That's Mr. Smith."

"Keep going."

"He is—" She caught herself. "I mean, he *was* a close confidant of Mr. Ducane. He was part of—" She leaned forward and whispered. "The Inner Circle."

Just the mention of it sent a strange chill down Castillo's spine. "Inner Circle?"

Debra leaned back in her chair and scoffed. "It's the small handful of people who make decisions about Ducane's companies. It's top secret—even *I* am not allowed to know anything about their meetings and dealings." Her eyes darted back to Castillo. "But I've done a little research on them myself—have to know what Ducane's looking for in his closest advisors, you understand?"

Castillo raised an inquisitive eyebrow. "So that *you* can take their place in the event that one of them is brutally murdered?"

"I told you!" Debra stood. "I had *nothing* to do with Mr. Smith's untimely death." She exhaled and settled back into the seat. "I'm just saying, a woman needs to be ready for anything. Things can move pretty quickly around here." Debra smoothed out the front of her skirt.

"So who do you think could've done this to Mr. Smith?"

The woman shook her head. "I don't know."

"One of Mr. Ducane's advisors, perhaps?" Castillo began to pace the room while he waited for Debra to consider the option. Another thought popped into his mind before the woman could speak: "Have you ever actually met Mr. Ducane?"

"Of course I've met him," Debra snapped. "His office is just upstairs."

"Is he here? Maybe I can speak with him?"

Debra exhaled. "No. He's been, um, *away*."

"Away?" Rico raised an eyebrow and stopped pacing. "Like on a business trip or something?"

"To be frank," Debra gulped, "no one has seen him for quite some time. He's been off the grid for a few months now."

"Don't you find that odd?"

"Yes—I mean, well, not exactly."

Castillo whipped around. "What do you mean 'not exactly'? He's your boss, isn't he? CEOs of extremely large and wide-reaching businesses don't typically just vanish for months at a time."

Debra shifted in her seat. "He travels a lot—or so I'm told."

"So what you're telling me is that you don't actually know much about him?"

The executive shook her head.

There was a sudden rap on the door. "Officer Castillo," came Tracy's voice from through the thick door. "You almost finished in there?"

"Yeah, almost!" He shouted back, then turned quickly to Debra. "The Inner Circle—do you have their names?"

The woman grinned and tapped her forefinger to her temple. "Up here."

Castillo puffed. "Can you write them down for me?"

Debra considered the request with a few heavy sighs, then opened the top drawer in her desk. She fished out a small pad of sticky notes and plucked a long black pen from a cup. While they listened to another impatient knock on the office doors from Officer Jones, Debra furiously scrawled out four names, then held out the yellow square. Castillo reached for the paper but the woman pulled it back quickly.

"You didn't get these names from me," she instructed.

Castillo nodded. "Of course."

The woman was once again about to slip the note into his hands when she placed it back on the desk and drew a line through one of the names: "Mr. Smith," she explained. Then she gave the note to the officer.

"Thank you, Debra—I mean, *Miss Underhill*." He nodded as he stood and folded the sticky note into his pocket. "You've been a great help." Castillo made a beeline for the doors, then turned at the last moment: "Be careful what ladders you ascend, Debra. The higher the climb, the farther the fall." He glanced at the dizzying heights out the window, then grinned at the woman and swung open the door.

Officer Jones was ready with a flustered expression, but Castillo moved right past her and headed toward the elevator. Tracy followed closely.

"Just *what* do you think you were doing back there?" She said in a harsh whisper as they waited for the elevator car to arrive.

"Using a little bit of creativity, that's all." Castillo smiled.

Tracy wasn't smiling back. The elevator dinged and the doors *swooshed* open.

As the two piled in and stood side-by-side, the doors shut once more and the car headed for the ground level.

"Under *no* circumstances are you to conduct an interrogation without me being present," Officer Jones chided him. "For both of our sakes—"

"Relax!" Castillo interrupted her and held out the folded sticky note between two fingers. "I got us our next leads."

Tracy crossed her arms. "Leads or no leads—you just earned yourself your second strike." She held up two fingers.

Castillo's jaw dropped. "Unbelievable..."

"Now we're doing the rest of this case *together*," Tracy gave him a stern look, "or you're going to be out of a job. Got it?"

Officer Castillo didn't respond, but clenched his teeth.

"So who's our first lead?" Officer Jones asked.

Castillo unfolded the small square and read from the top of the list. "First? A reverend—Juan Delacorte." He showed her the note. “And there’s two others: Viktor Gromble and Cameron Keene—any of those mean anything to you?”

“Nope. Let’s get back to the station—they should have the results on Smith’s toxicology report that we can examine while Marge runs the names.” Tracy gave another stern glance to Castillo. “I’m leading this investigation from here on out, Rico. Don’t you dare slow me down or cut me out again, or that’ll be the end of your career.”

There was much Castillo wanted to say to the woman—the officer who had stepped into his life from some faraway precinct—but he kept his mouth shut. The two officers remained silent as the elevator continued its descent.

CHAPTER 10

The late morning sun danced through the semi-opaque windows near the rafters of the warehouse as the members of the Dream Team folded up sleeping bags, blankets, and pillows from the night before and gathered around the stack of old television sets. After the late evening mission, the group had spent the remainder of the night resting. Declan stood near the bulletin board, placing a pin through the last of a series of recently-added words and phrases on slips of colored construction paper—words like *hedge maze, tower, boxers, chase*, and *cracks in sidewalk.*

"What am I missing?" Declan turned to the others, who looked away from the jittery, paused image on the monitors.

"The gold cube," Donna pointed to the TVs even though that particular image was gone. "That could represent Marcus, right?"

"Could be," said the man as he scribbled the words *gold*

cube onto another piece of paper. "But let's make sure we've got everything here before we start speculating about what it all means."

"There was that bird chasing him," Kiki said. "Was it some kind of stork?"

Buster shook his head. "It was a pelican. You can tell by the shape of the beak."

At this point, Mira rewound the tape, which played backwards like a grainy, first-person home movie on the numerous screens. She hit *pause* when they reached the moment with the bird.

"See? Definitely a pelican." Buster stood and outlined the curved lower portion of the beak with his finger near the screen. Quickly, Declan nodded and wrote the word on another slip, then pinned it with the others.

"So what does it all mean?" Donna moved toward the board. "How is this supposed to help us get any closer to finding Marcus or Angela—or getting to this vault, for that matter?"

For a moment, the others were silent, then Mira gestured to the words on the corkboard. "Every person dreams different things," she said. "But many of our dreams share a common language. People have been interpreting dreams for centuries."

Buster tilted his head. "Even the Bible tells stories of people knowing the meaning of dreams," he said. "Dreams of the future, of blessing—or of curse."

"Love the optimism," Kiki said, elbowing Buster. He

elbowed back as gently as he could, but sent the young woman toppling over her seat.

"Sorry," Buster winced.

Kiki chuckled as she picked herself up from off the floor and dusted off her jeans. "I probably deserved that," she grinned.

Declan held up two of the papers—*pelican* and *chase*. "Quite often, our dreams give symbolic meaning to experiences in our life—usually very recent ones. That's why we're doing this, after all. For example, the pelican bird is likely the Reverend's subconscious symbol to represent the larger Pelican Innovations company. Perhaps he feels guilty for his contributions, hence the bird chasing him in the dream sequence. Make sense?"

Donna gave a hesitant bob of her head.

"His lack of clothing could mean that he's worried about being exposed—that he's hiding something he doesn't want others to see," Mira noted, crossing her arms.

"That'd certainly line up with what he told me right before he zonked out," Donna affirmed. "He was hiding something."

"The hedge maze might mean he feels lost or trapped." Declan returned his attention to the other papers. "Perhaps the tower beyond it represents an unattainable goal. And the cube—"

"It's Marcus," Donna declared. "Like I said. The Reverend knows where he is."

"That certainly *might* be the case." Declan took a deep breath. "But we can't know for *sure* until we've seen more of the Inner Circle's dreams."

Donna seemed flabbergasted. "So that's it? We went through all of that last night and now that's all the analysis you're going to do? You've gotta be kidding." She shook her head. "What about the dream you got the other day—the one you showed me? How does it connect?"

The leader inhaled deeply. "Mr. Smith's dream seemed highly symbolic." Here Declan moved over to a set of words and phrases on a different color of paper. "Perhaps his loss of teeth and sinking beneath the tide were indicative of his own fears—fears of being too deep into something that he couldn't escape. And the dark blur could mean he felt like someone was out to get him."

"What about the number that kept showing up?" Donna inquired and pointed to the card with the four digits on it. "1,204—that means something, right?"

"Could be a secret code," Mira suggested.

Kiki rolled her eyes. "Or part of an ex's old phone number."

Donna hung her mouth agape. "So—*what?*—nothing we've got so far is of any value in helping us find Marcus or the vault?"

"I'm afraid we just don't have enough information yet," Declan said finally. "It's difficult to find the overlap between these disparate dreams with only these two to go on."

Gradually, Donna shook her head, then threw up her hands. "This is insane," she said. "I don't understand how getting symbols from dreams will get us *any* closer to finding Marcus." She started across the room toward the van. "This is a waste of time," she added over her shoulder.

"Donna, please!" Declan sprinted after her, while the others looked at one another with confusion. "Donna, come on," he said when he caught up to the blonde woman. "Give it one more job at least."

Donna whipped around and chuckled. "One more? What, so we can watch some other guy dream about his childhood fears and daddy issues?"

The man exhaled slowly and bit his lip. "Please, Donna. I really think this will work—we *will* find the vault and your Marcus. We just need another dream to connect the dots. The intelligence is there. I know it is!"

"Listen, I can't get caught doing this sorta thing," Donna said defensively. "This doesn't exactly strike me as the most *legal* operation in the world, and we nearly blew it last night at the club. Marcus' best friend is a cop, and if he starts asking questions and getting close, I need to be able to tell him the truth."

Declan sighed. "The truth, Miss Locke, can take many shapes. What's more important right now is completing our mission before more time has passed—before the memories of the vault have drifted out of the Inner Circle's minds and dreams." He paused. "At least give it *one* more mission before you throw in the towel? I think we're close."

Donna was silent for a moment, considering the man's comments. "Fine. *One* more. And if this turns out to be a dud like the last two, I'm out."

"Fair enough," Declan nodded.

"Alright then," Donna held her chin high. "Who's next?"

Declan smiled and nodded in the direction of the rest of the group. "How about we all have a bite to eat and I'll share the next briefing?"

The woman agreed and followed Declan back toward the others to prepare for breakfast and the mission ahead.

The Metro-Dade forensic scientist led Castillo and Jones down a hallway and into a darkened room, offering the two a pair of loose-fitting surgical masks to avoid contamination of the evidence. When they'd put them on, the scientist led the officers to a table upon which sat a microscope, several petri dishes, and glass squares that contained smaller samples of the liquids in question.

The young scientist had her hair tied up in a tight, practical bun and pointed to the first sample. "So we ran tests on the evidence you two collected at the scene of the murder the other night, concurrent with the autopsy procedures that allowed us to test the victim's blood for any of the usual suspects—" Here the woman turned to the officers. "Intoxication, accidental overdose, intentional overdose—you get the picture."

Castillo raised an eyebrow: "I mean, he was slashed with multiple blades of some kind. Are you saying you think he may have already been dead before that?"

"We don't like to rule out anything until we've run the tests," the scientist smiled politely.

"So what did you find?" Castillo crossed his arms.

"Well, we were able to get some samples from the shard of broken glass you found in the hotel room," she nodded. "Thankfully, we were also able to separate the blood from the citrus juice and extract enough from each to run the tests." Here, the woman rifled through a few sheets of paper in a manila folder and held out one. "In the sample of orange juice, we discovered a high concentration of a drug called lethepropol."

Now it was Tracy's turn to ask questions: "Lethe-*what?*"

"Lethepropol," the scientist repeated. "It's a newer drug, commonly used to induce sleep in insomniacs. Stronger doses are rumored to cause significant but short-term memory loss."

"So Smith was just trying to get a good night's sleep?" Officer Jones posited.

"Or," Castillo interjected. "Someone knocked him out so they could kill him easier."

"That's possible," the scientist nodded. "He didn't have a prescription." She pointed at the medical records in her notes. She then placed the sheet back in the folder and exchanged it for another. "We found other substances in the sample of the blood we were able to take from the glass," she explained as she held out the second sheet. "It was a little tough to be clear, but there were traces of some form of lithium along with an unknown substance that we couldn't identify."

Tracy leaned over the paper to get a better look at the numbers. "And what's lithium used for?"

"Usually, it's used to treat people who have bipolar," the scientist said. "Mood disorders—that sort of thing."

"*Very* interesting," Castillo noted as he processed through the data in his head. "So Smith was dealing with some kind of mood issue and knocked himself out to quiet the voices in his head—?"

The scientist shook her head. "I'm sorry, I should've clarified: the sample from the juice and the sample from the blood on the glass came back with two separate DNA signatures. The OJ had traces of Smith's DNA on it. We compared it with the blood from the autopsy just to be sure."

Castillo's eyes grew wide: "You mean—?"

"Yeah," the scientist nodded. "The blood and the juice—they're from two different subjects."

Officer Castillo grinned and nodded. "Now we're getting somewhere."

"Have you run the blood through the computer to see who it belongs to?" Tracy cocked her head.

The scientist nodded. "We already did," she said. "Unfortunately, it didn't match any DNA samples in our database."

"Naturally," Castillo grumbled.

"However," the woman raised a finger, "that was probably because the DNA from the blood sample *did* match the tuft of fur you collected."

Castillo leaned in. "So the DNA wasn't even human?"

The scientist was about to say something, but she closed her lips then started again. "I didn't say it wasn't human," she said slowly.

"So it *was* human?" Tracy's surprise showed in her big dark eyes.

"Let's just say the tests were, um, inconclusive."

All three let the silence linger for a moment.

With a deep inhale, Castillo said: "Whatever it is, this still doesn't explain the strange scars."

"I've told you everything we know," the scientist said, placing the sheet of paper back into the folder. She handed it to Tracy. "Let me know if you have any other questions."

"Thanks. Will do," replied Officer Jones with an amicable smile. Then, she turned to Castillo and started for the door. "C'mon, *partner*. We've got some digging to do. And I'm sure Marge has found something on the names from your sticky note by now."

When Tracy's back was to him, Officer Castillo rolled his eyes, then followed sluggishly behind as she led back into the hall and toward their offices.

As they rounded the corner, the office sounds became louder—fingers typing away on clunky keyboards, the occasional sonorous ring from the tip line, and an incoming fax. Jones and Castillo headed for the conference room from which they were conducting the investigation, but they were stopped by a short woman with puffy, graying hair and large, square glasses that boasted a rosy tint.

"Miss Marge," Castillo gave a side-mouthed grin. "What've you got for us?"

"I have some of the intel you were asking about." The woman looked irritated—but that may have just been due to the way her face was constructed, Castillo mused. The man reached for the thick folder, but Marge handed it to Tracy instead.

"I'm still working through the others," Marge elaborated. "But here's everything we've got on your guy Viktor Gromble."

Tracy flipped the top of the folder open to peek inside, then closed it and smiled to the older woman: "Excellent. This will be of great help, Marge."

"Don't mention it," she replied with a wave of her hand behind her head, as she had already started to hobble back to her desk.

The duo of officers entered the conference room and closed the door behind them. Tracy placed the folder on the table, opened it, and immediately began to sift through the items within—xerox copies of documents, photographs, tax records.

"Alright," said Officer Jones. "Let's find out what this Gromble character is all about."

"He looks like a half-melted marshmallow," Kiki said under her breath as Declan pinned the photo of an immense man with a bulbous, sagging paunch to the corkboard; it wasn't an entirely inaccurate description.

Declan tapped the photograph with his knuckle. "This is Viktor Gromble, and he's a terrible person."

Mira chuckled. "And why's that?"

"Besides the fact that he's been part of the Inner Circle, pulling the strings on Ducane's dirty work?" The leader turned to the others. "He's a womanizer, an embezzler, human trafficker, and an absolute slime. Thinks that just because he's got more money than a maharaja, he can do whatever he wants."

"When you put it that way, he actually sounds like a pretty nice guy." Kiki grinned at Declan, but he rolled his eyes and looked away. Buster and Mira shook their heads silently.

"So what's the mission?" Donna sensed the heist at hand might be more challenging than the last, and leaned forward to listen closely.

Declan picked up a pushpin and punched it into a city map on the corkboard. "Fortunately for us, Mr. Gromble has a regular weekday practice of visiting a specific Russian bathhouse in town," he said as he pointed to the spot he had just pinned. "That's where we'll find him this afternoon."

"Great," Kiki rose from her chair. "Massages all around!"

"Well, for some of us, anyway," Declan conceded. "Donna did such a fine job last night sweet-talking our Reverend, so she'll be the one to get Gromble relaxed."

Donna took a deep breath. "Of course I will," she mumbled.

"Each of us will pose as a member of the staff at the baths," the leader continued. "I'll run through each of our roles quickly as we'll need to get moving if we're going to make it in time for his mid-afternoon routine."

"I have a question," Mira said as she raised her hand.

Declan pointed to her to signal for her to speak.

Mira tapped her chin. "You said Gromble's there every day."

"Yes, is that your question?"

The woman shook her head, exhaled, and spoke again: "I mean, won't he notice that we aren't the usual staff?"

The leader paced the floor—a slab of unfinished concrete covered by a large rug. "Not likely. To him, every working-class employee is just another anonymous body that only exists to serve him. As long as we keep quiet and avoid attention, he'll go on ignoring us like he always does."

"Perfect," Buster smiled. "It's not every day that I get to be ignored." He made a sweeping motion with his hands to emphasize his conspicuous height and breadth, which prompted grins from most of the others.

"Speaking of the usual staff," Declan turned to Mira. "You've got some calls to make." He gestured toward a phone on a table with a long, coiled cord. "Think you can mimic the manager's voice enough to convince his staff to stay home?"

"If it's just the voice, I should be able to focus enough to make it work," Mira replied. "I've never successfully pulled off a visual illusion *and* an auditory one at the same time," she added to Donna, who was less familiar with the woman's powers.

With this, Declan began to run through his notes, assigning roles to each of the remaining members of his team as he outlined the plan of how they would infiltrate the famed bath and sauna to get Gromble alone. When they were all finished and the usual employees had been called and convinced their shifts had been canceled, the team promptly loaded the van and sped toward the old Russian bathhouse.

A patch of wispy clouds inched their way across the sky, barely covering the oppressive afternoon sun above as the squad car pulled up to a space across the street from the Russian baths. Officer Jones eyed the fading signage and eclectic facade with suspicion as she shifted the vehicle into park and squinted through the dirty windshield.

"Officer Castillo," she turned her head to her partner in the passenger seat, who was dressed in a loose-fitting short-sleeved Hawaiian shirt. "Don't you think this is a bit of a stretch?"

"Marge's intel found that Gromble comes here every day at three," Castillo reminded her, holding up his watch. "It's five minutes to three."

"I know that," Tracy scoffed. "I mean, do you think he's *actually* connected to the killing of Mr. Smith? All we've got to go on is your 'friend' Debra's forced testimony on a sticky note and not much else."

"Relax," Castillo urged Tracy. "I'm just gonna cozy up to him and see if he knows anything. Worst-case scenario? He knows nothing and I get a nice, soothing day at the spa." The man flashed his pearly whites. "I *promise* I won't do anything crazy."

His partner's eyebrow shot up. "You'd better not. You've only got *one* strike left."

As the two sat in the idling car, clusters of hairy-chested, pot-bellied sauna-goers filed out the front door—regulars, the officers presumed by the amicable laughter exchanged among the disparate groupings who hobbled off with wide smiles and glowing, tan skin. Officer Jones pointed to the clock on the dashboard.

"Better get in there," she said.

Castillo fumbled around with a lightweight bag, making sure it was filled with all of the items he needed, then adjusted a pair of reflective Ray-Bans. As he clicked open the car door and started to slide onto the sidewalk, Officer Jones tapped him on the shoulder.

"Aren't you forgetting something?"

The officer turned to find the woman dangling a pair of short swim trunks between her thumb and forefinger as if the item held some deadly contamination. Castillo rolled his eyes and quickly swiped the shorts from Tracy's hands, then stuffed the garment into his bag.

"Remember," Officer Jones leaned and held up a finger. "One strike."

Officer Castillo nodded, puffed, slammed the door behind him as hard as he could, then headed for the entrance to the baths, dragging his sandaled feet across the sandy sidewalk. As he pushed through the doors, the young officer caught a reflection in the glass: a glossy black van screeched up to the curb behind him, its windows tinted to the max.

Castillo grinned and stepped inside the building.

Well, hello there, Mr. Gromble. Right on schedule.

CHAPTER 11

Mira had just traded places with the attendant whose shift finished before the start of the three o'clock hour when she heard the jingle of a set of tiny bells on the front door. The sound startled her. She looked up expecting to find the obese character from Declan's photograph walking through the double doors of the compact lobby, but instead watched as a suave, slightly-unkempt young man entered and ran a finger through his hair.

"Oh!" Mira nearly shouted in surprise, then adjusted her volume to a more normal level. "I'm sorry, c-can I help you?"

The man removed his sunglasses and took a glance around the room before moving his gaze to Mira. "Uh, yeah, I'm here for the, um, Russian bath?"

Mira sensed something was off by the uncertain way he spoke. "First time?" She tried to play it cool.

"Is it that obvious?" This time the man smiled, revealing

an almost inconspicuous dimple.

The woman chuckled, then recalled her mission: *keep everyone but Viktor Gromble out of the sauna by any means necessary*. "Actually, this hour is reserved for one of our VIP guests," Mira said with an apologetic tone. "But we reopen for regular customers at four."

The dark-haired man glanced over his shoulder at the black van that had just parked out front. "You're sure you can't make room for a first-timer? I promise I won't get in the way."

Mira breathed in then exhaled quickly. "I'm afraid our distinguished guest prefers his own space when he's here," she explained, then leaned over the counter and rubbed her thumb and forefinger together. "He's paying a premium for that, you understand?"

The young man inside the lobby caught a glimpse of a pair of svelte men in black suits disembarking the van outside. They slid open its side door. The man turned back to Mira.

"I didn't want to do this," he said, reaching into a pocket, "but I guess I have no other choice." The dark-haired man whipped out a police badge and passed it across the counter.

Mira's eyes grew wide, but she tried not to show her fear. She picked up the badge. "I'm sorry, Officer—" The woman examined the attached credentials. "—Castillo. I didn't realize we had a member of Metro-Dade's finest in our midst. Is there something going on here that I should be concerned about?" She masked a nervous gulp as she handed the badge back to her guest.

"Not at all," Officer Castillo grinned, taking another glance over his shoulder. He scanned a small laminated sign that outlined the prices for various elements of the Russian bath experience, then reached into his wallet and plopped a few large bills in front of Mira. "Which way to the showers?"

Mira's hands were shaking as she counted the bills, then nodded toward a doorway in the corner of the room. "The men's area is right through there."

The handsome officer smiled once more and hurried in the direction she'd indicated. As he vanished through the doorway, Mira held her hand to her ear.

"Uh, bad news, team!" She whispered loudly into the comm. "Gromble just pulled up, but someone from Metro-Dade's here, too!"

"You guys hear that?" Kiki looked up from her inspection of an exposed panel on the Dreamcatcher and relayed the message from her earpiece. "Metro-Dade's sent someone here. You think they're on to us?"

In the back room of the old establishment, an area usually reserved for employees, the rest of the Dream Team finished their preparations. Buster fiddled with the settings on the Dreamcatcher device with Kiki, while Donna obscured herself behind a flimsy screen that doubled as a dressing room.

"There's no way they know," Declan said confidently, moving behind another of the dressing screens with a small wad of clothing in his hands. "Probably a coincidence."

Donna hollered back: "What happens if they catch us? I can't afford to go to jail."

Kiki shook her head. "Lady, if anyone here can afford something, it's you." She wiggled her fingers to allude to Donna's special powers.

The blonde woman puffed. "I have a kid I need to take care of, okay? So excuse me for showing an ounce of caution and care."

Kiki didn't respond to Donna's comment, but instead tried to focus on finishing the configurations to the machine.

"Buster, you sure the Dreamcatcher's gonna hold up to the heat and moisture in the steamroom?" Declan's voice echoed from behind the screen as he stripped off his usual neutral getup.

Buster squinted and turned a small dial with his big fingers. "It's never really been tested under those conditions," he shouted back.

Declan's disembodied head appeared around the corner of the screen. "So is it going to hold up?"

"Relax, Dec," Buster smiled back at him. "It'll work." He paused. "I mean, it *should*."

The leader of the group was clearly unamused by this answer, but ducked away again to finish changing. "Well, I suppose '*should*' is going to have to suffice. This is going to be a little more challenging now that Gromble isn't going to be alone in here—you two need to be ready for our signal to bring the device. Donna and I will take care of the rest."

As he said this, Declan moved out from behind the screen at the same time as Donna. She was garbed in a loose-fitting, bathrobe-like dress that fell just above her knees, with her thick blonde hair tied back in a large bun to keep it out of the way. Donna had exchanged her usual driving gloves for a thinner pair that resembled the disposable rubber kind—another specially-lined set that the doctor had crafted for her to assist in caring for her comatose sister.

"You look stunning, as always," Declan said with a mesmerized look in his eyes.

"You know I have a boyfriend, right?" Donna raised an eyebrow. "That's kinda the whole reason I'm doing this."

Declan sputtered defensively. "I-I didn't mean it like that—"

"If you say so," Donna teased him with a smile. "But thanks. Though, you know, my uniform's not *quite* as... *modest* as yours." Donna grinned and allowed her gaze to move from Declan's bare feet, up past the small towel-skirt that rested at his upper thighs, and across his bare, broad chest, arms, and neck, until her eyes met his. She noticed a scar about two inches long near his clavicle and a few small reddish dots clumped together on his forearm, but decided against bringing attention to either.

"Well," Declan proceeded awkwardly. "We'd better get to our places—Gromble and our other guest should be about ready to begin their first rounds in the sauna." He slipped on a pair of thin sandals and moved toward the entrance to an access hallway.

"Wait! How do we induce his sleep when we can't slip the powder into a drink?" Donna interjected. "You're not supposed to drink any liquids in there."

"We'll have to use the liquid that's already there," Declan started. "Kiki, since we're going to be occupied now that we have two guests to worry about, I'll need you to dump those ten kilos of the sleeping powder into the jacuzzi as *close* as possible to the time Gromble enters—not too early or too much will evaporate. Make sure the tub stays at 102 degrees so it all dissolves properly. The packages are in the duffel over there." He pointed to the lumpy bag.

Kiki nodded. "Sure thing," she said. "But what if the cop joins him for a dip?"

Declan bobbed his head slowly. "It's likely that he will. Since the substance will be entering the system through absorption instead of Gromble drinking it," the man explained, "it's going to take a little longer than usual to knock him out. Should be about five to ten minutes—it's a little harder to keep track of—but both of them *should* be out of there and onto their next steam bath by that time, and Donna and I will take it from there."

"There's that word again," Buster smiled. "*Should.*"

"So let me get this straight," Kiki started. "Gromble and the cop start out in the main steam room, then they dunk in the pool to cool off, take another stint in the sauna, then move to the jacuzzi full of sleeping powder, before they finally head to another steam room where you and Donna will give them their massages until they fall asleep. *Then* Buster and I show up with the Dreamcatcher and we just *hope* it works?"

"It's a little complicated, I realize," said Declan. "But that's how a Russian bath works. Alright, Donna? Let's go." Immediately, the two pushed through the door into the narrow, humid access hall.

Apart from the flopping of their thin sandals, the pair walked in silence toward the front of the building. The hall was dim, with most of its fluorescent lights burnt out.

"You a junkie?" Donna's voice echoed strangely.

Declan whipped around. "Huh?"

"You've been pretty coy whenever it comes to your past and present," the blonde woman explained. "Just wondering if that's because you're a junkie."

"I don't know what you're talking about—"

"The scars," Donna pointed to the dots on Declan's forearm. "My sister's been in the hospital for a year—I know a needle scar when I see one." As he didn't respond immediately, Donna added, "I'm not trying to be judgmental, we've just got a lot on the line; so I wanna know if you're hiding something from me."

The man took a deep breath and lowered his head. "You're right. They *are* needle scars. But I am *not* a junkie." Declan waved his hand defensively. "It's a special treatment for a rare condition that I have—I have to inject it every few hours. Heck, I just took a dose before we left the warehouse. Look, it's kind of sensitive so I'd rather not talk about it, okay?"

He turned and started back down the hallway as Donna lingered for a moment then took up the rear. At last, they reached a turn in the hall, which led to another segment from which several doors sprouted off.

"Steam room should be through that last one," Declan pointed and the pair proceeded to the door.

Donna peered through its small, porthole window. The other side of the glass was reflective, preventing the guests from seeing through to the faux-staff members on the other side, but Donna gasped when her eyes alighted on the man who sat on a bench in the room. She pivoted quickly to move her head out of the window and pressed her back against the wall.

"What is it?" Declan moved to look for himself, furrowing his brow.

"The cop," Donna answered in a rasp. "That's Rico Castillo. He's one of my oldest friends and he was—or *is*—Marcus' partner."

"*Your* Marcus?"

"Yeah. I can't let him see me or this whole operation goes out the window." Donna's face was flush as she turned to Declan. "This is gonna be more complicated than we thought."

Officer Castillo closed his eyes and inhaled a long, deep breath of the thick and moist air. The ground and walls emanated a ferocious heat, causing miniscule droplets of sweat to bead immediately on the man's tan skin, but something about it felt soothing—natural, rudimentary, primitive.

The man opened his eyes, glanced down at his bare stomach, and was starting to feel self-conscious about the size of his gut until a shadow filled the doorway. The swinging double doors opened at the same time, and a bloated, sluggish man pushed through. His girth required that he use both doors, and as the gargantuan figure turned to move toward the benches, the large man flashed a grotesque scowl at Castillo. *Or maybe that was just the way his face always looked,* the officer mused.

Layers of belly fat and skin drooped lazily, mostly obscuring the towel around his waist that was most certainly custom-made from four or five regular-sized versions stitched together. "I'd like to warm up before my massage," he sneered in a vaguely Slavic tone, pausing halfway across the small room to catch his breath.

It took a moment for Castillo to realize the man had mistaken him for an employee, so he sputtered out: "O-oh, I don't work here—"

Without a second glance at the officer, the large man lumbered to the wide bench nearby and orbited himself to prepare to sit. "Then... why are you here?" He grimaced as he lowered his mass to the seat.

Castillo was certain the slats would give way beneath the man, but found himself surprised when they seemed not to flinch under the weight. "Same reason you are," the officer started. The big man slowly turned his head to see how Castillo would finish: "To relax."

"But why are you *here—now?*" It sounded like it almost

pained him to speak.

The officer took another hot breath. "Because, I uh—"

"This hour is reserved." The man's face was red. Not even a minute had passed since he entered the steam room, but he was already engulfed in sweat.

"Oh!" Castillo feigned surprise. "The woman at the front let me in and didn't say anything to that effect. Perhaps she's new?"

The other man breathed in slowly, then expelled the humid air once more. "Perhaps," he replied finally. He wouldn't have noticed whether the woman at the front desk was brand new or had been there for decades—this man wasn't the sort to pay attention to those without power or status or something to offer him.

"Well," continued the officer, "since I'm already here—and drenched in my own sweat—I might as well go on with it." He offered a hopeful smile to the visitor. "My name's Rico—and you are?"

The other man's bulging eyelids sharpened to slits as he examined the officer's youthful form, then the corners of his lips turned up slightly. "Pleasure to meet you, Rico." The way he rolled the *R* made the cop cringe. "I'm Viktor." Gromble rubbed his pudgy hands in a circular motion over his protruding paunch.

The two passed the next couple minutes in silence, allowing the faint sound of steam to seep through the grates and cracks in the floor and walls. The heat was getting to Rico, who asked finally, "About how long are you supposed to be in here before going to cool off? This is my first time in one of these Russian baths."

"A few minutes more," Gromble muttered, his eyes shut. "Savor it."

Castillo wiped a drip of sweat from his brow using the back of his hand, then tapped his sandaled feet on the warm stone floor. He studied each corner, crack, and crevice of the room as he willed the time to move more quickly.

At last, Viktor groaned and stirred, opening his eyes. He held out a weighty arm and flailed a hand in Castillo's general direction. "Be a gentleman; help me up."

Before he could wonder how the man usually managed this routine unassisted, Castillo found himself rising from the bench and moving toward the man. Castillo took each of Gromble's hands in his own and began to heave and pull. Both men's faces contorted as they strained. Viktor finally budged, managing to stand to his feet. He gripped Castillo's sweaty palms just a moment longer than the cop would've preferred.

Need to find out what he knows, the officer reminded himself. Even being in the same room as the slimy creature known as Viktor Gromble made Castillo feel unclean, but there was a mission to carry out. *Just push through.*

"That way to the polar pool," Gromble again gestured lazily with a whole hand.

Castillo nodded and followed through the stony archway and into a room lit with vibrant, buzzing blue lights along the walls. In the center sat a pool—just slightly smaller than the type one might find in the backyard of almost every new Miami home built over the prior decade. Without warning, Gromble stepped to the edge and walked over it. He didn't even have a running start as he descended into the pool, but his body displaced gallons of the chilling water, spilling over the pool's low edge, then Castillo's feet.

The officer winced at the frigid temperature, but a moment later thought it felt soothing, having just emerged from the warmer room.

Gromble's head broke through the surface, and the man's upper body bobbed like a man-sized buoy. "Aren't you going to take a dip?" He waved Rico in.

Castillo quivered at the thought of the extreme cold, but nodded affirmatively. He shimmied off his sandals, then inched his way to the edge and looked down. He lowered a hesitant toe to the water, then recoiled as a ripple from Gromble splashed over it.

"Easier if you just jump right in," he chided with an uncomfortable smile.

The officer knew he was right, but Castillo needed a moment more. Finally, he took a deep breath, then launched himself from the edge. He sailed through the air, clutching his legs close to his chest in a cannonball position, then broke through the water with a shivering *splash!*

CHAPTER 12

Declan led Donna into the next room, where a number of slatted wooden bed-tables filled the warmly-lit space, with screens separating each to provide privacy whenever there were patrons present. The woman once again eyed the scar at the top of Declan's bare chest, noticing upon closer inspection that it appeared fresh—not more than a few days old by her estimation.

"What's that one from?" Donna pointed at the wound with a gloved hand as the man headed for a prep station near one corner of the room.

Declan briefly glanced down at the sweaty scar and shook his head. "You really like to ask a lot of questions, don't you?" The man reached for a pair of large buckets. Each was about halfway full with an aromatic oil and stuffed with oak sprigs. Declan handed one to Donna.

"What's this for?"

"See! Another question." He chuckled as she removed one of the thick sprigs, dripping with oil. "It's an oak broom—it's part of the Russian bath experience."

"So—*what?*—you *sweep* it across a person's back?" Donna practiced a slow, soothing motion in the air.

"No," Declan replied, reaching for the broom in his bucket. "It's a little more aggressive—like a thrashing." Here he made a sharp swat of the air, then another. A couple of leaf fragments and suds dripped to the ground. "You'll do this for a few minutes on either side, then offer a more hands-on massage to loosen out the shoulders and neck. Not much time to perfect it, but give the broom a few more tries. We can't let our guard down—Gromble will head to the jacuzzi next—the one where Kiki's dissolving the sleeping compound."

Donna raised an eyebrow and let out a playful chuckle. She whipped the oak broom back and forth a few times, each time growing more focused.

"Good," Declan grinned. "I think you've got the hang of it."

Even in the dim glow, Donna noticed a sparkle in the man's eyes. Maybe it was the fact that she hardly knew anything about him, or perhaps it was because he'd been so eager to help her and give her a place where her powers weren't a secret, but something intrigued her about him. And by his lingering glance, Donna presumed he felt the same.

"I'll take the officer—Rico, wasn't it?"

Donna nodded. "Yeah. Guess that means I've got Gromble."

"I'm sorry," the man contorted his smile. "I would've done it, but we can't risk your old friend seeing you, or the whole mission implodes."

She understood. Donna replied by nodding her chin, then she thrust the oak broom back into her bucket. "At least I don't have to touch him," she wiggled her fingers.

This sparked Declan's curiosity, and he cocked his head slightly. "What's that like?"

Donna held up her hands. "You mean wearing gloves? A little sweaty."

"I mean, what's it like to never be able to be close enough—to touch?"

His chest muscles loosened, Donna noted as she formed her reply. "To be honest?" She hung her head slightly. "It's... pretty terrible. My girl Starla—my niece—she's been like a daughter to me ever since my sister..." She trailed off, then started again: "After a little accident nearly a year ago, Starla won't get close anymore. It's like she doesn't trust me." Donna muttered, mostly to herself, "I never should have told her what happened."

"What *did* happen?" Declan took a half step closer, an empathetic instinct.

"Same thing that happened to Marcus." Donna's eyes met Declan's. "Turned to gold. I didn't mean for it to happen to either of them—" She was talking quickly now. "It was before we had these gloves. I didn't know. And now it's not just Starla who's scared—*I'm* scared. I'm afraid I'll never be able to protect her from myself. I'm afraid we'll never find

Marcus—that the doctor won't be able to replicate the cure. I'm afraid I'll never be able to be close to anyone again—to hold, to touch—"

"Donna!" Declan interrupted, grabbing one of her gloved hands.

"What?" She snapped her attention back to the man before her. Donna's eyes drifted slowly toward his fingers clutching hers.

"I think they're coming now," he said softly. Declan quickly released her hand and nodded toward the doorway from which the sound of wet, floppy footsteps seemed to be originating.

Donna took a deep breath then picked up her bucket. She silently followed Declan's lead and moved behind one of the dividing screens so she wouldn't easily be seen. *He wasn't afraid,* she noted. As she waited for the doors to open, Donna tried to push the thought from her head, but it returned just as fast.

The creak of the door prompted Donna to peer through a slit in the dividing screen. Her eyes widened as she saw the immensity of the man who entered first: Viktor Gromble. His facial expression looked even more grotesque in person, contorted and drooping from decades of discontent and malice, and his body dripped wet with cold, chlorinated water as he hobbled toward the bed-tables. To her relief, he was the only figure that entered at this time, so Donna walked toward him with a silent smile and motioned for him to enter her station.

Gromble scowled and huffed as he moved across the room. The wooden slats of the table creaked as he settled onto them. Just as Donna was moving to grab her oak broom, she caught the shadow-light of the hallway seeping through the doorframe. She turned her back to the door right as it swung open. Donna saw enough of his physique from the corner of her eye to recognize that it was Rico. She hid herself further behind the screen while Declan greeted the newly-arrived officer and led him to the table on the other side of the thin privacy barrier.

"First time?" Declan muttered with his head downcast and a hand outstretched toward the massage table.

"First time," Castillo nodded and smiled nervously. He hopped up and lay across the table with his chest pressed against the surface.

Declan rubbed his hands together. "Just try to relax."

Castillo closed his eyes obediently as Declan reached into his bucket and removed the oily oak branch. He wound back his arm and began to thrash it across the officer's upper back. *Thwack! Thwack!*

Castillo winced, opening his eyes for a moment.

"Too hard?" Declan inquired.

The officer took a deep breath, smiled, and shook his head. "No," he muttered. "Just wasn't expecting that." He shimmied back into the previous position and closed his eyes once more.

Thwack! Thwack! Oil and leaves dripped across both of the men, as Donna matched Declan's cadence. *Thwack-thwack!*

Thwack!

"That's enough of the branches," Gromble muttered to Donna after a few minutes had passed.

He hadn't said anything prior to that, so Donna presumed she must've been doing a decent job with her technique. *Either that or his mind is elsewhere.* The woman quietly returned the scrappy remains of the oak broom to her bucket of oil. Next came the part she dreaded the most.

"Pay special attention to the neck," Viktor said, his eyes still closed as he lay prone. "I've been feeling tense lately and need to be… loosened up."

Donna nodded, though her subject couldn't see the motion, and stepped to the side of the table. She held her gloved fingers above the bulge of the man's upper back and wriggled her fingers. She took a deep breath then gently settled her palms into the thick flab.

As the woman began to massage the area near his shoulders, the man writhed his head and emitted a groan of discomfort. Donna paused and lifted her hands a few inches from Viktor's back.

"Don't stop," he mumbled.

Donna winced and pushed her fingers back into the ripples of soft flesh and fat. After only a few more moments, the man opened his eyes and reached one of his grubby, sweaty hands up to grab Donna's wrist.

The action startled her and she immediately lifted her fingers from the man's back.

"The gloves," he said simply.

"It's... more sanitary this way," Donna stammered, trying to keep her voice down.

"I'm not concerned about... *sanitation*." Gromble ran his slimy tongue across his lips and leered at Donna out of the corner of his eyes. It was difficult for him to turn his neck while lying on his belly.

Donna quivered. "If it's alright with you, I'd like to leave them on."

"It isn't." The man's already narrow eyes became finer slits.

I swore never to let this happen again. Donna's mind flashed scenes of the moments in which those she held most dear were smitten by the power—the curse—that her fingers administered. *Not even this disgusting slime deserves that fate,* she thought. *Well, maybe a little—*

"Take them off." Viktor demanded softly.

"I don't think that's a good—"

The man's body undulated as he turned himself on his side so that he could see Donna more clearly while he maintained a grip on her wrist. "I said, take off the gloves."

The woman trembled and shook her head ever so slightly.

Gromble sneered and birthed his other hand out from underneath his side. Slowly, he reached it toward Donna's hand—the one held hostage by his vice-grip of her wrist.

"P-please," she sputtered. "I need to keep these on."

The man ignored Donna's words and delicately placed his thumb and forefinger over her gloved pinky and began to tug on the thick rubber-like material. The covering pulled away from her hand at that point, but the other fingers provided a safeguard. Next, Gromble moved to Donna's next finger. He gripped it strangely before smiling at her.

"No ring?"

Donna made no reply. She tried to pull away, but the man's strength overpowered her. He pulled on the glove again, this time freeing the ring finger.

Gromble then placed his pudgy grip on Donna's middle finger. As he started to remove this part of the glove, a pair of floppy footsteps appeared behind Donna.

"Well," came Declan's voice, "I think it's time to rinse off and take a warm dip in the jacuzzi, don't you?"

Donna had never felt more relieved as Gromble suddenly released his grip. She quickly tugged the loose glove tighter at her wrist and Declan began to help the man off the massage table.

"It was a pleasure," Viktor spoke from the side of his mouth as he gave Donna one last glance over. Then he turned and hobbled away toward the shower room to clean off the oils.

"Rico's gone on to the showers, too," Declan whispered to Donna when the man was out of earshot, then placed his finger to his ear. "Kiki, they're headed your way next."

"Roger." Came the static reply.

Donna let out a sigh and nearly collapsed against the massage table. She caught herself and leaned over the wooden slats. "That was *way* too close." She shook her head and looked down at her once-again gloved hands. "He could have turned to gold!"

"No time to worry about what *could* have happened,

Donna." Declan looked her in the eyes. "He might've deserved it anyhow."

She shook her head. "No one deserves that."

"Maybe you're right." Declan shifted the conversation back to their mission at hand. "Let's go make sure Buster's all set up with the Dreamcatcher. We'll only have a few minutes before the drowsiness kicks in."

Donna took a deep breath and nodded. When they were both ready, the two hurried out of the massage room and rushed back down the access hall.

Kiki better have done her part, Donna mused. *Or this all falls apart.*

"You're following me?" Viktor Gromble muttered as he pushed out through the shower room door and into the jacuzzi area.

Officer Castillo followed closely behind, still dripping from the quick rinse.

"Gotta learn how it's done." The officer grinned nervously.

Gromble's large, bare feet slapped against the slick tiled floor—the bathhouse didn't carry flip-flops in his size, but the extra layers of insulation that covered his body kept the man's soles from getting too hot in the other rooms. He came to the edge of the bubbling, circular pool and reached for a metal handrail. Viktor sniffed the warm, humid air that rose from the surface.

"Something wrong?" Castillo glanced at the man as he

peered into the waters.

Viktor shook his head subtly. "Chlorine's strong today." He dipped a delicate toe into the water. A satisfied smile came across his face, which prompted him to lower the rest of his body into the steaming jacuzzi waters. His body mass once more displaced the contents of the pool so that the water rose and spilled over its tiled edges, but the man paid little attention to this. Gromble closed his eyes as he allowed his lower body to sink beneath the surface.

While he did this, Castillo followed suit, stepping with a wince into the roiling tub. The water was hotter than he expected, especially after his quick, cold shower. *But this might be my only chance to get close enough to Viktor Gromble,* he remembered. *He has to know more about Smith—something that can help us solve the case of his murder.* With a deep breath, Castillo sat at the edge and gently descended into the nearly-scalding waters.

It's not so bad once you're in it, he tried to convince himself.

Castillo glanced at Viktor—his eyes were closed peacefully as underwater jets pumped a flurry of loud bubbles from beneath the surface. The rippling white noise echoed in the compact, tiled room, creating a claustrophobic ambience—the feeling that the half-soothing sound was closing in from every direction.

Now or never. The officer took a deep breath. "So, uh—Viktor, right?" He spoke in a voice louder than normal so that he could be heard above the bubbling din. "What do you do for a living?"

Castillo wasn't sure the man had heard the question, for his eyes were still shut.

Has he fallen asleep?

The question faded quickly as Gromble grunted. "What's it to you?"

"J-just making conversation," Rico stuttered.

"I prefer to soak *without* conversation." Gromble opened his eyes halfway, revealing a bloodshot glare, then closed them again.

The chlorine, Castillo surmised as an explanation for the redness. As a matter of fact, he could feel a slight stinging in his own eyes. He took a gamble: "C'mon, Viktor. Is that how you treat a public servant?"

Gromble exhaled slowly and looked back at Castillo, whose head, neck, and shoulders bobbed above the surface of the pool. "I prefer the private kind," he sneered, then rolled his eyes and continued. "Fine, I'll indulge. I run a number of profitable ventures throughout the Magic City—and some beyond. That enough for you?"

"It's vague enough," Castillo grinned, then shifted his legs underwater to keep from floating away. "Ever heard of a guy named Wesley Smith?"

Without hesitation, Viktor replied, "No. Should I have?"

Drat. Is he telling the truth?

"Not necessarily," answered the officer. *Keep going.* "How about Rolf Ducane?"

Castillo watched a very slow transformation of Gromble's face from a look of severity to a wide grin that appeared almost genuine. "Of course I have. You think I live under a rock?"

"Ever worked with him?"

"Perhaps." Viktor's gaze narrowed.

"Perhaps? What does that mean—?"

"I'm teasing you, Rico." Gromble cackled suddenly, again rolling the *R*. "Of course I've worked with Ducane; I'd be a fool not to. And don't you worry—all our dealings are in the public records."

He's hiding something. I can tell.

Castillo took a deep breath, inhaling more of the strongly-chlorinated vapors. "Not *all* of them," he said finally.

Viktor's face once again contorted into a look of disdain. "What is *that* supposed to mean?" He looked almost frightened.

"J-just that I know your connection to Ducane runs... deeper than that." Castillo had gone too far to back out at this point.

Gromble made no reply.

Rico took another deep, chlorinated breath. "I know about... about the Inner Circle."

Immediately, Viktor reached for the railbar and pulled himself up with a struggle and a splash, warm water cascading all over the tiled floor. He hobbled with haste toward an exit.

"Where are you going?" Castillo shouted as he, too, climbed out of the bubbling jacuzzi. He nearly slipped on the wet tile, but quickly caught himself.

"My hour's almost up—my *private* hour." He turned his

head to cast a glare at Rico before continuing toward the door. "I'd like to get one last, *quiet* moment in the steam room." His booming voice sounded more ominous as it echoed off the slick tiles that lined the walls. Gromble pushed through the door and stepped into the dark room, where the only light came from a trio of dim, reddish, heat-resistant bulbs mounted to the ceiling. A few highly-reflective mirrors on the walls indicated the one-way windows by which the bath staff could operate the heat and moisture controls without interrupting the bathers' experience.

Castillo followed closely behind, grabbing the door before it could swing back into place. "You know something about the Inner Circle," he insisted.

"I'm not answering any more questions," Gromble said, shaking his head as he took a seat on a sturdy bench and closed his eyes.

Rico sat down opposite him, so that the two faced each other.

I'm not leaving until he tells me what he knows.

Castillo took a deep breath and closed his eyes—but only for a moment. He tried to form a question that the man would respond to, but his mind raced.

CHAPTER 13

"Why aren't they asleep yet?" Donna peered through the one-way window at the pair of men seated in the steam room. She could barely make out the shapes of Gromble and Castillo through the foggy glass, both sitting comfortably but upright.

"It takes longer when the drug is administered through absorption and inhalation," Declan noted. He turned to Kiki, who stood near Buster and the Dreamcatcher in the tight, dark control room. "You *did* dissolve the whole dose in there, right?"

Kiki rolled her eyes. "Of course. Well, barely." She clarified: "I had one of my doubles do the job just in case I ran out of time—all I had to do was think it and she vanished." The young, pink-haired woman nudged Donna out of the way to get a look through the foggy porthole. "You know, *heat* accelerates the effect."

Declan glanced at a control panel that indicated the temperature in bright-red digital numerals: *180 degrees.* "I've heard about these Russian rooms," he said. "Supposed to be the hottest in the building. The best of them keep it mega-hot—190 degrees, sometimes higher."

"Holy cow," Donna muttered. "Is that even legal?"

"Sure, why not?"

"That's almost enough to slow-cook a roast in a crock pot!" Donna raised her eyebrows.

The bare-chested Declan started toward the panel when Buster cleared his throat.

"Declan," he chided. "The Dreamcatcher hasn't been tested in that kind of temperature *or* humidity. We're pushing our luck as it is." The big man wiped a bead of sweat from his forehead.

"And what about Rico?" Donna nodded toward the window. "They've already been in there fifteen minutes! They've got five—*maybe* ten—til the temp starts causing some serious brain damage."

"We can't risk missing this opportunity to get Gromble's dreams," Declan insisted. "If we don't crank up the heat, the dose may not take effect until it's too late. We have to get the dream while Gromble's in there." The man looked to each of his sweating partners. "Don't you want to find Ducane's vault?" His eyes shifted to Donna last. "And Marcus?"

None of the trio replied immediately. The mechanical huffing and puffing from an overworked furnace filled the silence while they considered what to do.

"You're the boss," Buster ceded finally, offering a shrug.

With a nod, Declan turned back to the control panel and cranked up the dial a few degrees. The machinery beside them made a greater effort and the cramped room felt stuffier and sweatier. "I'll continue increasing it until they go under," the leader stated.

Donna and Kiki crammed their faces next to each other to look through the glass once more, waiting for the men to slumber.

Castillo closed his eyes again and tried to breathe deeply to calm himself. His pulse was racing now. *Time's ticking. I've got to get something more out of him.*

The duo had been sitting in silence for almost fifteen minutes. *Or maybe thirty—I can't remember. It can't be healthy to stay in here this long, can it?* Rico's breathing was labored as he wiped beads of stinging-hot sweat from his brow. He missed a drop and felt its salty sting in his eye. It seemed like the room was getting hotter.

Gromble inhaled and exhaled in a measured rhythm, evidence of his lifelong experience frequenting Russian saunas across the globe. When Castillo opened his eyes to look at the huge man again, he felt his vision blurring for a split second.

Now or never, Rico.

The officer gasped for air, then spoke up: "You and Smith were both part of the Inner Circle."

Viktor's breathing pattern fluttered for only a moment before he continued his slow cadence. He kept his eyes shut, but Castillo knew the man heard him.

Keep going.

"You and Smith would have crossed paths," Rico continued. "The Inner Circle is small. I know you know him."

Still, Gromble made no reply. The room felt warmer. Castillo's vision dizzied, then focused once more.

"Talk to me," he demanded, again wiping his forehead with the back of his hand.

He thinks he can just evade my questions.

Then, the idea came to him. *Yes. That's it.*

Castillo leaned forward and spoke loud and clear: "Smith is *dead*."

Immediately, Viktor's bulging eyes shot open.

Bingo.

"A-ha!" Rico smiled. "You *did* know him."

Gromble's entire face contorted in contempt. "I haven't told you anything," he insisted.

"You've told me enough," Castillo noted. "Enough to make you a suspect."

The paunchy endomorph shifted slightly but said nothing.

"Did you have something to do with Smith's death?"

"No." Viktor shot back.

"Did Ducane?"

Gromble shook his head quickly, jiggling his gullet. "Ducane trusted Smith. He would never." Viktor's eyelids drooped slightly.

Then how does this all connect?

"If I were you," Viktor continued, "I would be looking for someone who's trying to get to Ducane."

Castillo took short breaths and felt his head spinning again. "D-do you know where Ducane is?"

Viktor yawned. "No more questions."

Rico would have been angry, but he felt his emotions fading fast. Suddenly, Viktor tumbled backwards onto the slick floor with a rubbery thud. Before Castillo could react, he felt his eyelids sinking, heavy, then shut. For a moment he was weightless, then he fell to his side along the bench, and everything turned to black.

"Go!" Declan demanded.

Buster burst into the sauna, where the humid air hit him like an invisible wall. He and Kiki hurried toward the two men whose bodies lay hunched in the positions in which they'd fallen, and Buster quickly placed the Dreamcatcher on the bench beside Viktor Gromble's pudgy legs.

Donna and Declan followed, with the woman hurrying to check on Castillo. "He's out," she nodded to Declan, who remained near the door. "Can we turn the heat down now?"

"I'm afraid not," the man replied. "We'd risk them waking up prematurely, and we can't have that." Declan disappeared back into the control room to keep an eye on the temperature.

Kiki finagled the head-piece for the Dreamcatcher onto Gromble's slimy, bare scalp and attempted to connect the clip at his triple-chin. "Strap's too small!" She glanced at Buster.

"Hold it in place, then," he instructed. Buster's dark forehead glistened in the dim light as he flicked in the final sequence of buttons and switches. "The device is pretty warm," he noted. "Better hope this works."

"Nothing we can do about it now," Donna reminded him of the obvious.

"Then here we go!" Buster moved his finger and hovered it over the large red button.

"Uh, guys?" Mira's voice crackled through their earpieces. "We've got a problem?"

Kiki shot back, "Just one?"

"That cop's partner is headed in here—looks mega serious."

"Partner?" Donna's heart fluttered.

"Some lady cop," Mira answered quickly. "Oh, shoot, she's heading for the front door. Hurry up in there!"

Mira's voice cut out and Declan reappeared. Donna noticed that he gripped his arm with the opposite hand, pressed over the needle scars. "Hit it, Buster!"

Buster gave a quick nod then took a deep breath and pushed the red button.

The tiny silver bells of the bathhouse front doors jingled as Tracy pulled on the handle, wearing high-waisted jeans, a light jacket, and a tucked-in t-shirt. Before entering, she forced an awkward smile at one of the two men in black who stood suspiciously beside Gromble's unmarked van. Jones turned back to the door and stepped inside the bathhouse lobby. The woman conducted a hasty survey of the small space before settling her gaze on Mira, the long-haired figure behind the front desk.

Mira looked up at Officer Jones with a hesitant smile. "Can I help you?"

Tracy sauntered to the counter, making another wipe of the room with her eyes. "How much for the full Russian package?" She tilted her head.

"Oh, um... our ladies' hours are on Wednesdays, actually," Mira said, fumbling over her words as she referenced a handwritten calendar taped to the register. She then reached for a stack of brochures and handed one to the newcomer. "All of our pricing's in there. There's some coupons on the back page, too."

The officer flipped over the flimsy brochure, then set it on the counter. "Do you have time for a little tour of the facilities?"

"A *tour*?" Mira repeated, trying to buy herself some time to think of a better response.

"Yes," Tracy eyed her with suspicion. "To take a look and make sure everything's up to my standards before I shell out this much cash." She gestured to the brochure again.

I can't let her back there. They need more time!

"Like I said, women are only allowed in the bathhouse on Wednesdays," Mira said. "Sorry, the owners are a little old-fashioned that way."

Tracy exhaled sharply, then took a shifty glance over her shoulder, eyeing the pair of serious men who stood outside the front door. "I didn't want to do this... but my name's Tracy Jones and I'm an officer with Metro-Dade," The woman flashed her badge. "I believe you've spoken with my colleague, Enrico Castillo, who's been back there for just a little too long." Jones pointed toward the doorway to the showers and sauna.

"Officer, um, Castillo," Mira nodded slowly. "Yes, he did enter the facility."

"And I'd like to check and make sure he's okay."

Mira didn't reply.

"Is that okay?"

"Um, uh," Mira stalled. She was interrupted by the jingling of the door's bells.

Tracy whipped around to view the pair of Viktor Gromble's bodyguards entering the sauna lobby. Neither removed the dark shades from their eyes.

"Oh, h-hello," Mira quivered. "You must be here to check on Mr. Gromble?"

"His hour's nearly up," said one of the men with little inflection.

"He doesn't usually stay in there for this long," added the other.

Tracy rolled her eyes back to Mira. "Guess we just gained a couple more for that tour you promised me," she grinned.

Mira nodded slowly. "Right. Of course. We can all take a walk back to check out the facility." Here she addressed the men in black: "And check on Mr. Gromble."

"Please." Tracy gritted her teeth.

The woman behind the counter orbited around it slowly and stepped toward the front doors. "Let me just lock this first." Mira clicked the deadbolt in place. "Alright, ready to go?"

"Yes," all three answered in impatient unison.

Mira forced another smile. "Okay, right this way."

She walked as slowly as she could without raising suspicion, ushering the trio of unexpected guests through the dressing room. "This," Mira explained, her voice echoing off the off-white tile floors and walls, "is one of our shower rooms. There's another at the end of the sauna loop where patrons can conduct a final rinse before returning to gather their things from these lockers." Here she gestured to the rusty-edged metallic lockers, which didn't quite match the aesthetic of the rest of the room. *Probably salvaged from some old school building.*

As Mira led the group of inquisitive guests through the bathhouse labyrinth, she listened closely in her earpiece for messages from the rest of the Dream Team. *Nothing. How much more time do they need?*

The woman could tell that Officer Jones and Gromble's bodyguards were growing impatient and worried that they'd seen no signs of the two men they were looking for. They paid little attention to the information Mira shared as they passed through several more rooms.

"And this is the jacuzzi," Mira said, trying not to inhale the vapors. *Could be residue from the sleeping powder Kiki dissolved in there.*

One of the bodyguards pushed to the front of the group. "Where is Mr. Gromble?"

"I, uh, think he's probably in our Russian room." Mira tried to sound uncertain. She knew that was the space in which the team was presently extracting Gromble's dreams.

"Take us to it," the second man insisted. "Now."

"Yes, of course," Mira sputtered. "It's right through the next door."

The two bodyguards pushed past Mira, nearly causing her to slip on the slick floor, and Tracy followed quickly behind.

They haven't come out yet! There's no way they're finished! Mira's eyes grew wide. *I have to do it: create an illusion to hide them.* She knew it was a risky attempt. If her compatriots weren't completely silent, the bodyguards and the officer would see right through the illusion.

The men reached the door and started to push through to the hot room. Mira shut her eyes and squeezed them tight, but it was too late. *They've already seen inside! We're done—*

Tracy's voice shouted over the bubbling of the jacuzzi and the steam: "Where are they?"

Huh? Mira opened her eyes. *It certainly wasn't my powers...* "They aren't in the Russian room?" She hurried toward the open door and looked into the dim, steamy space.

"There's no one inside," one of the bodyguards said. His hand moved inside his jacket, almost certainly toward a concealed weapon.

The momentary relief Mira felt was quickly replaced with fear. "I-I guess not," she stuttered, then pointed toward one of two inconspicuous doors on the far side of the dark room. "It's possible they're completing their regimen with a cool shower."

Mira followed the three as they moved quickly through the blazing hot—*but empty*—room toward the shower door. The sound of light, rushing water filled their ears, and Mira smelled the scent of a pleasant, minty shampoo.

Viktor Gromble was immediately visible, as he finished wrapping another long, fresh towel around his waist. He looked up to see his trusted bodyguards, followed by the two women. "What's going on here?" Gromble asked with a contemptuous scoff.

"Just checking to make sure you're alright, sir," one of the men replied.

Gromble puffed. "I'm alright. I was just leaving to get my things." He pushed past the two women and through another door that led back to the lockers.

Tracy raised an eyebrow and turned to Mira. "Where's my partner—?"

Mira ignored the question and hurried after Viktor and his bodyguards. "I'll need to let you out," she muttered, leaving Tracy behind as the group moved out of sight.

Jones shook her head.

"Castillo?" She said, louder than usual so that she could be heard over the sounds of running water. There was no reply. "You in here?" Again, she heard no answer.

Something's off. What if Gromble did something to Rico—hurt him?

Or worse.

Out of instinct, Tracy reached under her light jacket where her sidearm was strapped. She removed the weapon as she stepped quietly toward the rushing shower.

"Rico? You alright?"

The lack of response alarmed her even more. She saw a tiny rivulet of bloody water dripping along the floor. Tracy quickened her steps, moved toward the noise, followed the bloody trail, and whipped back the shower curtain, aiming her gun and—

"Hey! What the heck!" Castillo snatched the edge of the curtain and hurried to cover his dripping lower half.

"Ah! Sorry!" Tracy quickly turned away and half-closed her eyes. "I didn't mean to—"

"Can't a guy shower in peace?"

"I called out but—"

"Geez! It's bad enough with you breathing down my neck!" Castillo turned off the shower with a squeak then gestured toward a stack of cleanly folded towels. "Hand me one of those, will ya?"

"You were in here pretty long." Tracy holstered her weapon and picked up a towel. She kept her face turned away and handed the soft cloth to her partner. She spoke to the wall. "I was starting to get worried that Gromble or one of his people had done something."

Do I detect... genuine concern? Castillo dried himself off, then wrapped the towel around his waist. "I had things under control," he said defensively.

"But there was blood—!"

Through the doorway to the dressing room, Tracy heard the sounds of Gromble and his men rustling out and exiting the building—its signature jingling bells echoing faintly down the corridor.

Tracy sensed Rico was once again decent and turned to face him. A small, lumpy gash on the side of his head caught her eye and she instinctively reached for it. "Ah! There's the blood. What happened here?"

"Ouch!" Castillo winced and took a step back. "I said I had it under control."

"Doesn't look like it." Tracy crossed her arms.

The man inhaled then breathed out slowly.

Officer Jones raised an eyebrow. "What?"

Castillo avoided eye contact. "I, uh, fell asleep in the Russian room," he started bashfully. "Must've been the heat. It's a little foggy, but I think my head hit the bench." He touched the wound delicately and winced again.

Tracy rolled her eyes and smirked. "Well, I hope your spa day was worth it."

Again, Castillo tried to avoid meeting Tracy's eyes. "Not as much as I hoped," he began. "But, I found out Gromble knew Smith."

"You still think he had something to do with his death?"

"No," Rico shook his head. "He's slimy, but I think he was telling the truth."

"Anything else?"

"Yeah. Gromble doesn't think Ducane had anything to do with the murder; he insinuated that someone might have come after Smith to get to Ducane—not the other way around."

"Ducane seems like a hard man to find." Tracy took in her partner's words with a nod, then took a deep breath of the humid air. "Alright, get dressed," she snapped, grinning. "We've spent enough time in here and we've got that Reverend stopping by the station in—" she checked her watch. "In about thirty minutes."

"Yes, ma'am."

Castillo made a mocking salute, then the two filed out of the shower room with haste.

CHAPTER 14

"Here goes nothing!"

Kiki slipped the tape into the VCR. The warehouse was dim, as the day's fading light was beginning to cast orange and gold dapples on the milky upper windows, and the rest of the team stood with their eyes anxiously fixed on the towers of televisions that displayed blue holding screens.

The monitors turned to a crackling black image that intermingled with distorted color bars before smoothing out. A crisp cloudy sky appeared.

"That's it?" Mira wondered aloud.

"Shh!" Declan urged the entire group to keep quiet.

There was movement, a discreet motion to the whole scene. It wasn't the clouds moving, but the whole image. The rocking of the unseen camera—or rather, Viktor Gromble's point of view. There was a fairly steady cadence to the motion, a peaceful rhythm.

You can almost feel a breeze, Declan noted.

"What are those?" Buster pointed toward a series of brownish dots that appeared at the edge of the frame, too small and low-res to make out.

As the brown splotches made their way across the light blue sky, an alarming noise came from the VCR. Instantly, rotors accelerated as if they were fast-forwarding the tape, and the serene images on the screens were contorted and fuzzied.

Donna had kept quiet since they'd hurried into the van, but now spoke up: "What's happening?" She leaned forward, worried, as Kiki bent over the machine.

"I dunno!" The pink-haired woman flipped up the plastic flap that hid the tape inside the player, then flashed an anxious look back at Declan. "Not good."

"Kiki—what is it?"

"You're not gonna like this." As Kiki pressed the eject button, the screens' jittery images disappeared back to bright blue and the VCR tried to spit out the tape. Something got stuck inside, so Kiki tried inserting her fingers to yank it out. She couldn't get a good grip on it and glanced toward Mira, who stood nearest to a table of supplies. "Toss me a pencil or something?"

Mira scrambled and rushed to Kiki's side with a pair of writing implements in hand.

"Thanks," the smaller woman muttered, jamming the slender instruments into the gap.

The onlookers were skeptical of her methods, but Kiki

managed to wrench the videocassette out of its entrapment. She carefully removed it—forced it the rest of the way by hand—revealing a trail of melted, mangled, black cellophane ribbon.

"Gah, Kiki!" Declan rushed to her side. "Look what you did!"

The shiny ribbons were completely melted and gnarled as the pair examined the tangle.

"That wasn't me," she insisted. "It's totally warped and melted."

"I told you this would happen," Buster shook his head. "It was too hot in there."

Declan puffed through his nostrils, then asked Kiki quietly: "Any way to salvage it?"

Kiki yanked more of the ribbon off its plastic spool, unveiling another stretch of just-as-ruined tape. "I, uh, don't think so."

Donna's brow furrowed and she crossed her arms. "What—so that's it? We went through all of that for a few seconds of melting blue skies?"

Declan stood and moved toward her, noting the blonde woman's incredulous look. "Now, Donna—"

"Don't '*now Donna*' me!" She held up a stern, gloved pointer finger. "I just had to put *these* hands on that disgusting man's body, we narrowly evaded the cops (one of whom is a friend who I'm going to have to *lie* to), and I almost did the one thing that I *swore* I'd never let happen again!" Donna took a quick, deep breath. "So far, we've risked our lives twice—*more* for some of you—and we've got nothing to show for it but a couple of useless videotapes." She shook her head and threw her hands in the air. "I can't believe I thought this would help find Marcus; I can't keep doing this," she muttered, almost to herself, and started toward the warehouse's exit.

"Donna, wait—" Declan hurried after her, attempting to reassure the others with a glance as he did. "There's still one more member of the Inner Circle that could help us figure this out," he shouted.

"*Could?*" Donna paused and turned. "That's the thing—we don't even know if any of this is going to get us closer to finding Marcus *or* Angela *or* Ducane."

"So you're calling it quits? What about Marcus?"

"I'll find him another way." She started to turn away.

Declan grabbed Donna's arm before she could move any further from the group. "This is the only way."

He released his grip on Donna as she turned toward him. Their eyes met—his betraying a strange, animal fury; hers foreboding the calm before a storm of tears.

"I'm sorry about what happened with Gromble. I should've foreseen that. But please, Donna. The team needs you." Declan gestured toward Buster, Kiki, and Mira. "Finding the antidotes in the vault is of the utmost importance to them."

Donna considered his words and surveyed his trio of partners. "Why do you all care so much about finding Ducane's vault—what's so terrible about all of *your* powers that you'd risk everything for the chance to change it all?"

The three took glances at each other, waiting to see who

would speak first.

Mira was the first to answer. "Everyone hides," she started. "Everyone changes who they are to fit in, to be noticed—or to keep from being noticed. But when my *curse*—as you call it—became apparent, I took it to the extreme. Not just with changing the scenery, but changing myself. I could be anyone I wanted, appear any way I desired. With my powers, I was able to craft elaborate illusions, images of perfection that I had only dreamed of before—images of what I thought people wanted to see."

"But I don't understand," Donna cocked her head. "You're gorgeous—like *supermodel*-level. Girls would kill to look as good as you, Mira."

She took a deep breath. "What you're seeing isn't exactly *me*. There are very few people who have seen the real me." Mira lowered her head.

"What's wrong with a little supernatural makeup?"

"What's *wrong* is that people don't actually know *me*. I've spent so much time becoming this fake, curated version that I've lost the woman behind all of that."

Donna considered her words. "So why don't you just let down the facade?"

"I wish I could," Mira exhaled. "But it's not that simple. To be honest, I've been hiding so long that I'm afraid of what people will think when they meet the real me."

The room was quiet for a few moments until Mira added: "If we can find the vault—find the cure—then I can put an end to this, face my fear, and stop hiding from the world.

And then I won't have to face that choice every day."

Kiki waited to make sure Mira was finished, then chimed in. "My story's kind of similar to Mira's. Splitting myself so I can be in two—or three, or more—places at once? It's like this major high. I can do so much with my time now. But it also means that I have a really hard time being present. Being here and now, ya know?"

The others listened with rapt attention as the young, pink-haired woman continued:

"I started using my doubles to be more productive, help me make more friends—I could be studying with one friend while my double was off having fun. Still, something was off."

"I mean, look at what you're able to accomplish when there's more of you," Donna noted. "Isn't that worth it feeling *off* every once in a while?"

Kiki crossed her arms. "It was perfect until it started to take a toll on me and my relationships. My body and my brain were scattered in multiple places, but I was still just one person. We aren't made to be everywhere all at once."

"So can't you just stop splitting yourself?"

"I wish," Kiki puffed. "It's like an irresistible urge now. An addiction. It would be easier to just get rid of it, once and for all. With the cure."

"Just because it's the easy thing doesn't mean it's the right thing," Donna muttered. "What if you have these powers for a reason?"

Kiki shifted her weight from one foot to the other. "What reason?"

Donna shrugged. “Maybe to learn to control your powers—not to let them control you—and to use them for good. But what do I know?” Donna held up her gloved hands and shook her head. Finally, she turned her attention to Buster. “What about you?”

“I was married before,” Buster took a deep breath, fiddling with a band on his ring finger that Donna hadn’t given much notice of until that moment. “After the, uh, procedure, I went home. My wife came to greet me with an embrace—I hugged her back—” He lowered his head as his eyes became glassy. “I didn’t know I had developed that kind of strength. She died in my arms right then and there.” He sniveled then wiped his tears with the back of his hand.

Donna covered her mouth with her hand. “I’m so sorry, Buster.”

“Finding that vault,” Buster continued, now looking straight into Donna’s eyes. “It can’t bring her back, but maybe it can allow me to keep it from happening again—to allow me to live a normal life again.”

Donna broke free of Buster’s gaze. The sounds of distant vehicles whizzed by beyond the warehouse walls; inside, the vast room was filled with a palpable tension.

“Fine.” Donna took a deep breath. “One last heist. But if this doesn’t work, I’m out—no more Dream Team for me.”

“Fair enough,” Declan acknowledged. “I’m going to finish compiling the brief tonight. Be back here at nine in the morning—we’ll have some prep to do before tomorrow night’s mission.”

Donna agreed and gestured with her thumb toward the door. "I have to get back to Starla."

Before the man could reply again, Donna was gone. The warehouse door creaked and slammed shut, echoing through the cavernous space.

"Have you seen this man?"

Castillo slid a grainy black-and-white headshot of Wesley Smith across the table. Opposite the officer sat the Reverend Juan Delacorte, his lanky figure hunched and apprehensive as he studied the image before him.

"Why do you need to know?" The clergyman asked.

Rico shifted in the uncomfortable metal chair, one of the sterile interrogation room's few adornments. "That's irrelevant to the question at hand," he said with an impatient sigh. "Do you know him?"

The Reverend considered his answer—weighing the potential costs of truth-telling with the bliss of continuing on with his life of freedom from oversight or intrusion. Of course, he knew the situation was more complex than that, but he needed to decide quickly.

"It's a pretty simple question—"

"Did he do something wrong?"

"Do you know the man in the photo?"

"Something happen to him?"

Castillo gritted his teeth. "Do you know him? Yes or no?"

Delacorte slowly raised his eyes to meet Castillo's. "No."

The officer puffed then glanced toward the one-way glass window to his left. Rico could almost feel Tracy's inquisitive gaze inspecting his every move and every word from the other side of the mirror. *The only reason I won't pummel the truth out of this guy. I know he knows.*

Castillo felt a throbbing pain in his temple from his fall at the bathhouse. He rubbed the welt on his head, took a deep breath, and leaned forward. "I know about the Inner Circle," he said quietly.

The Reverend didn't flinch. "Am I supposed to know what that means?"

"Don't play games with me, Rev." Castillo chided him.

Delacorte raised an eyebrow. "Do you really want to toy with a holy man, Officer Castillo?"

The officer smiled. "Me and the big guy upstairs are square. I'm not scared of you." He paused, then added, "But maybe you should be a little more afraid—you could be next."

Slowly, the Reverend's demeanor drooped. "What's that supposed to mean?"

"The man in the photo—" *Who this guy definitely knows,* Rico reaffirmed to himself. "—died earlier this week. Did you know that?"

"I already told you, I don't know him—"

"It seems likely that he was murdered, and it's possible that you or your colleagues in the Inner Circle may be next."

The Reverend took a discreet gulp but said nothing.

"We can protect you." Castillo leaned back in his chair and folded his arms across his chest. "*If* you talk."

Several quiet moments passed, the Reverend's face betraying his worry.

Castillo realized the man wasn't going to speak about the Inner Circle or their dealings directly, so he shifted his approach: "Is there *anything* you can tell me about the last few days—anything out of the ordinary?"

"Such as...?"

"Did you notice anyone following you—watching you? Strangers? Friends?" The officer exhaled and thought through other ideas to jog the man's memory. "Did anyone try to get close to you or ask you about your, um, work—?"

The Reverend's expression changed, his eyes narrowed as he made eye contact with Castillo. "There was a woman."

Castillo took up a pen and notepad and held them as if he was going to write, but kept his eyes on Delacorte. "What woman?"

"At the bar—Casarosa," he elaborated. "It started normal enough—a pretty girl, blonde and flirty. We shared a couple drinks, things were going well, we went to find a quiet room in the back, and then..."

Here the Reverend's brows furrowed as he drifted into a thought, a recollection.

"Then *what?*"

"I don't remember." Delacorte shook his head. "I woke up in a dressing room. I don't even know if we, uh... if anything *happened* between us. She was gone." His eyes lowered. "She might've been an angel."

Castillo smirked. "In my line of work, we have *other* names for that kinda lady."

The Reverend didn't seem to think the joke was funny.

Rico leaned forward again. "Did you tell her anything... *sensitive*? Anything about your work, about the Circle?"

The Reverend snapped his eyes back to Rico. "I'm not falling for that."

Castillo sighed quickly. "Your life may be in danger, Rev. If this girl has something to do with it, I need to know—to protect you and the others."

"Of course," the man nodded and scrunched his eyes closed. "She told me her name was Demetria."

"What else do you remember about... Demetria?"

"She was blonde."

"Yes, you said that already."

The Reverend opened his eyes just to roll them dramatically for Castillo to see, then shut them again with a puff and continued. "She wore a short dress with those... what do you call them? Shiny circle things?"

"Sequins?" Rico suggested.

"Yes, sequins!" Delacorte pointed with both hands.

"So this blonde woman named Demetria was wearing a short, sequined dress," Castillo pretended to read back from his notepad. "Is there *anything* else?"

The Reverend thought for a moment, then spoke softly: "She had a nice smile. Oh—and she wore these, um—" He rubbed his hands together. "—she wore *gloves*."

"Gloves?" Rico repeated. His brow furrowed.

"Yeah, I thought it was odd, too. Not many people wear

gloves in the summer—especially not in South Florida."

Not many at all, Castillo noted. *There's no way she's involved in this—*

Castillo's mind raced with questions and far-fetched scenarios, before he returned his focus to the man across the table.

"I'm sorry, officer," the Reverend said at last. "That's all I know."

"Thank you, Reverend." Castillo nodded and feigned a smile as he rose from his seat. "I think that'll be all for now."

The other man stood up, too, and started for the door.

"If you remember anything or see anything out of the ordinary, you call me right away, okay?" Rico insisted with a raised eyebrow.

The Reverend nodded. "Of course, officer." An electric buzz could be heard, indicating that the door was unlocked. The man pulled it open and sauntered away down the hall. Castillo took a deep breath and exhaled sharply as the door opened wider.

Tracy entered.

"Not bad, Rico," she grinned and crossed her arms. "He basically admitted to being in the Inner Circle, though we already knew that."

Castillo nodded silently.

"You flinched," Officer Jones noted, taking a slow step toward him.

"Huh?"

"When the Reverend mentioned the blonde woman's

gloves, you flinched—your mind went somewhere else." Tracy cocked her head. "That mean something to you?"

Rico took a deep breath. "No," he said finally. "Just thought it was odd."

The woman raised one of her sharp, dark eyebrows. "You think there's something there?"

"I dunno," the man shook his head. "I'll have Marge run a search on the name Demetria and see if anything else turns up."

"Good idea." Jones nodded. "Then go get some rest. It's been a long day and I'm sure we've got another long one ahead of us while we link up with our final suspect."

Officer Castillo nodded again, then left the room to deliver his request to Marge and gather his things.

There's other people who wear gloves, right?

His mind wouldn't let it go.

Donna would never—she's got her sister and Starla and Marcus...

Rico knew it was unlikely that his old friend had anything to do with a gory murder case, but there was only one way to be sure.

The Corvette engine growled as its tires screeched around a sharp turn. Donna swerved out of a maze of alleyways and into a four-way intersection, then came to a momentary stop as the light turned red. She tapped the steering wheel with an impatient finger and let out a slow exhale. She pressed a button for the car's roof to retract. The sun had nearly vanished behind the city before her, but its gilded glow splashed its final rays over the woman as the thick canvas material sunk into the back of the car. The traffic light turned green.

Her sunglasses shielded her eyes from the whipping breeze, but Donna used a gloved knuckle to wipe a stray tear under the shades.

That was too close back there.

The glistening yellow car zoomed up the ramp to the causeway. Donna cranked the volume of the radio—a track by an obscure electro-pop group—and tried to tune out.

I just want this all to be over. Where are you, Marcus?

She zipped past a slow-moving conversion van.

I want us to be together—all together. Sondra, Starla, Marcus; the girls; and—Castillo! He can never know about all of this—

Finally, Donna turned onto the small offshoot bridge that led to Star Island. It was growing darker now, so she removed the shades as the car reached the gate. She rolled up to the front entrance, where her usual attendants helped her disembark and led her inside.

Donna's voice echoed through the vast, tiled entry room as the door closed behind her: "Starla, I'm home!" There was no response. The space seemed darker than usual. Donna flicked a switch, which did nothing. "Dang it! Bulb's out," she muttered under her breath.

The blonde woman continued toward the kitchen, from which she could see light seeping through the doorway.

"Starla?" She shouted again.

When there was no reply to her second call, Donna felt her pulse quicken.

Something isn't right! Someone's here...

She cautiously pressed herself against the wall beside the kitchen doorway and reached for a heavy candlestick on a nearby side table. A pair of footsteps moved slowly, quietly across the tile floors then paused. With a deep breath, Donna leaped around the corner, raising the candlestick over her head. She prepared to bring it down on the stranger in her kitchen. Her wide eyes softened when she recognized the man leaning against the counter.

"Rico!" She exhaled sharply, her rapid pulse slowing only slightly. "What are you doing?"

The officer eyed the blunt object in her hand with suspicion. "I oughta ask you the same question."

His comment didn't register, so Castillo pointed at the candlestick.

"Oh, sorry!" Donna hurriedly set it on the long counter. "Thought you were an intruder." She moved toward him. "How did you get in here? I didn't see your car."

"Your boys took it around to the side," the man explained. "Didn't want the neighbors to see a squad car and get suspicious."

"Thanks for that," Donna replied, still catching her breath.

Castillo moved toward Donna and went in for a hug, then paused. "Almost forgot—is it, uh, *safe?*"

Donna flashed a tired grin and held up her hands. "Yep, as long as I've got these on," she noted the gloves, then her demeanor sank. "But that hasn't convinced Starla yet."

The officer hesitated for a moment, his gaze dawdling on her gloved hands, then wrapped his big arms around Donna and held her tight. "She will, Donna," he spoke tenderly.

The woman lingered in Castillo's embrace; it had been so long since anyone had dared to be that close to her. Donna had forgotten how warm one could feel inside.

"You alright, Don? You're trembling."

Immediately, the woman stepped back, releasing herself from Rico's arms.

Does he know what we did? "Yeah, I'm fine. Just tired is all. Sondra's move, taking care of Starla, and—oh my gosh! What happened to your head?"

Castillo backed away as Donna reached a hand toward the bump on his head. It had started to scab over but it was still delicate and painful to the touch. "Just a little on-the-job injury," he said dismissively.

"Workman's comp cover that?" Donna quipped, trying to mask the fact that she knew *exactly* how he'd received the wound.

"I'm fine, Donna," he insisted. "It's already healing fast." Castillo touched the spot and winced.

Donna chuckled.

"Oh, she's upstairs, by the way."

"Huh?"

"Starla," Castillo clarified. "You were calling for her when you walked in. Probably has the headphones too loud—I showed her how to use the walkman."

Donna forced a grin, still wary of allowing the officer to know about the Dream Team and their secret missions. "So that's why you're here—to teach my girl how to use another piece of technology? You know they're saying those aren't good for children's development of social skills, right?"

Castillo held up his hands defensively. "She asked how it worked and I showed her," he said, moving toward the dining room table. "Actually, it's part of why I'm here." Here he moved so that Donna could see a cardboard box on the table. "It was in here."

"What's that?" Donna moved toward the box as Castillo removed the lid.

"See for yourself."

The woman peered over the cardboard edge to see what looked like a random assortment of odds and ends, including photographs, scraps of paper clipped together, a round button-pin bearing the emblem of a pizza parlor, one still-packaged action figure of a helmeted blue man with a rocket-launcher jetpack, and a stack of cassette tapes bound with a rubber band.

"Marcus' stuff," Donna muttered, rifling through the unorganized items. She held up a photograph of herself beside the handsome, dark-haired man. *So much has changed since then,* Donna mused. "Where did you get all of these?

"It's all stuff I kept when we had to clean out his apartment after the lease ended." Castillo thought back to the day several months prior. "I would've kept more, but this was all I had room for." He waved a thumb toward the doorway. "And the walkman, of course."

Donna grabbed the bunch of cassettes and began to read the labels. She gasped when her eyes alighted on one near the center of the pack.

"What is it?" Rico asked, trying to read the inky label.

The woman took the tape and moved swiftly toward a side table on which sat a brand new tape deck and a set of connected speakers. "It's from our first date," Donna said wistfully. She clicked the tape into place, closed the hatch, and pressed the play button. The woman adjusted the volume knob.

Immediately, the grainy sound filled the dining room. There was the crinkling of a windbreaker, the scraping of silverware at a far-off table, and the faintest ambient music drifting from what seemed to be a live band not far from the source of the recording.

"He took me to Jaci's Pizza," Donna explained quietly to Rico before being interrupted by a voice on the recording that sounded identical to hers:

"Do you *have* to record this?" Her voice crackled, a giddy, nervous laughter hiding under her words.

The deep, richer voice of a man replied: "It's a special moment. My first date with *Donna Locke*." Though the recording was only auditory, it was clear that Marcus was smiling.

Donna's younger voice shot back with a grin. "Careful, or it may be your last."

"All the more reason to record it."

The two chuckled.

"He had just bought this tape recorder and was begging to show me how to use it," Donna said to Castillo. "I humored him. We were almost done with dinner and then—" She rolled her eyes toward the ceiling and pointed a finger at the tape deck.

"C'mon, Donna," Marcus chided. "Just one song?"

Donna shot back with her mouth full: "In *here?*"

"Yeah, why not?"

"But there are *people* around, Marcus!" The younger Donna's unseen grin gleamed.

A fork and knife scratched a ceramic plate.

"I was just playing hard to get," Donna muttered to Castillo.

"Oh, Marcus told me *all* about it afterward." Rico smiled. "How he couldn't take his eyes off you."

"The band's ready for you," Marcus interjected, his head turned away from the recorder. The music had ceased, replaced with rising chatter from other restaurant-goers.

"Fine." The recording of Donna exhaled deeply. "I really wish I hadn't eaten all that cheese," she muttered as she could be heard sliding out of the pleather booth seat.

She and Marcus chuckled again, then her thick heels clacked hastily across the tile floors and faded away. Marcus sighed deeply as voices jabbered in the distance.

"The band *exclusively* performed songs in Italian," said Donna to Castillo. "I happen to have almost *zero* knowledge of Italian, so... I did my best." The band began to play a sweet, sultry tune and Donna closed her eyes, being transported from her dining room back to the moment as if she was living it for the first time.

"Buona notte." In her dining room, Donna's voice sang timidly over her own recorded voice through the speakers. "Buona notte. Piacere—" She hummed the next few lines, then opened her eyes. "This just doesn't feel right without a glass of wine," Donna quipped to Rico, starting for the kitchen. "You want something to drink?"

Rico waved a hand. "Water's fine."

Donna moved into the kitchen as her younger voice sang on: "È stato un piacere conoscerla. Buona notte."

A pair of glasses clinked together as Donna opened and closed a cabinet. She set them on the counter and poured from a pitcher of water. "So you gonna tell me how you got that lump on your head?" Donna leaned her head to view Castillo around the corner.

"Oh, it's really nothing. Kind of embarrassing, actually."

"You know you can tell me anything, Rico." Donna twisted a wine opener into the cork on a bottle of pinot noir.

Rico sighed. "I was, um, undercover," he started. "You're not gonna believe it—"

The cork popped. "Try me." Donna smiled and poured herself a glass.

Buona notte. Buona notte.

"So we're on this case—"

"*We?*" Donna interjected, remembering that she wasn't

supposed to know about his partner yet.

"Oh, yeah, the chief assigned me a new partner—"

Donna moved slowly with the pair of glasses in hand. "But Marcus is still out there—"

"Don't get me started." Castillo shook his head as Donna handed him a wineglass filled with ice water. "Thanks," he nodded, again noting her gloved fingers, her bouncing blonde hair, and the way she smiled softly.

Buona notte. Piacere.

"So, like I said, we're on this case—it's a murder case—"

Murder? Donna's pulse quickened. *Connected to Gromble or the Inner Circle?* It was the first she'd heard of it. She took another quick sip of pinot noir to hide her surprise.

"—you're never gonna believe this: I rendezvous with this creep in the Russian baths—you know the one across from the old bank downtown?"

Donna nodded.

"We get to talking and, must've been the heat, but I pass out right then and there. Hit my head on the bench, I guess. I woke burning up. Thank God I somehow made it to a cold shower in the next room or I would've been toast—literally."

"Sounds miserable." Donna took another sip. "Did you find out if he—uh, the creep—was the murderer?"

Castillo puffed and shook his head. "No," he muttered, taking a sullen sip of ice water. "But I know he's connected somehow. He knew the victim—this guy was found in an alley, it looked like he fell or was pushed out of a window."

Now Donna was intrigued. *Declan didn't tell me we were*

dealing with a killer. "Maybe it was an accident."

"I don't think so," the officer said confidently. He paused, measuring how much he should tell Donna—and wondering how much she knew already. "Can you keep a secret?"

Donna gulped and leaned in. "Of course, Rico. After all these years, don't you trust me?" *Cool it, Donna; he's going to get suspicious.*

"'Course I trust you, Donna." Rico swirled his drink. "Just some details about a case—I'm already skating on thin ice with the chief. But I gotta talk to someone about it."

Buona notte.

"I told you this guy—the victim—he fell out of a window. There were two strange things about this: the first was that—when we found him—he had these... *gashes* across his face and torso. They all ran perfectly parallel to each other, too precise to be multiple slashes from a single knife."

"That's terrifying," Donna said, genuinely disturbed by the image that populated her mind. "What was the other thing?"

È stato un piacere conoscerla.

"The other thing," Castillo's brows furrowed, "was that we found this weird tuft of what looked like animal fur—caught on the glass of the window."

Buo-na not-te! Donna's song came to an end and the restaurant crowd offered a round of sloppy applause. Marcus's claps, closest to the recorder, were loud and jovial.

"I've never seen anything like it." The officer's gaze drifted away as the images from the crime scene came to mind.

"There's something *off* about the whole case, but there's at least one more suspect I've gotta track down tomorrow—some lady—"

Again, Donna took a quick sip to hide her surprise. *Keene? The final member of the Inner Circle? Rico knew about Gromble, after all. This might complicate things...*

On the tape recording, Donna slid back into the booth with a giddy chuckle. "How'd I do?"

Marcus' smile was audible: "That was an excellent performance, Donna Locke."

Donna clicked the chunky button on the player and the tape stopped. She sighed as she pressed *eject* and took the cassette in her gloved hands.

"We'll find him, Donna. Soon." Castillo assured her, placing a gentle hand on her shoulder.

Donna nodded slowly, but couldn't bring herself to make eye contact. *He'll see right through me.* "I hope so," was all she could say.

Castillo glanced at a clock. "Well, I'd better go."

The two sauntered through the house back to the door. Castillo descended the front steps while one of Donna's attendants hurried off to get his car.

"It was good to see you, Donna," Castillo offered a faint smile.

Donna nodded in agreement. "Be careful out there, okay?"

The man didn't have time to answer, for his squad car rolled into the front driveway with a rumble. The young driver hopped out and held open the door for Castillo. He thanked him, got inside, and peeled off toward the gate.

Donna waved from the top step until the car was out of sight, then gripped the cassette tape that she still held in her gloved hands.

She sighed deeply. *Where are you, Marcus?*

CHAPTER 15

The next morning, the sky was gray and cloudy, obscuring the sun as it rose slowly over the Atlantic baywaters. Donna parked her car in the usual place on a hard-to-spot alleyway, then hurried and huffed down a block of barren warehouses until she arrived at the hidden headquarters of the Dream Team.

Donna barged through the creaky door. She zeroed in on Declan.

"Donna," he said with an innocuous smile. "Good morning. We're just about to—"

"Save it, Declan!" Donna's heels clacked along the concrete floor as she moved toward him. She pointed a stern finger in his direction. "Did you tell them?" The woman nodded toward Buster, Kiki, and Mira, who were gathered in the usual briefing area.

"Tell them *what*, Donna?"

"Did you tell the rest of the team that one of the members of the Inner Circle was *murdered?*"

The others rose from their seats, curious for Donna to expand upon the allegation.

"Donna, I—"

"What's she talking about, Dec?" Kiki approached the pair.

"Miss Locke is just a little worked up—"

Donna puffed. "Worked up? What is this operation you've got us involved in, Declan? Did you know that someone was *killed?*"

The man exhaled slowly. "Yes. I knew it." Declan nodded and kept his face downturned. "It was Mr. Smith."

Mira gasped. "Smith was murdered?"

"I'm afraid so," Declan answered softly.

"And on top of that," Donna continued, "the cops are closing in. My good friend Officer Castillo paid a little visit to my house last night."

"Does he know you're involved with us?" Mira held a hand over her chest.

Donna shook her head. "I dunno. But he knows about the Inner Circle, which means we're racing against time *and* Metro-Dade."

Buster gave a thoughtful look and scratched his chin. "This does not bode well for us."

"Yeah, that's what I'm saying!" Donna said, throwing her hands in the air for emphasis.

Kiki moved closer. "Are we in danger, too?"

Mira added: "Is someone going to pin the murder on us?"

Donna's voice spoke again, quickly. "Remember, I wasn't even *part of* the team yet when you guys harvested Smith's dream—"

"Let's all calm down," Declan's voice rose then became quiet again. "I believe someone knows we're after Ducane and his vault. They're trying to tie up loose ends. Remember, the members of the Inner Circle are the only people who know where it is."

"Then we can't delay," Buster said, bobbing his head. "We have to carry out our dream heist on the last member of the Circle before this mysterious killer has the chance to strike again."

"*And* let's try not to get caught by the cops!" Kiki pleaded.

None of the others replied immediately. Buster and Kiki's words hung ominously in the large, dusty space until finally Declan started for the rugscaped seating area.

"Buster's right. We can't expend our energy worrying about what *might* happen: we've got a mission to do." Declan waved for the others to follow. Reluctantly, they obeyed.

Donna's eyes narrowed as she watched the man move to the corkboard. *There's something else he isn't telling us,* she thought. *Something he doesn't want us to know.*

The briefing began without further delay. Declan pointed to a newly-pinned photograph on the board. "This is Cameron Keene. She's the final member of the Inner Circle and, therefore, our last chance to get the information we need to find Ducane's secret vault."

Donna raised her hand.

"Yes, Miss Locke?"

"Is there any concern that Miss Keene's dreams will be in—how do I say this?—um, less-than-stellar condition, given the amount of time that's now passed since the Circle met?"

"It's a valid question," Declan affirmed. "But we have reason to believe she's been in regular communication with Ducane, which means her mind is likely to have continued to reinforce the associations it has with Ducane—including, but not limited to, the location of his vault."

The answer did little to assuage Donna's concerns.

She crossed her arms as Kiki spoke up:

"So how we gonna do this?"

Declan grinned. "I'm glad you asked. Miss Keene is a hard woman to pin down, but I've managed to settle on one fact that may work to our advantage."

May? Again, Donna's confidence was waning.

"She's a bit of a snob when it comes to fine dining," Declan continued. "She's obsessed with being the first to patronize and offer reviews of new restaurants in the city."

"So, what?" Kiki stood. "We sneak some sleeping powder and laxative in her food while she's out to eat at a fancy restaurant, then suck the dream out while she's running to the bathroom?"

"Close." Declan's eyes glimmered. "But you're thinking on far too small of a scale, Kiki. We're not just going for her plate of food—we're going to fake the *entire* restaurant."

Donna's jaw hung loose. "You're kidding, right?"

"We told you before, Don," Kiki smiled. "Declan doesn't really *kid*."

"Just *how* are we supposed to fake an entire restaurant?" Donna's eyes were wide.

Declan grinned and slowly turned to face Mira.

Mira immediately shook her head. "Wait a minute—no! I know what you're thinking and it *won't* work—"

"Sure it will," he insisted. "You can make any illusion—small or large."

"That's correct," Mira said. "But there are a few key kinks to work out—like what happens when someone talks, or if this Cameron Keene goes to touch something that's not really there? I'm telling you, I don't think it's possible." The dark-haired woman shook her head.

"I believe in you, Mira." Declan grinned. "And I think I've got it all figured out." At this point, the leader explained the remainder of the plan, making frequent reference to maps and notes pinned to the board.

Declan conveyed that he had managed to secure the rental of an empty storefront—just off Ocean Avenue—that once housed a seafood restaurant. It was on a quiet side street free of too much inquisitive foot traffic, but still close enough to the main drag to avoid raising suspicions in Cameron Keene's mind. The elaborate plan involved everyone: first, Buster's brute strength would be put to use outfitting the space with a couple sets of tables and chairs—he'd then act as cook and chef, operating from an extremely limited prix fixe menu crafted by Declan; Declan himself would serve as waiter and de facto handler for Keene; Kiki, Declan explained, was to use her powers to create a crowd to fill the room.

"Uh, Dec?" Kiki raised an eyebrow. "Won't it be just a *tad* suspicious if the restaurant's just filled with seventeen girls who look exactly like me?"

"Yes. It would be *very* suspicious. Which is why Mira's going to make sure no two Kiki's look exactly alike." He turned to the long-haired woman, whose jaw hung agape.

"You're putting a *lot* of faith in me, Declan. You know I've never done anything this elaborate before, right?" Mira hoped he would change his mind.

"I know," he answered. "You'll do fine. There's a spot in the back of the restaurant where you'll be able to do your thing without being interrupted. Kiki, you'll need to be seated in the dining room so you can keep an eye on your, um, *selves*."

Kiki rolled her eyes and nodded. "Whatever you say, boss."

Mira interjected again: "We still haven't solved the issue of what to do if Keene talks to someone or touches something that isn't really what it looks like."

"That's what the tables and chairs are for," Declan explained. "Real, tangible items to give her senses confidence in what she's seeing, hearing, touching—"

"And tasting," Buster added with a grin. "I make a mean etouffee."

The comment lightened the room a little, and Donna raised her hand. "What about me?"

Declan smiled. "You get to use your gift."

Donna's face contorted. "Turning things to gold? I'm not sure how that's going to be helpful—"

"I mean your *voice*, Donna," Declan interrupted. "You're going to provide the ambience. Some things can't be faked."

It had been nearly a year since the last time she'd performed publicly. In a way, it felt like a part of her she always associated with her relationship with Marcus. After all, he was the one who had pushed and encouraged her to pursue that dream.

Before she could protest, Declan added, "Don't worry, I've already hired a band."

"Phew!" Kiki feigned relief. "My upright bass skills are a little rusty."

Donna considered all that she'd heard. She still had serious apprehensions and questions, but knew that this was presently her only hope of finding Marcus—however dim the outlook appeared at the moment.

Finally, Donna exhaled slowly and nodded. "Alright. I'll do it."

"Well, then," Declan clapped his hands together. "We've got a lot to do before the big opening tonight. Miss Keene's already been invited and her secretary assured me it's on her calendar. Donna, I'll need you to gather a couple sets of dishes, cups, silverware. Buster, you and I will grab the furniture. Ladies, you're responsible for any other adornments that Mira doesn't feel comfortable creating illusions of—we should only need enough for Keene's table. Alright—let's get to it."

"One quick question," Kiki pointed as the group started to disperse. "Does this real fake restaurant have a name?"

"Oh, yes, of course," Declan answered. "For tonight, you are all employees at South Beach's newest, hippest spot: the Midnight Lion Cafe."

Officer Jones hunched over a stack of file folders on the conference room table. She flipped through a few pages, skimming her finger quickly to pick out the details transcribed on the crinkled document. On the opposite side of the long table, Officer Castillo did the same, though perched and leaning in a squeaky swivel chair, only half-looking at the pages gripped by his sweaty fingers. The gray, late-morning light basked both of the officers in a soft glow that issued through the frosted windows.

A dusty fan in the corner hummed. Castillo tossed his file on the table and let out a tired sigh. "How far back do these go anyway?"

"I had Marge pull incident reports from the past ten years involving any sort of knife wounds or gashes," Jones noted without looking up from the page. "There's files from surrounding jurisdictions as well. She's working on the next decade once we get through these."

Rico shook his head and reached for a new folder. "I just don't see how you think we're going to find anything relevant to Smith's case this far back."

"You never know," Tracy answered.

Castillo exhaled slowly and opened the file. The numbers and typewritten notes were starting to blur together, barely forming coherent sentences on the page, when Tracy shouted: "Wait a minute."

"What?" Castillo leaned forward, the chair creaking. "You found something?"

"I think so," her eyebrows were pointed and focused as she studied the pages before her.

Rico stood and walked to the other side of the table, where he hovered over Tracy's shoulder to get a look at the file. "Homicide?"

"Not exactly," she said, removing a small, faded photo. Tracy handed it to Castillo. "Those marks look familiar?"

Castillo studied the picture, noting the same parallel cut-marks—like claws across the subject of the photograph—as those they'd found on Smith's cold corpse. But this time the victim was not human. The photograph appeared to have been taken in the dark, so it was difficult to make out through the blood. Castillo squinted. "Is that... a cow?"

"Yeah," Tracy nodded as she skimmed the write-up of the case. "This case happened on a cattle farm near Homestead—almost ten years ago. Looks like the farmer reported it: one of his prized cows went missing in the woods and he found it like that."

Rico leaned over Tracy's shoulder and pointed a finger at the printed text. "Report says they determined it was just a wild bear that wandered on to the property." He shrugged and tossed the photo back on the table in front of her.

Tracy stood and held out the picture. "Does it *look* like a bear did that?"

Castillo was silent as he reluctantly re-inspected the photograph.

"Listen," Jones continued. "I may be a city girl, but we spent a lot of time in the Catskills growing up. I know a bear wound when I see one." She pointed to the picture. "And that is *not* a bear wound."

"Fine," Rico agreed. "But that happened ten years ago. Do you think there's any way it's connected to Smith—or this mysterious Inner Circle?"

"Maybe. Maybe not." Officer Jones slid the photo back into the file, closed the folder, and started for the door. "But I know a way we can find out," she grinned and exited the conference room.

Castillo hurried after her into the open central space of the station. "Wait! You want to go visit this cow farm? Now?"

"Why not?" Jones answered without looking back, quickly navigating the bustling maze of desks and cubicles with haste.

"Because," Rico insisted, "we're supposed to do surveillance on the Inner Circle tonight—"

Tracy spun around, stopping Castillo in his tracks. "We'll be back in time, Rico." Her eyes narrowed. "Wait a minute—you're not *scared* are you?"

"Course not." He straightened up.

"Good. Then let me make this call and we'll pay a visit to the farm."

Officer Castillo inhaled deeply as Tracy disappeared into her office. Something about the situation made him uneasy. Rico was certain the gashes in the photograph and on Smith were *not* from a bear.

And that was quite concerning.

Donna knocked lightly on the cracked-open bedroom door.

"Come in," came Starla's soft reply.

The woman pushed through into the room, where her sister Sondra lay in her usual peaceful state. The blips and beeps of life-supportive machines were audible but faint, and they all but faded from Donna's consciousness as she laid eyes on the scene of Starla with her mother. At present, the girl was holding up an oversized notecard with unintelligible writing scribbled on it.

Donna raised an eyebrow as she sat down in the empty chair on the opposite side of the bed. "What are you up to in here?"

"Just doing some flash cards," Starla replied, placing the card into a short stack. "Just because mom can't talk doesn't mean she can't learn. I'm introducing her to all of my friends from school." The child held up an example featuring a stick figure and an accompanying name scrawled in crayon.

The girl's aunt forced a smile and sighed at the child's naiveté.

Someday, when she's older, she'll understand all of this better.

Donna took a deep breath. "So I've gotta go out again

tonight," she said to the girl. "Sue and Lisa will be here any minute—they're going to watch you and take care of you tonight."

"Like a sleepover?" The girl's face lit up.

Donna chuckled. "Yes. Exactly."

"Can we get pizza?" Starla's big eyes pleaded.

"I don't see why not," the woman conceded. "I'll leave them some cash so you guys can order a couple."

"Soda, too?"

Donna exhaled quickly. "You know it makes you hyper, Starla."

The girl's lip became puffed and pouty—her usual tactic for winning over her aunt. "Please?"

The woman rose from her seat. "Fine," Donna said, moving toward the door. "You be good for the girls, okay?"

"I will, Aunt Donna," Starla answered sweetly.

A warm smile flashed across Donna's face. "I love you, little Starling."

"Love you, too."

The doorbell chimed, echoing through the whole house.

"That'll be the girls," Donna explained, heading out the door. "Be good!" Without waiting for Starla to respond, Donna hurried down the hall to the staircase. One of her attendants opened the door, ushering in two women in sunglasses.

"Girls!" Donna extended a welcoming gesture as she descended the remaining steps to greet Sue and Lisa.

"Hey, Don," Sue smiled, taking off her shades. She wore

large golden hoop earrings that jingled as she moved in for a hug. "How's it going?"

Donna embraced Sue, then moved in to do the same for Lisa. "Fine," she answered quickly.

"Been busy lately, huh?" Lisa asked, raising an eyebrow.

Sue nodded. "You and Rico have *both* been busy—I think my brother's been working too hard. Closing in on some case. And what's your excuse, Don? More philanthropic stuff?"

"Uh, sure, you could call it that," Donna replied with a coy smile. She started toward the kitchen and motioned for the ladies to follow. "I've gotta grab a few things for a, uh, good cause—"

The three women moved into the kitchen, where Donna began to open cabinets and remove various items—plates and cups. She set them on the counter.

"What are all these for, Don?" Lisa inquired.

"Some friends need to borrow them," she answered cryptically. "There should be some boxes in that closet." Donna pointed and Lisa scurried to open the narrow pantry door.

"Any news on Marcus?" Sue leaned back against the counter.

Donna shook her head without looking at Sue and opened a drawer. "Not yet," she replied. Donna hurriedly picked out a few sets of silverware. "I've made some new friends, though, that might be able to help."

Lisa returned with a large cardboard crate and began to relocate the dishes from the counter into the box. "How's Starla doing now that your sister's back home?"

"She's okay." Donna grabbed two handfuls of the silverware and shoved it into the box. "Actually, she's been acting kind of weird—acting like Sondra can still hear her or something. Should I be concerned?"

"Kids are like that," Lisa replied. "They deal with hard things differently than we do."

"I guess." Donna returned to the drawer for another load of forks then put the top on the box. "I'll probably be gone all night." She lifted the crate and started for the door, then stopped and set it on the edge of the counter while she fished into the pocket of her jeans. "Oh, almost forgot—Starla wants pizza." Donna stuffed a wad of cash into Sue's hand then heaved the box back into her arms.

"Don, you sure you're okay?" Sue followed the woman down the hall.

She shouted over her shoulder: "Yep, I'm fine."

Sue shot Lisa a worried glance.

Donna paused at the small curtained window, looking out at the growing midday storm above the baywaters. The foreboding scene unsettled her for a moment, but she hastily proceeded into the garage. She hit the button to open the overhead doors and stuffed the cardboard box into the back of her open convertible.

"Make sure she's in bed at a decent hour, will ya?"

"Of course, Donna," Lisa replied from the top step.

The car engine revved and Donna slammed the door shut.

"Pepperoni!" Donna shouted. "Starla likes pepperoni pizza. No sausage!"

"Donna—"

"Sorry, gotta run!" She revved the engine again and screeched backwards out of the wide garage, then zipped down the driveway and out of sight. As the garage door slowly motored back into its closed position, the two women returned to the house to locate Starla.

CHAPTER 16

Heavy stormclouds gathered overhead as the squad car sped down the two-lane country road on the edge of Homestead, zipping past groves of parallel orange trees and native plant nurseries. The officers sailed past the town limits, entering a vast, multi-mile stretch of farmland.

"Slow down." Tracy consulted the Rand McNally map, holding its crisp pages closer to the window's dim light. She had allowed Officer Castillo the privilege of driving this time so that she could navigate.

Castillo reluctantly complied with his partner's instructions. There were few other vehicles in sight, save for an impatient semi in the rearview that used this opportunity to honk in an obnoxious manner before swerving to pass the police car in the opposite lane.

Officer Jones pointed at a chain-link fence up ahead. "Turn in there."

"Yes, ma'am," Castillo mumbled.

The car pulled off the pavement and onto a short, dusty driveway. The fence was secured with a mismatched, closed gate with what appeared to be a pulley system.

"Didn't you say this guy's expecting us?" Castillo raised an eyebrow as he waited for something to happen.

Jones nodded. "Yeah, give it a minute—"

Honk! Rico slammed on the horn.

"Are you kidding?" Tracy snapped.

"What? Just wanna let the guy know we're here!"

Jones scoffed and shook her head. A moment later, the rickety gate began to buzz and retract slowly, bumping along the uneven dirt and grass. When the gate was open wide enough, Castillo pulled forward along the gravel driveway, where they could now see a small farmhouse.

The house was painted a warm white, its outer walls paneled in wide wood siding. A low sloped roof covered a generous screened-in front porch, through which Tracy and Rico now saw the shadow of a man watching them pull up. Rico parked the car behind a rusty pickup truck. Beyond that sat a small shed and an old muck-stained pontoon boat atop a trailer hitch—it looked as if it had lived in that exact spot—unmoved—for years.

"Let me do the talking, alright?" Tracy's stern expression pierced Rico.

He exhaled slowly. "Sure thing, *partner.*" Castillo quickly exited the vehicle.

Tracy did the same, surveying the rest of the vast property beside her. One half of the land featured a long field, wherein livestock grazed on weedy grass. The other side of the plot was filled with a dense forest—an overgrown grove of mature, native slash pines.

A man's voice shouted from the house. "You made good time."

Rico and Tracy followed the sound to the porch, where the man pushed open the creaky screen door. Jones hurried around the front of the car and extended her hand: "Hank Rochester?"

"In the flesh." The man gave a slight nod and reciprocated Tracy's gesture. "Which one of you's Officer Jones?"

"That'd be me, Mr. Rochester," she half-smiled.

Castillo came up beside her and took his turn shaking hands. "And I'm Officer Enrico Castillo—"

"My *partner*," Tracy added, with a subtle glare to Rico. *He'd better not get in the way.*

"I gotta say," the man huffed, "didn't think they was ever gonna send one of them city officers out here—let alone two." Hank turned and started back toward the door. "Come on in—storm's gonna break soon."

Rico and Tracy glanced at one another then followed Hank into the house.

The wooden floorboards were creaky, painted in a dark and homey stain. The living room smelled musty, and a thin layer of dust covered the items on a pair of matching bookcases.

"Please, make yourselves comfortable." Hank motioned

toward a faded blue-gray sofa with a pattern of off-white dots.

The officers obediently took their seats, sinking into the well-worn cushions, while Hank settled into a wooden rocking chair across from them.

"Sorry, it's not much in the way of entertaining," their host muttered with a wave of his hand.

Rico forced a silent smile.

"It's... lovely," Tracy started. "Uh, Mr. Rochester—"

"Please, call me Hank."

"S-sure. *Hank*, we don't want to waste anyone's time here, so let's get right to it. What can you tell us about the, er, mysterious incident with your prized cow?" Officer Jones produced a small notepad and pen.

Hank took a deep breath then leaned back in the rocking chair, lulling himself into its rhythmic motion as he spoke. "Well, been a long time," he began with a sigh.

"Ten years," Rico mumbled. "Give or take?"

Officer Jones shot him a piercing glance.

"Sounds about right." Hank nodded, oblivious to the tense nonverbal exchange. "I'd only had Bev a few years when it happened." He glanced over at a series of framed photographs on crooked nails attached to the far wall.

Tracy followed his gaze to an image of a woman, faded, youthful. "So, uh, what *happened?*"

He inhaled and turned back toward the officers. "Well, one evening I went to check on Bev and the others in the pen, but she wasn't there. Sun was already setting and it was getting dark, but I searched as much of the woods as I could—that patch out back. Wasn't grown up as much as it is now, but you could still lose your way in it when it was dark out."

"And you found her?" Jones sat poised with her pen hovering above the page.

"Couldn't find her." Hank shook his head. "Called in the Florida City police—couple of unhelpful knuckleheads finally showed up after a few hours. But after searching all night, we found her. Somehow she'd wandered out. I don't know how it happened—"

"And when you found her," Rico interrupted, "Bev was... wounded?"

"I'll ask the questions, Officer Castillo," muttered Tracy through gritted teeth.

"Slaughtered's more like it." Hank's eyes and tone were fiery as he sunk back into the memory. "Four parallel slash marks—something got 'er."

Tracy leaned in. "*What* got her?"

Mr. Rochester exhaled slowly as he made another couple of lazy rocks in the chair. "Police said they thought it was a bear. That's what they put in the report when they closed the case."

"But you don't think that's what happened?"

Hank bellowed. "It sure as hell wasn't a bear, that's for sure."

Tracy's eyes narrowed as she pressed the butt of the pen to her chin. "Sorry to belabor this, Mr. Rochester, but if it wasn't a bear, then what *do* you think did this to your, um, Bev?"

The heavy clouds outside the window stirred and

grew darker.

"You ever hear about all that weird experimental stuff they did down in the everglades back in the early seventies?"

The cops looked at each other, dumbfounded, shook their heads, then waited for Hank to continue.

"Some cultish science camp where they took the kids a while back. Most people think it's all just some made-up conspiracy crap, but you know in every wild, crazy story there's some nugget of truth."

"Sure," Jones offered to keep him talking.

"Soon as I started talking about my theories, the officers up and left. Said I wasn't right in the head. Never heard from 'em again. Even stopped answering my calls after a while."

Rico cleared his throat. "So let me get this straight: you think some kid from a cult camp snuck onto your farm and stole your cow, then slashed it to pieces as part of—what—some religious ritual?"

"Religion ain't got nothin' to do with it." Hank shook his head and rose from his seat. He walked toward the kitchen then turned back. "I'm sayin' one of them experiments got loose and slaughtered my old' Bev."

"You think a *person* did that?" Jones spoke loudly so Hank could hear from the kitchen. The two police officers gave each other another worried glance. Tracy rose from her seat to move toward the kitchen, stopping to examine the photographs on the wall.

Hank ran the sink and filled a glass of water before meandering back into the threshold of the living room. "A mutation—variation on reality." He took a drink.

"That's an interesting theory—" Rico started. Tracy's glaring eyes grew wide.

Hank puffed. "That's exactly what the Florida City folks said right before they wrote me off as crazy." The man moved back into the kitchen.

Castillo fumbled: "I didn't mean that—"

The man ignored him, set his glass down, and reached into a basket on the kitchen counter. He held up a plump, red apple. "You hungry?"

The officers shook their heads.

Hank proceeded to unsheath a large knife from its wood block home and began to chop the apple on a cutting board.

"Look," Hank raised the knife and waved it toward the officers. "You've seen those marks. Now, no knife coulda got them that evenly-spaced" He chopped. "—not with a creature livin'" *Chop!* "And movin'" *Chop!* "And writhin' like my ol' Bev woulda been doin'." *Chop!* "And I sure as heck know that a bear didn't do that to her. So, the only logical explanation—"

Chop! Chop!

"—is that it was an experiment from this, um, camp?" Smirking, Castillo now rose, too, so that all three stood.

"That's right." Their host's expression was sincere as he glanced from one officer to the other, then puffed: "You don't believe me, do ya?" He set down the knife and began to munch on one of the apple slices.

Jones clicked her pen sharply then inhaled quickly. "Mr.

Rochester, I think what Officer Castillo means is—"

"Nah, I've heard it all before," he took another swig from his glass of water, then slammed his glass on the counter and leaned over the sink, his back to the cops. "You cops are all the same..."

Tracy whispered harshly to Rico over her shoulder. "What part of '*let me do the talking*' didn't you understand?"

Her partner held up his hands in defense. Jones shrugged and shook her head, then stepped foot in the kitchen. "Mr. Rochester—I mean, Hank. It's not that we don't believe your story," she searched for the right words. "It's just that we need to, uh, *understand* it more."

The weathered man half-turned his head. "Understand?"

"Yes. Help me understand how you came to this theory. There's got to be something that made you come to that conclusion."

"I already told you. No bear coulda made those marks. No knife, either." Hank's face was red and roiling, and he avoided eye contact with the officers.

There's something more, Tracy suspected. *Something he isn't telling us.*

Still standing in the living room, Castillo studied a picture nailed to the wall. "This your wife?" He pointed to the photo of the young woman that Hank had fixated on earlier.

Rochester turned now and made a sweeping motion with his hands. "Get out!"

Tracy was dumbfounded. "Please, Mr. Rochester—"

"I said *out*!" He moved back toward the living room

doorway, a movement that forced Tracy and Castillo back toward the seating area.

"I just asked a question—" Castillo replied.

"No respect," Hank mumbled as he continued to push the officers toward the front door. "Couple a no-good crumby officers... come in here and think I'm a lunatic—"

They were thrust onto the porch now, and Tracy interjected: "Wait. Hank, please. I believe you."

The angry host finally paused and took a deep breath.

Jones turned to Castillo. "Wait in the car," she snapped.

Rico thought about making some smart retort, but held his tongue and slowly made his way down the steps to their vehicle.

When Castillo was inside the car, Tracy turned back to Hank and said softly, "Now, I promise, I *want* to believe you. And I'm sorry we upset you. That was not my intention. Is there anything else that makes you think that this was some sort of rogue science experiment?"

Hank breathed in the cool air and took another look at the dark, gathered clouds, mediated by the screen. "Me and Beverly used to attend this little church in town together," he started, his eyes still fixed on the sky.

Tracy raised an eyebrow, "You and the cow?"

Rochester's expression softened only slightly. "Bev's the cow. *Beverly* was my wife. Bev was born the day she passed."

"I'm sorry—"

Hank seemed not to hear Tracy's condolences and continued with his story: "The minister there at the church used to talk about faith—you know how much they like to talk about '*faith*' at these churches? '*Walk by faith and not by sight*,' he'd read. '*Faith is the substance of things hoped for*,' and all that. But the one sermon I remember was when he talked about 'blind faith.'"

"I'm sorry I'm not really a religious person—"

A thunderclap rumbled in the distance.

"I'm getting there," Hank assured her. "D'you know that 'blind faith' isn't in the Scriptures?"

Tracy wasn't sure if it was a rhetorical question or not, but Hank continued before she could form a reply anyhow.

"The minister said that people get this wrong all the time. He said we ain't need a faith that's blind; we need one that's *informed*."

"I don't see how this is relevant—"

"Footprints." Hank interjected.

"What?"

"Evidence that informed my theory, officer. I found footprints that night—the night Bev was slaughtered."

Jones leaned in. "Not from a bear, I presume?"

"Nope. Looked like some sort of big animal at first—paws with claws. At least the ones nearest to where we found her. But I followed them into the woods."

"And?"

"Well, uh, they, uh, *changed*. As they got farther away—eventually they weren't big claw prints no more."

"Then what were they?"

Hank took a gulp, his eyes glazed over as he remembered

the image. The man reached a hand into his pocket and produced an old photograph, folded in half. He opened it and held it out to Tracy. "They were footprints—from a *person*."

Tracy's jaw hung loose as she stared down at the black-and-white photograph: pairs of indentations that transitioned from massive paw prints to small human footprints—just as Hank had described. Before she could ask another question, she heard the piercing horn from the squad car. She whipped around and glared at Castillo in the window. Small droplets of rain began to trickle and fall on the dirty hood of the vehicle.

"Thank you, Mr. Rochester. Uh, *Hank*." She shook his free hand.

"You believe me," he stated with a half-raised eyebrow. "Folks thought the photo was a hoax—something I staged."

Tracy inhaled deeply, then nodded. "I believe you."

"Take it." Hank handed the photo to Tracy. She received it with a grateful nod.

With that, Officer Jones hurried through the screen door and down the steps to the car. She gave a final quick wave to the man on the porch, then slid into the passenger seat and slammed the door. Rico fired up the car.

"So, anything helpful—"

"Drive." Tracy snapped and Castillo pulled the car down the dirt driveway and back onto the main road.

The car sped down the old country road as flecks of rain spattered across the windshield. Tracy quickly explained what Hank had revealed to her about his wife, the mysterious morphing progression of footprints, and the old photograph.

"So what's next?"

"What's next is that you've just earned your third strike," Tracy said sharply.

Castillo took his eyes off the road for a split second. "What? Are you kidding me?"

"You almost blew it back there."

"Hey," Rico said defensively. "Without me he wouldn't have even told us about his crazy science theories."

Officer Jones exhaled through her nose. "Three strikes. You're out."

Rico's jaw hung open. "But what about the meeting with the lady from the Inner Circle tonight?"

"I'll handle it," Tracy said smugly. "Keene was hoping it would only be one of us, anyhow—draw less attention. You can turn in your badge when we get back to the station. It's been a pleasure working with you, Rico."

Castillo squeezed the edges of the steering wheel as his anger began to rise. Before he could respond, Tracy flicked the volume of the radio up, blasting a country-rock song to cover over the tension. The duo sped on the rest of the way without speaking as the storm grew stronger and darker.

A bolt of sizzling purple lightning pierced the sky, brightening the downtown sidestreet with a sudden flash like daylight. Declan shuddered and jolted, taking a step backwards from the tall glass windows that lined the front of the makeshift restaurant. He checked his watch then exhaled slowly. The man rubbed his forearm with his palm, sensing a slight tingle. A rumble of thunder masked a set of soft footsteps that approached from behind.

"Are you sure she's gonna show?"

Startled by Donna's voice, Declan moved his hand to his side and turned toward her.

"Positive," he said, swallowing a subtle gulp. "Ready?"

"We're all set." Donna turned and gestured to the open dining area with one of her gloved hands. The team had managed to mostly mask the odor of seafood that had lingered from the building's previous use. "Band's in a room in the back. Figured we'd wait until Kiki and Mira were running their con before we brought them out—less risk and less to explain if they're not in on the con."

"Good." Declan eyed the few tables and chairs that littered the room. Only one, in the center of the room, was set with a full place setting and centerpiece. *Keene's has to be real. Mira's illusions aren't strong enough yet to convince Keene of something she can't touch.*

Donna inspected the flickering neon light that hung in the window, spelling *Midnight Lion* in a solid, pseudo-cursive lettering. A second ribbon of light formed a simple outline of a lion. "What's with the name?"

"Nothing special. We found the pieces of the sign in a salvage yard. Figured it wouldn't hurt to repurpose something old and give it another life—and we're a little too pressed for time to be able to get a new sign fabricated."

"It's catchy, I guess," Donna shrugged.

Another burst of lightning illuminated the small restaurant and the street outside. Rain droplets began to pelt the glass, tapping indecipherable Morse-coded messages before trickling into puddles on the sidewalk.

"Alright," Declan nodded. "We'd better get everyone in their places." Mira and Buster peered through the swinging kitchen door. Declan moved swiftly toward them and Kiki, who had just returned from the restrooms. "Time for you to split up," he told her with a grin.

"I'm on it." The pink-haired girl closed her eyes and scrunched her face. Donna and Declan watched as the side of Kiki's body stretched out, melting and separating into a second, identical iteration of the young woman. Donna covered her mouth. There was nothing that prepared one for the weirdness of such a sight, even if they'd seen it before.

As the thunder rumbled on, Kiki repeated her full-body mitosis, producing more than a dozen identical clones of herself—all dressed the same. "How do we look?" The small troupe of Kiki's doubles twirled in sync.

"Mira will take care of how you *look*," Declan reminded her, with a nod toward the woman in the kitchen door. "*You've* got to make sure all of your, um... *selves*... can *act* properly. Are you going to be able to sustain this many of you?"

The original Kiki inhaled deeply then nodded. "Yeah, of course." Her expression did not convey the same confidence as her words.

Declan moved in closer and put a hand on her shoulder, then spoke softly so only she could hear. "You haven't done this many before. You told me the more you do, the more it puts a strain on your mind. You sure you can handle it?"

"I said I'll be fine," Kiki assured him. "It shouldn't take much mental energy once we're all sitting and eating—I could do those things in my sleep."

"Please don't." Declan rolled his eyes then stepped back. "Alright, places!"

All of the Kikis hurried to take seats at the various dining tables, leaving the one in the center—the one reserved for Keene—empty. Declan pointed at Mira, who nodded, then took stock of the room. She then moved out of view and into the back of the kitchen.

In the main room, Declan and Donna watched in amazement as the room transformed before their very eyes. First the tables, once devoid of all but napkins and silverware, now appeared to be covered in dark tablecloths. Ornate floral centerpieces sprouted from surfaces. A warmer ambient light and modern art on the walls offset the former cold and barren look of the restaurant shell. Lastly, the dozen or so identical copies of Kiki morphed one-by-one into unique and distinctive individuals—women and men, couples on dates—all of varying sizes and physiques.

Donna's jaw hung agape as the process came to its finish. The room had completely transformed from just a moment ago, and it now actually appeared to look like a bustling and successful restaurant. The only thing off was that it lacked both the ambience of music and the usual chatter.

"You'll have to keep your voices low," Declan spoke to the fake restaurant guests. "Otherwise our guest of honor will pick up on the fact that you all sound like an eighteen-year-old Korean girl." He turned to Donna. "Bring out the band."

As Donna hurried to the green room, Declan met up with Buster just inside the kitchen door. After a quick glance over his shoulder, Declan shut the door and spoke quietly. "You packed my doses right?"

Buster thought for a moment.

"Buster?" Declan raised his eyebrows.

"Mhm," Buster answered with a hurried nod. "Should be in the office with Mira." He pointed a thumb toward the back of the kitchen.

"*Should* be—?"

Before he could make his way to the office, the kitchen door swung open and a large bearded stranger put his face through the gap. "It's Keene," said the incongruous voice, which was now clearly identifiable as Kiki's. "She's pulling up now."

"Thanks." Declan dismissed her then turned back to Buster. "Try not to burn or break anything back here, okay?" The leader of the group then tugged on the edges of his jacket to tighten it and returned to the dining room.

Declan arrived to the front of the restaurant just in time. At Donna's instruction, the band began to play a vaguely familiar Italian melody and she took her place beside a microphone. The room immediately felt more alive—and not a moment too soon. Along the dark, wet sidewalk came a tall woman with a trenchcoat and an umbrella. She ducked under the overhang of the front door, folded the umbrella, then gave it a quick shake. The woman in the long coat turned and pushed through the door, allowing the sweeping sound of the rain to intermingle with the music within. Donna took a deep breath and began to sing.

Buona notte...

CHAPTER 17

A thunderclap rattled the thin glass windows at the front of the Midnight Lion as Cameron Keene shook off her umbrella, folded it, and closed the door. She glanced at the small stage area to her left, where Donna and the band crooned and swayed. The newly-arrived woman ran a flat hand along the side of her head to slick back her hair, which was pulled up on either edge above her ears with a voluminous, modern flare at the top. The rest of her hair was pinned together tightly at the back of her neck, giving her a serious and severe expression. She licked a sliver of dark, waterproof lipstick and turned to Declan, who approached her with a rehearsed smile.

"Welcome to the Midnight Lion." He half-bowed. "Do you have your invitation, Miss—?"

"Keene," she said, reaching into a coat pocket that was almost as deep as her voice. "Cameron Keene." The tall woman handed the thick invitation to Declan, who inspected it, nodded, then motioned for her to follow him to a table.

The woman's eyes narrowed as she sauntered behind Declan. "You look familiar," she said, trying to place the man's face in her mind. "Have I seen you somewhere before?"

"I... don't think so." Declan gulped, and spoke over his shoulder: "You must have me confused with some other man, Miss Keene. But people often tell me I look like someone famous—just one of those faces, I guess."

Declan took short breaths as they walked, but he was grateful for the conversation which diverted her scrutiny from the restaurant's other guests. Mira and Kiki were convincing—*but every illusion breaks down if one looks too closely*, Declan thought.

"Here you are," he smiled again and pulled back the seat as they reached her table.

Cameron settled gracefully into the chair, raising an instinctive eyebrow as if making an assessment of its comfortability before she slid it forward.

Declan started to gather the pieces of the second place setting that sat on the opposite side of the table when Keene raised a stern hand.

"I'm expecting someone," she said.

Declan blinked and tried not to show his surprise. The team hadn't prepared for the variable of an extra guest at the table. He gulped, forced a grin. "Expecting someone?" *This could get interesting...*

"The invitation allowed for a guest," Keene noted.

The man nudged the plate back into its spot. "Of course, Miss Keene. And when shall we expect this guest to arrive?"

Cameron checked an octagonal, silver wristwatch. "Any moment now." The woman did little to mask a sharp, disappointed sigh.

"We'll be on the lookout," Declan replied. "May I offer you anything to drink in the meantime?"

"Water, to start with—no ice." She answered. "Ice isn't good for digestion."

"Of course, Miss Keene." Her host tipped his head in her direction, then the man walked briskly toward the kitchen.

Declan pushed through the swinging door and motioned for Buster to come close.

"What is it?" Buster observed the worry painted across Declan's brow.

"Keene's here," he said, reaching for a pitcher and a glass of water. "But she's expecting a guest."

"And?"

"We didn't plan for this," Declan replied, placing the full glass on a circular tray.

"We'll adapt," Buster grinned. "We always do." Something caught Buster's eye through the small serving window.

"What is it?"

Buster took a deep breath. "Time to adapt," he said, shaking his head. "It's Metro-Dade."

Declan's eyes grew wide as he peered through the cutout toward the front of the restaurant. A uniformed Metro-Dade cop stood outside the door under an umbrella, ready to enter.

Declan balanced the tray and pushed through the door. *This just had to get more complicated, didn't it?*

Officer Jones collapsed her umbrella and entered the dim, crowded restaurant. It had a vaguely-Italian theme, accentuated by the angelic voice coming from the small stage to the left and the scents of garlic and tomato and buttery bread wafting throughout the space. The officer eyed a tall woman at a table near the center of the space and consulted a small xeroxed photo folded in her pocket: *That's her—Cameron Keene.*

A handsome, suave host—Declan—appeared. "Good evening, officer. Is there a problem?"

Something in the way he asked it told Tracy she should be suspicious, but she had no reason to suspect anything foul at play. Besides, she had a mission: get Keene to talk. "Oh, sorry—didn't have time to change out of the uniform. There's no problem," she smiled. "I'm meeting someone."

"Ah, of course. Miss Keene, I presume?" The man said, nodding toward the tall woman's table with the empty seat.

"That's right," Tracy answered.

Declan made a soft smile, rubbed his upper forearm, then motioned for Tracy to follow. The officer noted his perfectly-pressed slacks, black dress shoes with wingtips, and the forced smile. *He's out of place here,* she thought. *The shoes are expensive—must've been a gift.*

When they approached the table, Keene looked up and

seemed to size up the sturdy officer.

"Here you are," Declan gestured and stood by. "Miss Keene, your guest."

The serious woman rose from her seat and extended a hand to Jones. "Officer Jones, I presume," she stated, towering over the officer. "Cameron Keene. It's a pleasure." The words rolled between her dark-painted lips without a drop of joy or anything that could remotely be described as *pleasure*. In unison, the two women took their seats.

"Something to drink, officer?" Declan leaned forward.

"Water's fine."

"Ice?" The man's eyes flitted to Cameron's hand, lifting her own lukewarm glass to her lips.

The officer followed Declan's gaze, then answered, "Yes. Ice, please."

Cameron rolled her eyes and did little to mask a scoff while she took a sip of her drink. Declan disappeared into the back of the restaurant, leaving the two women to linger in the tense moment.

"I thought I made it clear that I wanted to draw as *little* attention to this meeting as possible." Keene glared across the table, her eyes flicking between Tracy's badge and uniform.

Officer Jones took a deep breath to offer a frustrated retort, but decided against speaking her mind. Instead, she exhaled quietly. "Thank you for agreeing to meet with me—"

"This conversation ends the instant I finish my dessert." Keene's icy eyes pierced Tracy right as a muffled thunderclap rumbled the whole building.

"Of course." Jones puffed. "And I thank you for your time." She took another breath to begin when the man reappeared with a serving tray and her glass of water. He set it before Tracy with care. "Thanks."

"It's my pleasure," Declan said as he moved the tray and his hands behind his back. "Do you need a moment to inspect the menu?" He pointed to a pair of identical cards upon which the options were printed beneath a designer's hasty recreation of the neon sign outside. "We're running a limited menu tonight for our special soft opening."

Tracy opened her mouth to share her order: "I'll have the—"

"A good waiter always has a recommendation ready to share," Keene interrupted in a firm voice as she scanned the menu without looking up at the man.

He gulped, rubbed his arm with his free hand, then returned to his poised position. "Yes, Miss Keene. I, uh, recommend the special of the night—chicken parmigiana, served with house-made angel hair pasta and a side of steamed mixed garden greens."

"Two of those, please." Keene averted her gaze from the menu and observed Tracy to see how she would react. The officer took a quick breath and nodded her reluctant agreement with the order.

"Two orders of chicken parmigiana," Declan repeated for accuracy. "May I interest you ladies in anything else to drink?"

This time Officer Jones waited for Keene to speak.

"I'll have a glass of cabernet sauvignon."

"Excellent choice," the man affirmed. "Tonight's selection is Three Sisters out of Ocala—fruit-forward taste, barrel-aged to perfection."

"Perfect." Cameron crossed her arms and looked to Tracy.

Declan pivoted. "And for you, officer?"

"The cab sounds fine, thanks."

With that, the man gave another nod and hurried gracefully back to the kitchen area.

"Well?" Keene tilted her head as she took another sip of her iceless water.

Tracy leaned forward, her forearms pressed against the edge of the table. "Miss Keene," she started. "Did you know a man named Wesley Smith?"

"Smith's a common surname," the woman replied. "*Should* I know this particular one for some reason?"

"That's… what I'm asking you," Jones pressed. *She's being even more difficult than I imagined.*

"I've known many Smiths in my day," Keene continued. "But I can't say I know a *Wesley* Smith."

"You *can't* say or you *won't* say?"

Keene set down her glass. She answered with a level calmness that—Tracy noted—seemed slightly contrived. "I can't *and* I won't because I don't know him. Why is Smith so important anyway?"

Jones inhaled. "Well, for starters: he was murdered."

"You don't say?" Cameron took another sip of her lukewarm water.

Tracy noted that Keene didn't appear surprised. Or perhaps it was merely a complete lack of empathy for the loss of a human life. *Not surprising in the slightest.* "I *do* say," Jones said. "Did you know about that?"

"Smith's murder? How *could* I know about it if I've just told you I don't know the man?"

Officer Jones was about to speak when she saw the waiter returning. His small tray contained a bottle of wine and two glasses, each exactly one-third full. *That's odd,* Jones noted. *Normally they pour it in front of you.*

"Here's your cabernet." Declan placed the first glass in front of Keene with careful poise. As the man went to set down the second glass, Tracy noticed his hand waver slightly. The surface of the wine sloshed back and forth like a tiny burgundy tide, but all liquid remained inside the glass as it touched down on the table. "And one for you, officer."

"Thanks," Jones muttered.

Declan nodded then turned and hurried away again.

The kitchen door swung open forcefully, startling Buster. Declan quickly set down the tray of wine and hurried toward the back office while gripping his upper forearm, moving past the big man who slowly stirred a large, bubbling vat of spaghetti.

A few moments later, Declan returned to Buster's side with a serious expression. "Where are they?"

"Where are *what?*" Buster continued stirring.

"My doses," the other man said through gritted teeth. "You said they're in the office but I can't find them."

"I said they *should* be in the office," the cook corrected.

Declan exhaled sharply. "You didn't pack them—did you?"

Buster made no reply, but adjusted the heat knob on the industrial stovetop.

"Buster...?"

The large man took a deep breath and shook his head.

"What?"

"I'm sorry, I forgot! With all of the moving and getting the restaurant up and running—"

Declan turned away and muttered to himself: "This is not good. I can feel it coming—we've got a few minutes max."

Buster tried to be optimistic. "You already slipped the sleeping drug and the laxative in Keene's drink, though, so we'll be good, right?"

Now Declan's breathing became heavy and he shook his head. "I don't know, Buster. I don't know how much longer I can hold it off." The man was already beginning to sweat more than usual.

"Then have Kiki fill in," Buster suggested.

The other man shook his head. "The second she speaks, she'll give it all away. Mira isn't strong enough yet to be able to mask Kiki's voice with mine."

"Well do you have a better idea?"

The muted sound of Donna and the house band filtered through the closed kitchen door while the two men stood considering their options.

"No," Declan said at last, speaking softly. "You're right. If I start feeling worse, I'll tap out and Kiki and Mira can take it from there on." He returned his attention to Buster and clenched his teeth. "How much longer on the chicken parm?"

Buster smirked and peered into the oven. "Almost ready. Just another minute or two."

Declan took a deep breath and began to pace across the sticky kitchen floor.

Between Donna's songs, the various pseudo-patrons—the Kiki clones—of the fake restaurant interrupted their meals and conversations to offer a round of applause. Officer Jones followed the lead of Cameron Keene, who made no such gesture but instead took another swig of wine. As the music began once more, Tracy again pressed into her interrogation.

"So what is it you do for a living, Miss Keene?"

"You spoke with my secretary, didn't you?"

"Yes, but she was a little vague and short on pleasantries—," Officer Jones replied. "Can't imagine where she picked that up," she added under her breath.

Keene took another sip.

"Usually when someone's that coy," Tracy said, "it's because they work for the government—*or* they're into something a little more... illicit."

The woman across the table snickered. "And which do you think is true in this case, officer?"

Jones smiled. "As much as I'd like to drag you into the station right now, I'm going to have to go with the former."

"You're astute; I'll give you that."

Tracy shifted in the uncomfortable seat. "So which is it? FBI, CIA?"

"I really shouldn't say," Cameron said, turning her face away from the officer.

"No, I really think you should," Tracy leaned forward. "Or perhaps I just charge you with obstruction and call it a day? Though, I was really looking forward to the chicken parm."

Keene sniffed and glanced over her shoulder. "What's taking them so long?"

"Dodging the question, Miss Keene?"

The woman crossed her arms, sunk back against her chair, and glared at Officer Jones. "You really don't let up, do you?"

"Not in the slightest."

"Fine," she smirked. "Defense."

"You work for the DOD? No kidding?"

"Not kidding at all," Keene answered.

"See, that wasn't so hard, was it?"

Cameron didn't respond.

"And what interest does Ducane have with the DOD?" Tracy continued to press.

"He—" Keene started, then backtracked. "Ducane? *What* Ducane?"

Tracy smiled victoriously. "The one you were just about tell me about."

Realizing that she'd been tricked into revealing her association with the man, Cameron took a deep breath and became silent.

"Don't worry," Jones said in a mock whisper. "I already know you're part of his *Inner Circle*."

"You know nothing of the kind."

"Miss Keene," Tracy started calmly. "I'm afraid you—and possibly Ducane—may be in danger. Whoever killed Smith: I believe they may be coming for one of you next. Can you tell me why someone would be trying to get to Ducane?" Keene seemed lost in a thought, so Tracy pressed again. "Did you hear that, Keene? Your life may be in danger."

Up until this point, Keene had remained poised and prim. But now, her face contorted and she placed a hand near her abdomen. "I'm sorry. Please excuse me for just a moment, will you?"

Officer Jones raised an eyebrow in suspicion. "Trying to run, are you?"

Keene rose from her chair and shook her head, her face suddenly drained of all its color. "I'll be right back, officer."

The cop let out a long breath and leaned back.

Sure, she thought. *She'd better be.*

CHAPTER 18

Declan peered around the edge of the kitchen door, looking out at the dim restaurant as Keene rose from her seat and scurried toward the bathrooms. The man clenched his fists and warm sweat dripped at the edges of his dark hairline.

"It's happening!" He shouted to Buster, who delicately placed sprigs of basil as garnish on two steaming plates. "Keene's headed for the restroom and I can feel my instincts overtaking me—any minute now. You have to go and get the dream—*now*!"

"We can't leave the cop hanging," Buster reminded him of the obvious, setting the plates on the serving tray.

Almost on cue, a large bearded man burst through the kitchen door, nearly slamming into Declan. Declan recognized the figure from earlier.

"Kiki—thank God," Declan gasped, then motioned for her to follow him around the corner of a large silver shelving unit so that they could get a clear view into the small office in the back. The lights were off, but Mira sat inside, barely visible in what little light snuck through the door. Her back remained turned to them as Declan panted: "Mira, we need you!"

"What is it?" The big bearded man said in Kiki's small, snappy voice.

"The cop didn't see you come back here, right?"

Kiki shook her head.

"Good. You're going to be me."

"Why can't *you* be you?"

Mira took deep breaths, listening to their bickering.

"Because," Declan said through gritted teeth, gripping his arm. "I can't go out there like this."

Kiki glanced back to Buster and rolled her eyes. "You forgot his dose again?"

"I could've sworn we packed it in the van!" He raised his hands in defense.

"Shut up and listen!" Declan snapped. "Take these plates to the officer out there. We can't let her get suspicious *or* go after Keene."

"Get suspicious?" Mira's voice was haggard as she did her best to maintain the elaborate illusions in the other room of the restaurant. "So you don't think Kiki's voice on *your* body will seem suspicious at all? I can't mask her voice, remember? Not while keeping the rest of this intact." Mira faced the office wall once more. She took short breaths and inhaled through her nose.

"We have no choice," Declan said. "Now go!"

Sensing the urgency of the moment, the members of the party began to disperse. Buster grabbed the large suitcase in which the Dreamcatcher was stored and issued through an access hallway; Kiki took a deep breath and lifted the tray of plates while she watched as her body morphed to mirror Declan's; Mira remained in the office, straining.

"I'll be out back," Declan shouted as he hurried toward the back door. "Whatever happens, don't let me back in!" With that he clutched his upper forearm again and pushed through the rusty door into the thunder and rain.

Kiki, dressed in Declan's skin and attire, took a large, nervous gulp and pushed back through the swinging kitchen door.

Tracy took a sip from her water glass, which was by that time mostly fragments of melting ice. She tapped a finger on the table and surveyed the dim room. Votive candles flickered at each of the tables, illuminating the jovial faces of the restaurant patrons. *Something's off*, the officer thought, but she couldn't quite place it. The band finished a song and the room erupted in a light round of applause. Tracy offered her own clapping and turned in her seat to get a better look at the stage behind her.

The blonde singer smiled and gave a nodding curtsy. Officer Jones noted her elegant dress, feathery blonde hairstyle, and the pair of gloves she wore on her hands. *An odd choice,* Tracy thought. The officer began to turn back in her seat then suddenly stopped.

Wait—the gloves! She did a double-take and zeroed in on the soft material that covered the singer's hands. *A blonde woman with gloves—just like the Reverend described. There's no way...* But her mind couldn't shake the idea. *It's the summer: no one wears gloves in Miami—or at least no one in their right mind.*

Officer Jones tried not to look suspicious as she attempted to take in more details of the other woman's persona. Tracy's eyes narrowed. *It would be quite the coincidence for the same woman to show up in the same place as two different members of the Inner Circle.* Tracy turned back and eyed the hallway that led to the restrooms. *What's taking Keene so long?*

The officer considered going after her, but her thought was interrupted by the return of the waiter. The man smiled, placed one steaming plate in front of Tracy and the other at Keene's empty place, then turned and began to walk back toward the kitchen.

"Excuse me." Jones flagged him down. "Can I get some more water?"

The waiter gulped, noted the empty glass, then nodded and hurried off.

Weird. He was super attentive to our table earlier, but my glass has been empty for a while. Officer Jones caught a whiff of the hot dish in front of her and picked up her silverware to eat. Out of the corner of her eye, she took another look at the gloved woman. *Who is she?* Tracy put the sizzling bite into her mouth—

"Oh-oh—hot!"

The officer nearly spat up her bite, loosening her jaw to let air cool the half-chewed molten meat as the waiter—Kiki under the guise of Declan—returned with a clear plastic pitcher.

"Holy crap, that's hot!" Tracy finished the slightly-cooled bite. "But not bad," Tracy conceded as she swallowed and took her next bite with greater caution.

Kiki filled the officer's glass to the brim, splashing a little over the edge where it quickly soaked into the tablecloth. The difference in the size and shape of the two bodies—Kiki's own body and the one she now appeared to inhabit—created all sorts of challenges when it came to hand-eye coordination. *Don't mess this up,* Kiki chided herself.

"Are you okay?" Tracy asked.

The waiter quickly nodded and smiled. *She's suspicious. She totally knows something's wrong—I'm gonna blow it.*

Jones raised an eyebrow. "You sure? You were pretty talkative earlier."

The waiter who looked like Declan swallowed, his pronounced adam's apple bobbing conspicuously. *Just get back to the kitchen as fast as you can.* Kiki nodded again and started back toward the kitchen.

"Wait," the officer said, holding up a pointer finger.

Kiki took deep breaths, then pivoted to return to the table. *If I speak, she's going to hear my voice—not Declan's—and this all goes south.*

"The singer up there," Tracy continued, nodding over her shoulder. "What's her name?"

Can't speak. Kiki inhaled and tried to stall by looking unsure about which person on the stage Tracy was referring. *Don't do it.*

"The blonde woman," the officer clarified. Donna hurried off the stage and vanished down the hallway in the back of the restaurant. "Her," Tracy pointed.

Kiki nodded slowly and scrunched her—or rather Declan's—brow as if deep in thought. *If I stay silent, the officer will be even more suspicious than she already is! I'm about to ruin this whole thing...*

She opened her mouth to give an answer.

At that exact moment, a soaring note from the band on the small stage signaled the start of the next song. Kiki uttered, "I don't know," in the deepest tone she could muster, offered a smile, then hurried back into the kitchen as the instrumental music filled the restaurant.

Kiki burst through the door, sloshed the water pitcher and tray onto the counter, and leaned against a stainless steel side table, heaving deep breaths. After a moment, she tapped an earpiece, switching it on. "Buster, you got that tape yet?"

"Almost," his voice crackled.

Through the kitchen's tiny window, Kiki could see Keene and Tracy's table. Her eyes grew wide as she watched Officer Jones rise from her seat and start toward the restrooms.

"Mayday, mayday!" Kiki's voice shrieked. "The cop's

heading your way!"

"Not finished yet," Buster snapped.

"Hurry it up and get out of there!"

"We *need* the rest of this dream," he answered. "It's our last chance at finding Ducane's vault."

"But Buster—"

"Grab Mira and start the van!"

"The further away Mira gets, the harder it's going to be for her to sustain the illusion."

There was no answer from Buster this time. Kiki watched in horror through the plexiglass porthole as the officer reached the hall that led to the restrooms.

I guess this is it, Kiki inhaled sharply. *It's all over!*

Tracy crept down the dim hallway toward the restrooms. The band's instrumental sounds faded slightly into bassy blips and the officer scanned the wall for the women's room.

It's so dark back here. Whoever designed this place—

The officer's eyes landed on the door.

There.

Officer Jones moved cautiously toward it and took a deep breath.

I swear, if she slipped out the back...

Tracy pushed on the door, but it caught on something. Confused, she tried again.

"It's one of those individual kind," a voice spoke from the shadows.

Jones whipped around, startled. "Huh?" She squinted to see better. *The blonde woman from the stage.*

Donna stepped forward. "The bathroom—it's just the single kind. Somebody's in there." She smirked and gestured toward the door with a gloved finger.

The gloves.

"You alright?" Donna raised an eyebrow.

Tracy nodded brusquely. "I'm fine. Just looking for my, uh, dinner companion."

The music crescendoed, issuing waves down the corridor.

"Did you knock?" Jones asked.

Donna nodded.

Tracy took a breath and exhaled slowly. Her mind again drew her to the gloves. "Sounded good up there. You perform often?"

The blonde woman grinned, a tinge of nervousness in her expression. "Thanks. Not as often as I'd like." Donna extended her hand to the officer. "I'm Goldie. It's my stage name," she added quickly.

Jones reciprocated, shaking the gloved hand. "Pleasure to meet you. Tracy," she added. With a brief pause, the officer pursed her lips and pointed to Donna's hand. "What's with the gloves?"

Immediately, Donna tensed. There was more to the question—she could tell. "Just part of my, uh... act," she answered.

"Right." Jones narrowed her gaze and returned her attention to the bathroom. She gave a heavy knock on the door with the bottom of her fist.

"I think she'll come out when she's ready—"

Tracy shook her head. "Been too long." She rapped again. "Keene! You in there?"

"I'm gonna go—" Donna muttered.

"She'll be out any minute," Jones explained.

Donna shook her head. "I can hold it," she half-smiled and started off down the hall back to the main portion of the restaurant.

Jones puffed and knocked once more. There was no answer. The officer's pulse quickened. She knocked a few more times. "Open up, Keene. You better not be hiding—"

Finally, Tracy heard the click of the deadbolt lock on the other side of the door. She stood at the side of the threshold as it swung open. A strange humid gust drifted past her—like air displaced by a large object—and she took a step back out of instinct. *Huh?* When she returned her attention to the restroom, Jones saw Keene through the gap of the open door; she was leaned up against the back tile wall of the room with her eyes closed and head wilting to one side.

"Keene!" Jones rushed through the door—only briefly wondering how it had opened and unlocked all by itself, for the higher priority was the woman in the bathroom. "Miss Keene, can you hear me?" She knelt beside the limp body and felt for a pulse at her neck. After a few harrowing seconds, Tracy exhaled. *She's alive.* "Cameron? Miss Keene?"

A sudden gasp for breath signaled Cameron Keene's apparent resuscitation and her eyes blinked open. "Where am I?"

"The Midnight Lion," Tracy said. "Are you okay?"

Keene's eyes drifted lazily around the room before landing on Jones. "Who are you?"

"I'm Officer Tracy Jones," she answered with an air of both impatience and puzzlement. "You met me here for dinner—you remember?"

She didn't have that much wine...

Cameron took another deep breath and started to stand. Jones took a hand to help her up.

"Was someone—" Tracy started, searching for the words. "—*in here* with you, just a minute ago?"

The tall woman shook her head slowly. "I don't think so."

What in the world is going on here?

"Let's get you some water, Miss Keene," Jones said, leading her toward the bathroom door.

As she pulled open the door, Tracy noted that the music had stopped. It was replaced by the sounds of voices speaking loudly. *Huh? Is that—Italian?* The voices sounded concerned.

Jones became worried immediately, as well, for when she stepped into the hallway guiding Keene, she noted that the floors had changed. Gone were the well-kept patterned tiles she'd stumbled across moments earlier; now the ground was solid concrete.

What the—?

The Italian voices grew louder, and Tracy and Cameron rounded the corner to witness a truly shocking sight: the entire room had been stripped bare of its accoutrements. The glamorous furnishings of the Midnight Lion had vanished, along with every single one of its guests. Tables and chairs were mismatched and grimy. Only the floral arrangement and the dishes on their own table remained. The members of the band hurriedly packed their instruments while uttering conversations in their foreign tongue.

"What's going on?" Jones snapped.

One of the Italian musicians shook his head quickly. "Gone! One minute: there. Next minute—gone. *All* gone!"

Tracy's head spun. *The silent waiter. The strange breeze in the doorway. The blonde woman. The gloves—this doesn't make sense.* Her mind and eyes turned toward the door to the kitchen. *Escaped out the back, no doubt.* Officer Jones released her grip on Keene and sprinted across the room.

"Where are you going?" Cameron's groggy voice trailed off behind her.

Jones glanced over her shoulder but kept moving. "I'm *not* finished with you!"

The officer hurried into the kitchen. It was empty. She scrambled around the maze of stainless steel cabinetry and rusty freezers until she spotted the back door. Tracy took a deep breath, placed one hand on the gun at her side, and punched through, splashing down into a shallow puddle.

The storm had turned to a light drizzle by this time. Drips snaked down Tracy's determined face as she whipped her body and weapon in either direction. The alleyway was mostly unpaved, covered in thick, sedimentary mud. *They can't have gone far—not that fast.* Her eyes landed on a set of thick tire tracks a little way off. *A-ha!*

Before she could reach the tracks, something else caught her eye. A couple of small, dark lumps under a flickering streetlamp. Tracy's eyes narrowed. *Shoes?* Men's black dress shoes, to be exact. Jones approached cautiously.

Brand new, she noted. Jones withdrew her gun and used the barrel to flip over one of the polished shoes, which looked like they had been tossed haphazardly across the wet dirt. *Wingtips—just like our waiter wore! But why'd he toss them? Certainly not to get away faster—it would have cost him precious seconds to untie and jettison them...*

As her mind raced with questions, she searched for a trail. *There.* The rain hadn't completely wiped his tracks yet, and Jones treaded carefully to avoid stepping on what remained. There was a pair of footprints sunk deep in the mud. *He was moving fast.* Tracy stood beside them, noting that the footprints followed roughly the same route as the vehicle. *He tried to catch up to the getaway car—did they leave him behind?*

She discovered a second pair of shoes, also strewn or thrown—women's heels. *Those belonged to the singer. What did she call herself... Goldie?*

Officer Jones wiped another few drips of rainwater from her eyes and continued to follow the tracks and treadmarks. Then she froze. Her pulse quickened and her eyes grew wide. There, in the mud, where the next steps of the barefoot waiter should have been, were a set of enlarged prints that appeared to be anything but human. *This isn't possible—*

With a gulp, Jones kept a tight grip on her handgun and moved forward. The successive marks grew larger as they moved away from the restaurant—animal footprints that suggested fur and claws—until finally they were nearly a foot and a half long. At last, the prints came to a stop where the mud ended and a paved road began.

Tracy swallowed again and reached into a pocket of her uniform, shaking. She removed an old, folded photograph—the parting gift from Hank Rochester—and held it beside the last set of enormous, beast-like footprints. The human-to-animal progression was the opposite of the pattern in Hank's photo, but the large imprints in the two images were undeniably identical. Jones began to shake her head slowly, involuntarily. *The thing that killed Smith? And Hank's cow? This can't be real. This can't happen.*

But it *was* real—the footprints morphed as they progressed, leaving a muddy record for Tracy to witness with her own eyes. A more pressing thought rushed to Tracy's mind:

He's still out there.

CHAPTER 19

Just a few minutes prior to Tracy's discovery, she stood near the restrooms, the romantic and wordless strains of ambient Italian music drifting down the restaurant's dim corridor. Donna Locke stood outside the bathroom door, attempting to respond to the Officer's bevy of questions in the most succinct and inconspicuous way possible.

"What's with the gloves?"

Donna felt her entire body lock up as the stern officer posed the question. There was something more than curiosity behind it. *She's suspicious.* "Just part of my, uh… act," Donna stuttered, trying to buy time without giving herself away.

"Right." The officer narrowed her gaze and allowed it to linger on the gloves for what seemed to Donna like minutes. Finally, she turned back toward the bathroom door. The officer gave a heavy rap with the bottom of her fist.

Buster isn't finished! Donna took a quick breath. "I think she'll come out when she's ready—"

Officer Jones shook her head. "Been too long." She knocked again. "Keene! You in there?"

The minute she steps in there and sees Buster, we're done! I can't wait around any longer. She bit her lip. "I'm gonna go—"

"She'll be out any minute," Jones answered.

Donna shook her head. "I can hold it." She half-smiled and started off down the hall back to the main space of the restaurant. Behind her, she heard the frustrated officer continue knocking, shouting, "Open up, Keene. You better not be hiding—"

The blonde woman rushed past the band and hurried toward the kitchen. As she did so, the dozens of fake patrons began to vanish in silent wisps as Kiki and Mira's powers ran their course, expiring as the women shifted their focus. Donna burst through the swinging door just as Kiki reached the back exit.

"Hurry, Donna!" Kiki waved her on.

Donna slowed her steps momentarily. "But Buster and—"

"I'm right here," an unseen voice spoke just a few feet from her ear, near the swinging door through which Donna had just passed.

Donna whipped toward the sound. The big man slowly appeared, as if an invisible cloaking blanket was pulled from over his body. "Thanks, Mira!" Mira stepped out from the restaurant office and Buster flashed an anxious grin as he gripped the Dreamcatcher in one hand. "That was too close."

Kiki's eyes were wide. "Did you get it?"

Buster nodded and held up the item in his other hand: a clunky VHS tape in its generic striped sleeve. "Got it all. Let's go!"

Mira held the door as the group exited into the alley. The light rain quickly soaked their clothes. The keys jingled as Kiki fished them from her pocket and unlocked the van from the driver's side. Mira took the front passenger seat and Buster entered through the side sliding door. The engine rumbled to life.

"You coming or not?" Buster waved Donna in.

Donna lingered and looked back toward the door. "What about Dec—"

A blood-curdling howl resounded off the alley walls. Donna whipped around and screamed. A hulking and disfigured creature moved swiftly in the wet shadows—hurtling right toward her!

Through the open side door, Donna heard Buster's terrified voice shout: "Kiki, drive!"

The van lurched forward through the thick mud, spinning chunks of dirt on Donna's dress as she hurried after them on foot.

"Wait!" Donna cried, only catching a brief second glimpse of the beast that pursued her. In most respects, it appeared human—the bare feet looked like they belonged to a man—but the upper half was definitively inhuman—a hairy, ferocious monstrosity. The creature seemed to be changing before her very eyes, morphing into something further and further from a person.

Donna screamed again as the beast gained on her. She kicked off her cumbersome heels and ran after the van with as much strength as she could muster. The creature bent itself so that it ran on all fours and reached out a talon-like paw toward Donna. As her arms swung to keep up her pace, Donna felt a brief, cold sting as the tip of a claw scraped through her glove and pierced her forearm and wrist. The woman winced but kept moving, gaining a second wind.

The van neared the end of the alley. The gaps between Donna, the monster, and the van narrowed. For a brief moment, the vehicle slowed to round the bend onto the paved street and Donna leaped through the air toward Buster's outstretched hand. His strong grip pulled her in effortlessly. He quickly slid the door shut. The beast slammed into the closed door and bounced back, momentarily disoriented. It was all the time they needed; Kiki hit the gas and the van screeched down the street and into the dark midnight.

From the passenger side mirror, Mira watched the hunched and hairy figure shrink away in the distance, then slink across the road toward the dark ocean and disappear. Donna's pulse raced and she allowed herself to lean into Buster's warm shoulder.

"What the hell was that thing?"

Buster exhaled slowly and shot a pensive glance toward Kiki, whose eyes met his in the rearview mirror. "Donna," he began. "There's something we haven't told you about Declan."

Donna's eyes grew wide. "You mean..." Her voice trailed off

and she shook her head instinctively. "That's not possible."

"I'm afraid it is." The large man sighed. "That *thing* was Declan."

The van sputtered along the barren midnight streets in silence. Donna studied a trail of rain droplets down the side window, illuminated by the rhythmic passing of yellow-orange streetlights. It was either the exhaustion, the lack of a square meal since lunchtime, or the shocking revelation that the creature in the alley was the man in whom she had put her trust the last several days. *Why did he lie? Why did he keep that a secret? All the rest of us shared our abilities freely. Why didn't he trust us—trust me?*

Kiki's frantic voice from the driver's seat snapped Donna out of her thoughts: "Donna, you're bleeding!"

As Donna looked down at her wrist, Mira shouted. "Kiki, watch it!"

The vehicle swerved and skidded. The young driver quickly righted the car and turned her eyes back to the road.

Donna now felt the sting and throb of the bleeding wound on her forearm. She winced as she inspected the oozing blood that dripped on the van's corrugated metal floor. A long cut split the wrist of her protective glove in two. *He was lucky he didn't cut closer to my hand, or he'd have ended up just like Marcus...*

"Does it hurt?" Buster's voice was calm.

"A little," the blonde woman replied, trying not to look at

the gash.

The big man reached for a first aid kit under the driver's seat and produced a cloth, a roll of gauze, and a small brown bottle of hydrogen peroxide. "This is going to sting," he muttered as he unscrewed the plastic cap and dabbed some of the pungent liquid on the cloth. Donna willingly extended her arm toward the man, who gently applied the substance to her cut.

The woman gritted her teeth and scrunched her eyes. "So you three knew about Declan?" She asked, inhaling sharply. "You knew this whole time?"

Mira was the first to answer. "He made us *swear* not to tell you," she said.

"But all the rest of us have weird powers, too. What made his so different?"

"He's done things, Donna," Buster said softly. "When he has one of his... episodes. Things that would be too dangerous for someone like you to know about."

"Someone like me...?"

Buster took a deep breath.

Kiki snapped from the front: "It's because of who your friends are, Donna—Metro-Dade. You're too close to the cops. They can't know about all this."

Donna's brow furrowed. "If we were trying to prevent the cops from getting suspicious, I think we failed majorly back there. That officer—and Keene—just saw the Midnight Lion vanish before their very eyes." She puffed and took a deep breath as Buster finished wrapping her wrist in gauze. "Will he be okay?"

"Declan?" Buster raised an eyebrow then nodded. "It'll wear off before long. Usually only lasts an hour, give or take."

The rain began to pick up again, and the van slowed as they reached the bay doors that led into the team's warehouse headquarters. Kiki pressed a button on a remote control and the door began to retract.

"This is my fault," Buster shook his head. "I forgot to pack his dose—he takes them regularly to prevent this sort of thing from happening."

Slowly, the van rolled into the dark space as the door shut behind them, drowning out the pattering storm. They came to a stop and the crew disembarked. Buster carried the Dreamcatcher and handed the videocassette to Kiki.

"Let's hope whatever's on here was worth us blowing our cover back there," Kiki said as she grabbed the tape and hurried toward the viewing area.

"Keene was the last member of the Inner Circle," Mira reminded her. "So this was pretty much our last chance any way you slice it."

The group crowded around the stacks of television monitors as Kiki blew on the tape then inserted it into the VCR. She rewound it to the beginning and was about to hit play when a loud clattering noise made them all freeze.

The sound bellowed through the warehouse again, a metallic clanging audible above the droning rain. It came from the retractable door. Buster started toward it, then paused when he heard another sound: a ravenous howl.

"It's him," he whispered. Quickly, he moved toward a cabinet and withdrew a long-barreled rifle, which he loaded with a small vial. "I think he's ready for his dose." Buster took a deep breath and nodded to Kiki. "On the count of three."

The small woman stood beside him with the door's remote in hand. The banging and scraping grew louder, as if the beast's claws could penetrate the door at any moment.

"One."

Graaarrr—

"Two."

Scrape-screech.

"Three."

Kiki hit the button. The door began to roll upward. As soon as the wet, dark brown, hairy legs of the beast were visible, Buster took aim.

"Uh, Buster?" Kiki trembled and took a step back. "What are you waiting for?"

He paused a moment longer. Then the creature's torso to come into view.

"Shoot! Now!"

The beast started to crouch on all fours and splashed across the rainy pavement to scramble under the half-opened door, a fire in its eyes. Donna gasped and clenched her fists instinctively. She was about to run.

Splink. The quiet ampule shot down the barrel and lodged itself squarely in the creature's neck. It scampered toward Buster then quickly flopped to the concrete floor with a heavy *thud.*

With caution, the others moved closer to inspect the large, hairy monster, lying flat on its chest. Ever so slowly, the long, thick hair began to retract, and the several-inches-long claws at its finger tips shrank. In a few moments, the figure of the beast was gone, leaving only the dripping wet shape of a human man. Donna now recognized the familiar, short-cropped brown haircut as Declan's, though his face was turned away from her.

"Grab me that blanket, will ya?" Buster nodded to Mira, who complied and tossed a thick, textured cloth to him while Kiki sealed the garage door once more. The large man wrapped Declan's bare body in the blanket and picked him off the cold floor. Carefully, Buster carried the unconscious Declan over to a sofa near the monitors and propped him against the couch's arm.

Donna approached, trembling.

Mira nodded beside her. "He'll be fine."

As the group looked on, Declan's eyelids began to flutter. He awoke and flashed quick looks in all directions before settling his gaze on Donna and the others. He noted Donna's bandaged wrist immediately.

"Was that from me?"

Donna nodded.

"I hope I didn't hurt you too badly," he said softly.

Donna raised her wounded hand: "Just a flesh wound." She tried to smile, then winced as a throbbing pain shot down her arm. There were many more words she wanted to say, but she held her tongue.

"I'm sorry you all had to see me like this," Declan continued. "Did we get what we needed?" He turned to Buster.

Buster shrugged. "I sure hope so. Because that lady from Metro-Dade is going to be on our tail in no time."

Declan's expression shifted, and he raised his eyebrows. "You mean they saw through the illusion? It broke?"

Mira held her arms across her chest and nodded while letting out a deep sigh.

"Which means we don't have a lot of time," Kiki reminded them, moving over to the VCR once more. "It's only a matter of hours before Keene alerts Ducane and causes him to move or destroy the vault—and then all of this means nothing." No one else spoke up. She continued. "We ready to watch this?" It was a rhetorical question, so Kiki didn't wait for a response as she grabbed the remote and moved back toward a seat. "Here we go."

Kiki took a deep breath and pressed play.

The living room was almost pitch black, save for the bluish glow from the boxy television set. The sound of pattering rain was barely audible over the TV volume. "I'm starving." Starla rubbed her belly to emphasize her point.

"Pizza should be here any minute," explained Sue. She and Lisa sat on either side of the girl, sinking into the comfortable, modern sectional sofa.

"I'm thirsty, too," the girl groaned.

"I ordered a bottle of Coke. You want some water?"

The girl didn't reply.

"I'll get you a glass of water."

Lisa leaned toward them and whispered loudly. "Shh! This is the best part!"

On screen, a massive great white shark emerged from the ocean and beached onto the side of a fishing boat, instilling pure panic in the vessel's crew. As the small boat began to sink and fill with water, the toothy creature bared its massive jaws. One of the boat's crew—a man with a black bandana—lost his grip and slid down the now-slanting boat, directly into the maw of the beast.

Sue threw her hand over Starla's eyes. "Gosh, Leese, what's this rated?" Sue checked the back of the cassette's cardboard box.

"I'm going to check on mom." Starla jumped down from the sofa and scurried across the rug and disappeared upstairs.

"PG?" Sue exclaimed when she'd found the rating. "You gotta be kidding me. Starla's too young for this—"

Sue puffed and got up from the couch to move into the kitchen, and the film's dramatic soundscape seemed to follow her from the other room. The woman tried opening a couple of different cabinets before finding the cups. She set a pair on the counter. As she moved to the fridge, lightning flashed and Sue froze. Through the back window in the momentary electric glow of the lightning flash, she thought she saw movement. She looked closer, squinting across the darkened, wet backyard and out to the baywaters, waiting for it to happen again. Seconds passed. Lightning flashed again.

Nothing.

The woman continued to remove a pitcher of water from the fridge, with which she quickly filled the pair of glasses. Sue's eyes once again drifted toward the window. She was sure she'd seen something.

Just your imagination, Susana, she told herself. The woman put the pitcher back in the refrigerator, then listened closely. A gust of wind spattered rain against the glass, causing Sue to tense. She breathed in then exhaled slowly.

Bingggg!

The doorbell pierced Sue's thoughts and she jumped.

It's the pizza, she reminded herself, nodding to boost her confidence. Sue started into the entryway to the house and approached the front door. *This is why I don't watch scary movies at night—or ever, for that matter.*

Donna's usual young doorman and valet had gone home for the night, so Sue moved slowly toward the door to open it herself.

Bing-bingggg!

Sue gulped and reached for the handle.

Just the pizza delivery guy...

With a deep breath, Sue unlatched the door and pulled it open. Another sharp gust of rainy-wind swept up onto the barely-covered outside entry area. Sue's body loosened as she recognized the signature red visor of the pizza boy and the damp cardboard boxes in his hand.

"Two pizzas for Sue?" The teenage boy was dripping wet and read off a moist receipt. His car idled in the long driveway, the headlights casting dim but solid beams toward the neighboring hedge.

Sue nodded quickly and reached into her pocket for the cash. "Yeah, I'm Sue. Thanks." The pair exchanged money and the boxes.

"Oh, almost forgot the Coke." The boy hurried back to his car.

The tense John Williams score echoed from the living room as Sue glanced over her shoulder back into the house.

The sloppy footsteps of the delivery guy prompted Sue to turn back. The teen handed Sue a plastic bag with a bottle of soda, which she managed to grab with her fingers underneath the pizza boxes. She thanked him with an awkward half-nod, then the boy drove away as Sue headed back inside and shut the door.

"Pizza's here!" Sue shouted.

Thunder rumbled the whole house as Sue tramped across the floor, leaving a slick drip-trail of water on the tile leading into the kitchen, where she placed the pizza boxes side-by-side on the island countertop and flipped open their flimsy tops.

"Mmm," she wafted the aroma of bread and cheese and processed tomato sauce. "Come 'n' get it!" The audio from the movie drowned her voice, so Sue started toward the living room, but stopped abruptly when she caught a glimpse of the sliding glass door in the adjacent dining room: it was *open*—nearly a foot wide gap—and the rainy breeze licked at the foot of the gauzy, drawn curtain.

Sue's heart raced. She couldn't move. The sliding door had *absolutely* been closed right before she greeted the pizza boy—*without a doubt*. She was about to call out to Starla when she heard a loud *thud!* come from the ceiling directly above her. The volume of the movie playing in the living room was still so loud that it made it hard to tell for sure, but Sue was certain she heard a girl's shout.

Starla!

A more definite, shrill scream came from the living room, muffled slightly: "Help—!"

Sue immediately recognized it as Lisa's voice. Sue hurried to peer around the corner, then quickly changed course and flattened her back against the wall—eyes wide—as she caught the glint of a shiny metallic item in the hand of a darkly-garbed figure in the other room. She hadn't seen much, but she'd seen enough to know what was happening: the person in black—a man—had his hand gripped over Lisa's mouth to quiet the scream.

To her other side, Sue heard more sounds of struggle coming from upstairs—it now seemed that whoever was up there with Starla was dragging her down the hallway.

A million questions raced in Sue's mind, but she knew she had to act fast. The dark-haired woman ducked behind the kitchen island and pressed herself against its obscured side as tightly as she could.

From the small gap between the corner of the island and the cabinets opposite it, she watched as the man in black forced Lisa out the back door with a sack over her head—

guiding her at gunpoint into the pitch-black, rainy night. She noted his pair of pure white sneakers with blue stripes—an odd choice for a break-in.

Ay, Dios mío—

Several heavy footsteps thumped down the stairs and Sue's attention now darted toward this noise at the opposite side of the kitchen. Though she again had only a sliver of visibility, Sue watched as more masked men in black carried two bodies down the stairs—one was Starla while the other was her limp, comatose mother Sondra. A figure at the back of the pack carried the machinery that kept Sondra alive. Sue held her breath as the footsteps sloshed through the rainwater puddled on the tile floor of the kitchen. The men stopped, and Sue could feel them hovering just on the other side of the island. Sondra's heavy, mechanical breathing apparatus emitted a steady, almost rhythmic rasp.

No, no, no—they've seen me!

A hand reached across the island—Sue could hear that much. It rustled something sloppy and gooey, then lifted it.

"Pepperoni," the man said, his mouth full of a cheesy bite. "Still warm."

Another of the figures chided him. "Hurry up, Sal! Before someone sees us. We're on a tight schedule."

"Joey's already outside," the one called Sal replied as he swallowed the bite, then exhaled sharply. "Fine."

Sal shrugged and tossed the slice onto the counter, where it landed with a floppy slap. Sue heard the group shuffle quickly across the room and into the dining area. Sue squinted through the gap, taking inventory of those passing: *one man, Starla, two, Sondra, three with the life support, and four—four intruders, plus the other—"Joey?"—that dragged Lisa outside.* The last figure carefully but quickly slid the glass door shut on the way out, muffling the rain and thunder once more.

With great hesitation, Sue crept up to the counter and peered out the edge of the kitchen window. A well-timed lightning flash illuminated the cadre of kidnappers, their quarry, and their destination: a small boat lashed at the seawall of Donna's property. The image disappeared as suddenly as it had arrived. Sue took labored, anxious breaths and braced herself against the counter. Part of her wanted to run after them, but the woman knew that she'd only endanger all of their lives. The men had guns. *And besides*, thought Sue, *they didn't seem to know I was here.*

Another flash revealed that the group had made it to the boat. Like a stuttering, stop-motion scene, a flutter of successive flashes showed the moments: the figures lifting Lisa and the unconscious Gordon ladies across the space between the shore and their craft; a soaked getaway boat driver starting the vehicle's motor; then the boat turning to change directions.

The last image Sue saw was the faded lettering on the opposite side of the boat:

The letter *o* (or maybe it was a zero). A wide space. Then the word *stone*.

She took a quick breath. *No. This can't be happening.* Sue maintained what little of a view of the boat that she could in the dark night. Then the craft vanished across the tumultuous obsidian waters of the bay.

They were gone.

CHAPTER 20

Tick. Tick. Tick. Tick.

The woman opens her eyes to find the source of the sound. It's her alarm clock and it hasn't gone off yet. Her bedroom is dark and sparsely decorated. The tall woman sits up and inspects the far wall: there's a shaker-style paneled door with a crystal knob, a portrait of a dog in a business suit, and an eclectic assortment of clocks that fill nearly every other space.

A quarter after midnight.

She throws the linen quilt off her body, revealing that she's been sleeping in her favorite gray pantsuit.

No time to change.

The tall woman checks her hair in a side table mirror—pinned up tight—then hurries for the door, her long strides drawing out each step.

Is it far to never-never land? A strange thought echoes.

Not if you're Peter Pan, comes the rehearsed reply.

The knob turns easily enough and the woman begins to descend down a flight of stairs. The ticking continues, echoing louder now. The steps spiral downward; the journey seems infinite until, finally, she spots a cold, bluish glow below her.

When she reaches the foot of the stairs, the woman passes through a large archway. Her steps slow, for she now realizes that her feet are ankle-deep in thick, pink sand. The lady looks back over her shoulder to plan her escape, but the passage has vanished.

Tick. Tick. Tick.

With considerable effort, the woman is able to lift one of her long, heavy legs from within this sudden desert. She looks up at the sky to find that there is no sun visible—just a soft, ambient glow that causes her armpits and forehead to sweat more and more.

Tick. Tick. Tick.

A grainy trickle of the rosy sand streams like a waterfall before her, filling the boundless room at a steady pace. Now it grows faster, quicker. The level of the sand rises to her knees. She attempts to continue her steps forward, but with every passing moment this becomes more impossible, bogged by the rising desert.

The sand isn't like desert sand, though, she notes between deep breaths. *It's coarse and textured—made up of fragments of eroded shells and other debris from an ocean.* The lady has little time to ponder this, though, for now the sand has risen to her neck. She can't move.

Tick. Tick.

The ominous noise grows louder and louder, a deep echo.

She struggles to swim up with the sand, but her legs are anchored and fixed so she makes no progress. She expends much effort and energy as the sand creeps up her chin, then over her mouth, then her nose.

She becomes curious, confused, and angry at the last thing she sees before she is buried alive in the pink sand: the painting from her bedroom—the dog in the business suit, grinning like a canine devil. Then everything goes black.

The members of the Dream Team sat in silence as the tape came to an end and Kiki clicked the *stop* button. The warehouse suddenly felt enormous and empty.

Kiki finally broke the quiet. "Uh, did that make sense to *anyone?*"

The others slowly shook their heads. One could almost feel the discouragement rising in the air.

"Great," Donna muttered under her breath.

Declan inhaled deeply, wrapping the large blanket tighter around his body. "I'm sure there's some message hidden in it," he suggested. "We just need to think."

"Think?" Donna now rose from her seat and crossed her arms. "There's nothing to think about. This dream—and all the others we've risked our lives to acquire—are just a bunch of subconscious bullcrap."

"Now, Donna—" Declan started to stand.

"Don't do that." She directed a stern finger at the man. "Don't treat me like I'm some dumb blonde who's overreacting. Everyone here can see that this entire operation was absolutely futile." Donna took a breath, then continued. "You know what, actually? Maybe I *am* dumb for thinking this could actually work."

"I had a plan—"

"*Had* a plan," Buster emphasized. "It didn't work."

Mira stepped forward. "And now Metro-Dade's going to be on our tail for the stunt we pulled at the restaurant. What now, Declan? Do you have a plan for getting us out of this mess?"

"Yeah," Kiki added. "You promised we would find Ducane's vault—that we could *fix* us, so that we could be normal again."

The man stood in front of the sofa, surveying the hopeless, frustrated faces of his team.

"I'm sorry," he said finally. "You're right. I let you all down. I thought that this would work, but I miscalculated. If you want to leave, I'll understand." Declan took a slow breath as his eyes drifted to the corkboard upon which a smattering of notes and photos were pinned.

Donna nodded. "Well, then. I guess this is goodbye." She maintained eye contact with Declan for a long moment, as if there was more she wanted to say, then turned and started for the exit. "It was nice meeting all of you—" Donna nodded to each of the other three in turn.

"But Donna, where will you go?" Declan asked.

"I guess I'm going to go back to looking for Marcus on my own," she shrugged. "Now if you'll excuse me, I've got a family to get to."

Declan lowered his gaze for a moment, then glanced at the board again. Donna's heels clacked away, echoing off the large walls of the barren space. Declan shifted closer to the board, still clutching the blanket that shrouded him, and examined a few of the scribbled notes and drawings.

Donna reached the door and rotated the squeaky handle.

"Wait!" Declan shouted. Donna and the others turned toward him.

"For what?" Donna puffed impatiently.

"I think I may have an idea of where this all leads after all," Declan answered.

Kiki, Buster, and Mira looked at each other, waiting for the man to speak again.

Donna released the door handle and sauntered quickly back toward him. She stood inches from his face with a fiery look in her eyes. "Oh, so *now* you've got an idea—just can't bear to see me leave, huh?" The man didn't respond, so she continued. "What makes you think you can crack this dream code all of a sudden?"

The man looked down and gulped. "Because, there's something else about which I haven't been entirely honest with you all," Declan said quietly.

"Spit it out, Dec." Kiki said.

"I think I may know where Ducane's secret vault is hidden

after all, because—" He took another deep breath. "Because Rolf Ducane is my father."

The rain could hardly be heard over the hubbub inside The Fountain of Youth—the miniscule but crowded watering hole sandwiched between two bustling storefronts on South Beach. Rico Castillo frequented this bar—along with a slew of others—so often that the men and women behind the counter knew him by name. Rico lumbered across the smokey room, barely glancing to inspect the patrons squeezed into dark wood tables and booths along the far wall as he made a beeline for the bar. He settled onto a round stool.

"Why the long face, hun?" The bartender set a small glass of water and a square napkin in front of the man as he took his seat.

"Thanks," he muttered and took a sip, swallowed, then answered: "I don't even know where to begin."

"How about your usual?" The woman smiled and lowered her eyes to the level of Rico's own downcast pair, eliciting a subtle but fleeting grin from the man.

"That'd be great."

The woman turned and moved away to concoct the beverage while Castillo surveyed the room: a raucous party of university students; couples on dates. A drunk reveler bumped his head on one of the stained-glass lamps that hung from the ceiling, just a little too low, and made a startling shout, which quickly devolved into laughter from his companions. Rico inhaled then puffed a long, drawn out sigh, as if expelling the day's events.

"Here you go, hun."

The bartender set the drink in front of the man. It was a light, creamy color, and it had a tiny fake umbrella lodged in it at an angle.

"Thanks." Rico pulled the beverage closer and caught a whiff of rum and coconut, then took a large, sloppy sip. He licked his lips. "You ever feel like you're living in some kind of dream—your own reality that's totally disconnected from everyone else's?"

The woman could tell he was in the middle of a thought, so she simply nodded politely.

"You're sure you know what's real, but no one else seems to buy it. It makes you question everything." He took another few gulps of his drink.

"Sounds tough," the bartender inserted.

"Darn right, it's tough." Rico nodded. "Especially when they've already made up their mind that they don't like you—don't *trust* you. Just waiting for you to mess up so they can expose you as phony, crazy, delusional—take your pick."

A loud crash prompted both of them to whip their focus across the room. A patron had knocked a full glass off the table by accident, causing it to shatter and splatter over the dark, sticky floor.

"Can you get that, Tito?" The bartender hollered to another staffer, who harumphed off to clean up the mess.

Rico continued with his stream of thought: "Where was

I? Oh, yeah: some people just have it out to get ya. But what they don't understand is that most of us—we're just trying to do our best, right? Just trying to get by when everything we knew turned upside-down in an instant. And what do we get for trying? You get your gun taken, your badge taken—kicked off the force without a chance to explain or anyone even bothering to ask you, 'what's wrong?' Ya know?"

"Sorry, hun." The bartender nodded. "But surely there's gotta be *someone* who understands, right? Someone who believes you?"

Castillo thought for a moment as he took another drink. He set the glass back down slowly. "Yeah," he replied softly. "There is someone."

"Maybe you should give 'em a call?"

"You gotta phone?"

"There's a payphone 'round the block." The woman motioned toward the door. "Rain's slowed a little."

Rico sighed again and chugged the final dregs of his piña colada. He rifled through his pockets to produce a few bills, which he slapped on the counter. "Thanks for everything."

With that, the man rose from the stool, staggered his first few steps before regaining his balance, and exited onto the slick sidewalk. Rico glanced both ways as the rain dripped down his face. He wore a light rain jacket that he pulled tighter to fight a chill. When he'd located the phonebooth at the end of the street, he started toward it, keeping his head down.

A car drove by, splashing a light mist from a deep puddle

onto the sidewalk and Rico's ankles. He reached the plexiglass-encased booth and stepped inside to keep dry. A small crack in the ceiling allowed a steady drip of water to fall right in the center of the compact space. The man rearranged himself in the booth a few times before resigning himself to the fact that he would not be able to avoid getting wet.

With his back pressed up against one of the transparent sides of the booth, Castillo produced a handful of quarters and inserted a few into the phone's slot, then pounded out a number on the keypad and waited for the phone to start ringing.

Donna's enormous mansion felt cold and empty as the rain splattered lightly down the glass. Sue couldn't bring herself to step away from the kitchen window, the portal through which she had just watched Starla, Sondra, and Lisa disappear into the dark in the clutches of the masked home invaders.

A tear formed at the edge of Sue's eye. She wiped it, then started. The sound of a closing door echoed down the hallway.

More intruders?

Sue's nervous breathing turned to fury. She reached down and carefully slid open a drawer full of knives, then withdrew the largest one she could find. Without a sound, the woman slowly moved toward the doorway from the kitchen to the foyer. Footsteps approached. Sue raised the knife above her head, gripping it with both hands.

No one messes with me or my friends. I won't let this happen again...

She readied to bring down the blade on the unseen subject, took a deep breath. The steps were at the kitchen now. Sue wound back her arm and—

"Hello?"

It was a man's voice—familiar.

A slight amount of tension released in Sue's arms, and a lightning flash pierced through the darkness. The momentary burst startled the approaching man as he stepped through the doorway and adjusted his glasses.

"Doctor Lansing!" Sue exhaled sharply and loosened her grip on the knife.

"Miss Castillo," he replied, his eyes growing wide at the sight of the sharp blade in her hand. "What exactly were you intending to do with that?" Roger pointed a hesitant finger.

"Oh, sorry—" She set the knife on the counter, then turned back to the man. "They're gone, Roger! Lisa, Sondra, Starla—gone!"

"What do you mean, *'gone'—?*"

"*Kidnapped*! I don't know who they were but they just came in—"

Sue quickly told Roger all that had happened, barely maintaining her composure.

"What do we do?" Sue sniveled. "We can't just let them get away!"

Roger nodded and took a deep breath. Before he could

speak, the pair froze again.

Brrring!

It was the phone across the kitchen.

"Do we answer it?" Sue asked in a hushed tone.

Brrring!

"What if it's a ransom call?" Roger suggested. "The kidnappers stating their demands—?"

Brrring!

It seemed like the sound was growing louder.

"We have to answer it, then!"

Brrring!

"No!" The doctor shook his head furiously. "That'll give them the upper hand."

Brrring!

"We have to act like we didn't get the call—to buy ourselves more time to find our dear friends."

Sue wasn't sure about the doctor's plan, but held her breath as she awaited the next ring. The kitchen grew silent. Then, a *click* and a long *beeeeeep!*

"Hey! Donna?" A man's muffled voice echoed through the room over the speaker, conveying the voicemail message in real time. "You there?"

"It's Rico!" Sue gasped in relief, starting for the phone.

The doctor held her back. "What if they're listening in?" Roger whispered loudly. "They don't know you and I are here yet!"

"—I'm sorry to call you so late," Rico's voice was sluggish. "But I just wanted to see if you, uh—if you could talk. I've been having a pretty rough time—and I bet you have, too—I miss him every day. And I wish there was something we could've done—*I* could've done differently. I guess what I'm saying is that I need someone to tell me I'm not crazy for believing everything—that it all really happened. That Marcus is still out there and that we'll find him—"

Sue's tension softened as her brother spoke, and she moved toward the phone once more.

"Well," Rico continued. "I guess you aren't going to pick up, and I've only got so many quarters—" Change jingled in his pocket. He muttered under his breath: "Was worth a try—"

Sue grabbed the receiver. "Rico!"

"Sue? Why are you—"

"No time to explain," she interrupted. "They're gone, Rico!"

"Who's gone?"

"Starla, Sondra, Lisa—they took them!"

"*Who* took them?"

"I don't know," Sue answered frantically. "They came in from the back, dressed in masks—there were a bunch of them. They took a boat—oh, Donna's going to be mortified."

"Slow down, sis," Rico urged her. "Are you alone?"

"No, Roger's here with me," Sue took a deep breath.

"Hello, Officer," the doctor shouted into the receiver as Sue held it up.

Rico's voice started again. "Alright, stay there! I'll be there as fast as I can—we're going to find them, Sue. It's going to be okay." His assurances seemed directed at himself as much as his sister.

Sue thanked her brother then reluctantly hung up the phone as the line went cold.

Roger nodded to her. "You heard him. It's going to be alright. Your brother knows what he's doing."

The woman nodded slowly, inhaling and exhaling with a measured cadence.

Lightning flashed through the window again.

Come on, Rico, Sue thought as she looked out the window at the water once more.

Time's running out.

CHAPTER 21

"That *slime* is your *father?*" Donna's mouth hung agape as she took an instinctive step back from Declan.

Kiki, Buster, and Mira waited in silence for the man to respond. It didn't seem possible that they could have known him for so long without ever learning this vital secret.

"Yes," Declan muttered, pulling the soft blanket close across his chest. "Draven's my mother's maiden name—I was born Declan Albert Ducane."

Kiki let out a chortle and slapped her hand over her own mouth to try and keep it in.

"What's so funny?" Declan raised an eyebrow.

"I'm sorry," Kiki shook her head. "Your middle name's *Albert?*"

"It's an old family name," the man said defensively.

Donna took a deep breath. "So you lied to us about your *name* as well? Great. This just keeps getting better." The blonde woman started to move away, but her curiosity kept her from leaving.

"It was to protect all of you—all of us." Declan's words felt genuine—as if he actually believed them. "I don't expect you to understand, but I felt it was the right thing to do."

Mira took another look at the bulletin board behind the man and pointed. "You said you know where the vault is?"

Declan shook his head. "I have an idea, at least."

"Better than anything we've had thus far," Buster muttered.

"And isn't it a little convenient that you *suddenly* know where the vault is—after we've gone through three harrowing missions of questionable legality?" Donna was nearing the end of her patience for the man's apparent inability to reveal the whole truth.

"The pink sand in Keene's dream," he answered. "That's what clued me in. I should have figured this out sooner. But now I see that there was no *single* dream that could have given us the answer. Each one provided merely a fraction of the whole picture—probably because each member of the Inner Circle took in different details based on his or her perspective, desires, hopes, fears—that sort of thing."

Kiki sighed. "You're going to tell us the answer, right?"

The man nodded. "When I was young, I remember my father taking us to a place not far off the coast—an island. The small island was formed of a porous reef—he called it Coral Island—and its beaches and shores were covered in strange, beautiful pink sand—I'd never seen anything like it before."

"Couldn't it be a coincidence that the sand was pink?" Donna suggested. "I'm sure there are lots of other places with pink sandy beaches."

"All of the other clues line up, too, though," he replied. "I remember there were tons and tons of seabirds that would sun themselves between their dives into the water for fish—they were pelicans. Like the ones in a couple of the dreams."

"I'm guessing that's where your dad got the name for his business," suggested Kiki.

"It's likely."

"So what if it is the place you went when you were a kid?" Donna pressed. "Do you think this vault could really be there? And how do we get there?"

"I'm *sure* that's where his vault is—it has to be." Declan's breathing was heavy now. "I searched for it when I was younger, but I could never find it. The name Coral Island doesn't appear on any maps of the area."

Donna threw her hands up. "Great!"

"*But*—" Declan continued, nodding toward the dream elements depicted on the corkboard. "I think the dreams may give us even more of the clues we need to find this mysterious secret island." He turned to Mira. "Do we have a map of the Miami coastal region?"

The quiet woman nodded in the affirmative and fished around in a tall locker. Mira withdrew a large, rolled-up map and removed its rubber band. She unfolded it on the table as the others gathered around to press down its corners.

"First, we'll need to discern any landmarks that may have been hidden in the dreams," Declan instructed.

Immediately, Donna's gloved finger pressed onto the southern tip of Key Biscayne on the wrinkly map. "The lighthouse," she explained. "From the Reverend's dream, remember?" The woman hurried over to the bulletin board where she unpinned a grainy image xeroxed from a frame of the Reverend's dream tape. "Look closely. That tall tower—it's a lighthouse."

"It could be *any* lighthouse, though," Kiki snapped.

Donna smiled and shook her head. "No. It's the one on Key Biscayne. Marcus took me there once—I could never forget the shape of it, the chipping white paint, the dark triangular shapes that make up the metalwork at the top, that little window on the side there." She pointed at the piece of paper.

"So the island can't be too far from there, right?" Mira posited.

Buster's brow furrowed as he stood over the map. "You said the island was made of coral, right?" Declan nodded and the large man continued. "Then perhaps we can follow the contours of the reef that runs near the Key—the area that would be in view of the lighthouse. *That* view—" He pointed at Donna's grainy photo. "The area is probably quite small."

"And look at the shadows on the lighthouse," Donna said quickly, her excitement building. "In the Reverend's dream, it was morning. The shadows are on the left side, which means the sun's coming from the east—still rising—so our

Coral Island's got to be to the south of the old lighthouse."

Declan bobbed his head in agreement, then took another look at the pieces of information strewn across the bulletin board.

"Did you remember something else about the island?" Donna wondered, moving to his side.

"I'm afraid so," he said quietly. "I remember that we could only stay there for a short time—only a couple hours at most." Declan closed his eyes, recalling the hazy memory. "As soon as we'd arrive, my father would moor the boat to an old wooden dock post—the dock itself had been long-gone by the time I first visited. Then he'd go off into the mangroves to take a walk while I played in the shallows of a rocky tidepool. Like clockwork, father would return just as the waves were beginning to grow and lap up over into the area where I played. Then we would leave."

The others waited for Declan to continue with his story, hoping he had a relevant point.

"Father said the island was special—that it would disappear when we left and only be visible the next time we were to come to it." The man smiled to himself. "Back then I believed it was magic. In each of the videos we gathered—except for Gromble's warped tape—the dreamers were concerned with the time. In Smith's, water came up around his ankles. Keene's was similar, except for her it was sand she was sinking in. Now I know father was just talking about the tide." He turned to the team. "I believe Coral Island—and likely the vault, too—is only accessible when the tide is low."

"That would make sense with Keene's dream," Mira suggested. "Low tide's around half past midnight and half past noon this time of year. In her tape, Keene's clocks read a quarter to midnight. She must've had to catch a ride out there at just the right time."

Declan tensed and scanned the room for a clock. "What time is it right now?"

Kiki checked a watch. "A few minutes to midnight."

The man cursed under his breath. "Then we don't have much time."

"You want to go right *now*?" Donna asked.

Declan turned to her, moving close. "You want to find your boyfriend or not?"

"Of course—"

"Then we have to go tonight. If we wait, they'll likely change the location of the vault, or strip it bare, and we'll be back to the start with nothing to show for it." The man's eyes flicked from one member of the team to the next. "Are you with me—for one last mission?"

The room was tense but bubbling with hope that their efforts might actually pay off.

"We're with you, Dec," Kiki grinned. "The Dream Team sticks together. But," the young woman pointed at the large blanket wrapped around him. "Maybe you should find some pants first."

Declan nodded and grinned.

"Alright, then," the man answered. "Time to find ourselves

a secret island vault."

The Midnight Lion crawled with Metro-Dade officers, their muddy footprints tracking across the concrete floor. Rhythmic flashes of blue and red from the squad cars outside bounced through the large front windows of the barren storefront, where the only things left to indicate the presence of a restaurant in the space were the weather-worn neon sign near the entry and a couple of sets of mismatched tables and chairs.

A burly, uniformed officer approached Officer Jones with a tiny notepad in his hand.

"Anything?" Tracy's hardened eyes betrayed a desperation for answers.

The man took a deep breath then let it out slowly. "Officer Jones," he started. "Tell me again what you *think* happened here tonight?"

"*Think?*" Her eyes narrowed. "I *know* what I saw." Tracy gestured to the walls. "There was art hanging there; those tables were set; heck, the floors were a fundamentally different material! One minute it was there; the next? It's all like you see now. How does that happen?"

The officer raised his eyebrows and clicked a pen. "It doesn't."

"I'm telling you what I saw, officer." Tracy clenched her teeth.

"Seeing isn't *always* believing, Jones." The big man offered.

"Right. Well let me know if you find anything." The

woman puffed. "Thanks for your help," Tracy muttered and stormed toward the back of the restaurant.

Jones pushed through the swinging door into the kitchen, where the harsh white-green light cast a sickly glow over an irritated and slightly disoriented Cameron Keene. The tall woman sat in one of a pair of cheap stacking chairs with her arms and legs crossed, barely acknowledging the weary officer as she entered the room.

"Thank you for your patience." Tracy settled into the seat opposite Keene.

"May I go now?" Keene's eyes fluttered condescendingly.

Jones exhaled quickly. "Not yet. I've just got a few more questions."

Cameron sighed. "I can't guarantee that I'll have answers."

The officer gritted her teeth and smiled. "Just do your best, okay?"

The tall, poised Keene rolled her eyes.

With the pleasantries sorted out, Officer Jones leaned forward in her chair. "Was someone in the bathroom with you?"

"You were," the woman replied curtly.

"No, before that," Jones snapped. "What happened in there? How did you end up on the floor? You were totally out of it when I walked in, but somehow you—or someone—unlocked the door."

Cameron closed her eyes and strained to recall. "I don't know."

Tracy scooted her chair closer to Keene. "Then *think*—you

have to remember something."

"I must've passed out—I think I hit my head pretty hard," she answered, placing a gentle hand on her hair.

Jones stood and walked briskly to the woman's side, placed hands on both sides of Keene's head, and yanked it so the light spilled on it more evenly.

"Ow—hey!" Cameron struggled.

"Hold still!"

"Just what do you think you're doing—?"

Tracy tilted her head to get a better look at the other woman's scalp, then pressed a hand against the spot. "Does this hurt?"

"I said, what do you think you're—!"

The officer pushed harder. "Does it *hurt,* Keene?"

Keene winced. "You're pressing your palm into my scalp—of course it hurts!"

"There's no wound, no mark, no bruise." Jones released the woman and stepped back. "You didn't hit your head."

Cameron's eyes narrowed. "What are you implying?"

This doesn't make sense. Jones breathed slowly. "I'm not sure," she replied finally. "But now would be a good time to fess up about your involvement with Mr. Ducane."

"I already told you—"

"*Talk,* Keene!"

"What about my lawyer—?"

"Cut the act, Keene. Lives may be in danger—including your own—so if you don't start talking, we're going to take this to the station and, to be honest, I don't think we have time for that." She paused for a breath. "What's your involvement with Mr. Ducane and his company? Tell me about the Inner Circle."

The tall woman lowered her eyes in silence then took a labored breath. Finally, she made eye contact with Tracy once more and held her chin high. "Mr. Ducane and I have an um, arrangement—a mutual agreement, if you will. Our department provides the technology and resources, and in return Ducane ensures we benefit from the latest advancements."

"And a generous sum of money, I presume?" Tracy raised an eyebrow.

"Naturally," the other woman smiled. "Ducane is a true patriot, you see."

Tracy's thoughts suddenly drifted to the muddy footprints in the alleyway. "Do you know if Mr. Ducane was ever involved in any... experiments?"

"He owns the region's largest and most successful research laboratory," Cameron answered quickly. "Of course he's involved in experiments."

"I mean on *humans*—anything really weird or off the wall?"

Suddenly, Cameron's expression changed and she tensed. "You know, officer, all of this commotion almost made me forget that I have somewhere to be. What time is it?"

The officer checked a watch. "About midnight. You didn't answer my—"

Keene's eyes widened and she rose from the chair. "I need to go—are we finished here?"

Jones stood and used an arm to block Cameron's progress

toward the door. "Not so fast, Keene. We're in the middle of an interrogation, remember?"

"If I'm not there in fifteen minutes, they'll leave without me."

"If you're not *where*? And *who's* going to leave without you?"

Cameron licked her lips, which had grown parched from all the talking. "The Inner Circle," she said the words in hushed tones. "There's a boat that's supposed to take me to the location where the Circle is meeting tonight."

"Seems a little late for a meeting," Jones quipped. "Where's this *boat* taking you exactly?"

She shook her head. "I don't know. It's a secret location. We're blindfolded during the boat ride every time. That's why I can't be late—"

"What's the meeting about?" Tracy pressed.

Cameron puffed. "Something big. It couldn't wait. I don't know any further details, okay?"

Though the tall woman had been evasive all evening, Tracy could now sense that her words were sincere. *Getting close to Ducane—this could be the key to solving the mystery of Smith's murder. And finding out what that* thing *was.* Jones was ready for answers. "Alright," she said finally, lowering her arm. "You're going to get on that boat."

Keene nodded her thanks.

The towering woman started toward the kitchen door again, when Jones added:

"And I'm coming with you."

A Sunshine Cab splashed through a deep puddle as it came to a screeching halt at the front gate of Donna Locke's waterfront mansion. The rain still pattered lightly as one of the side doors of the goldenrod-striped taxi clicked open and Castillo stepped out onto the street. He wobbled to gain his balance, handed a few bills up to the driver, and slammed the door harder than he intended.

When the gatekeeper recognized Donna's disheveled old friend, he activated the electric motor to retract the gate, allowing Rico to make his way up the driveway to the huge house.

Sue had been waiting anxiously behind the door and swung it open when she heard her brother's knock. "Oh, thank God!" The dark-haired woman threw herself into Rico's arms while Roger nodded a quiet greeting.

"Hey, sis," he said. "I'm here—it's gonna be okay."

Sue sniffed as she stepped back. "You've been drinking again." She furrowed her brow and let out a subtle, disappointed puff.

Castillo rubbed the back of his neck and avoided eye-contact. "Just a little," he muttered. "Been a rough day, okay?"

"It's been a rough *year*," Roger noted with a raised pointer finger. "How about we continue this conversation inside. Looks like this storm's about to pick up again."

The siblings agreed and followed the doctor into the house, where they gathered around the kitchen island. The smell of lukewarm pizza caught Rico's attention. He lifted a splattered, solitary slice from the counter and took a bite.

"Tell me what happened," the man spoke through a mouth full of cheese.

His sister moved to the sliding glass door. "They came in through here—the movie was so loud that none of us heard them. There were five or six of them—all men, I think. Wearing masks and dark clothes." Her eyes drifted as she had a thought. "One wore white sneakers with blue stripes on the sides—I couldn't forget that."

Castillo dropped the crust back on the counter and moved toward the glass doors. "So they came in here. Then what?" He knelt to examine now-dried mud prints on the tile floor, caked dirt that had fallen loose from the suspects' shoes.

"One grabbed Leese in the living room," Sue pointed. "And the others went upstairs for Starla and Sondra."

The young man wandered the living room in search of a clue. "Has anyone heard from Donna?"

"She said she'd be out all night," Sue explained.

"Can we reach her?" Roger asked from the dining room threshold.

Sue shook her head. "She didn't say where she was going. She just packed a bunch of things from the kitchen and left."

The sweep of the living room yielded no further clues, so Castillo headed upstairs, followed by his sister and the doctor. They entered Sondra's bedroom.

"Donna's sister's been on oxygen tanks since she came back," Rico noted with a slight slur in his words.

"They took the tanks, too."

Rico cocked his head. "Really?"

"Yeah, *really*." His sister crossed her arms and stood by the window. "What is it?"

"Then maybe there's some good news: this wasn't just some random break-in," Castillo said, rounding the bed. "Whoever these men were, they knew exactly what they were doing—everything about this was deliberate. That's why there were so many of them— they knew they needed a few to get Sondra out of here."

Sue raised an eyebrow as her brother looked under the bed. "What's the good news?"

"The good news," Rico rose, "is that they clearly wanted Sondra *alive*." Before the other two could respond, he declared: "Nothing here. Do you remember *anything* else, Sue?"

As the group wandered back to the second-floor hall, Sue caught a glance out a window down at the backyard. Her eyes drifted toward the slippery seawall. "They left on a boat—came on it, too, I guess."

"What boat?" Her brother joined her at the window, trying to visualize the scene.

"A small white boat—barely big enough for all of them to huddle inside the cabin, I would guess. I could only read part of the name on the back. It looked old, faded, scratched off," Sue said. "Uh, what was it? I remember an *o* and the word *stone*. I'm pretty sure it was missing some letters—the spacing was off."

"Port of origin?"

"Couldn't read it from that far."

Rico exhaled sharply. "Great."

Roger spoke up. "Can't you run the name through the databases you all have at Metro-Dade? That would surely turn up something more for us to go on."

Castillo's eyes wandered quickly to the carpet, avoiding contact with the doctor.

"Well, Rico," Sue pressed. "Can't you?"

The man gulped and shook his head slowly.

"*What*? Why not?"

"I, uh—" he started. "Like I said, it's been a rough day."

Sue's shoulders loosened. "You lost your job?"

The former officer nodded.

"What the heck happened?"

"Well, my partner thought I was acting out of line and—" He shook his head. "You know what? It's a long story that we don't have time for right now."

"Well it seems we've got nothing but time," the doctor said. "At least until we come up with a solution to finding our friends. What do you propose, officer—I mean, uh, *Rico*?"

Rico, weary, leaned slightly as he considered their next steps. "I can't go back into the office," he muttered. "But there may be someone who can help."

"Who—?" Sue started to ask, but Rico had already started for the stairs. They hurried down to the kitchen, where her brother punched in a number on the phone and waited for it to ring.

CHAPTER 22

A gust of wind and rain splattered down the sliding glass door of the dining room. Sue tried to keep from biting her nails and started pacing nervously.

"You sure this is going to work?"

"She'll call," Rico assured her. "If anyone can find that boat, it's her."

"And what happens when we *do* find it?" Doctor Lansing asked with a gulp. "Your sister said these men were *armed*."

Castillo sighed. "Still working on that part."

A few more quiet moments passed. A flash of lightning pierced the room, startling everyone. The phone rang.

Rico grabbed the receiver before it could complete the first ring. "Hello?"

"I think you're in luck, Rico," the woman's voice crackled. "I may have just found your mystery boat."

The man let out a breath of relief. "Thanks, Marge. You're

a real life-saver." The others gathered around. "Ready when you are."

"Alright, so there were only two boats on our registry with *o* and *stone* in their names," Marge said. "You're not gonna believe this, but one of them's got Miami listed as the port of origin."

"Go on," Rico nodded.

"Name's *Moonstone*," Marge continued. "And I don't know how up-to-date this is, but I've got a note about the place where it's usually docked. Ready for the address?"

Rico grabbed a piece of paper and a pencil and scratched out the address as Marge dictated it through the phone.

"What's all this about anyway? You sure you don't need me to call in backup?" Marge asked when she had finished.

"No!" Castillo answered quickly. "Let's keep this on the down-low for now. Don't want the bureaucracy slowing us down, if you catch my drift? I'll tell you all about it... soon."

"This better be worth me losing a good night's sleep," Marge sighed. "I'm putting my job on the line for this—you realize that, right?"

"Yeah," he replied softly. "I know."

"Don't make me regret this."

"Understood. Thank you, Marge."

"You got it, Castillo." The woman hung up with a click.

Rico held up the address. "Looks like we know where we're headed."

"Um, excuse me," Roger said. "How do you suggest we get to this mysterious mooring place, exactly?"

Sue grinned and her eyes drifted toward the doorway that led to the garage. "I think I've got an idea."

Castillo nodded. "Excellent choice," he smiled and took a few faltering steps toward the hall. "I'll drive us—"

Roger swooped in and caught the man as he lost his balance. "I, uh, think your sister better do the driving," he smiled nervously. "This should be interesting," he muttered.

Vrrr-ra-ra-room!

Sue revved the engine of the hot-pink convertible—a vehicle that Donna used far less frequently than her golden Corvette—as she waited for a traffic light to turn green. The silent sequence initiated, basking the wet car and the mostly-empty streets in the vivid, viridescent glow. With the car's top up to shield them from the rain, Sue gunned the engine, sped down the slick street with the wipers working at full-speed, then zoomed around another slant of the long causeway. Roger sat in the front passenger seat with the slip of paper upon which the address was scribbled while Castillo leaned through the gap between the seats with a woozy look in his eyes.

"Gosh, Rico, how much did you drink?" His sister snapped a look of concern in the rearview mirror.

His eyes drooped. "Not too much."

The doctor squinted to read a street sign. His eyes flashed wide. "Go right!"

The car made a sharp turn and Castillo tumbled to the side.

"At least put your seatbelt on, please," Sue insisted.

"Sure thing, sis," Rico slurred his words a little as he grabbed a buckle. He struggled for several moments to find its matching slot then finally clicked it into place.

"The marina should be just up ahead," said Doctor Lansing, pointing at an intersection viewable through the blurry windshield. Sue barely slowed the car as they approached it, then slammed the brakes at the last minute.

Rico's belt caught him this time, preventing him from being launched through the front of the car. Roger gripped the passenger door with one hand and braced himself on the dashboard with the other.

"We're here," Sue said with a quick sigh of relief.

Roger and Rico groaned.

"Better park somewhere they aren't going to see us," Rico suggested.

"Good idea."

The dark-haired woman swung the car into reverse, skidded into a five-point-turn, then slowly brought the vehicle to a stop in a nearby darkened alley. As the trio disembarked and hurried down the street in the pattering rain, they froze in place; the once-empty street now lit up with a pair of approaching headlights. Castillo motioned for his companions to step slowly back toward a chain-link fence that bordered the sidewalk. The car passed by, splashing an arc of muddy water in their general direction, but then turned away onto a street and continued toward the denser part of the city.

"Alright, let's keep moving," Sue suggested. "Lisa and the girls may not have much time." The group continued moving in and out of the shadows and the occasional dry spot brought about by overgrown shade trees that hung across the pavement.

The rain slowed a little, devolving into a misty sprinkle. When they rounded the corner, the three stopped again, their heads peering inquisitively around a small structure like disembodied faces on a totem pole. The whole area seemed to be devoid of civilians or passersby.

"C'mon," Castillo waved to Roger and Sue as he took off across the puddle-ridden parking lot toward the marina entrance. They watched carefully for any signs of life, but moved on when they deemed the area clear.

The marina itself was a maze of interconnected floating dock segments, jutting out into a number of smaller sections. The area was packed full of boats, with only a few slips unoccupied. The trio found another shadow in which to lurk just beyond the open gated entry.

"How are we going to find the Moonstone now?" Sue threw her hands up in exasperation then wiped a trickle of rainwater from her face. "All these boats look the same in the dark." She was right; the dusk and the dearth of lights or lamps meant it would be nearly impossible to spot their missing boat unless they were right upon it.

"We could split up?" Rico suggested.

The others quickly shook their heads in unison to note their disagreement with the idea.

"I think it'd be best for us to stick together," Roger inserted. "We've lost enough of our friends already."

"Good point." Sue gave a quick nod. "I guess we start on one end and work our way around?" No one else made any another proposal, so the three friends walked swiftly down the dock.

It seemed that most of the boats had their lights turned out. On one or two occasions, the trio encountered a moist, sleepy seafarer puffing a cigar in the sprinkling rain or hanging a lazy line into the water in hopes of luring a midnight catch. In these instances, Sue, Rico, and Roger smiled and continued walking, hoping to avoid suspicion.

For some time the group searched the docks, doubling back down dead-end paths and repeating their sloppy steps on the occasion that they lost track of their location due to a handful of nearly-identical motorboats. Sue was growing more anxious at each turn. There was no sign of the vessel called Moonstone. *We don't even know if that's the boat that took them, for crying out loud!* Sue kept the thought to herself and curled her arms close as a wet shiver moved down her spine.

As they rounded another bend in the winding, floating docks, the group felt the floor shift slightly. Rico grabbed the others by their sleeves and pulled them back.

"What is it?" Roger wondered.

"Did you feel that?" Rico looked down. "Someone's coming."

He was right. Now Sue could hear voices—distant and unintelligible, but most certainly voices. The faint light of one of a few fluorescent lamps swayed with the bay's breeze, making a pair of silhouettes visible at the end of one stretch of moorings. One was abnormally tall. Both appeared to be women holding umbrellas, Sue noted. *Lisa? Sondra? What about Starla?*

She didn't have much time to wonder or speculate, for the figures were moving toward them briskly and the rain was starting to pick up again. Rico yanked Sue and the doctor back, where they found a place to hide on a narrow strip of slats, shielded by a tiny fishing vessel.

As the women moved closer, it became clear that the figures were not her missing friends. The taller one wore high-heels and had her hair slicked in a modern, asymmetrical way—Sue recognized the style from the department store catalogs she often perused. The second woman was more of an average height. Her hair and complexion were dark, shaded even more by the dim light of the night.

Rico's brow furrowed and his vision blurred. *Jones?* He'd only seen half of the second woman's face for a split-second and his earlier drinks hadn't quite worn off, but he was almost sure it was her. *What's she doing here? And out of uniform—is that the informant we were supposed to meet with earlier?* "We need to follow them," Castillo mumbled to Roger and Sue.

"Are you crazy?" Sue's eyes were wide. "We can't let anyone see us—we haven't found the Moonstone yet!"

The two ladies sauntered on across the slatted platform and made their way down one of the long dock sections that stretched out furthest into the bay. They were nearly out of view.

"That was my partner," Castillo explained, pointing toward the women.

His sister cocked her head. "Don't you mean *ex*-partner?"

"What if she's undercover?" Roger suggested. "Do you really want to blow it?"

Rico shook his head. "I don't have a clue why she's here, but I've got a weird feeling about all of this," he said. "We *need* to follow them. It can't be a coincidence that they're here."

Sue inhaled deeply and pursed her lips. "Fine." They started to move from their space in hiding and slinked down the dock. "But keep an eye out for our missing boat. It's got to be here somewhere." She wasn't as certain as her words seemed to suggest, but Sue was not about to give up hope of finding her friends. Time was running out.

Tracy rarely allowed her nervousness to be outwardly apparent, but she was struggling to maintain her composure as she followed closely, a half-step behind Cameron Keene. Going into an undercover mission without a partner was *not* proper protocol, but there had been no time to loop in another officer from the force. *Or Rico—maybe I shouldn't have been so hard on him.*

Jones took a deep breath and gripped the handle of her umbrella. The scent of seawater and sun-dried fish guts wafted across the long stretch of dock. She smoothed out her blazer and adjusted the pair of stiff shoulder pads. The officer still wore her uniform slacks, but they were bland enough to pass for something corporate. As there were few shops open at such an ungodly hour, Jones had to settle for a blouse and a blazer from a storefront that sold more high-end, avant garde fashion items to complete the ensemble. It was far from her style, but was the best she could do on short notice.

"How much further?" The usually-stoic officer asked her guide as she played with the itchy collar on her blouse.

Keene's long steps kept her pace swift. "Slip 46," she said. "End of the jetty."

Jones glanced over her shoulder. She was certain Keene had people with eyes on them, but they had yet to make themselves apparent. "Remember, if you say *anything*—"

"I know, I know," Cameron shook her head as she walked. "Not a word about you working for Metro-Dade—"

"Would you keep it down?" Tracy rasped.

Keene puffed and spoke more quietly. "I told you, they aren't exactly expecting any guests."

"You'll stick to the script," Jones insisted, moving closer. "I'm your special guest and Ducane's looking forward to meeting me."

Cameron did not reply. The rain began to tap loudly on the surface of their umbrellas.

"Is it gonna fly or not?"

Keene took a deep breath. "These men are hired hands. They won't dare question someone of my position."

"Good," the officer answered, backing off slightly, and

noted the slight coolness of the handgun hidden at her side beneath her blazer. The pair kept moving.

The tall woman slowed as they reached the final few slips of the dock. She looked in all directions before extending her hand toward a small silver bell that hung from one of the wooden posts that supported the mooring. *Ting-ting-ting!* It gave off a soft, tinny sound.

Tracy raised an eyebrow and orbited slowly. "Do you think anyone heard that—?"

"Shh!" Keene placed a sharp finger over her own lips. "Wait."

A few long seconds passed before a light turned on in the cabin of the nearest craft. Tracy heard a door open and shut, then watched as a large, salty man approached, shifting the weight of the boat ever-so-slightly. From the other side of the boat, two more weathered men showed up. All moved to the small platform that connected the vessel to the wooden slats of the dock.

"It's not far down to paradise," said the first man, his arms crossed over his torso. A tuft of salt-and-pepper chest hair escaped from beneath the neckline of his shirt.

Tracy immediately felt her body tense and tried not to let her observation show: *they're speaking in code. I should've predicted this...*

"Only if the wind is right," Keene replied casually.

The imposing man eyed Tracy, then flicked his gaze back to Keene. "Not far to never-never land, either, eh?" The men on either side of him slowly moved their arms to their sides.

Cameron gulped, but spoke confidently. "What Tiger Lily says goes."

At this, the pair of men slackened their posture.

"Who's our guest?" The salty captain asked curtly.

"She's a special guest of Ducane. She's coming with us," Keene said without a hint of hesitation. "Ducane's looking forward to meeting with her."

She started toward the ramp as the captain stepped aside.

Keene turned and saw that Tracy hesitated. "What are you waiting for? Come aboard." She offered a hand and a fake smile.

Tracy inhaled slowly, glanced at the men—each nearly double her size—then forced a grin and took Keene's hand. She stepped up onto the boat and began to follow Keene toward the cabin as the men pulled in the gangplank.

"Now, they're going to have to put blindfolds on us, you understand?" Keene started to explain.

Before she could finish, Tracy felt two sets of strong hands grab her arms. "Hey, what the—?"

She couldn't move. Her eyes grew wide. *It's a trap!* Immediately, her vision was obscured by a pungent piece of cloth tied tightly over her eyes from behind. She started to struggle and writhe but knew it was useless. *My gun—I can almost reach it—*

Tracy gasped as she felt the weight of the cold pistol being removed from its hidden holster under the side of her jacket. She was powerless to stop it. The men yanked her hands behind her back and quickly bound them with a zip-tie. The thick plastic dug into her wrists and she winced.

This can't be happening!

The boat's engine rumbled to life. The firm grip of the sweaty, silent pair of men nudged and guided Officer Jones forward. The rain began to drizzle harder. She surmised that they were entering the cabin, for the sound of the engine and splashing became muffled. Tracy started to scream when she felt another binding cloth being wrapped around her head, this time covering her mouth so that her shouts became dampened.

The young officer wriggled but realized her efforts were futile. Now the only thing to do was wait. *They're taking us to Ducane. I'll think of something. There's got to be a way out of this.*

Jones took labored breaths and tried to calm herself down as the low roar of the engines and the sweeping rain drowned out most other sounds.

Where's a partner when you need 'em?

"They're getting away!" Rico rose from behind his hiding place and started down the jetty, but his sister grabbed him by the shirt.

"Wait a minute!" She stood and let go. "They'll see you!"

"You both saw what I did, didn't you?" The man's wide eyes flashed from Sue to Roger then back again. "They took Trac—I mean, Officer Jones. We can't just let that happen. They're getting away!" He gestured up the dock, where the boat swiftly pulled away into the dark, roiling waters of the bay.

Sue threw her hands up. "But what about the Moonstone? We still haven't found the boat that took the girls."

"And," Roger interjected, "while I appreciate the valiant sentiment, we currently have no vessel of our own."

Castillo glanced around. They were surrounded by boats. Before this evening, he could have called for a Metro-Dade skimmer or compelled a civilian to offer their boat for law enforcement purposes; but now, with his credentials stripped, the man held little sway or influence. "The boat's not here," Rico sighed. "The Moonstone—the girls—their captors would be foolish to come back here so soon." He turned to check on the other boat speeding away. "If we don't get on their tail stat, they're going to get away, too."

"So, *what?* You just want to abandon Lisa and Starla and Sondra?" Sue was furious. "Can you even imagine what Donna will do when she finds out?" The woman began to pace.

"We're going to find them," her brother insisted. "But right now, we have nothing else to go on. Heck, I've got a weird feeling about all this—I bet the Moonstone and that other boat are connected somehow."

Sue wasn't convinced. She avoided eye-contact with Rico and shook her head.

Roger gulped and smiled awkwardly. "May I point out again that, regardless, we have no way to follow the boat that has your partner?"

Rico took a deep breath and nodded. "Thanks, Doc.

Working on it." He surveyed the area. Immediately to the side of the trio was a small speedboat, lashed to the dock post with a soggy rope. The former officer looked both ways then—seeing no bystanders—leaped off the dock and into the small craft.

"Rico!" Sue gasped and spoke in a loud, raspy whisper. "What the *heck* do you think you're doing?"

The man knelt under the controls and yanked open a small panel. "I can't let them get away," he pointed toward the horizon. The boat upon which Tracy had been taken continued to shrink away.

"Um, Rico," the doctor muttered. "Are you sure this is legal—?"

Sue spoke over him. "Didn't you say she got you *fired?*"

Rico puffed and floundered with a set of colorful wires. "*I* got me fired," he explained. "She was just doing her job. I should've been there tonight—this never would have happened." The man put the ends of two wires together, eliciting a spark. "Tracy needs our help." The lights on the console flickered briefly. Castillo clicked a few switches and the small boat rumbled to life. "I've gotta do something about it," he glanced back to the pair of friends on the dock. "You coming or not?"

Sue looked to Roger, who shrugged his shoulders, sighed, then hurried to lower himself into the speedboat. The rain and wind swept Sue's dark hair across her face as she stood, arms crossed, towering above them. The low roar of the other boat in the distance grew almost indiscernible. Finally, she let out a sharp exhale.

"Fine," she muttered. "But we can't forget about the girls!" Sue carefully made her way into the tiny boat.

"We won't," Rico assured her. "Now, hang on tight!"

The man threw the boat into reverse and quickly motored away from their slip. When they were clear of the other vessels, Castillo adjusted the throttle and pushed ahead into the dark, wet night, his eyes locked on the faint dot—the only remaining visible presence of the boat they intended to follow.

CHAPTER 23

Donna clung to the railing as the speedboat bounced from wave to wave across the bay. The growing rainstorm made the water extremely choppy, but the team had no choice but to press on. *Marcus—we're so close.* Donna winced as raindrops pecked at her skin, accelerated by the boat's velocity. *So close—*

A voice interrupted her thoughts:

"We almost there?" Kiki shouted from the backseat of the compact motorboat. In the daytime, one could see its sleek sky blue color and the hot pink stripes down either side, though the colors were now muted by the dark.

Declan turned his head to answer, his brown hair whipping across his face. "Almost," he nodded and pointed ahead while he kept one hand on the steering wheel. "Once we round that bend, we should have a little better visibility."

Sure enough, as the speedboat skimmed beside a sandbar,

it cleared a row of waterfront homes that blocked the view. A tiny speck of light floated above the otherwise dark treeline ahead, now.

"The lighthouse," Mira noted the landmark.

Maybe he isn't so crazy after all. Donna tried to slow her breathing, but adrenaline was kicking in and her heart rate quickened.

The boat traveled swiftly along the coastline. They rounded the tip of the cape and the lighthouse loomed large. Making a quick assessment of the distance, Declan veered out to where the baywaters met the wider sea.

In the backseat, Buster had remained silent for several minutes, staring off the stern as rain snaked down his smooth-shaven head. He turned to face forward and his low voice bellowed: "Someone's following us."

Donna noticed Declan's hands tense on the wheel as he replied: "You sure?" The man glanced over the heads of the three passengers nestled on the back bench. Through the rain, all he could see was darkness and the distant, shrinking skyline of the city. "Probably just some fishermen or smugglers who don't want to be seen," the boat's de facto captain shrugged, trying to reassure himself.

A few moments passed, silent save for the sputtering and splashing of the engine across the sea. The rain had soaked most of the party's clothing by this time, and they felt the chill as the wind whipped over their damp coverings.

"They've stayed on the same course," Buster spoke again. "They're definitely following us."

Donna leaned to Declan. "Can we lose 'em?"

The man licked his lips. "If we veer too far, we might overshoot the island," Declan muttered. "Can't risk it. Gotta keep moving."

"We don't even know for sure if this mystery island is out here," Donna reminded him. "We're going off strangers' dreams and your vague childhood memories, remember?"

"Coral Island is real and it's out here." Declan kept his eyes ahead. "I *know* it is."

Declan thrust the throttle and the boat's engine growled, speeding faster across the tumultuous waters. He glanced back over his shoulder; he still couldn't quite see the boat to which Buster was referring.

As he swiveled to look ahead, Declan slowed the small vessel's speed. Straight ahead of them was a dark and fuzzy silhouette framed against the deep purple sky, with a jagged edge reaching up from the horizon line.

Donna followed the man's squinting gaze. Slowly, more elements became clear: Trees. Land. An island. *Coral Island,* she smiled in disbelief.

"Guess this is where I say 'I told ya so,'" Declan grinned to Donna.

Her wet blonde hair clung to her cheeks as Donna kept her eyes fixed on the small land mass ahead. "You were right," she nodded. "I can't believe it—we're so close." *Marcus.* She couldn't bring herself to form the words on her lips—couldn't garner too much hope. *Not yet.*

"I'm going to take the long way and loop around the far

side of the island," Declan explained as he swung the wheel. "Kill two birds with one stone: lose the scent of whoever's following us and make sure no one knows we're coming."

The rest of the team agreed with this plan and held on tight as the boat rocked and swayed on its new course. Though all felt relief that the island did, in fact, exist, Donna's mind started spinning with the possibilities and scenarios. *How are we going to find Marcus and get him off this island without being seen or caught—?*

As if reading her thoughts, Declan turned to her. "We'll figure this out, Donna. We're not leaving this island without Marcus."

Donna took a deep breath then nodded slowly.

The boat made a wide arc and pivoted around to the far side of the island. The mass of land was small enough not to draw attention—a person could likely traverse its entire length within a few minutes on foot. Thanks to its size and the rhythms of the tide, Coral Island had remained mostly untouched and secret over its lifetime, often mistaken for a common, uninhabitable tangle of mangrove shrubs. As they rounded its edge, Declan moved in closer. Buster confirmed that they had shaken off the craft that was tailing them.

The Dream Team disembarked and stepped onto the mushy shore. Declan handed Donna a rope to fasten to a nearby mangrove tree, instructing her to chose one a little further up the beach. "Remember, it's low tide now," he said. "We've only got a little while before it starts rising again—and covers this entire beach."

Each member of the team had changed into more comfortable, versatile attire before they left the warehouse—durable shoes, dark and neutral colors. The rushing breeze off the boat dried them a little bit, but the rain continued to pepper them with light, misty drops that kept each member uncomfortably damp. Mira now slung a nondescript backpack over her shoulders to carry a few of the items she thought they might need, while Declan moved up to the edge of the thicket and clicked on a flashlight.

"We can use the trees as cover," he explained. "I would guess the entry point to the vault is close to the moorings on the other side of the island, so we'll have to do our best not to be seen." Declan started into the trees then turned to Mira. "Got my dose this time?"

Mira nodded then reached into her bag. She pulled out the small vial so he could see it clearly then tucked it back into the pack. Buster puffed and rolled his eyes.

Satisfied, Declan led the the way into the dense mangroves with the others in tow. The ground was moist and covered in flecks of debris and stray refuse—signs that the tide's reach extended beyond the island's sandy edges and further into its lush core. Buster's feet sank deeper into the ground than the others, but this did little to slow his pace as he took up the rear and the boat faded from view.

A few minutes in, Declan cut out the light. The group stopped walking.

"What is it?" Donna whispered.

"You hear that?"

Donna strained but heard the gradual approach of a muffled motor. *The boat that was on our tail.*

"I told you someone was following us," Buster muttered in his usual deep voice.

"They weren't following us, after all, were they?" Donna said softly. "They were already headed to the island."

The engine cut out. Declan waved the others forward to a place where they could see through the trees down to the beach, now on the opposite side of the island from where they had moored their own vessel. There were two figures—one on the shore and one on the boat. Mira shuffled around in her pack and pulled out a pair of binoculars to inspect the scene.

"You're never gonna believe this," Mira said, passing the binoculars to Donna.

"What is it?" Kiki asked, squeezed beside Buster.

Donna squinted through the viewfinders. "It's Keene!" She handed the instrument to Declan. "But who's that with her?"

"I dunno," Declan answered, his eyes pressed to the lenses. "He's tying up the boat." He waited and watched. "There's more of them—two men and a woman."

Kiki reached out for the binoculars, but Declan didn't see this. "Who?" The young woman asked.

"What the—?" Declan leaned his neck forward. "It's the cop from the restaurant!"

"What's she doing here?" Donna gasped.

"She's bound and gagged," the man continued his inspection. "Couple a goonies got her." A moment passed. "They're headed up the beach now—into the trees." Declan lowered the binoculars. "We have to follow them—they're here for the vault. I'm sure of it. And they'll lead us right to it."

As the group started to rise from their hiding place, Kiki snapped. "Guys! Wait!"

The others turned and saw her hand pointing in the dark toward the vast bay. A small, barely-visible light appeared, growing quickly. Suddenly, it disappeared.

"We need to go," Declan muttered, starting to press on into the thicket again. "We can't risk losing Keene's trail."

"But somebody else is out there," Kiki rasped. "They'll see us!"

"Whatever it is, it's gone. Stay low." The leader of the group kept walking, his feet mushing slowly and carefully through the soft earth.

Kiki puffed and followed reluctantly, keeping her gaze transfixed on the dark spot on the horizon where the light was last seen. The group followed Declan through the trees. It could hardly be called a path; the mangroves wove gangly webs of waxy branches and salty tendrils that pressed in all around the team, making progress difficult.

Declan's makeshift trail led the group down closer to the beach and spat them out on the sand. They headed toward the actual path, through which Keene and her goons had disappeared with the bound officer.

Suddenly, the team was hit with a bright and powerful searchlight. Momentarily blinded, they froze and strained to see from where it was coming—likely whatever vessel Kiki had spotted.

"We've been found!" Donna exclaimed. "What do we do?"

Declan furrowed his brow, attempting to peer through the light. He made no answer.

The boat with the light rumbled its engine and moved quickly toward the other vessel moored to the small dock. The spotlight remained on the Dream Team. Instinctively, the five raised up their hands in a sign of surrender.

"It's no use running," Declan muttered.

Finally, those on the boat killed the engine and one of them lashed the craft to the dock post. As the blinding spotlight shone on the helpless group, a woman's voice called out.

"Donna?"

Donna's expression contorted. The voice was familiar. *It can't be—*

With a loud click, the light switched off. In the dim darkness, with a circular ring of light now burned temporarily into her retinas, Donna could only tell that there were three figures aboard the boat. Two men and a woman.

"Donna, is that you?" The voice rang out again. The entire group on the beach loosened a little as a woman with dark hair hurried off the watercraft, onto the dock, and down to the beach. In the glow of the moon, her familiar face became visible.

"Sue?" Donna gasped. "What the heck are you doing here?"

The women ran to embrace one another. "I'm here with

Rico and the doctor," Sue answered, squeezing her friend tight. As she let go, Sue examined the eclectic group of strangers that accompanied Donna. She whispered in her ear as they released their hug: "Uh, Don? Who are your pals?"

Before Donna could answer, she caught sight of the men moving down the dock: Rico and Roger. She could tell from the expressions—and their sudden appearance on this same island near midnight—that there was something terribly wrong.

Rico gave Donna a silent hug. Roger nodded and gave a quick, awkward grin.

"What are you guys doing here?" Donna asked again, baffled as she flicked her gaze from Rico to Sue and back. "Did you leave Lisa to fend for herself with Starla back at the house?"

"Actually, Donna," Rico exhaled slowly, his face downcast. "That's why we're here. Something, uh, happened—"

"Your partner," Donna interjected, recalling the captive officer who had just been lugged into the mangrove jungle. "They've got her!"

Rico nodded. "I know. We followed them here. But, Donna, something *else* happened."

It was dark, so no one could see the color drain from Donna's face as she began to put the pieces together.

"They took them, too—" was all Sue could get out before her voice cracked.

"Who?" Donna feared she already knew the answer.

Rico's eyes narrowed as he noticed the faces crowded

on either side of Donna. "Wait a minute," he said as he recognized Mira, her chin lowered. "I know you—you're the woman from the bathhouse the other day! Donna, who are these people?"

"They're okay," she assured him. "They're my friends. Now, what *happened*, Rico?"

"Uh, Miss Locke, if I may," Roger interjected when neither of his companions brought forth an answer. "Your sister and her daughter and Lisa—they were taken."

Donna's ability to form words vanished as the doctor's voice echoed in her mind above the lapping tide. *Gone. Taken. Everyone I hold dear—what is happening? How is this happening? And why—?*

Rico spoke, still wary of the four mysterious individuals who stood beside Donna: "We're not sure, but we think the same people who took Tracy also have the others—we were following them and they led us here."

Donna threw her hands up. "Wait a minute: you *think—?*"

"It's just a hunch," he said. "We don't have a lot to go on. Sue barely escaped herself."

"It was terrifying," Sue added. "They pulled a boat up to the seawall out back and broke in through the slider—"

"You mean that boat?" Mira nodded toward a third vessel that was barely visible just a short distance up the coast, obscured by trees and shadows.

Sue leaned to get a better view as Declan clicked his flashlight toward it, revealing the name along its side—with three missing letters.

"That's it!" Sue pointed. "The Moonstone! They're already here."

Declan muttered. "This has my father written all over it—I can feel it."

"I hate to interject," said Kiki. "But may I remind everyone that the tide's coming in *and* Keene and company are way ahead of us by now?"

"Who's the kid with the pink hair?" Castillo raised an eyebrow.

Kiki started to lunge at the one-time officer, but Donna held her back. "She's with us. Sue, Rico, Doctor Lansing—meet the Dream Team." She gestured toward them. "That's Kiki, Mira, Buster, and Declan." They made quick introductions. "I don't have time to explain it all right now, but the short of it is that they're helping me find Marcus."

"Find Marcus?" Rico's eyes widened. "Where is he?"

"We think he's here—on the island." Donna took a deep breath. "But Kiki's right—we don't have much time. Let's go."

Though both groups had numerous questions about the other, the large posse hurried across the wet sand and found the entrance to the path. They spotted the jumbled footprints of Keene, Tracy, and the captors. "This is the way," Declan said, clicking the flashlight back on and starting into the thicket. The others followed quietly and quickly, grateful to have the bushy tree canopy provide a slight reprieve from the sputtering rain.

The path was narrow. It snaked in wide curves across the island, though Declan had a sense that they were moving closer to a place near the isle's center.

At one point, Roger slowed his steps, holding up the majority of the Dream Team who walked behind him. In the darkness, Kiki stumbled into him and the two nearly toppled over. Buster grabbed them both by the collars and set them back on their feet.

"Thanks, Buster," Kiki puffed. "What do you see, Doc?"

By this time Declan, Donna, and Rico, who walked near the front of the pack, had slowed to see what the commotion was about.

Roger peered into the dark, then waved for the flashlight. Declan handed it back to Sue, who stood beside the doctor and aimed it a few feet into the trees.

"It appears to be some kind of nest," Doctor Lansing observed, squinting his eyes. As the others set eyes on the large, thatched nest, they noticed a fluttering motion in it. A large, brownish bird flapped a feathered wing but remained in place, guarding a group of speckled eggs.

Declan sighed gruffly. "Hey, I hate to be the downer, but we're not here to birdwatch—"

"Just a moment, if you will." The doctor kept his eyes fixed on the nest, and muttered under his breath: "Why aren't you running away?" Roger nudged his feet forward a few inches, then loosened his shoulders as he got a better look at the bird. "I think it's hurt."

"What is it?" Kiki whispered so as not to frighten the creature.

"I could be wrong, but it appears to be a pelecanus occidentalis," the doctor answered.

Kiki raised an eyebrow. "In English?"

"Pelican," Mira said softly. "Think it's a sign?"

"It's a sign that we're in the right place." Declan exhaled sharply. "Now let's go, *doctor*." He held out his hand for the light and Sue reluctantly returned it to him. Roger stepped out of the foliage, leaving the pelican behind.

The team returned to their mostly-silent trek down the winding path. Soon they reached a spot where the path came to an end. The sound of the lapping tide could be heard louder now, indicating that they had drawn closer to another edge of the small island. The footprints terminated near a large porous rock, but there appeared to be no sign of where their quarry had gone from this point.

"Uh, guys?" Kiki looked around. "Is it just me, or does it look like Keene and company just vanished into thin air?"

Rico knelt to examine the mucky footprints. A few of them were cut in half by the big rock, as if the stone had been placed over them. Castillo ran his hands along the edges of the stone, wiggling his fingers into the soft, sandy, wet earth. "They didn't vanish," he said, then heaved, pulling up from the bottom of the small boulder.

There was a low *click* as Rico's fingers felt something under the mud. To everyone's surprise, Castillo lifted the large rock straight up, revealing that it was, in fact, only a facsimile of a boulder attached to a rusty hinge. Some skilled artist had cleverly crafted the strange fake rock to throw curious island-goers off the scent of what lay beneath it. The group stared at yet another obstacle under the hinged fake rock: a solid metallic hatch sealed with a lock and a keypad.

The squishy sand spilled along the edges of the hatch as the onlookers wondered what to do next. Rico tried the handle. It was locked.

"Ducane's vault *has* to be in there," Donna speculated. "Along with the people I love. We have to get it open!"

"Alright," he said, stepping away. "Anyone have any idea how we get in here?"

"Buster?" Kiki suggested.

Buster stepped forward. He knelt to the ground and placed a hand on the metal hatch, pressing with only a little force at first, then with all of his strength. He rammed a fist into it, then winced. "This is some impermeable wizardry of Ducane's invention," he said. "Built to withstand anything—including me." Buster rose from the ground and brushed the sand from his knees.

Rico flicked his eyes across the group. "Okay, any better ideas?"

"The combo," Sue suggested. "Anyone know what it could be?"

The members of the group thought silently for a moment, the trickling rain beginning to patter more loudly on the tree-cover above.

"1-2-0-4," Mira spoke suddenly.

Everyone turned to her.

Kiki crossed her arms. "Huh?"

"Smith's dream," Mira continued. "The number 1204 was

repeated over and over."

Rico raised an eyebrow and turned to Donna. "Did she just say *Smith?*"

Donna bit her lip and gave a shrug, avoiding an answer that might connect her with the man's untimely murder.

Declan bent down to the keypad. "Worth a shot," he muttered. Quickly, he typed in the four digits, each numeral appearing on a rudimentary digital screen.

Almost immediately, the interface beeped a warning, playing back a computer's synthesized voice: "Passcode incorrect. Two more password entries remaining."

Donna tensed. "Two more tries? This is not good."

"Anyone else?" Rico asked the eclectic group.

Declan rose and ran a hand through his hair.

Donna turned to him. "This is Ducane's vault, right? And Declan's his son," the woman thought out loud. "Do you think the passcode could be connected to *you* in any way? An important number, a year, a date—"

"2-1-5-6," Declan muttered, kneeling again beside Rico and the hatch. "February 1, 1956: it's when I was born." Declan extended a shaky finger to begin to enter the code.

"Wait," Kiki interjected. "Are you sure?"

"Sure of my birthday? Yeah."

"No, I mean *sure* that your estranged father would use that as the passcode to his vault?"

Declan sighed. "To be honest? No—I'm not sure," he lowered his head. "But maybe he actually did care about me all this time. I wouldn't mind being wrong about that."

Donna, bending low beside him, placed a gentle, gloved hand on Declan's shoulder. "We don't have a lot of time left," she whispered. "Marcus—my sister—"

"Okay," the man nodded. "Here goes nothing."

With a nervous gulp, Declan tapped in the numbers: 2. 1. 5. 6.

As the final number was pressed, the hatch let out a brief contrarian beep, then repeated a new iteration of the message from before: "Passcode incorrect. One more password entry remaining."

Declan's shoulders sank as he felt the collective gasps of the rest of the group, but he tried to force himself to focus on the task at hand. "We can do this," he muttered, mostly to himself, but stood to address the others. "We can crack this. We've infiltrated *dreams* for crying out loud. Now, anything else that we can think of that could possibly work as the code?"

For several moments, no one said anything. The gentle lap of the nearby waves grew louder and choppier, crashing and grasping over an exposed coral reef just beyond the mangroves that shrouded the group from the growing rain.

Then Mira spoke up. "I may have an idea," she said, closing her eyes. "There was something else in Smith's dream."

Kiki made an impatient flourish with her hand. "Well? Spit it out!"

"In the dream, a man sat in a desk to take a test," explained Mira, with particular focus on Sue, Rico, and Roger, who weren't familiar with the scene. "What was obvious was the answers he kept writing to the test—1204, the number we already tried. But I noticed that the entire time, the man tapped on the desk with his free hand. And by the time he was finished, his feet were sinking into the wet sand—the tide coming in, just like it's going to here." She paused for effect, listening to the rise of the lapping waves. "The tapping," Mira emphasized. "It was Morse code."

Buster crossed his meaty arms. "I take it you're going to tell us what the message was?"

Mira grinned. "Yes, Buster. It was a word—*cade*. I didn't think anything of it, but it struck me as odd. Does that mean anything to anyone?"

Sue glanced down at the hatch then back at the other woman. "Uh, hate to break it to you, but this thing needs *numbers* not words."

"What if the word is a number?" Roger suggested.

"Exactly," Mira pointed.

Roger continued. "Each letter corresponds to a number of the alphabet. C is three, A is one, and so forth."

"Ah," Sue nodded her understanding. "So D would be four and E is," she ran through the letters in her head. "Five?"

"3-1-4-5," Rico repeated as Declan lowered himself to his level once more. "Do we go for it?"

Declan inhaled deeply. "If this doesn't work, we need to be ready to run," he said. "It'll likely set off an alarm, and who knows what's going to come for us if we trip it." Finally, the dark-haired man returned his fingers to the keypad. "Alright, here goes."

3. 1. 4. 5.

Bleeeep! The keypad flashed the numbers. The same ominous, robotic voice began to speak the message as the entire group held their collective breaths.

"Passcode correct."

A wave of relief rushed over the group. The hatch clicked and the large, circular door opened slowly, revealing a darkened tunnel that led into the ground at a steep incline. Declan reached for the flashlight and waved it inside just as a series of dim, wall-mounted lights began to flicker on, one after another. Concrete steps slanted down into the earth, a hellish staircase into what appeared to be some sort of bunker.

Declan turned back to the others and gulped.

"Well, I think we found our vault."

CHAPTER 24

Tracy took deep breaths, inhaling the musty scent of the burlap sack that covered her head. Through the miniscule, cross-hatched gaps in its weaving, she caught speckles of dim light. As they waited, standing, the woman felt the pair of sweaty hands clinging loosely to her wrists, which were bound behind her with a zip-tie.

Footsteps approached, echoing softly. An unfamiliar male voice spoke from that general direction: "He wasn't planning on any extra subjects for tonight's demonstration."

"I had no choice." This voice, a near-whisper, belonged to Cameron Keene. "She's Metro-Dade."

The man's voice snapped. "What were you thinking, Cam?"

"We'll take care of her, won't we?" Keene replied.

Take care of me? The woman's tone made Tracy uneasy.

"We're about to begin," the man continued. He turned

slightly, speaking directly to Tracy's captors. "Take her to the storage wing. And bring the other three to the aquarium."

Other three?

Officer Jones felt the weathered hands tighten around her wrists then push her forward. Tracy nearly tripped as the unseen captor guided her to make a turn down a slight downward incline. *Further under the island,* she noted. The slant mirrored the entry to the undersea bunker—the spot where the gruff boatsmen had traded out Tracy's blindfold and gag for the sack that now covered her head.

As she couldn't see, Tracy did her best to take note of every turn, attempting to burn the route into her memory so she would be able to find her way back out as soon as she contrived an escape plan. The group navigated down a few more narrow hallways.

Tracy discerned a faint buzzing sound. It grew louder as they proceeded down the present hall, and the woman could see a reddish glow through the burlap bag over her face. The buzzing noise increased to a near-deafening throb, which Jones could feel rumbling her entire body. The group continued walking, though, and soon the mechanical sensation faded behind them.

They wound down a few more corridors and finally came to a stop. A finger tapped out a four-digit passcode and Tracy heard a click followed by a swooshing servo. A slight gust of air issued from a now-open door. The young officer heard the sound of shuffling steps—small ones. *A child.* And heavy breathing, as if through machine.

"Get in there!" The hands shoved Tracy. She stumbled forward into the room and was guided to a far corner.

"Let us go!" The invisible little girl's voice shouted from the other side of the room.

From the echo, Tracy surmised that the room was small, with a low ceiling and walls of some thick, impermeable substance. *Concrete?* It was dim, too, judging by the hints of grayish light spilling through her head covering.

"Quiet, girl!" The gruff voice—the boat captain—spat. "And who told you to take off that sack?"

"But my mom," the child pleaded. "The tank is almost empty. If she doesn't get more of that, she'll die—" Her voice was muffled as someone stuffed a bag over her head once more.

"Don't worry, we don't want that either," the man answered. He turned and muttered over his shoulder. "Grab one of those canisters on the way. Don't want her gone before Ducane sees her."

Ducane! Tracy's pulse pounded. *So he is here after all.*

"C'mon!" One of the unseen men muttered to the strangers in the corner. The captain took hold of the girl's wrists with one hand and guided another silent woman with the other. The two remaining thugs struggled to lift a quiet third figure—Tracy presumed this was the girl's mother, attached to some special breathing apparatus. Finally, the officer could feel the room become empty. She hurried in the direction of the door but heard its signature *swoosh*. It slammed and latched shut.

Tracy exhaled sharply and stood in the center of the barren room.

Now what? Ducane's here, but what's going on? That girl—she's here against her will, too. Something bigger's at play here. I have to help them.

But first, Tracy sighed. *I have to find a way out.*

Declan moved down the sloped tunnel, stepping with caution from one concrete step to the next. Rico and Donna followed closely behind, with the rest of the team assembling single-file after them.

At one point, the staircase curved off to the side. Declan slowed the group's pace as he could no longer see much further ahead. Eventually, they reached the end of the steps. The space terminated in a sterile hallway, which forked in several directions.

"Now what?" Kiki asked from the back of the pack.

Donna's worry showed clearly on her face in the dim light. "We search the place. They're keeping all of them down here somewhere—Starla, Sondra, Lisa, Officer Jones. And Marcus."

"We're not leaving without *any* of them," Declan affirmed, placing a gentle hand on Donna's own gloved one. "Or the formulas that can fix us—that can reverse the experiments my father subjected us to."

"Is this the part where someone suggests we split up to cover more ground?" Sue raised a timid hand.

Her brother nodded. "I think that's our best plan of action at this point."

No one disagreed. With haste, they settled on three groups to ensure no one explored alone. Before they headed off in their designated directions, Declan stopped them.

"Remember," he said. "We don't have much time. Once the tide rises fully, we'll be stuck down here with no way out." He checked his watch. "I'd say we're looking at about thirty minutes—or less."

Mira rifled through her pack and handed the small vial and syringe to Declan. "In case you need it," she smiled and stepped back. The man tucked it into a belt pouch.

Quickly, the divided teams hurried off down the diverging corridors, leaving Declan and Donna alone at the bunker's forked hall. The two gave each other a knowing nod and started down their assigned route.

The corridor was long and dim, peppered with support ribs that jutted from both sides of the wall every dozen feet or so. Several doorways and passages splintered off in an elaborate concrete maze. Given the fact that it was buried underwater, far from view, Donna found it odd that the bunker seemed so clean and well-kept. Apart from the exposed pipes and conduits running above them, the hallways were immaculate and sparse. One could almost feel the lull of the ocean pressing down on the whole place—Donna tried not to think about it.

Declan nodded to the piping that lined the ceiling. "Those conduits are carrying power somewhere important," he said.

"I think we're headed in the right direction."

Without words, Donna continued to follow at Declan's side. Soon they came to a bend in the hall. Both peered around the corner but ducked back when they saw a pair of figures standing guard near a door.

"Do you think the girls and Marcus are in there?" Donna whispered.

Declan took another furtive glimpse around the edge of the wall. "Maybe," he muttered. "They're guarding it for a reason. If we have any hope of getting out of here without being caught ourselves, we're going to have to find a way past those guards."

"What do you propose?"

"There's gotta be another way into that room," Declan said. "A back door, an air duct, something like that."

The two peered again. Declan noted a door with vented slats just a short way down the corridor. A janitor's cart rested beside it. *That could work.* If they moved from one support beam to the next, staying flat against the wall after each, he and Donna could keep out of view of the guards. The dark-haired man whispered this to Donna and she agreed to follow his lead.

Declan stole another glance, verified that the guards were occupied in conversation with one another, then rounded the bend in the dim light. Donna followed closely. The two pressed themselves flat against the wall, now blocked by the first chunky beam. The man looked again, moved swiftly around the support beam, then flattened once more.

After repeating this a couple more times, the pair reached the vented door. Declan jiggled the handle and found it locked. He cursed under his breath when he saw an electronic keypad. With a furtive glance to verify that the two guards were still distracted, Declan typed in the code they'd used to enter the bunker. To his surprise, nothing happened. No lights, no beeps, no messages.

"What is it?" Donna mouthed, a breathy near-whisper.

Declan shook his head. "I don't know. Something isn't working right." He breathed deeply then moved his fingers to the edges of the keypad panel. With a little bit of work, he was able to pry the panel away from the wall. Inside, a tangle of cords taunted him, but Declan's eyes moved to a fried, melted wire. "Crap. Wire's frayed too much. Can't hotwire it without that."

Donna gave him a dumbfounded look and raised her eyebrows. "So now what?"

The man bit his lip and let out a silent exhale. His eyes drifted to Donna's gloved hands. "Wait a minute: gold is a conductor. And it's malleable."

"What—Declan, I can't—"

"C'mon, Donna. It may be our only chance."

"I swore I wouldn't let what happened to Marcus happen again."

"Don't worry," Declan cut her off. "That *won't* happen." He looked around, then bent down to his shoe and quickly began to tug the thin lace free. The man rose and held it out to Donna. "This oughta do the trick."

Donna glanced at the distracted guards, then puffed. "Fine." She slowly, carefully removed one of her gloves. "Drop it in my hand. Careful you're not touching it when I am."

The man held the shoelace delicately at either end and moved it over Donna's hand. Then, with a deep breath, Declan released it. The string fell quickly. As soon as a part of it touched Donna's skin, the entire lace turned to thin, solid gold. From the force of gravity and the speed of the transformation, the object looked like a thin pair of prongs jutting downward. Donna managed to set it down, slip her glove back on, then hand the golden wire to Declan.

"Impressive, as always," he smirked. Declan began to bend and ply the golden shoelace, fitting it into the exposed circuitry of the open panel. With haste, he wound it in place of the frayed wire. A slight shock startled him momentarily as he made the final connection. The panel lights flickered on. "Bingo."

Donna grabbed Declan's arm. "Do you hear that?"

The man angled his head slightly. Declan and Donna froze.

Footsteps!

They were headed right toward them.

Kiki and Mira ended up in a group with Doctor Lansing, winding through the narrow corridors that seemed to move deeper and deeper below sea level. The trio proceeded with caution, peering around each corner before stepping into it to avoid any potential run-ins with whatever sentries might be guarding the place.

"So you two have, um, *abilities*—just like Donna?" Roger asked in a hushed tone.

Kiki grinned. "Not *just* like Donna—"

Mira rolled her eyes as the group rounded another bend. "You'll have to excuse Kiki," she said. "You'd almost think she *wants* to keep her powers."

"I can't imagine why you'd want to get rid of them," the doctor replied.

"Secret super powers aren't all they're cracked up to be, Doc." Kiki sighed. "Sure, they're great at first. But it turns out when you try to split yourself so you can do lots of things and be lots of places all at once, you end up just being nowhere at all."

The pink-haired woman peered around a corner then waved for the others to follow.

"Seems like that would be an enticing option, though," said the doctor. "To be in more than one place at once—if you could, I mean."

Kiki nodded silently as they kept walking.

"How about you?" He turned to Mira. "What are your powers?"

She lowered her head. "I can make things appear different than they truly are."

"I see." Roger noticed the slight sink of her posture. "You seem... disappointed. What's so bad about that?"

"Nothing, usually," Mira explained. "It's just that, like Kiki, it's tempting—tempting to only portray what you think others *want* to see. And it's just as well, because they don't want to see who I really am."

"And what would happen if they do?" Roger cocked his head as they came to another bend in the corridors.

Kiki and Mira surveyed the next hall.

"It ends," Mira said finally.

Roger sputtered and contorted his eyebrows. "I beg your pardon?"

"The end of the hall," she nodded around the corner. "It doesn't go any further." The trio moved into the wide space, where they approached a set of doors. A small sign beside it read: *Refrigerated Storage.*

"Well, I sure hope Donna's friends aren't in there," Kiki muttered.

"It's not likely," Roger agreed. "But this is very similar to the sort of facility we had when I worked for Pelican—it's how we stored many of our proprietary compounds to keep them from spoiling or expiring."

Kiki's eyes grew wide. "Proprietary compounds? You mean like—"

"The cure," Mira finished the thought. "The way to reverse what Ducane did to all of us?"

"Perhaps," the doctor nodded, then pointed to a strange device built into the wall that had no buttons but appeared to offer some sort of secure entry to the lab storage beyond. "But let's not get ahead of ourselves. This appears to be some sort of secure access, but I can't for the life of me imagine how we could get through this—"

Suddenly, Kiki threw a hand over the doctor's mouth and gave a *shushing* motion with her finger. The trio became quiet. They could now hear voices echoing down the corridor from which they had just come.

"What do we do?" Kiki whispered.

Roger's breaths were heavy. "This would be a great time for one of you to showcase your abilities."

"I'm on it," Mira said with a tilt of her chin. "Get back against the wall."

The others complied just in time. Two figures in labcoats rounded the corner and headed directly toward the large door. Roger held his breath. *They've seen us.* He shut his eyes instinctively, as if it would make the approaching scientists go away. *This is it.*

The doctor waited what felt like many long seconds for the figures to speak up—to make some remark of alert. But no such outcry occurred. Hesitantly, Roger cracked open one eye, then the other, and watched as the two scientists—a man and a woman—completely ignored the three interlopers pressed against the cold wall. The woman turned and seemed to direct her gaze right at Roger. He froze.

What the—

The woman continued talking as the other scientist stood in front of the strange interface beside the door.

"I'm just saying," the woman addressed her partner. "Science hasn't *disproved* the existence of parallel worlds—"

The male scientist placed his face close to the interface, then held up a finger to quiet the woman. He then spoke in a loud, clear voice: "Julian Leach."

A red light blinked through a glossy black panel then, with a pleasant chime, the door clicked open. The man pulled the door open the rest of the way, emitting a cloud of wispy condensed vapor.

The woman continued: "So I guess what I really mean is that we should be trying to study spacial phenomena—"

"I suppose it's possible," the man finally replied, ushering her inside. "I just don't know if it's *likely*—"

Their words faded away as they closed the heavy door behind them. It clicked again, signaling that it had locked once more.

Roger let out a large exhale and turned to look to the women at his other side. Kiki and Mira grinned at him.

"What just happened?" He raised an eyebrow. "Did you just—"

Mira nodded. "Yep."

"Incredible. Why someone would want to get rid of a power like that is beyond me," he muttered under his breath as he moved back to the electrical panel beside the door.

"It looked like some sort of voice scanner," Kiki noted. "That guy just said his name and it let him in."

"I suppose it's time to see the further extent of your abilities then," Roger said to Mira. "Can you fool a computer?"

She started to shake her head. "I've never really, actually, successfully replicated someone's voice when they haven't been around to give me a reference point." Mira wrung her hands. "And... even then I wouldn't call the results *successful.*"

Roger inspected the panel, then turned back to her. "Are you willing to give it a try?"

Mira bit her lip. "Do I have a choice?"

The doctor and Kiki shook their heads in unison.

"Alright." Reluctantly, Mira stepped forward and placed herself before the shiny panel. Now she noticed a series of small dots indicating the presence of a vented microphone just below the blinking red light. She gulped, then opened her mouth to speak the name: "Julian Leach."

The voice that came from her throat sounded nothing like Mira's typical voice. It carried the same timbre and depth as the scientist who had successfully gained entry a few moments prior.

All three waited anxiously for the interface to respond. Finally, it chimed.

This time, though, the sound was different than the all-clear signal that occurred at the scientist's voice. The warning sound made it clear that Mira's impression of the man had been less than perfect.

"What happened?" Roger asked, appearing over Mira's shoulder.

"I told you," she said, louder. "I've never successfully produced a perfect vocal illusion."

"It doesn't have to be perfect—" Roger tried to assuage her doubts.

"Apparently for a computer it does." Kiki crossed her

arms. "Try again, Mira!"

Mira nodded and readied herself. "Julian Leach."

The warning chime beeped again, louder.

Kiki stood by. "This one of those 'three strikes you're out' kinda locks again?"

"Shh!" Roger waved for her to be silent.

Mira took another deep breath and tried a third time: "Julian Leach."

The interface seemed to be computing, calculating the accuracy of the deep vocal pattern that came from Mira's mouth. Then it beeped again. This time, it wouldn't stop. The red light started flashing more aggressively.

"Uh, guys?" Mira stepped back. "What now?"

"We need to get in there!" Roger said as the women backed away.

"That has to have alerted someone that we're here!" Kiki pointed to the flashing light, nearly shouting over the now-blaring sound.

They almost didn't notice the click of the door. It cracked open. Someone pushed on it from inside the storage chamber.

Mira grabbed the doctor and Kiki by the shoulders and pointed directly at the widening gap. *We're done for!*

CHAPTER 25

Mira didn't have time to push the group back to the far wall. As the door began to open, revealing the two scientists, she pulled all her focus and energy to the two friends whose shoulders were in her tight grip, standing with their backs toward her.

Please work.

The trio vanished from sight.

Mira could sense the fear in Kiki and Roger, but they all stood motionless near the blinking access panel. The two scientists pushed the door all the way open so that they were now fully visible. They started toward the alarming flash. As the thick door began to swing shut behind them, Mira whispered, "Go!" and guided her two companions in a wide arc away from the panel just as the two scientists moved toward it. With another quick motion, Mira propelled the doctor and Kiki through the closing gap of the door. It slammed and latched shut behind them, sealing them in the frigid, dark space.

The three panted as they became visible once more.

"Sorry about the vocal illusion," Mira said. "Told you it's not my forte."

"Don't worry about it," Roger said. "You got us in regardless."

Mira gripped her arms, shivering from the cold. The doctor and the women scanned the dark space in which they now stood. The chamber was narrow and long, lined with row after row of sealed, translucent cases. Roger noted that those closest to them contained glass vials full of fluorescent, gooey substances. Each case also had a temperature control and a gauge to ensure that its contents achieved a specific, fine-tuned level of refrigeration.

Kiki crouched to inspect one of the lucite cases. "So what are we looking for exactly?"

"The vials should be labeled with a serial number," Roger answered mindlessly as he searched the immediate area with his eyes. They landed on what he was looking for and he hurried toward it: a binder on a pedestal near the door. "A-ha!" He exclaimed as he flipped it open. Inside he found a series of typewritten pages behind plastic page-protectors. Roger ran his finger down one page, then flipped to the next.

"Doc?" Mira asked from beside another case.

"Just a moment," he said. "This is an index of sorts. I'm hoping it will help us find the formulas we're looking for." He flipped a page. "All of the projects have codenames, so this could be challenging. For example, the codename for the project that led to Donna's powers was *Midas*."

"Fitting," Kiki snickered while she stood looking over one of the man's shoulders.

Mira approached and perched at the other. "Looks like the codenames are listed by year. The two of us and Buster were part of trials in 1977. Declan's dates much farther back."

"And Project Midas concluded last year," Roger nodded. The listings started with the most recent, so it was easy enough to find the first code. The doctor skimmed the page. His finger landed on a long sequence of numbers and letters. Roger fished in a pocket, withdrew a wad of gum wrappers, and began unfolding and flattening them. Then he produced a pen from his shirt pocket, clicked it, and scribbled the serial number on one of the wrappers.

Roger flipped a few more pages until he arrived at the experiments from 1977. "Any idea what they may have called the experiments you participated in?"

Neither of the women had an answer. They scanned the names down the page. *Starsaber. Crockett. Hercules—*

"Hercules," Mira interjected. "That's *got* to be Buster's formula."

Roger transcribed the sequence on the paper-side of the wrapper.

Penelope. Starthorn. Nephele. Medea.

"The goddess of magic and illusion," Mira muttered. "Medea. Do you think that could be me?"

Kiki nodded. "Sounds likely enough. But none of these

really scream 'person who can clone herself instantly' do they?"

While Roger scribbled the serial numbers for the formula they believed to correspond to Mira, he took another look at the page. "If precedent is anything to go by, Ducane seems very fond of his ancient mythology. I'd wager it's one of those—Penelope, Nephele, or perhaps Chronos—just skimming the page."

"Roger's right," Mira added. "I'd put money on Nephele—if I remember right, she was an exact copy of the goddess Hera."

The others agreed that this made the most sense, so the doctor hurriedly scratched the number onto the gum wrapper then flipped a few more pages to search for the project that Declan was subject to. "When did you say his experiment took place?"

"About ten years ago, he says," Kiki recalled. "Around 1971, I think."

Roger exhaled and lowered his voice. "These records only go back to 1974." He flipped through a few pages just to be sure there wasn't a hidden section stuck to another.

The two women looked at each other, then back at the doctor. "I guess there's not a lot we can do about that now," Mira said softly. "For the time being, he's at least got his doses to keep the powers at bay." She took a deep breath. "We're running out of time."

Doctor Lansing quickly copied the serial numbers from one gum wrapper to two others then divvied them up so that each of the trio held a copy of the list.

"Now," the doctor explained. "We search the place."

Kiki turned to face the expansive chamber and placed her hands on her hips. She sighed. "This could take awhile. They don't look like they're in any particular order."

Mira raised an eyebrow and elbowed Kiki. "It would help if there were a few *more* of us."

Kiki crossed her arms. "I hate it when you're right." She rolled her eyes then closed them.

Roger watched with curiosity as her body started to contort a little. Then, in an instant, a second identical version of Kiki stepped out from the other and stood at her side. She winked at the doctor, whose eyes grew wide.

"Impossible," he muttered to himself, shaking his head. "Full-body mitosis?"

The original Kiki kept her eyes shut as the process repeated itself and another identical copy morphed into existence.

"How many of these replications can you produce?" Roger inquired, inspecting one of the copies. He poked her arm and his eyes grew wide again when he realized she was an actual living, breathing, tangible person.

"The more I do, the more it puts a strain on me," the original Kiki answered, opening her eyes. "Each of their minds is linked to mine, so I can only process so much at once."

Satisfied, the doctor nodded. "Then let's get to it."

Immediately, the now five members of the group began to scour the long room for the specific formulas indicated on the gum wrappers. They moved with haste, recalling the rising tide outside, but had to inspect each vial individually to ensure they didn't overlook any of importance.

Rico, Sue, and Buster lumbered down another narrow corridor, moving past a vented door from which a low, mechanical rumble emanated. They continued on, feeling the floor slant downward with each step.

Sue noticed a slight stagger in her brother's steps. "Rico," she took him by the arm. "You gonna be okay?" The trio stopped walking.

"Yeah," Rico pulled back, tilting his face away. "I'm fine."

"You're *not* fine." Sue grabbed his chin in the way she had so many times when they were children, forcing him to look her in the eyes. "What is it, hermano?"

He gulped and took a deep breath. "I'm worried," Rico slipped a hand inside his jacket and pulled out a small Polaroid photograph. "I'm afraid I'm going to lose her, too."

Sue examined the photo: a woman in uniform, shielding her face from the bright camera flash in what looked like a hotel room. "Your partner. But what she did—"

"—was my fault," Rico interjected. "I couldn't stand her because I wasn't ready to accept that maybe Marcus was really gone forever. I haven't been the same since he left—I know that. I would never tell Jones this, but I was actually starting to like her."

Buster, who had listened silently up until this point, spoke in his deep voice: "We need to keep going."

Rico nodded. "Yeah, you're right. Sorry."

"Rico." Sue placed a hand on his shoulder again. "We're going to find her—find them all. Tracy's here. Donna said Marcus is here, too—in the vault. We can do this." Her final words seemed to be aimed as much to herself as to Rico.

"Do me a favor," her brother answered. "If we find Jones, don't tell her I said any of that, okay?"

"*When* we find her," Sue smirked. "Deal."

Immediately, the siblings started up again, following Buster's lead as they made their way down the spartan hallways.

A few minutes later, the party reached a section of the compound that contained a number of solid, identical doors on either side of the hall. Each of them appeared to be locked with an electronic keypad fixed to a section of wall beside it.

"She's gotta be in one of these," Rico pointed and hurried to one of the keypads. He pressed the button to open the door, but it buzzed at him. The locking mechanism held tight.

"Try the comm," Buster pointed at the speaker embedded in the panel.

Rico complied, holding down a button to talk: "Hello? Tracy? Lisa? Girls? You in there?"

There was no answer. Only static.

"Give 'em a sec," Sue suggested. "Maybe they're tied up or can't respond."

Rico exhaled. "We don't have time for this. The tide is rising, remember?"

"All these rooms are locked." His sister made a sweeping gesture. There were nearly a dozen doors. "What do you suggest?"

After a slight pause, Rico slowly looked up and met Buster's eyes.

Buster made a defensive wave of his hands. "It's too risky," he said in his deep voice.

"What's the point of special powers if you never use them?" Rico countered.

"There's more to it than that," Buster replied. "What if I accidentally damage something more... structurally significant? I could bring this whole place down on us."

The former officer thought for a moment. "It's a risk we have to take. Our friends—Donna's loved ones—could be behind any of these doors!" Rico pleaded. "If not for me, will you at least do it for Donna?"

The large man puffed and squeezed his hands, cracking his massive knuckles. He took a deep breath, then spoke softly: "Fine. For Donna."

At this, Buster moved closer to the door, sizing it up. He looked over his shoulder. "You might want to stand back," he said with a half smirk. The siblings complied and moved to the far side of the hall, trying to peer around Buster's hulking figure to watch the action that was about to unfold. Rico and Sue held their breath. Then, with a wind-up, Buster threw his fist squarely into the center of the metallic door.

The laboratory room glowed with an ominous, sterile light that was almost green. Mira scanned the dozens of beakers and vials in the case before her. Her eyes flicked back to the ink-scrawled gum wrapper in her fingers. None of the serial numbers matched. She bit her lip and moved on to the next case, beside Kiki. *Or one of her copies.* Mira had lost track when they dispersed throughout the long room. *They're all connected, anyhow.*

"I got one," another Kiki exclaimed from behind Mira. "I think it's Buster's." She hurried over to Mira, who took it from the young woman's hands and placed it carefully into her backpack. "Does this seem morbid to anyone else?"

The third Kiki—one of the copies—shouted across the room. "You mean how we're looking for something that will make some of us cease to exist? Yeah, pretty weird."

Mira chuckled and the women resumed their quest for the other compounds.

"What's the first thing you're gonna do?" A voice rang out beside Mira—the original Kiki, she concluded.

Mira looked up. "I beg your pardon?"

"When we're fixed," the pink-haired woman replied. "What's the first thing you'll do?"

The woman thought about the question as she crouched to view a low shelf of compounds. "I guess I'll stop pretending," Mira muttered, glancing at the wrapper notes, then back to the case.

Kiki raised an eyebrow as she studied the case before her. "How do you mean?"

Mira reached the end of the shelf and rose to view the next one. She glanced over her shoulder to make sure the doctor and Kiki's copies were out of earshot, then spoke softly: "If you could change the way that people see you, don't you think you'd take advantage of that ability every chance you got?"

"I guess so..."

"Well, that's what I did. What I've *done*."

Kiki lost focus of the vials. "You mean like on all of our missions, right?"

"Well, yes," Mira answered, her face downcast. "But I mean that I've changed the way *everyone* sees me—for as long as I've been able." She took slow breaths. "Ever since the experiments, all those years. When they told me I was chosen for the trial, it felt amazing. No one had ever picked me before. I always assumed it was because I wasn't good enough, didn't look right—my nose protrudes too much; one of my ears is lower than the other; I'm not the 'right' proportions. So when I realized I could adapt to be whatever kind of *beautiful* another person wanted, I did."

"Sounds exhausting," Kiki said.

"It is." Mira sighed. "It takes a lot of energy to maintain. But it's hard to break a habit."

"Have you tried?"

There was a lingering silence as the others rifled through the lucite cabinets and jingling glass containers. Mira looked to Kiki. "No one would want that version of me. Even you guys."

Kiki abandoned the case in front of her and moved quickly to Mira's side. She took the woman's hand in her own and looked at her with wide, sincere eyes. "We didn't invite you to the team because of the way you look, Mira. You're on the team because, no matter what, you're one of us."

Mira gulped and looked away, but said nothing.

"And when we're all fixed, you'll still be one of us—because you're our friend."

The dark-haired woman nodded slowly, cracking a grateful smile.

A sudden outburst from the other side of the room drew their attention.

"Found one!" Roger shouted. He held up a small, glass vial. "Two actually!" The women listened as he read from the vials. "These should correspond to the experiments on the two of you."

"So, what, we just drink that and we're back to normal again?" Kiki asked.

The doctor forced a grin as he inserted the two containers into Mira's backpack. "Not exactly." Roger could sense the growing skepticism in the room, so he quickly added: "They're meant to be delivered through injection. Don't worry. I helped create and handle many similar formulas. We'll take these back to the surface and I'll be there to walk you through it every step of the way."

This seemed to put the women at ease, for they quietly went back to their search for the final compound—the formula administered to Donna nearly a year prior.

"Is this it?" Mira exclaimed after a few more moments of searching. Roger and the three Kikis ran and crowded to look over her shoulders. "Serial number matches the one for codename Midas," she referenced the stamp on the slender test tube. Mira handed it to the doctor, who verified that this was the correct compound.

"That's it then," he stated as he added the formula to their collection in the pack. "Now let's get out of here and find the others!"

Kiki turned to her identical counterparts. "Thanks for the help," she said.

"I guess this is goodbye," one replied somberly. "Maybe forever."

The original nodded. "I guess so." The three women stepped forward in unison, embracing each other in a group hug.

Kiki closed her eyes. Roger and Mira watched as the two copies of the pink-haired woman vanished into thin, wispy air. When Kiki opened her eyes once more, she nodded and the trio moved quickly out of the lab back down the hallway.

"Hurry," Donna urged, hovering over Declan's shoulder as he twisted the gold wire into place.

Declan tried repeating the passcode that had brought them into the bunker.

3. 1. 4. 5.

A light flashed green. The latch clicked. Declan swung open the door just enough for the two to enter the darkened space. As the footsteps grew louder, Donna and Declan closed the door behind them and crouched to peer through the vented slats.

They could only see the feet of the several passersby heading toward the guarded door at the end of the corridor outside, but Donna's heart skipped when she caught a glimpse of a pair of small, bare feet pattering along the cold hall.

"Starla!" She whispered involuntarily, covering her own mouth.

It took everything in her not to burst back through the door at that moment. *We'd never escape.* Donna heard the struggling guards carrying a heavy load, and the machine-assisted breathing that told her Sondra was with them, as well. *We'll find a way.*

Declan yanked Donna's arm and nodded at the space ahead of them. The closet housed a tangle of duct work, lending cool, breathable air and ventilation to the underwater compound. The woman followed Declan as he started forward, moving to the far wall. He removed a grate from one of the wide duct segments and gave a flourish of his hand.

"Ladies first."

"You want me to go in *there?*" Donna stared into the vent's metallic throat.

Declan pointed up, allowing his finger to follow the path of the ducts. "This connects to whatever's on the other side of this wall—wherever they're taking them." He tilted his head back toward the door. "We'll fit easily," he assured her. When Donna didn't seem convinced, Declan started toward it. "Fine, I'll go first."

The two crouched into the tight space. It was wide enough for them to traverse it on hands and knees, shuffling with their heads low and at an odd, uncomfortable angle given the duct's limited height. It was dark, but Declan could see a bluish light emanating from somewhere up ahead, along with the low drone of indistinguishable, distant voices. He carefully led Donna toward the spot with as much haste as possible.

As they neared the blue light, it became apparent that it was emanating from a vent on the floor of the present stretch of duct. The two interlopers squeezed next to one another and lay prone so that both could see through the vent's slats. Donna instinctively clenched a hand to grip at the wall of the duct when she realized how high up they were.

Below them stretched a vast room that looked to be several stories tall. The blue, undulating glow came from the farthest wall of the chamber, which consisted of a single, solid glass window that looked directly out into the ocean depths. Donna thought it reminded her of an aquarium. Blue lights along the base of the window illuminated passing fish and clumps of living coral, though the night lent a shallower view than she surmised was typically visible in the light of day.

Their attention was drawn quickly from the aquarium window to the main entrance to the room—the door through which a large group presently entered. It was Donna's loved ones—*most* of them. Starla, Sondra, Lisa, she presumed, though the bags over their heads made it difficult to be certain. *But where's Marcus?*

A burly group with scowling faces and dark clothes led the captives across the vast room. The commotion at the door had taken so much of her attention that Donna hadn't noticed the five, large seats that formed a semicircle around an oblong dining table, the members silhouetted by the blue glow of the glass and water. Four of the chairs were occupied, and the individuals seated in them shifted slightly when the prisoners approached.

Declan let out an almost inaudible gasp. "That's him."

"*Him?*" Donna asked without taking her eyes off the captives.

"Yeah," Declan nodded. "That's my father."

CHAPTER 26

Crack!

The thick, metal door burst to pieces, a massive hole forming in its center—right where Buster's fist had landed. The edges of the door frame had created slight cracks in the concrete wall as they pulled away, but this seemed to be the furthest extent of the damage. He and the Castillo siblings—overcoming their momentary shock at the man's brutish, inhuman strength—crowded around to peer through the large hole.

It was clear at a glance that this room was used as a sort of holding cell. In one corner there was a small iron cot. In another sat a plastic bucket. A short chain hung from the wall at about average waist-height.

Rico raised an eyebrow and his shoulders sank. "No one here," he muttered.

"But I think we're on the right track," Sue affirmed.

The trio moved on to the next cell. Buster repeated his action again. For how utterly powerful Buster was, the whole thing seemed nearly effortless as Rico and his sister observed the big man. There was another deafening metallic crash. A small bit of concrete dust crumbled from the wall. The group looked into the now-open cell.

Empty. Drat!

"Keep going," Rico urged.

Buster quietly complied. They made their way down the hall, crashing through a half-dozen more empty cells. Sue noticed a hairline fracture along the concrete ceiling, but shrugged it off quickly as they came to the next door.

The group was becoming discouraged, but once again Buster wound back his arm and let it fly toward the door. The metal caved like flimsy cardboard under the force. A frightened shout emanated from inside the room.

"Jones?" Rico's eyes grew wide as the dust cleared.

At the far wall of the room, sitting on another metal cot, was a woman with a burlap sack over her head. "Who's there?"

"Tracy, it's me—Rico!" He hollered, his heart racing as he stepped through the opening—carefully clearing a disfigured piece of metal at the level of his knees.

"Rico!" Tracy shouted. "How on earth...?"

Finally, the former officer reached Tracy and yanked the thick bag from her head. She blinked a few times, her brown eyes wide with wonder and disbelief.

"Rico, what the heck are you doing here? How did you

find me?"

"I'm here to save you. We followed the boat." He reached in his pants for a pocket knife. "Are you okay?"

"I'm fine," Jones answered. The two locked eyes. "Why are you doing this, Rico?"

Rico began to saw at the thick plastic zip-tie that bound her wrists. "Because it's one of the first things they teach us in the academy," he looked up and his eyes met hers. "Never leave your partner behind."

"*Partner*," Tracy's expression softened. "I like the sound of that." She caught sight of the two figures outside the door. "Who are your friends?" She tilted her chin toward them.

Rico snapped through the zip-tie, freeing Tracy's hands, and waved for her to follow him out of the room. He pointed to the hulking man first. "Tracy, this is Buster. You can thank him for the, um—" He nodded at the gaping hole in the door. "—renovation."

"Thanks," she smiled uneasily.

"And this," Rico turned to Sue, "is my sister Susana."

"Just *Sue* is fine." The women shook hands. Sue shot a worried glance to the ceiling. "Is it just me or did that crack get bigger?" She pointed up.

Buster furrowed his brow. "It's not just you. We need to go. Now."

"We're not leaving without the others," Rico said firmly, moving to the next locked cell.

"Others?" Tracy asked.

"My friend Donna—her sister, her niece, and her best

friend were all taken. They've gotta be in here somewhere." He motioned for Buster to join him at the door. Buster wound back his arm.

"Her niece," said Tracy. "She's a little girl?"

Rico held up a hand for Buster to wait. "Yes! Have you seen her?"

"There were others in the cell before they threw me in," she explained. "I didn't get a good look, but it was definitely a kid's voice I heard. And some sort of mechanical breathing apparatus. There were three of them."

"That's them!" Sue exclaimed. "Sondra's on a ventilator."

"You're sure there were just *three*," Rico verified.

"Yeah, that's what they said." Tracy nodded. "Why—?"

"Marcus," he interjected. "Donna said he's here, too.

"He's *here?*" Tracy's eyes grew wide. "Rico, I'm sorry I didn't believe—"

He held up a hand to cut her off. "It's okay. I know I sounded crazy." He continued. "Donna said they're keeping him in some sort of *vault*."

"You think it could be one of these cells?"

"Not likely. Sounded like something more protected—more heavily guarded."

Sue piped up. "Do you know where they went—where they took the girls?"

Tracy closed her eyes to think back. "The aquarium," she said. "That's what they called it. Said they were taking all three of them there to see Ducane."

"Anyone have any bright ideas about where this aquarium

could be?" Rico consulted the group.

No one answered. Buster shook his head.

"I guess we double back the way we came then," Rico concluded. "We'll find the others and the vault."

In agreement, the four hurried back down the long corridor, sloping upwards in the direction they had come. Sue took a final, fleeting glance at the cracked ceiling. A tiny spurt of concrete dust fluttered to the floor. She gulped, then quickly followed the others away from the cell block.

"That's my father," Declan pointed. "And the rest of his Inner Circle."

Donna's eyes followed his gesture through the slats of the air vent down to the man who sat in the center seat in the dim chamber below. Most of his body was cloaked in shadow, but as Starla, Sondra, and Lisa were pushed closer to him, he leaned forward into the light. Donna could immediately see the family resemblance—Ducane had the same chiseled jawline and handsome features as his son. His hair was a similar dark chestnut color, though flecked with bits of gray at the edges.

"I have to say I'm impressed, Sal," Ducane spoke in a commanding, unhurried tone as he swallowed a bite from his plate. "Bring them closer."

Sal, one of the meaty thugs, led the three ladies closer, the burlap sacks still covering their heads.

Starla let out a squeal that echoed throughout the aquarium room. "That hurts!" She snapped as the man's pair of gruff hands nudged her forward against her will.

Donna clenched her gloved fists, watching helplessly from her perch behind the AC vent.

"Save it, kid," Sal answered. "Joey, c'mon."

The one called Joey directed Lisa forward by kicking his white sneakers lightly at the back of the woman's legs. She whimpered, trembling as she stepped closer to Ducane and the others, as another handful of the darkly-garbed goons brought Sondra and her breathing apparatus before the table and semi-circle of chairs.

When all three were lined up, Ducane stood and grinned as he spun to address the other three seated near him—the Reverend, Viktor Gromble, and Cameron Keene, looking stern and cross as ever. "My esteemed colleagues," said Ducane. "Thank you each for coming on such short notice. I trust your travel was smooth—you understand the need for secrecy and heightened security given all that's transpired this week, and the nature of what you're about to see."

Donna's brow furrowed and she shot a glance to Declan. *About to see? What?*

"For many years I waited for another anomaly to emerge," Ducane continued. "As you all know, they are rare specimens that often seem to follow rules of their own—defying what we've known to be true about genetics and heredity. But not *all* such specimens are created equal. Some are in a class all their own." Here he began to pace. "Some require, er, *intervention* to realize their maximum potential, while others need no such prodding."

The man moved nearer to little Starla, the bag covering her face as she tried to make sense of what was happening.

"Now, I know that all of you are apprised of the latest ongoing projects here. Unfortunately, work has stalled as some of our, um, *resources* have dried up." Here he eyed the prisoners. "But as fate would have it, we've secured a veritable trinity of subjects who possess qualities of great interest to me and the work we're doing here."

Ducane quickly snatched the burlap sack from Starla's head. Frazzled, she blinked and took in the dim, blue room with wide, frightened eyes. The seated members of the Inner Circle inspected the disoriented child with their own piercing gazes.

Next, Ducane moved to Sondra, supported by a cadre of sturdy men. He took the covering from her head, revealing that she remained in a coma, her breathing tubes still fixed snuggly to her nostrils.

"Mom!" Starla cried and hurried toward her.

Ducane stretched out an arm and pushed the girl away, addressing his distinguished guests. "As you all may have guessed, the quality of greatest interest is exactly what it appears to be: the subjects are *family*."

Once again, Donna's face contorted, viewing the scene from above. *Family? But Lisa—wait a minute! He thinks that she's—*

Ducane removed the sack from the third captive, letting loose a mass of reddish hair. Lisa appeared just as stunned as

Starla as she took in the surroundings. Ducane's expression of glee quickly reddened as he realized that the woman was not the one he had hoped for.

"Who the hell are you?" He gritted his teeth.

"I-I'm L-Lisa," she stuttered helplessly. "Lisa Jorgenson. What are you doing with us—"

Ducane snapped his attention to the cronies that stood behind the prisoners. "Where is she?"

The one called Sal sputtered a defensive reply: "We took all three of 'em that were in the house, just like you said—"

"I was *very* specific." Ducane inhaled quickly, then gestured toward Lisa. "Does that look like blonde hair to you?"

Up above, Declan shot a glance to Donna. She nodded. *He wanted me instead—because of my powers, no doubt. But what do Starla and Sondra have to do with this?*

Joey, the man with the striped sneakers, gulped and groveled. "It was dark—"

"Dark!" Ducane's hands turned to fists.

Cameron Keene finally spoke up from her seat. "Is there a *problem*, Rolf?"

Gromble nodded his agreement with Keene: "Are we going to have a demonstration or not?"

The leader took a deep breath and pivoted toward his Inner Circle. "A slight hiccup," he forced a smile. "These two will still be of use. However, it's not the spectacle I'd hoped for. I'm sorry I dragged you all here for nothing." Ducane turned to the men behind the unmasked prisoners. "Take the girl and her mother to the labs immediately. Dispose of the redhead."

Lisa gasped.

"Make it look like an accident," Ducane added as he moved back toward his seat.

"What does that mean—?" Lisa shouted after him as the gruff guards began to push her back toward the door, along with Starla and Sondra. "Hey! Ow—!" Joey kicked her in the legs again and she tumbled a few steps forward.

Donna's breathing quickened. "They're going to do something terrible. We have to save them!"

"My father's likely the only one who knows how to get into his deepest vault," Declan answered in a whisper. "You want to find Marcus, don't you?" The longing in Donna's eyes was the only answer he needed. "We have to face Ducane."

"Are you crazy? You just wanna waltz into that room? What about the guards?"

"I'm still working on that part," he replied. "Either way, we need to get down there!"

With some reluctance, Donna agreed and the two began to shuffle their way back down the vent as quickly as they could move.

Declan reached the slatted doorway and heard footsteps just outside. With a glance at Donna, who nodded and pulled off one of her gloves, he turned the handle and pushed the door open.

The small group of thugs walked past the janitor's closet with the trio of unmasked prisoners, pushing and carrying them along at a brisk pace. The one called Joey led the group, shoving Lisa forward at gunpoint with a smile, while Sal took up the rear, his hand clutching a fistful of Starla's ruddy hair.

Donna and Declan spilled into the hall just as the group passed by. Declan snatched a janitor's mop from the wheeled cart near the door and tossed Donna an empty bucket. The two stood their ground. The blonde woman held her ungloved hand at her side and shouted down the hall.

"Hey, you!"

Sal was the first to spin around; the others followed—there were five thugs in total—with looks of confusion painted across their faces.

Starla's eyes grew wide. "Aunt Donna!" The girl squirmed. "Help!"

"Don't worry, little Starling," Donna said softly. "I'm here."

When he saw that the two were unarmed and that the child recognized her, Sal smiled. "Donna," he repeated, drawing a gun from his side with his free hand. "Hey, Joey—isn't she the one we were looking for? The one who should've been at the house tonight?"

Joey grinned from the back of the group, exposing browning gums. "Sure looks like her," he replied. "Pretty blonde." He nestled his face near Lisa's thick red curls and whispered: "No offense, red."

Lisa retched at the goon's repulsive remarks and salty breath. "Donna, I hope you got a plan—"

"Shut 'em up!" Sal hollered.

Joey shoved the barrel of his handgun into Lisa's side. She quivered and quieted.

"Let them go," Donna demanded, taking a step forward.

Sal puffed. "Or *what?*" The gruff man smiled widely, wickedly, revealing a couple of gold teeth. "You're going to mop us up?"

Donna slowly raised her hand and gestured at the glint in the man's golden grin. "Nice crowns—how about I give you a few more of those?"

The men in black chuckled. Sal took a step forward, cocking his gun. Donna and Declan moved back to maintain the distance between them.

Declan muttered out of the side of his mouth. "What now, Donna Locke?"

"I'm thinking," she whispered back. Donna clutched the handle of the bucket in her gloved hand, then raised it up. "See this?"

Sal glanced back to Joey and chuckled. "Yeah, I see it."

Donna gulped and moved her ungloved hand to the drab plastic pail. As her skin touched it, the grimy bucket quickly turned to shiny, shimmering gold. Donna strained to keep it raised, as its solid gold state caused its weight to increase nearly five-fold. "If you don't let them go right now," she said confidently, "*this* is what I'm going to do to *you*."

The man's jaw sank slowly as he stood mesmerized by the strange trickery before him. Then with a contemptuous scowl, Sal gripped the gun tightly and aimed it straight at Donna. "Not if I shoot you first." He pulled the trigger.

Craccckk-pinggg!

The bullet fired off. Donna winced and shoved the golden

bucket in front of her face. The shot ricocheted off the metallic surface and clattered to the floor. Donna's eyes were wide as she realized what had just happened. Declan yanked her back by her sleeve as he watch Sal take aim once more.

"Get back, Donna!" Declan shouted. The pair split off to either side of the hall, hurrying behind the protruding concrete support columns just in time to avoid another deafening shot. It splintered the edge of the beam behind which Donna crouched, sending a flurry of debris flying past her shoulder.

Sal, Joey, and the rest of their group advanced slowly, keeping the prisoners in tow. The men aimed and fired a few more shots, each time getting closer to Donna and Declan's hiding places. The pack of thugs moved up, just past the janitor's cart, and held their ground as they awaited the inevitable capture or wounding of the helpless duo.

As Sal paused to reload, Donna glanced around the corner. She grunted and hurled the golden bucket toward him with all of her might. At the last minute, the man stepped aside, pushing Starla with him. The bucket landed on the foot of one of the goons supporting the comatose Sondra. The man wailed but maintained his grip.

"You've got nowhere to run, Blondie," Sal seethed. "You and your boyfriend are outnumbered, outgunned, and out of options. Put your little gloves back on and come out with your hands up and *maybe* we can arrange a deal where you get out of this alive."

From her spot behind the column, Donna met Declan's

eyes across the wide hall. He shook his head slowly. *He's right though,* she thought. *We can't hold them off much longer. We're toast.*

As her mind raced, Donna heard a shrill voice shout out from behind the thugs:

"Get your slimy mitts off of them, losers!"

Donna's eyes grew wide and she bent to look around the corner. The group of armed men also pivoted slowly, lowering their weapons ever-so-slightly.

Lisa was closest to the voice and recognized the speaker instantly. "Sue!" She nearly shouted.

Sue's dark hair draped over her shoulders as she gripped a broom from the janitor's cart with both hands. Behind her stood Rico, Tracy, and Buster. A pair of white sneakers with blue stripes caught Sue's attention and she nearly gasped: "You!" Sue allowed her gaze to drift up to the face of the sneakered man holding Lisa captive. "*Joey*, right?"

Joey's eyebrows contorted. "Uh, yeah—?"

Before he could finish his reply, Sue interjected: "Nobody messes with my friends. Got it?" With all her might, Sue swung the heavy broom handle in a graceful, sweeping motion. The thick, solid wood crunched as it met the side of Joey's head. The man's body slumped to the floor, limp, and his handgun slid across the ground and landed at Tracy's feet.

For a split-second, Sue stood with her mouth agape, baffled by her own adrenaline-fueled actions. Her focus widened as she took in the rest of the scene: the thugs—more angry than ever; the prisoners; Donna and Declan beyond them, still crouched behind the support beams.

Tracy lunged for the gun and scooped it up, then aimed ahead. "Get down," she hollered at Lisa, who pulled Sue with her as she threw herself to the floor.

The two friends pressed shoulder-to-shoulder in a quick pseudo-hug. "Boy, am I glad to see you," Lisa muttered. "That was amazing!"

"I got lucky," Sue quipped then slapped her hands over her ears as Tracy fired off a couple shots just above them.

One of the thugs dropped his gun and crumpled to the floor. Rico was right behind Tracy to snatch up the weapon. He assisted in swiftly dispatching the final few men. The last of the lackeys had carefully set down Sondra and her breathing apparatus against the side of the hall before they each took bullets to the legs.

The two officers pivoted at the same time, turning their weapons in sync to aim at the remaining enemy. Sal took a nervous step back and shoved the barrel of his gun to the side of Starla's head.

"Not a step closer or the kid goes, too," he shouted, rivulets of sweat issuing down his hairy neck.

The child whimpered and winced at the cold metal against her scalp. "Please don't hurt me—"

"Shut it, kid!" Sal snapped. He nodded to the officers. "Put the guns down or I pull the trigger."

Tracy and Rico made eye-contact, but kept their barrels focused on the man.

"I'll do it!" He threatened, applying more pressure.

"You don't need to do this," Tracy tried to calm him, inching forward.

Sal noted the step and waved the gun toward her. "I said, don't come any closer!"

Officer Jones put up her hands apologetically and ceased her steps. The man returned the cold barrel to Starla's hair. The girl winced and closed her eyes. Sal heard a sound behind him and whipped around to see Donna and Declan approaching.

"You, too—not another step or she dies!"

He waved the gun at them and shifted so that his back now faced the wall.

"Now," he continued, a frightened finger rattling the trigger. "You're going to put the guns down like I asked, and you're going to let me and the girl pass on our way and—huh?"

As he spoke, his hand began to move the gun away from Starla's head. The others looked on in confusion.

"What the—?" Sal gasped, struggling to fight against what appeared to be his own involuntary movement.

His arm continued to move, aiming the gun upward, toward his own head now. For a moment it lingered. "What? Cut it out!" There was sheer panic and fear in Sal's eyes.

Then the arm shifted slightly in a quick, jaunted movement, pointing the gun toward the ceiling. His finger pulled the trigger.

Crack! Crack! Crack! Click. Click.

The magazine was emptied. Sal wore a dumbfounded

expression. He flew suddenly backward toward the wall and the gun tumbled to the ground. As the group looked on, they watched as a young woman materialized—it was Kiki. She turned to the group:

"So much for sneaking around in secrecy."

The members of the group breathed sighs of relief as they recognized Kiki. Tracy moved to Sal's now-limp body to verify that he was unconscious. Donna slipped her glove back on and hurried toward Starla.

"Aunt Donna!" She smiled faintly as they moved toward one another. Starla paused a step before reaching her aunt. Her eyes moved to Donna's gloved hands.

"It's okay, kiddo," Donna assured her, crouching to the girl's level. She stretched out her hands to invite Starla closer. "It's safe. I promise."

Starla took a deep breath, nodded, then threw herself into Donna's arms.

Donna breathed in deeply, the familiar scent of the girl's thick, ruddy hair bringing her immediate comfort. "I was so worried for you," she muttered. "I love you, little Starling."

After a few moments, Starla loosened her grip on Donna, and they turned back to the others.

Donna rose and turned to Kiki, Starla still clinging to her aunt's side. "Wait, how did you—?"

"Teamwork." Kiki smiled and nodded toward the end of the hall, where two figures now approached from the shadows between the widely-spaced overhead lights.

Buster was the first to recognize them: "Mira—and the

doctor!"

With a collective sigh of relief, the rest of the party waited for the newcomers to reach them. Mira placed an arm around Buster, then Kiki.

"We found the compounds," Mira announced to the group.

"Doc says he thinks he can finally fix us!" Kiki added.

"That's incredible," replied Buster, turning to Roger. "It's amazing that you managed to find all of them."

The three members who had found the formulas sunk slightly. Roger shifted his gaze to Declan. "Not quite *all*."

Declan exhaled slowly. Donna placed a gentle, gloved hand on his arm.

"But," the doctor interjected hopefully, "we did manage to acquire a certain formula that I believe will help us rid Miss Locke of her own curse—and cure your Marcus, whenever we find him."

Marcus! In the flurry, Donna had nearly lost sight of their remaining objective. *He has to be here*—

Her thoughts were interrupted by a sudden burst of sound. A woman's garbled voice spoke out through a hidden speaker system: "Seven minutes to maximum tide level. Please exit the facility immediately."

"Guess that means it's time to go," said Kiki. She started to turn down the hall.

"No," Donna said more firmly than she intended. "I'm *not* leaving here without Marcus!"

The corridor was silent, save for a distant, indistinct

throbbing.

Donna continued. "We have to find Ducane's vault," she said, clutching Starla in her arms. "Marcus *has* to be there—has to be *here*." The woman turned to Declan. "You promised to help me if I helped you. Does our deal still stand?"

Declan inhaled deeply, then nodded. "It stands. You're right. We're so close. We have to confront Ducane and get him to reveal the vault."

No one seemed opposed, so Donna gave quick orders. "Buster, can you carry my sister? Rico, get the girls out of here."

Rico started toward her. "But Donna, I can help you find Marcus—"

Declan raised a hand. "We need to keep it small," he said, glancing at Donna. "Just me and Donna. The others need you."

Donna offered Rico an earnest, soft smile. "Get Starla home safe, okay?"

The team began to move. Sue and Lisa wrangled Starla, while the doctor followed behind Kiki and Mira.

"Wait," Declan shouted as they started off. "Actually... Kiki, Mira. I've got an idea."

Mira reluctantly removed the backpack full of vials and carefully handed it to Roger.

Donna hurried to give Starla one last squeeze then watched as the large group took off down the corridor and disappeared around a corner. When they were gone, Donna turned to Declan and the two ladies.

Kiki crossed her arms. "Alright, Dec, so what's the plan?"

Declan smiled. "Time to bring down Ducane."

CHAPTER 27

Rico and Tracy tarried near the back of the pack while Buster led the way, carrying Sondra's limp body and medical equipment in his massive arms. Sue and Lisa followed with Starla between them, the girl holding their hands. At the tail end of the group was Roger, lagging a few steps behind, who seemed to be lost in his own thoughts as he scurried to keep up. The backpack of compounds was draped across one shoulder.

Tracy kept her sights on the maze-like corridor ahead and muttered softly to Rico, "It's them."

"Huh?"

"I recognize them from the restaurant," Tracy clarified. "The waiter, the singer—with the gloves—your friend?"

"You mean Donna?" Rico, who hadn't attended Tracy's dinner meetup with Keene, slowed his steps. "They were all there? You're sure?"

She nodded. "And that lady with them we just left back there was the attendant from the bathhouse." Tracy took a deep breath. "You think they're involved in Smith's murder?"

"Donna would never involve herself with something like that," Rico assured her, though doubt began to creep into his own thoughts on the matter. "There's gotta be something else we don't know yet—something that explains it."

Realizing that her accusations seemed to be upsetting Rico, Tracy changed the subject as they rounded a corner. "I'm sorry."

"You said that already," Rico said quickly, trying to avoid eye-contact.

"No," Jones put a hand on his arm, prompting the man to turn toward her. "I mean I'm sorry for what happened earlier. The 'strikes' and all."

Rico exhaled sharply. "You were just following orders."

"Orders from a chief who thought you were losing your mind," Tracy grinned as they continued walking. "I'm sorry he didn't believe you either."

Rico shook his head. "He was right to do it—and you were, too. Marcus vanishing like that—it put me in a bad place. I wasn't exactly a sterling example for the Metro-Dade ranks."

"We'll get you the help you need. No one should go through something like that alone." The woman's voice was sincere and empathetic—Rico wasn't accustomed to hearing such tones from his colleagues.

Maybe she's not so bad after all.

"It's still bothering me, though," Tracy continued. "The

case—Smith's murder, the weird fur in the hotel room. When we get out of here, I'm going to tell chief everything so we can get you reinstated and finish the job. I need you." She added, "And of course Marcus will be a great help, too."

Rico tried not to smile but failed. "I appreciate it, Jones."

Just a few steps in front of them, Sue made a furtive backwards glance at the snaking hall to their rear. She spoke loudly for Buster to hear: "How much longer til we're out of here?"

Buster kept up the pace. "It should be just around this bend."

"Good," Sue muttered. "I have a bad feeling about all this."

Lisa shot her a brow-furrowed look. "About *what?*"

Sue angled her head back and lowered her voice. "Did you hear that?"

"Hear *what*, Sue?"

Ahead of them, Buster slowed his steps as he was the first to round the corner. Straight ahead was a fork in the path, the corridor diverging in several different directions. A reddish glow filled the space.

The others caught up and saw the split for themselves.

"Great," Buster puffed. "I don't remember us passing this fork in the road."

Roger piped up, his breathing intensifying. "So we're lost?"

Tracy chimed in quickly. "Don't worry. I think I can get us out. I made a mental map when they brought me in blind. It's a little rough," she clarified then squeezed her eyes shut, "but I think we passed by this spot." Jones seemed to be listening for something, mapping out the space in her mind.

She opened her eyes and pointed to a vented room up ahead, wherein a droning generator emanated its familiar thump. "We came this way. Take the center hall."

Her confidence gave the group another boost of energy. Tracy moved to the front of the group and led as Buster and the others fell in behind her, now picking up the pace again.

"See, Sue," Lisa whispered. "You must've just heard that generator, right?"

Sue stole another look over her shoulder. "No," she said as she turned back to Lisa, her face growing pale. She gripped Starla's hand tightly. "That's not what I heard."

The guards outside Ducane's audience chamber moved swiftly down the hall, guiding the three remaining members of the Inner Circle toward some unseen exit of the undersea bunker. The Reverend and Cameron Keene moved with purpose, while Viktor Gromble hobbled along, lagging at the rear. When they had rounded a corner and moved out of sight, a slatted door creaked open. From the janitor's closet appeared two heads, which quickly materialized into two bodies—Donna and Declan—running quietly down the hall in the opposite direction that the Inner Circle and their entourage had gone.

Donna stopped in front of the sealed doors to the aquarium room. She looked to her side, inspecting Declan's rugged, nervous figure clutching a handgun he'd swiped off one of the fallen guards minutes earlier. The two took deep breaths.

"Ready?" Declan spoke softly.

"Are you sure about Mira and—"

"They're right where they need to be. You remember the code?"

"Yeah." Donna's gloved hand was shaking a little as she punched in the four digits. She allowed her finger to hover over the green *enter* button and closed her eyes. *Marcus,* she thought. *I'm coming.* With a deep breath, Donna opened her eyes and pressed the last button. The interface chimed. A locking mechanism clicked and the door swooshed open.

"Here we go," Donna muttered and the two stepped forward into the chamber. The door closed quickly behind them.

The audience chamber appeared even larger from this vantage point. The undulating blue light from the giant, ocean-viewing window masked the edges of the space in shadow, such that the room appeared empty at first glance. Donna caught sight of a slight movement on the far side of the room—a man with his back to the two new arrivals.

She took another deep breath and then shouted. "Ducane!" Her voice echoed back to her just as loudly.

Ducane turned slowly, remaining shrouded by the shadows. "Well, you're just a few minutes too late, Miss Locke," he said as he began to saunter toward the woman. "Your absence caused me a great embarrassment with my top investors." Here, Ducane now entered a more well-lit part of the chamber, revealing half of his devilish grin and his salt-and-pepper hair. He cocked his head when he saw the man at

Donna's side. "Hello, son. I didn't realize you and Miss Locke were so well-acquainted."

Declan shifted. "You know why we're here, father."

Ducane flinched. "Do I?"

"Marcus Myles," Donna snapped. "We know you've got him here—in your vault. Tell us where the vault is and *maybe* we'll let you out of here alive."

Ducane burst into amused laughter, which grew ominously loud as it ricocheted off the walls and glass of the wide room. "Ah, Donna," he spoke slowly, taking a few steps closer to pair. "So uninformed—so ignorant about so many things."

Donna shot a quick glance to Declan. The two made eye-contact, worried.

The menacing man before them continued, still half-shrouded in darkness. "What makes you think you have any say in whether I live or die, Miss Locke?"

The woman exhaled slowly. "You seem to know who I am," she said, slowly pulling off one of her gloves. "So I presume you know what I'm capable of." Donna held out the exposed hand. "With the touch of a finger, you'd suffer the same fate Marcus has—only I have a feeling there's no one who cares enough to come and rescue you."

"You wouldn't dare," Ducane smirked, inching forward.

The woman clenched her fists instinctively. "Gold sinks fast. What do you say you spend the rest of your days at the bottom of the ocean?"

"I'd rather not," he replied.

"Or I could just shoot you and get it over with." Declan raised the handgun.

"You and I both know that wouldn't help anyone. I'd be at the bottom of the ocean and you'd have channeled your anger but failed to learn the way into my vault."

"So you admit it," Declan said with a subtle sigh of relief. "You *are* keeping Marcus in a secret vault. Where is it and how do we access it? Tell us now!"

"I don't think I want to do that," Ducane muttered.

Declan gripped the gun tighter and moved forward.

Ducane grinned and stood his ground. "Aren't you just a *little* bit curious, Miss Locke?"

"Curious about *what?*"

"Oh, come on," Ducane puffed. "You know what I'm talking about: aren't you interested to know what makes you so... *special?*"

Donna's breaths became quick. *Special. That's the word Roger used all those months ago.*

"But you're not the only one," Ducane continued. "Surely you must have realized this by now. I'm surprised *he* didn't tell you." The man nodded toward his son.

For a brief moment, Donna turned her gaze to Declan. *There's more to the story,* she thought. *That's what Declan said when we met. He knew about me, and—*

"Donna," Declan said, his hands still clutching the cold gun. "He can't be trusted."

"Says the man who hid the truth of his own abilities," Ducane taunted.

"You're only jealous," the son snapped.

"What are you talking about?" Donna held her hands out once more, shifting her attention from father to son and back. She moved closer.

Declan offered Donna an earnest look. "My... curse," he said. "*He's* responsible for making me like this—you know: the monster. The beast."

"Go on." Donna shifted her feet.

"My father used me as his guinea pig—his lab rat—to test his crazy experiments. He was too much of a coward to do it on himself." Declan's hands were sweating now as he turned back to Ducane. "What kind of father does that to their kid?"

Ducane lowered his head. "What's done is done," he muttered. "And I assure you it wasn't cowardice that led me to this. You were special, too. And you're right. I was envious—jealous to have blood like yours—and your mother's."

"Don't you *dare* speak her name!" Declan now reached his father's side and aimed the barrel of the gun at his chest, only a few feet away.

"You weren't the only ones subjected to my experiments," Ducane said slowly. "For so many years, I hoped and wished that I could be like you. Nothing worked—until now."

The shadowed man gulped and slowly took a step forward. As the scattered blue light shimmered across his face, Donna could now discern grotesque scarring on one half of the man's visage. Ducane began to writhe his neck. It made a loud cracking noise, then he began to convulse. Declan loosened his grip on the gun, lowered it ever-so-slightly, and watched with wide eyes as his father transfigured before his eyes.

Ducane's body began to bulge and grow, his musculature increasing in size as the hair on his body quickly amassed. Soon he was nearly a head taller than before, and his entire body was covered in thick brown and gray animal fur. The tips of his fingers extended and sprouted razor-sharp nails that appeared almost metallic in the dim light. He made a guttural growl as he finally lifted his head to look once more at the two nervous bystanders.

"We're not so different from each other after all," the beast grinned at Declan, baring a set of glistening incisors.

Declan barely had time to take in the scene when Ducane swiped one of his sharp talon-like claws at his arm. The gun tumbled across the floor and skidded toward the aquarium window. The son clutched his hand in pain. Blood. Skin torn from his hand. Before Declan could react further, the beast lashed out with his other claw, digging the blades of his fingers deep into his son's chest.

Donna screamed. She watched in what felt like slow motion as Declan's eyes rolled back into his head and his body crumpled to the floor. Almost instantly, Donna could tell that the body wasn't breathing. She started forward but stopped after a couple steps, returning her attention to the menacing creature before her.

The beast licked his lips with a long, slimy tongue. Blood dripped from both of his hands as he turned his attention to Donna and bared his teeth. "What was it we were saying about who controls life and death?"

"Sue, you okay?" Lisa tried to follow the woman's gaze while maintaining her grip on Starla's hand.

Sue shook her head. "Nope. We are *not* okay," she muttered. "Big guy!" She hollered up to Buster. "I think your little breakout is coming back to bite us."

The large man's eyes grew wide as he heard it, too: the sound of cracking concrete. Buster's jaw sank a little as he cradled Sondra in his arms. "We have to move *fast!*"

Officer Jones maintained her lead of the group, guiding them around a corner. "The exit should be just around the next bend," she assured them as they picked up the pace.

"At least we're still ahead of the tide, right?" Lisa quipped to try and lighten the mood.

Almost instantly, a bright red light began to flash and a voice garbled over the loudspeaker system: "Tide level critical. Evacuate immediately."

Lisa said nothing. Rico nudged her back. "Keep moving—faster!"

The party moved swiftly, nearing the compound's final exit stairway. Tracy pressed a button, activating the hatch door, which slowly creaked open up ahead. Buster was the first to exit, carrying Sondra up to the mushy surface of the island. The rest of the women and Starla followed. Rico tailed them, but stopped cold when he saw a look of fear in Tracy's eyes.

She spoke quietly: "Wait—where's the doctor?"

"He was right behind me—" Rico spun around. The doctor lagged far behind, holding one of the vials and inspecting it in the hall's dim light. Beyond him, down another section of the hall, Rico witnessed a set of double doors with small porthole-like windows. His heart rate spiked at what he saw through the windows: a wave of seawater gushing down the corridor.

Rico took a few steps toward him so he could get a clear view: "Doc! Run!"

When the wave hit the back side of the sealed doors, it splashed a mist over the glass. The water level quickly rose to cover the glass. The pressure forced tiny spurts of water through the crack in the double-doors, leaking rapidly into the long stretch of the hallway in which Roger now ran.

"A little faster," Rico said, taking backward steps up the steps again while keeping his eyes on the doctor.

Roger fumbled with the backpack and the loose vial as he hurried along.

Suddenly, there was a loud metallic *crunch*. The double-doors gave way, and thousands of gallons of water poured into the corridor. The waves moved swiftly, rushing around the doctor's ankles and up toward the stairs. Roger lost his balance, tripped, and fell headlong into the cold, salty water. The backpack tumbled ahead of him and the loose vial disappeared under the wave before popping to float along the surface.

"Doc, c'mon!" Rico urged as the water now lapped up toward his elevated ankles.

Roger lunged for the backpack and yanked it out of the water. When he pulled it out, he realized that the top flap was wide open. "The formulas!" He shouted frantically, watching as the remaining vials bobbed on the surface, swirling away from him in the tumultuous white waters. The strength of the rising waters carried them away—further from the exit.

The doctor took a deep breath. *I'm not leaving without those vials!*

CHAPTER 28

Donna froze, her eyes wide. She took short breaths. Declan's rugged features appeared softer to her as she inspected his body once more, motionless and bleeding. Ducane's hairy, beastly form approached the woman slowly, his jagged toenails clacking along the polished floor.

The woman took a step back, inching toward the aquarium glass. She held out her ungloved hand. "Don't come any closer!"

The beast smiled. "Aren't you afraid of me, Miss Locke?"

Donna didn't reply, but continued to back away. Out of the corner of her eye she could discern the shape of the fallen handgun—just out of reach.

Make a run for it.

As the woman eyed the weapon, Ducane suddenly reached out one of his sinewy arms and grabbed a plate from the still-set dining table. He chucked it at Donna. She ducked and held out an ungloved hand to stop it. Her finger grazed the edge as she crouched low. The ceramic plate instantly turned to gold and clattered across the floor beyond her.

Ducane smiled. "Ah," he said. "I've never seen your abilities in real-time, but they're more impressive than I thought."

The creature took a few steps forward, reaching for a piece of silverware: a butter knife. Donna lunged for another plate from her end of the table as Ducane wound back his arm to hurl the dull blade at her. The dish turned to solid gold, which Donna wielded swiftly to parry the projectile knife in a quick downward motion. The butter knife fell to the ground.

"If you kill me," Donna said through labored breaths, "you'll lose all of the progress you made with your experiments." She tossed the plate aside and managed to take a few steps back—closer to the loaded weapon.

Ducane licked his slimy lips and followed suit. "If I kill you, your blood will still give me what I need. It makes no difference to me whether you live or not—it's what's inside of you that interests me. Besides, cadavers have better manners—just ask Mr. Smith." He bared his fangs and readied to pounce.

As he did this, Donna watched the long hairy ears on the sides of his head twitch slightly. The monster's head tilted toward the entry to the chamber. Then she heard it too: the sound of a distant, deep cracking. A sudden, blaring alarm began, basking the room in a blinking red light.

"Tide level critical," an automated recording rang out. "Evacuate facility immediately."

Donna's eyes grew wide.

The beast shifted his attention from the sound out the door to the shadows on the opposite side of the chamber, then quickly scurried in that direction. Puzzled, Donna threw herself to the ground, picked up the handgun, then ran after Ducane.

"Hey! Where do you think you're going?" She shouted as she attempted to catch up. Donna slipped her glove back on the exposed hand so she could grip the gun with both. "I'm not finished with you!"

Ducane reached a panel on the far side of the chamber. Though it was dim, Donna could discern the seam of some sort of door, hidden from all but the most careful inspections.

"Is that your vault?" Donna shouted, her hopes rising as her gun gripped the trigger. *It has to be!* "Stop right there or I'll shoot!"

The beast whipped around. "If *you* kill *me*, Donna," he said through short breaths, "you'll never find Marcus. And you'll never know the truth about *them*."

Donna's brow furrowed and her grip loosened. "The truth about *who*?"

Ducane grinned unnervingly. "Your *family*, Donna."

"What are you talking about?" She tightened her hold on the gun, taking a step forward.

"You, your sister, her offspring," said the monster's gravelly voice. "You all share something vital: your blood."

Of course. It's why he wanted all three of us—

"But of course, there's more to the story," the beast bared

his teeth.

More? Donna shook her head. *That's not important right now—he's just trying to distract you. Focus. Marcus. The vault.* "That's your vault, isn't it?" She waved the gun at the hidden door, then aimed it back at the beast's heart. "Open it!"

"I underestimated you, Miss Locke." The beast held his ground. "Who knew you were so heartless? I thought for sure that you and my boy had a connection—that you wouldn't just leave him to rot." He gestured a sharp talon-nail toward the limp body.

Donna maintained her gaze and her grip. "Yeah, you underestimated me, alright." She said with a hint of a smirk. "You'd think the guy who created the experiments would recognize when they're being used against him." Donna nodded toward Declan's bleeding corpse.

Ducane raised a hairy brow and shifted his attention back to his lifeless victim. Slowly, the body morphed from the shape of Declan into a smallish, pink-haired woman. Then, the woman's body dissolved, vanishing in a cloud of misty, particulate matter. It was gone.

"Clever." The beast clenched his sharp fingers and readied himself to lunge at Donna.

Immediately, the sound of rushing water filled their ears. Both Donna and Ducane turned toward the door to the aquarium chamber. A look of fear came over Ducane and he used this moment to run.

"Donna!" A woman's weary voice shouted from above. "Get out of there!"

The blonde woman flicked her gaze to the vent above, where she could see Kiki through the slats.

"Get out now!"

Before she could respond, the doors to the chamber swished open, letting in a gush of ankle-high water and a familiar, worried face: Declan, alive and well.

"He's getting away!" The man shouted, pointing toward another corner of the room near the aquarium window where Ducane now disappeared into a narrow door that shut quickly behind him. Moments later, a rumbling sound filled the room, and a small submarine craft passed beyond the thick glass, then vanished into the dark depths of the sea.

Declan cursed under his breath, then ran toward Donna, his steps sloshing as the water began to level out across the wide space. He slowed when he reached her. The two embraced.

"You did great, Donna," he assured her. "But we *have* to get out of here—now!" Declan motioned to the water that was slowly rising over their shoes.

"But we're so close. Marcus—the vault!" She now led Declan to the strange seam in the wall. "This is it—I know it."

"How do we get in?" The man felt his fingers along the thin outline.

Donna did the same on the opposite side. Her gloved fingers felt the border of a piece of ornamentation on the wall, which suddenly rotated away to reveal a full alphanumeric keyboard.

"I'm guessing this is how."

Declan hurried to her side. "Shoot. It needs another passcode. Try the number from before."

Donna nodded and punched out the numbers. The interface beeped antagonistically. The woman tried the word—*cade*—to no avail. "We *have* to get it open! Think!"

The water rippled up to their shins.

"I'm trying," Declan nodded, closing his eyes.

Donna's mind was still swirling. She replayed Ducane's words in her head to try and garner some clue. *My family. The special blood. Ducane's family*— "Your mother," she sputtered.

"Huh?"

"What was her name?"

"Donna, I really don't see how this is relevant—"

"It's the only other idea I have," she insisted. "What was your mom's name?"

Declan took a deep breath. "Her name was Rose. Try it!"

With a hurried nod, Donna punched in the four letters and hit *enter*. The two held their breaths for a long moment. The door mechanism clicked, and the secret door creaked open a few inches.

"It's stuck!" Donna wrapped her fingers around the now-exposed edge of the door. "The water's coming in too fast." *Almost there, Marcus.* "Help me push!"

The two waded through the knee-deep ripple and pushed their full weight against the door. It budged a little. They shoved and strained again, finally managing to swing the heavy vault door wide enough for them to enter the space beyond.

Donna's pulse quickened as she rounded the door. The search for Marcus had taken nearly the entire past year of her life, and the harrowing missions of the Dream Team had led them finally to Ducane's secret vault.

Finally.

Donna took a deep breath, cleared a corner, and peered into the vault's main space.

The woman froze in place, the water trickling and rising up her legs. Her jaw lowered instinctively. Declan stepped beside her and slowly placed a gentle hand on her arm.

"I'm sorry, Donna," he muttered, barely heard over the rising water. "I'm so sorry."

Donna scanned the compact room. The walls were lined with small, sealed compartments—what looked like lockers. She knew in her gut that there was no way a full-grown man, shaped in gold, could fit inside one of these, but the woman hurried to open one. Inside was a stack of binders, appearing to house financial records of some kind. Donna hurried to the next, then the next. All filled with trinkets and documents—nothing related to Marcus.

"Donna, we have to go—"

"You said he'd be here, Declan!"

"I said he *might* be here, and I *wish* he was, alright?" The man gritted his teeth. "But we have to leave now if we want to survive this."

Donna couldn't bring herself to look him in the eye as she continued to work her way around the room. *There has to be something here. Some clue, some information.* Donna opened one of the cases and paused. Something inside caught her eye: an airtight, lucite case containing a collection of about a dozen floppy disks. Her spirits rose and she held up the case. "Look!" Donna pointed at a label on the front.

Declan sloshed across the room to inspect the label: *A. Hyde.* "Angela?" His eyes grew wide.

Donna's voice cracked. "Do you think—?"

He placed his hand on hers. "It has to be. She was the last one seen with Marcus, right?" Donna nodded and Declan offered a soft smile. "Now, can we get out of here?"

Donna wiped a few drops of ocean water and tears from her cheek. She inhaled deeply and clutched the clear case to her chest, then nodded. "Yeah. Let's go!"

The waters roiled and rose, lapping up the stairs as Rico watched Roger begin to wade through waist-deep water—*away* from the compound's exit. Through the distant gushing, Rico saw two figures emerging. *Kiki,* he realized. *And Mira?* Kiki limped along with an exhausted woman slumped over her shoulder—she resembled Mira, but something was different about her features. Rico couldn't quite put his finger on it.

"A little help?" Kiki shouted when she saw him.

Rico hurried over and helped Kiki walk Mira the rest of the way to the hatch, where Tracy assisted in guiding the two women to the surface above.

Castillo looked back to find the doctor. The flashing red

alarm sirens heightened the tension in his voice as Rico shouted after him.

"Leave the vials," the officer insisted as he stretched out his arm. "Take my hand, doc!"

The doctor ignored Rico's pleas and continued down the hall, following the flow of the bobbing vials. He managed to scoop one up and quickly tuck it into the soggy backpack, which he slung tightly over his shoulder. *Three more to go.*

A drizzle of ocean water began to seep in through the hatch edges. Rico exhaled sharply and shouted up to Tracy, who looked in from the ground level. "Get the others to the boats. We'll be right behind you."

"The water's coming in, too fast, Rico," she replied. "Are you crazy?"

Castillo forced a half-grin. "Only a little." The man then turned away and sloshed down the steps into the deeper water.

The water was now at the level of their chests and rising even faster.

"Doc, let's speed it up!" Rico waded toward him. The powerful current sent one of the vials near him and he reached out his hand. It caught a small whirlpool and was whisked away, just inches out of his grip. Rico dove after it.

Gotcha. His fingers wrapped around the clear test-tube and he held it up for Roger to see. "Got one!" Rico passed it into the doctor's hands.

A moment later, the doctor managed to grab another vial. Roger tucked it into the backpack with the others. "Excellent," he shouted over the hallway rapids. "One more!" The doctor scanned the roiling surface of the waters.

There was no sign of the missing vial.

Rico, who was now paddling sideways, adjusted to touch his feet to the ground. As he leveled out and his shoes met the floor, he stood and realized the water was now up to his neck. "No time! This is it!"

Roger continued to look across the waves. *Where are you?*

"Roger! If we don't go now, neither of us are going to make it and those vials will drown with us—!" He gurgled the last of his words as the water lapped up against his chin.

"It's Donna's," cried Roger. "The last vial is the one to fix Donna. And Marcus. I *can't* leave without it. I *have* to fix my mistake!"

The doctor was determined. His head bobbed, rising with the water so that his feet were lifted slowly off the floor. His eyes fluttered across the waters, bathed in flashing red like an ocean of blood, and the reality sank in.

It's gone. Roger shook his head slowly and doggy-paddled to stay afloat. "I'm sorry, Rico," he said, finally turning to the man. "I'm so sorry."

"Apologies later. Swim *now!*"

Rico and Roger paddled furiously toward the hatch. The tide waters were pouring in now, rushing down the stairs to meet the corridor flood. The two men struggled up the wet incline, slipping and backsliding.

A firm hand appeared in the hatch opening. Rico looked up. It was Tracy.

"Give me your hand," she shouted, "*partner.*"

Rico's eyes flashed a glimmer of hope. He shoved Roger from behind to boost him up. Jones grabbed his outstretched arm and pulled the doctor up out of the tunnel. Then, the two on the surface lifted Castillo.

"Thanks," he nodded as he caught his breath.

"Don't mention it." Tracy panted and pointed ahead down a marshy path. "Now let's get off this rock. Boats are that way."

The island was nearly submerged in the rising tide. The three trudged through the ankle-deep saltwater and took off toward the place where the watercrafts had moored. Roger clutched the backpack of vials over his shoulder, taking one final glance back at the gaping hatch. The red flashing lights were barely visible now, drowned out by the roiling water and mangrove silt that bubbled over the opening.

The doctor took a deep breath. *I'm sorry, Donna.*

Roger turned away and splashed after Rico and Tracy, leaving the underwater compound and the lost vial behind forever.

As Roger, Rico, and Tracy emerged from the trees, they swam across the submerged beach. The two vessels upon which their parties had arrived were now gone—likely taken by the island's other evacuees; only the Moonstone was left behind, idling near its mooring behind the trees, and the dock was no longer visible as the dark waters had engulfed it.

The trio reached the edge of the vessel and climbed up a metal ladder. Sue appeared from above and helped her brother and the others onto the boat as Buster throttled the engine from inside the cockpit. They broke away from the island and drifted out to sea to avoid being swept into the tide's current.

Rico collapsed and leaned his back against the railing near the back of the boat.

His sister crouched near him. "Are you okay, Rico?" Sue placed a gentle hand on his shoulder, and spoke softly so she was out of earshot of Starla and the others. "Did you see Donna?"

The man glanced across the narrow deck to where Starla sat shivering, wrapped tightly in a blanket and Lisa's maternal embrace. Rico returned his gaze to Sue, gulped, and shook his head slowly.

Kiki appeared and asked, "What about Declan?"

Rico lowered his head. "They didn't make it out," he muttered.

The boat rumbled on in silence, skirting the edge of the now-submerged island. Roger stood looking off the railing at the aft, twin trails of foamy water churning in the vessel's wake. The man clung to the wet backpack of vials. His eyes started to gloss over as his mind replayed the earlier scene.

Then something caught his eye. His vision narrowed and he bent in closer. "There's something out there," he said, barely loud enough for the others to hear.

Mira, weary and tired as she sprawled across a bench

cushion, mumbled, "What is it?"

Doctor Lansing pointed. "Don't you see it? Under the surface—it looks like—"

"Lights," Kiki exclaimed. "Two of them. Buster, slow us down!" She shouted through the open door, and the driver brought the boat to a slow drift.

"They're growing," Roger noted.

Soon, most of the boat's passengers were crowding along the back railing to get a glimpse. The lights grew brighter until finally, with a splash, they broke through the rippling waters. It appeared to be a tiny vehicle—its yellow color and large bubble window indicating that it was some sort of compact submarine. The twin headlights blinded the passengers aboard the Moonstone, who covered their faces and squinted through their hands to get a better look.

Finally, the lights clicked off. The little craft motored over to the side of the Moonstone so that it was now in range of a fading floodlight.

Starla's eyes grew wide when she saw the figures through the misty glass bubble. She threw her blanket aside. "It's her! It's them!"

The tiny submarine made a clicking noise, prompting a small hatch at its top to open. Two weary faces appeared in the space: Donna and Declan.

"Aunt Donna! Aunt Donna!" Starla jumped up and down. "You made it!"

Donna smiled up to her. "We did, little Starling. We made it."

Tracy watched Rico's shoulders sink as he realized there was no third passenger in the submarine. *Marcus,* Jones thought. *He wasn't down there.*

Buster throttled the engine again and brought the larger boat closer to the sub so that their two friends could climb aboard. As Donna ascended the ladder, she handed up the clear lucite case filled with floppy disks, which Rico quickly grabbed.

"What are these for? Doing some coding?" He handed the case to Sue and helped lift Donna the rest of the way.

Rico pulled her close and gave her a lengthy embrace.

Donna crumpled in his arms. "We looked for him," she choked up, then shook her head. "I think—I *hope* there's something on those disks that can help us find him. They were in Ducane's vault, so they've got to be important."

He nodded. "We'll do everything we can to find him," Rico assured her, then glanced up at Declan, who Tracy now assisted onto the deck.

Starla ran over and wrapped her arms around her aunt. Donna smiled and continued her soggy greetings with the others as Buster kicked up the throttle and the boat soared across the bay, leaving the submerged Coral Island in its wake.

CHAPTER 29

The sun was just beginning to rise, painting the glass of the Miami skyline in brilliant blues and soft violets. A van reached a dusty warehouse, where a sliver of heavenly light seeped through the building's upper windows and garage door cutouts. The vehicle entered and the large door closed behind it. Doctor Lansing and the members of the Dream Team piled out of the van.

Buster's deep voice bellowed as they traversed the large space toward their main seating area. "So the two of you were able to convince Ducane of the illusion—that it was Declan standing before him—*talking?*" He slipped an arm under Mira to support her as she started to droop.

Kiki nodded as she anchored Mira's other arm. "Yep. He was with us, watching and listening through the vent so we knew exactly how he'd sound responding to his dad. It was crazy."

"You said he killed the copy," Buster continued. "Did it, um, *hurt?*"

"Yeah. Like hell." She glared at him. "Almost lost control of her sooner, but when the pain finally got to be too much, I had to let go."

Here the two helped Mira onto the sofa. Her eyes fluttered. In the overhead lights, Buster could now see that Mira looked quite different than before—slight alterations in her features and body—so that he almost didn't recognize her.

Buster pulled Kiki a few steps back and whispered: "Is she okay? What happened to her?"

"I think she'll recover," the pink-haired woman answered. "For her to be able to mimic Dec's form *and* voice—even when she had *me* to work with—it took everything in her. She let down her guard—this facade she'd been showing us for as long as we've known her. It took a lot to keep up. But all of it—creating an illusion that intricate for that long—it wiped her out."

By now the others had assembled nearby and Roger began shuffling through the soggy backpack. He inspected the first vial he grabbed then handed it to Buster. He proceeded to distribute the remaining pair to Kiki and Mira, then stood back and crossed his arms.

"I'm sorry, you two," he said to Declan and Donna. "We were only able to secure the formulas for these three."

Donna's shoulders sank and she looked to Declan.

"I'll be fine," Declan said somewhat unconvincingly. "I'll just keep taking my doses. They're easy enough to come by.

It's *you* I'm worried about."

"I can get by. I've learned how to manage it—and these gloves make it easier. But what about Marcus?" Donna asked softly. "If we don't have that formula, we can't change him back even if we find him."

"*When* we find him," the doctor corrected gently. "It's *possible* that the disks you secured may contain information that could allow me to recreate the formulas more quickly. Regardless, I've been working on it, and I won't rest until I've finished it, Donna. You have my word. I created the original compound that gave you your abilities, remember? I've done it once. I can do it again. It's only a matter of time."

This gave Donna a small bit of reassurance and she nodded silently.

Kiki eyed the oozing material in her test tube. "So, you said we're not supposed to chug this, right?"

"My understanding," piped Roger, "is that these formulas should be *injected*. You don't happen to have a few pneumatic injection guns lying around do you?" The doctor's eyes jumped from one member of the team to the next for an answer.

Declan moved to a locker and swung it open. "We've got plenty—just in case." He distributed the devices to Kiki, Mira, and Buster. The trio loaded the vials into their syringe guns and looked around the room.

Kiki held the needle near the crook of her arm. She gulped nervously and her breathing became heavy. Finally, she moved the syringe gun away.

Donna saw her lower the injector. "What's wrong?"

Kiki kept her eyes down. "Now that we're here—now that we've *finally* found the way to change things—I don't know if I can do it."

The blonde woman started toward her: "I can help you if want—"

"No, no," Kiki shook her head. "I mean I don't know if I want to go through with it. I don't know if I want to be *fixed.*"

Buster nodded to himself. "Kiki's right," he muttered. "We've tried so hard to find a way to get rid of these... *abilities*... that we didn't stop to realize that they're part of what make us *us.*"

"Wait a minute," Declan interjected. "We went through *all* of that to get these formulas and now you're just going to throw this opportunity away?" His jaw hung agape as he surveyed the expressions of the team to be sure they weren't pulling some kind of prank on him. "What about you, Mira? You feel the same way?"

By this time, Mira had regained some of her energy. She looked at the injection gun and the oozing formula within. "I thought I needed this to stop pretending—thought the only way I was ever going to be able to let down my guard was if I had this cure. But it turns out the only person I was really fooling was myself. I don't need some formula to become someone else—don't need to put up a facade. I can let my guard down—*without* the formula. I just need to learn when to use my abilities for *good*—just like Donna said."

"Besides," Buster said. "It doesn't feel right for us to get a cure when the two of you can't have the same."

"That's very sweet of you, Buster," said Donna gently. "But don't hold back on account of us. I haven't given up hope. Doc'll find a way."

Declan surveyed the team again. "Then you've made up your minds?"

Kiki, Mira, and Buster gave confident nods.

"Well that settles it, then," said Roger. "And I suppose we'd better hang on to those concoctions just in case you change your mind." The doctor slowly moved around the seating area and collected the vials, removed them from their injection guns, and placed them in a durable satchel.

"So all of the missions—the dream heists—were a waste?" Donna asked.

Declan shook his head. "They weren't a waste. We found my father, and you're one step closer to finding Marcus."

"Thank you all," Donna replied. "Thank you for risking everything for me." Here the woman checked a clock and started. "Oh, I need to get back to the girls. I hope I'll see each of you again someday." She moved around the group and exchanged hugs, finishing with Declan.

"Someday *soon*, I hope," he grinned.

Donna nodded back as she started for the door. "Yes. Someday soon."

Three Weeks Later

The blazing noonday heat made the Metro-Dade police station feel stuffy and humid. The old slatted jalousie windows did little to keep the cool air inside from the sputtering, recently-repaired AC window units.

Rico stood before a closed office door. He fanned himself with a folder he swiped from a nearby desk and tugged at his collar to let some of his body heat escape. He was clad in a light-colored suit and a geometric tie. He mumbled: "And *why* did I need to wear all this again?"

"Because," Tracy turned her head, arms crossed with a folder in one hand, and rolled her eyes. "We've gotta convince the chief you've cleaned up your act."

"I *have* cleaned up my act!"

"I know," she nodded. "But chief needs to *see* the progress to believe it." Tracy reached out and adjusted his tie. "You're a little crooked."

"Thanks."

At that moment, Marge smashed down her phone receiver and hollered across the room. "He's ready for you."

The duo nodded and smiled, then made nervous eye-contact.

"Let me do the talking," said Jones. "Okay?"

Castillo agreed with a bob of his head, then Jones swung open the door and the two filed into the office. The chief swiveled around in his chair when they entered, swirling a wispy cloud of cigarette smoke. "Well look what the proverbial cat dragged in." He snuffed out his cigarette remnant in a small ashtray then stood up. "Officer Jones," he nodded to the woman as he orbited the desk, then shifted his gaze to the freshly-ironed Rico. "And Mr. Castillo. Didn't think I'd be seeing you back here."

There were about a dozen things Rico wanted to say—none of them wise or kind—but he nodded politely instead.

Tracy started: "Chief, if you'll allow me to explain—"

"You'd better."

The woman took a deep breath. "I believe that Rico—er, Mr. Castillo—deserves to be reinstated to the force."

The chief, now perched on the corner of his desk, almost lost his balance but caught himself. "You think *what* now?"

"She thinks I should be reinstated to the—"

The small man shot Rico a stern look. "I didn't ask you, Castillo." The chief turned back to Tracy. "Give me one good reason why I should even entertain the idea."

Jones hesitated, then spoke up again. "I'll give you three."

She tried to ignore the smile she caught spreading across Rico's face out of the corner of her eye. "For starters, he's responsible for the major breakthrough that enabled us to solve the case of Mr. Smith's murder."

"Your prime suspect—this *Mr. Ducane*—is nowhere to be found," the chief noted.

"He'll turn up," said Tracy optimistically. "The important part is that we now know who's responsible."

"You *think* you know who's responsible," the man muttered under his breath. The chief cocked his head. "But go on: what's the second reason?"

"This may be the hardest to believe," Tracy began, "but Mr. Castillo has been going to therapy."

The chief's eyebrows fluttered as he tilted his head toward Rico. "*You*? In therapy?"

Rico nodded. "For a couple weeks now. Turns out its not as scary as it sounds. I didn't realize how much the stuff with Marcus affected me—"

Tracy elbowed him in the side.

"Ow!"

She whispered through gritted teeth: "I'll do the talking, remember?"

"You know what?" The chief uncrossed then crossed his arms. "I'm glad you're doing that—I really am. Good for you, Castillo." Here the man once more directed his attention to Tracy. "You said you had *three* reasons."

Officer Jones gulped and nodded. "The third reason I think Rico should be reinstated—" Tracy paused. Rico noticed a glistening at the edge of her eyes. "He saved my life." The two made brief eye contact. Rico smiled softly.

The chief stood up and began to pace, waving his hands in the air. "Alright, alright. Don't get all mushy on me."

"So," Tracy raised an eyebrow. "You'll do it then?"

The chief paused, pivoted, then continued pacing. "Gimme a minute to think."

The annoying box fan in the corner whizzed and buzzed. Rico twiddled his thumbs.

Finally, the chief stopped walking and turned to his two guests. "I've made up my mind," he said with a serious tone. "I know it's been a tough year for all of us. And we could really use all the manpower we can get. So, Castillo? Consider yourself reinstated."

A wave of relief washed over Rico. It took everything in him not to reach out to Tracy for a grateful embrace.

"On *one* condition," the chief's words interrupted Rico's thoughts. Castillo's expression became more somber as the man continued: "You and Officer Jones here will be partners."

Neither of the pair protested. Rico offered a heartfelt, "Thank you, chief."

"Yeah, yeah, you're welcome, whatever. Now run along and fight some crime."

Rico and Tracy started for the door. When they had nearly reached it, Officer Castillo turned back. "Um, chief? One more thing."

"Yeah?"

"Can I have my gun back?" He smiled awkwardly.

The chief took a long breath and let out a deep sigh, then slowly hobbled behind his desk. The man opened a drawer, reached his hand into it, and withdrew Rico's gun and its accompanying holster. "Do me a favor: try not to shoot it when there's civilians around, okay?"

Rico accepted the weapon and nodded his agreement. "You got it, chief."

With that, the man returned to Tracy at the door and the two left the chief's office. As they moved down the hall, Tracy leaned close to Rico.

"Congratulations, Officer Castillo. Looks like you're stuck with me." Jones grinned, exposing a dimple on her cheek.

"Looks like it," Rico smiled back. "*Partner.*"

Bing-binggg!

"Can one of you get that?" Donna shouted from the kitchen. She listened until she heard the sound of pattering little feet scurrying down the staircase.

Starla shouted over her shoulder: "Miss Lisa, c'mon!"

"I'm coming," the red-haired woman said, moving a few steps behind.

Bing-binggg!

The two reached the front door only moments apart. Starla clicked the big door handle and swung it open with all her might as Lisa appeared at her side. A smile washed over the little girl.

"Uncle Rico!" She dove at her surrogate uncle, wrapping

her arms around his waist.

"Hey, Starlita," Rico smiled and tried not to drop the pair of large cardboard pizza boxes in his hands. He glanced behind him, where his sister and Tracy approached from the car.

Lisa moved in to hug Rico then reached to take the boxes to the kitchen while Donna appeared behind her.

"No valet tonight?" Castillo smiled.

Donna gave the man a heartfelt embrace, her gloved hands sensing a bit of tension in his back. "I gave the boys the night off."

Sue and Tracy finally reached the steps and greeted Donna.

"Come in! Come in!" Donna waved them through the foyer and latched the door behind them. The blonde woman clicked the deadbolt in place—a recent unconscious habit she had developed since the kidnappings. "Everything's pretty much ready. You bring the drinks?"

Sue held up a narrow brown bag. "Merlot to celebrate the occasion," she said as she fished through drawers. "A-ha!" Sue exclaimed, holding up a corkscrew.

As the group gathered around the table to take their seats, Sue popped the cork from the bottle and began to fill the glasses of the adults, skipping over Starla. "How about a Coke for you, Star?"

The girl nodded eagerly. Sue grabbed a red can from the fridge and clicked the cap, then set the fizzy caramel-colored beverage in front of Starla. Everyone settled into their seats and began to divvy up slices of the warm pizza. The friends laughed and enjoyed one another's company until everyone was full and content.

When they were finished eating, Sue and Lisa were whisked away by Starla to play with her dolls. Tracy joined the ladies somewhat reluctantly while Rico moved to the kitchen to help Donna with the dishes. Rico stood at the sink, scrubbing plates under the running water, then handed one to Donna to dry. She seemed to be in a daze.

"Whatcha thinkin' about?"

Donna shook her head. "Nothing, sorry." She ran the towel over the dish.

Rico raised an eyebrow then shut off the water. He leaned back against the counter and crossed his arms. "Really, Donna? I know you well enough to know when your mind is somewhere else."

"I'm just thinking about something Ducane said," Donna muttered, keeping her eyes on the plate. "He said he knew why I was *special*," she said. "He seemed like he knew something more about me and Sondra."

"You mean your powers?"

Donna nodded.

"What do you think it means? You think she has powers, too?"

"I don't know. But for starters, it means that there are a lot less coincidences in my life than I thought," she said seriously. "It means Ducane was planning for a long time—watching us—" She trailed off in a thought.

"Donna, you're safe now," Rico assured her. "Starla and

your sister are home. We're here. I'm going to protect you."

"Yeah. I just wish I knew more. But Ducane got away before I could press the matter."

Rico took the dry plate from Donna's gloved hands and placed it in the cabinet. "He's gone for now. Who knows when he'll turn up again. What matters is that you're safe and we're one step closer to locating Marcus."

Suddenly, Donna's eyes grew wide. "Oh, gosh!"

"What is it?"

"I almost forgot about Roger," she said, starting for the kitchen table. "Lemme bring him a couple slices—the man probably hasn't eaten in days." She slid a few lukewarm pizza slices onto a clean plate and then trudged back across the kitchen toward the hall.

Rico followed closely behind as Donna navigated the house and ascended the narrow staircase to the above-garage lab and studio. Donna gave a light rap on the door and listened for any sign of life. A few moments later, the door swung open.

"Miss Locke!" Roger said with a look of surprise and delight, then nodded to Rico as well. "And Officer Castillo—what a pleasant surprise!"

"We brought you a bite to eat." Donna handed the plate to him, which the doctor received eagerly. "Thought you might be hungry."

"A very astute presumption," the doctor nodded and took a large bite from one of the slices as he hurried across the room, waving for the duo to follow. A glob of congealed cheese slid across the plate as he set it beside his desk. "Miss Locke—you are *not* going to believe what just happened."

"What just happened?" Donna raised an eyebrow.

"I believe," he said with a smile and a few clicks of the keyboard, "that I may have just discovered the whereabouts of your dear Marcus."

Donna's legs almost gave out beneath her. She braced herself against the desk. "What! Where is he?"

Rico's eyes were wide as he awaited the response.

"You recall those floppy disks you and Declan salvaged from Ducane's compound?"

"Of course," Donna snapped. "That was only a few weeks ago, Roger."

"Right." The doctor continued. "Well, I've been working through the files and data on each of them—there isn't a ton, but it's all encrypted and encoded, so it's taken me quite some time to sift through it—"

"And?" Rico interjected impatiently. "Where's Marcus, doc?"

Roger puffed a little then focused once more on the screen in front of him. "As I was saying, the disks contain loads of data. I managed to recover what appear to be the travel and communication logs of many of Ducane's top employees—"

"Angela," Rico muttered.

The doctor raised a pointer finger. "Exactly right. Shortly after the date that your precious Marcus was, um, transformed, there was a communication between Ducane and Angela Hyde."

Donna bent in closer. "What did it say?"

"I haven't been able to decrypt that portion of it yet," explained Roger. "But I was able to transcode the first lines of it—the items that denote the routing location of the transmission."

"In English?"

Roger took a deep breath and exhaled. "Angela's message pinged from a location in the Caribbean—the Bahamas, to be more exact."

Donna's heart was beating fast. She made eye-contact with Rico.

"You thinking what I'm thinking?" Rico asked.

"Yeah," Donna answered softly. *Marcus.* She could hardly believe it was true. *I'm coming for you.* Donna nodded slowly to Rico and smiled. "Time to call my travel agent. It looks like we're headed to the Bahamas."

The story continues in

Nightmare Array

A Magic City Wonders Novel

(Coming in 2024)

If you enjoyed *The Dream Team*, would you be so kind as to leave a review for it on Amazon or your preferred book vendor's website? Every review helps my books get found by new readers!

Thank you for reading,

- Taylor

ABOUT THE AUTHOR

Taylor Thomas Smythe is a native of West Palm Beach, Florida, which has been a source of inspiration for a variety of his creative works. In 2019, Taylor released the first installment in his acclaimed seven-book *Kingdom of Florida* middle-grade fantasy series, which was a silver medal winner in the Florida Authors and Publishers Association President's Book Awards and a finalist in the National Indie Excellence Awards. *Goldie*, the first installment in his *Magic City Wonders* series, was a gold medal winner in the Independent Publisher Book Awards and silver medal winner in the Florida Book Awards. Taylor enjoys creative writing of all kinds and topics, but he especially likes to write stories about imaginative places and secret, magical worlds.

Visit ttsmythe.com *for more from Taylor Thomas Smythe.*

www.ingramcontent.com/pod-product-compliance
Lightning Source LLC
Chambersburg PA
CBHW020307030826
48979CB00029B/2288/J

* 9 7 8 1 9 5 9 3 4 5 1 2 1 *